PRAISE FOR THE SANGREAL TRILOGY

THE GREENSTONE GRAIL

"A promising start."   —*Kirkus Reviews*

"*The Greenstone Grail* has the feeling of an epic story, yet it retains all the elements of [a] fairy tale, told [in a] wonderful evocative tone. . . . A pleasure and a treat."   —SFRevu

"Whether it's clumsy teenagers, ancient guardians, calculating immortals, or menacing supernatural entities, Hemingway's a dab hand at character and evokes atmosphere deftly and vividly."   —*Starburst* (UK)

THE SWORD OF STRAW

"This spellbinding adventure will leave readers enthusiastically awaiting the third book, which promises answers to myriad mysteries."   —*Publishers Weekly*

"Hemingway does a superb job of blending British folklore, plot elements, and characters from the preceding book and an excellent portrayal of contemporary teenagers into a real page-turner likely to please a broad readership."   —*Booklist*

"Engagingly written with an appeal to fans of Grail fiction and the Harry Potter series, this fantasy adventure and its predecessor belong in most fantasy and YA collections."   —*School Library Journal*

By Amanda Hemingway

THE SANGREAL TRILOGY

The Greenstone Grail
The Sword of Straw
The Poisoned Crown

The
Poisoned
Crown

BALLANTINE BOOKS
NEW YORK

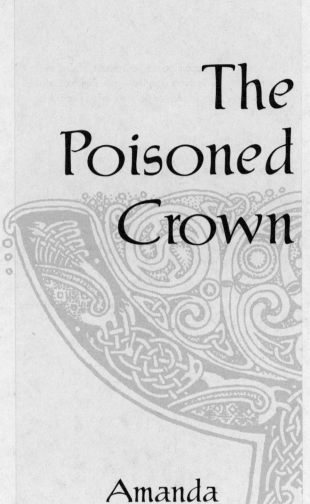

The
Poisoned
Crown

Amanda
Hemingway

A Del Rey Trade Paperback Original

Copyright © 2007 by Amanda Hemingway

Published in the United States by Del Rey Books, an imprint of The Random House Publishing Group, a division of Random House, Inc., New York. Originally published in Great Britain by Voyager, an imprint of HarperCollins Publishers Ltd., in 2006.

DEL REY is a registered trademark and the Del Rey colophon is a trademark of Random House, Inc.

ISBN 978-0-345-46082-0

Printed in the United States of America

www.delreybooks.com

9 8 7 6 5 4 3 2 1

The
Poisoned
Crown

Prologue: The Albatross

He was the bird, and the bird was him. He was Ezroc, son of Tilarc, fifteenth grandson in a direct line from Ezroc Stormrider, the greatest albatross who ever lived. He had flown the Four Oceans and the Ten Seas, and had seen the South Pole rising like a spire of emerald from the violet hills of the Land-Beyond-Night, and the white foam of the combers on the pink coral beaches, and had smelled the perfume of the last flowers that ever were, before the hungry waters took it all away. He had lived to 102, and died in the season his fifteenth-generation grandson was born, so the name had been passed on, but young Ezroc knew he could only dream of touching the legend.

They had set out from the Ice Cliffs more than two moons past, the albatross flying on wings still short of three spans from tip to tip—three spans would mark him for an adult—leaving the cold clean seas of the north far behind, heading south, always south. Keerye could not match his speed, for all his seal-swiftness, and from time to time the bird would descend onto the rocking waters, waiting for his friend to catch up. Some nights they would rest together, sea-cradled, half-human Keerye steadying himself on the swell with his tail flippers, while they gazed up at the unfamiliar stars.

"Do you think we've reached the Fourth Ocean yet?" Ezroc said once.

"There are no Four Oceans anymore," said Keerye, who was older and wiser, or at least more knowledgeable. "No Ten Seas. When people speak of them, it's just words. Now it's all one big ocean, without any land in between to divide it up."

"But we're looking for land," Ezroc pointed out. "We're looking for the islands in the stories—the Jeweled Archipelago, and the Giant's Knucklebones, and the Floating Islands of the utter south. There must be land somewhere."

"Islands are different," Keerye said sagely. "Islands grow, like plants. They come out of the sea sprouting fire and when they cool down there are great weeds on them with stems as thick as a monster eel, poking up into the sky all by themselves."

"I don't believe it," Ezroc said. He had dismissed such tales before. "Without water to support them, they'd fall down."

"I heard it from Shifka," said Keerye, naming the most venerable of the selkies, "and *he* heard it from the great whales, so it must be true. Whales don't lie."

Ezroc duly tried to picture weeds growing on dry land, standing up by themselves, and failed. But it was something to search for.

The seas were growing warmer now, and more dangerous. They were coming to the realms of the seakings, where they worshipped the Goddess, who hated all creatures of land and air. Ezroc was anxious, since it was said the merpeople would kill a selkie if they found one in their territory, but Keerye was scornful. "They are *fish*," he scoffed. "I can outswim any fish. Let them catch me if they can." Ezroc wanted to know why the Goddess should hate them, but Keerye said there was no why. The Goddess was an elemental, who felt but could not reason, as strong as the currents that circled the world, in fury like the tempest, with a heart as black as the uttermost deeps where nothing could live. She was supposed to have a Crown of Iron that never rusted, but was kept in a mysterious cavern of air under the Dragon's Reef. Had anyone seen her? Ezroc asked. What did she look like? In their rest times they speculated about it, visualizing her as a huge ray, a hundred spans wide, whose creeping shadow brought death to the seabed, or a squid as big as an iceberg, belching poisoned ink, or a merwoman tall as a tidal wave with coiling sea snakes for hair and fins that crackled blue with electricity. Once, they met a great purple grouper that Ezroc thought might be her, but Keerye tickled it under its prognathous jaw and it mooched along with them for a while with no sign of hostility.

"Do you know any islands?" Keerye asked, but the fish didn't answer.

"Maybe it doesn't speak our language," Ezroc suggested, so Keerye tried the other tongues he knew, the click-click of secret Dolphin-speech, the croaking of Penguin, the burble of Smallfish, and even a few words of Shark, but the grouper never spoke at all. Presently, it turned aside, heading west toward the shadow of sunken rocks.

This was reef country, and now they grew very wary. Above the corals the shallow water was green with sunlight and teeming with smallfish, but there were deep blue chasms in between where the mer-folk might hide, and cruising sharks in search of more substantial prey than yellowstripe and fairyfin, and dark clefts that might conceal mon-sters they had heard of but never seen, creatures of the tropical waters who didn't venture into the north. Giant sea scorpions, crabs whose pincers could slice a selkie in half, things part fish, part reptile, that had no name and no real species, armored with spikes and spines, their flip-pers halfway to feet, their mouths agape with rows of dagger teeth. Ezroc felt himself safe enough in the air, sustained on near-motionless wings, but concern for Keerye made him fly low, and the selkie was both reckless and curious, diving to peer under every rock. They met a turtle coasting the reefside who told them he was the last of his kind; his mate had been gone twenty years, searching for a place to lay her eggs.

"Do you know any islands?" Keerye said.

"If I did, my mate would have buried her eggs there, and I would have found her again," the turtle replied. "The islands are all gone. Swim to the absolute south, and you'll find only sea swirl around the Pole, and the sun that never sets shines on the endless waters without even a rock to break the surface."

Keerye asked the same question of those smallfish he could persuade to listen, a green octopus that was slithering over the coral, a frilled purple sea slug, and even a passing shark. The smallfish responded with bubbletalk, meaning little, the octopus turned red and disappeared into a crevasse, and the sea slug tied itself into a slow-motion knot and rippled away. Only the shark snapped a coherent answer.

"There are islands," he said, "but you must move fast to catch up with them."

"Which way?" asked Keerye. "South?"

"South—west—east." The shark flicked his tail by way of a shrug and glided on.

"The Floating Islands," Keerye said. "That's what he means."

"I don't trust him," Ezroc said. "My father says, a shark is a stomach with fins. He doesn't talk, he just opens his mouth."

But Keerye was too eager on their quest to take warning.

THEY MET the mermaid on a night of shooting stars, at the full of the fourth moon since they'd left the Ice Cliffs of home. On an unknown signal the corals released their spores, uncurling like smoke into the sea surge, glittering with reflected light, until both sky and sea seemed to be heaving with the dust of stars, and leaping fish, come to feast on the coral's beneficence, left phosphorescent tracks like meteor trails through the black water. Keerye lay on his back in the sway of gentle billows, made careless by the beauty, luxuriating in the night magic. "The sky fires of the north are lovelier," he insisted, but the star glitter was mirrored in his dark eyes as he turned his head this way and that. Ezroc sat on the wave beside him, sculling with webbed feet, dazzled by the wonder of it. Neither of them saw the watcher until she was very close.

Her hand brushed Keerye's tail, feeling the strangeness of his fur, flinching away and returning to touch again. The selkie, whose reflexes were lightning, somersaulted and caught her arm, holding her though she wriggled, fish-like, trying to escape. Her skin felt cold and slippery, like bladderwrack. He forced her head out of the water and saw the gill slits in her neck widen as she gasped in the alien element. Her wet hair looked black in the starlight but he guessed it was darkly purple, and the sheen on her arms was like pearl. Her eyes were unlike his, narrow and slanting, with no whites; he could not tell their color.

She was small, barely half his size. He guessed she was still a child.

"You're merfolk," he said. "Are you alone?" And when she didn't answer: "What is your name?"

Her mouth opened and shut, but no noise emerged.

"What is your name?"

"Maybe she can't talk out of water," Ezroc suggested.

Keerye had never met merfolk before, but he knew enough of them from rumor and hearsay. "She can talk," he insisted.

And again: "What is your name?"

"Denaero," she said at last. Her voice sounded thin and strange in the air, more accustomed to carrying underwater. "I am Rhadamu's daughter. If you hurt me, he will kill you."

"We won't hurt you," Ezroc said. "We wouldn't hurt anyone."

"*If* you answer my question," Keerye amended.

"I answer or not, as I please," said the girl, trying to toss her head, but Keerye held her by the hair. "I am not afraid of you, even if you eat me."

"Why should I eat you?" Keerye demanded, startled.

"Selkies eat merpeople," Denaero said. "We are fish. Lungbreathers eat fish. That is the way of things."

"I won't eat you," Keerye said. "You are too small. When we catch fish that are too small, we throw them back."

"My father is the High King," Denaero declared. "When the Festival of Spawning is over, he will come looking for me and hunt you with spears. You will be stuck full of spears till you bristle like a sea urchin. You won't be so scornful then."

Keerye laughed out loud at her defiance and her pride, and the girl sulked, then laughed, too, ducking her head underwater when he let go of her hair to inhale her native element.

"Why must we talk like this?" Denaero asked, meaning above water. "Can't you talk undersea?"

"I can, but Ezroc can't. He's a bird," Keerye explained.

"I heard there are birds that fly through the water," Denaero said, not wanting to appear ignorant, "called pinwings. If you can fly underwater, why can't you talk there, too?"

"I'm not a penguin," Ezroc said. "I'm an albatross."

The girl shivered and shrank away. "A windbringer," she said. "I thought they were only in stories. Is it true, you can fly around the whole world in a day, and you bring ice storms from the north to destroy us? Did you bring the ice now?" She glanced from side to side as if expecting ice floes to emerge from nowhere.

"I don't bring ice," said Ezroc. "I don't want to harm you."

"The stories say you are much bigger," said Denaero, recovering her courage.

"He's only young," said Keerye. "Like you. When he's fully grown, his wings will be as wide as—as the entire reef."

"Could I ride on you, then?" Denaero begged suddenly. "Could I fly—really fly—up in the sky among the stars?"

"Well . . . ," Ezroc temporized.

"One day," said Keerye. "But now we are on a quest. We are looking for islands. Do you know of any?"

"Only in stories," Denaero said. "The Goddess ate the islands. She is always hungry. Once, there were whole kingdoms above the sea, full of creatures that didn't swim, and strange people, neither merfolk nor selkie. I wish I could have seen them. But the Goddess swallowed them all up. Then she devoured the islands, one by one, crunching up the rocks that were their bones. There are no islands anymore."

"We heard there were Floating Islands," Keerye persisted, "south of here, or east, or west. Have you seen them?"

The girl's face changed; her hair lifted of its own accord, rippling with sparks.

"Those are not *islands*," she said. "Don't go near them . . . Listen!" She dipped below the waves, the better to pick up vibrations, reappearing a moment later.

"The festival is over," she continued. "My father is coming to look for me. If he finds you, you will be stuck full of spears like a sea urchin. I do not want that. You must swim fast, fast, till you come to the Great Reef Wall where the sea boils and the steam goes up a hundred spans into the air. If you can cross that, you will be safe. But you must go *fast*. Your swimming makes an echo pattern that we can detect from far away; that was how I found you. If my father senses it, he will hunt you down."

"How far to the Great Reef Wall?" asked Ezroc.

"Can't you stop the king?" Keerye said.

"I will leap and dance in the water and make a great splashing that will overlay the echo pattern, but you must go *now. Please!*"

"Thank you," said Keerye, and he kissed her cold little cheek.

"Thank you!" cried Ezroc, and he spread his wings, driving himself into the air.

The mermaid held her hand to her face for a second or two, as if she feared to lose the imprint of the kiss, though it was a gesture she had never known. Then she forgot it in the wonder of the bird's rising.

"Come back when you're grown!" she said. "Come back and fly me to the stars! Promise?"

"I promise!" Ezroc called as he veered southward. Below, Keerye streaked like a javelin through the still-gleaming water.

Behind them, Denaero arced and plunged and dived, churning the midnight waves to a tumult of foam.

IT WAS dawn when they reached the Great Reef Wall and saw the steam of the boiling sea like a cloud over the sun. Keerye swam to the edge of the shallows, where the reef fell away in a submarine cliff down to unguessable depths. Far below there must have been vents in the seabed, emitting gas from the planet's core, and so the water beyond the wall bubbled like a cauldron, and the stink of sulfur hung in the air. Ezroc flew high above, soaring on the thermals, but he could see no way for a selkie to pass. "The steam barrier stretches as far as the eye can see," he told Keerye, "and at its narrowest it must be more than twenty spans across. We might travel a sennight and find no way through."

"Show me the narrow part," the selkie said. "In seal form I can leap high and far, higher and farther than any from the Ice Cliffs."

"Not that high and not that far," said Ezroc. "You'll scald in the water and bake in the steam. It will kill you."

"If you were to lift me, I could do it," Keerye said.

"I cannot bear you. I am not yet strong enough."

"But if you swoop as I spring, and hold my foreflippers, the joint impetus of both leap and flight will carry us over the barrier," Keerye declared.

"Maybe, maybe not," Ezroc said doubtfully. "The risk is too great. Let us turn west. Somewhere there will be a break."

"You said there were none," Keerye pointed out.

They might have argued about it long, but Ezroc, rising to scan the seas again, saw shadow shapes skimming the reef toward them—the vanguard of the hunt. Mermen mounted on blue sharks wielding spears of bone tipped with blood coral, barracuda trained for the chase with fin rings that rattled to denote their route, and behind them on huge hammerheads the king and his court, trailing cloaks of whalehide and brandishing axes of polished obsidian. The king himself wore a helm or crown adorned with the claws of a giant lobster and mail of oyster shells gleaming with mother-of-pearl.

"*Now* we have no choice," said Keerye. "Swoop on me as I leap—catch me and hold firm—and we will make it."

"Suppose I cannot . . . ? If I let you fall—"

"I have faith. You won't let me fall."

Keerye could not go deep—the reef was too near the surface—nor give himself a long run, for the hunt was drawing close. But he swam back as far as he dared and then arrowed toward the wall, driving himself forward with his powerful tail, all seal now, breaking the water and rising up . . . and up . . . The sun glittered in the spray around him, then the sea smoke stung his eyes, and he felt the talons of the albatross digging into him, tugging, lifting, sweeping him through the fume toward clear air and cool sea. Sudden pain scorched his flank—a well-aimed spear glanced off him and dropped into the fog. And then before he knew it he was plunging down, betrayed by his own weight, torn from the albatross's grip to fall into the seething water . . .

It was hot, but it did not burn. He was through the barrier. They had done it.

THEY SWAM south for many days at leisure while the spear wound healed and fur and feathers, singed in the sulfurous vapors, grew again. The days were longer, and the sun had barely dipped below the horizon before reemerging to resume its orbit of the sky. Once, they came across a great shoal of silvertail and fed until they were almost too full to float, but they saw no creatures they could talk to save a few small-fish who spoke a dialect they did not recognize. Another time they found a vast mat of kelp, rootless, drifting on the current with all its mobile populace. Ezroc thought it might be one of the Floating Islands from the stories, but Keerye said no, islands were solid and did not wallow in the water.

"I think there are no islands anymore," Ezroc said.

But they kept on searching.

And then they saw it, on a day without sunset, a great hump looming out of the water ahead of them. It looked like a boulder or cluster of boulders, sea-smoothed, rose-tinted, marbled in blue, with occasional fan-like growths sprouting from cracks and testing the air with feathery tendrils. Keerye swam eagerly toward it, ran his hands over the boulders, then pulled himself out of the water and sat in the sun, shedding even the semblance of a tail, naked in his skin and gilded with light. Only his long silver hair and velvet-dark eyes showed him for a selkie.

"This is what we sought," he said. "A Floating Island. Where there's one, there will be more. Maybe there's real land still, in the utter south, land with roots that go all the way to the world's heart. The stories must be true after all."

"Are you sure it's an island?" Ezroc circled the atoll, still too wary to land there. "Denaero warned us—"

"Denaero was a child, afraid of ghosts. This is solid: look!" He slapped the boulder, making a wet sharp *thwack!*, but to Ezroc's ear it didn't sound quite right.

"It doesn't feel like rock," he said, alighting beside Keerye. "Rock should be hard."

"It's hard enough. I'm going to sleep here for a while. It's been too long since I slept out of water."

"I'm not tired," Ezroc lied. "I'll keep watch."

He took off again and drifted on the high air, scanning the sea in all directions, but he could see no other island nor any living thing. The translucent water seemed to be empty even of smallfish, clear and limpid as a lagoon. That troubled him, though he couldn't define why, and he widened the radius of his flight, covering a large area around the atoll, but still there was nothing to be seen. At last he settled on the water close to the island, folded his wings, and slept.

When he awoke he was alone. The sun was low, though it would not set; sky and sea met on the horizon in an arc of reflected fires. And in every direction there was only water. The island—and Keerye—had gone.

Ezroc hurled himself into the air with a great cry that seemed to carry to the ends of the world. He told himself it was a Floating Island: it had simply floated away. He would find it soon, and Keerye still sleeping, stretched out on the blue-veined boulders. He had only to fly high enough and he would see it: how could you lose an island?

Those are not islands, Denaero had said. *Don't go near them . . .*

The dread lay coldly on his heart, dread and worse than dread, the terrible foreknowledge that it was too late, it had been too late from the moment he fell asleep. The island was gone and Keerye was gone and he would never see his friend again. The wide wastes of the ocean ached with his desolation, a void that could not be filled. He flew higher and higher, and the sun fell away beneath his wings, and the huge solitude of the sea unrolled below him, without land or life, empty now forevermore. He would fly all the long lonely miles back to the north, and tell his tale to those who would mourn, or curse his name—Ezroc the faithless, who lost his childhood playmate and dearest friend—and return to the south, traveling the seas for countless moons, until he knew every wave, every tug of the world's current, every whim of the winds. His journeys would become a legend to outdo his ultimate grandsire, his adventures a fairy tale for children; but he would never find Keerye again. His keening wail echoed over sky and sea, harsh with longing and despair.

"Keeeeryeee . . . *Keeeeeeryeeee* . . ."

No answer came.

HE WAS the bird, and the bird was him. He felt the air under his wings, bearing him upward, the sun warming his feathers, the huge angry pain of his heart. It was too much pain, too much to endure, and he pulled his mind away, letting the bird go, watching its flight track into the sun while his thought sank seaward and drifted into a dim blue realm, no longer sharp with the awareness of the bird but soft and dream-like. In the azure gloom he saw the island, not floating on the surface but moving through deep water, the rose-stained boulders swelling and shrinking like the bulb of a vast jellyfish. A skein of tentacles trailed behind it, fifty yards long or more. Something pale was tangled in their grasp, something that barely struggled now. Vision dipped under the bulb and he saw a dozen mouths opening and closing, each with a ring of needle-tipped teeth. The pale thing, still wriggling slightly, was maneuvered toward them, passed from one to another as each took a bite. Blood smoked on the water, but not much: the feeder did not believe in waste. Above, the bulb turned from pink to crimson as it gorged, pulsing with a glow of its own; the blue veins empurpled and swelled into ridges. Briefly, he touched its mind, such as it was—the mind of a glutton enjoying a rare special feast.

He wrenched his thought away in horror, out of the sea, out of the dream, through the veils of sleep to his own world.

Ripples

"Define the Irish Question between 1800 and 1917," Nathan read aloud.

"If we knew the question," his mother said, "we might be able to work out the answer."

"I don't think that'll satisfy Mr. Selkirk," Nathan said, sighing. He pushed his history essay aside and replaced it with a plate of buttered toast with honey and cinnamon, a recipe of his uncle's. The honey had oozed just the right distance through the toast and he bit into it with enthusiasm, if a little absentmindedly.

His mother noted his abstraction and knew or guessed the reason, but was prudent enough to say nothing. He was fifteen now, too old to press for confidences. She only hoped, if there was trouble, he would tell her in the end. The summer had been long and uneventful, a summer of normal teenage preoccupations: success (and failure) at cricket, doing homework, not doing homework, friends, fads, hormonal angst. They had managed a trip to Italy, looking at palaces and pictures in Florence and then staying with Nathan's classmate Ned Gable and his family in a villa in Umbria. Annie had feared they would never afford their share of the rental but somehow Uncle Barty had found the money, though he wouldn't accompany them. These days he rarely left the old manor at Thornyhill, deep in the woods.

Yet he wasn't really a stay-at-home sort of person. He had told Annie once that he was born in Byzantium before the fall of the Roman Empire, which, she worked out, made him about fifteen hundred years old. He called himself Bartlemy Goodman, though it was probably not his name. She might have thought him mad or unusually eccentric if she hadn't known him so well and seen what he could do, when the occasion demanded it. He had taken her in on a cold lonely night long ago when she was pursued by invisible enemies, becoming an uncle to both her and Nathan, and as her son grew up into strange adventures Bartlemy had been their counselor and support. But there had been no adventures this summer, and now autumn was failing, and the wind blew from the north, plucking the last ragged leaves from the treetops, and Nathan was restless with the feeling of deeds undone, and worlds to be saved, and time slipping away.

Soon, Annie thought, *he'll start sleeping badly,* and there was a tiny squeeze of fear at her heart that she could not suppress.

I sleep too deep, Nathan thought, *and I dream too little and too lightly.* The portal was closed, the connection broken: he could no longer roam the multiverse in his head, following trails he could not see on a quest he did not understand. He had dreamed his way through other worlds— the ghost-city of Carboneck in Wilderslee, and the sky-towers of Arkatron on Eos, where the Grandir, supreme ruler of a dying cosmos, sought for the Great Spell that would be the salvation of his people. Nathan had retrieved the Cup and the Sword to bind the magic, and now only the Crown was wanting—the Crown and the sacrifice and the words of power, whatever they might be. But there had been no dreams for nearly a year, and the pleasures of cricket and the problems of history were not enough to fill his life.

"How's Hazel?" his mother asked, helping herself to a piece of his toast. "I haven't seen her lately."

Hazel was Nathan's closest friend: they had grown up almost as brother and sister, though getting on rather better than most siblings. Adolescence had brought friction but had never driven them apart.

"You know Hazel." Nathan spoke around munching. "She didn't exactly *like* her mum's old boyfriend, but I think she *approved* of him. She doesn't approve of the new one at all."

"Because he's so young?"

"Mm."

Annie smiled. "Well, all I can say is good for Lily. I think Franco's very sweet."

"He's *Italian*," Nathan objected.

"How insular! Besides, you didn't mind the Italians last summer."

"That was in Italy!"

"Suppose *I* got myself a toyboy," Annie said. "How would you feel about that?"

"You are joking, aren't you?" Diverted from thoughts of other worlds, Nathan looked really alarmed.

"Maybe."

"Look, you know, if there's someone, it's cool with me—as long as he's nice and really cares about you—but . . . well, I'd rather have a stepfather than an older brother!"

"Nicely put," Annie said. "Still, I doubt if the situation will arise."

Nathan couldn't ever recall her having a proper boyfriend, even though several men had been interested. He said: "You must have loved Dad very much." Daniel Ward had died before he was born, killed in a car crash when he fell asleep at the wheel.

"Very much," she said. *Only he wasn't your dad . . . Your father was a stranger who waited beyond the Gate of Death, waited for my love and longing to open the unopenable door, and when I would have given all that I had for all I had lost he took me, body and soul. He seeded my womb and sealed up my memory, and until you grew up so unlike Daniel—until I found the courage to unclose the old scar in my mind—I never knew the betrayal and rape hidden there.*

But she loved Nathan, conceived in treachery, child of an unknown being from an unknown world, so she kept her secret. She saw his father's legacy in the mysteries that surrounded him, but she told herself, over and over, that he did not need to know. One day, perhaps, but not yet. Not yet.

That night, Nathan went to bed thinking of the Irish Question, and dreamed of the sea.

AT THORNYHILL Manor, Hazel Bagot was having a lesson in witchcraft.

"But I don't want to be a witch," she protested.

"Good," said Bartlemy. "That's the way to start. Now you need to learn what not to do. Otherwise you could bumble about like you did last year, conjuring dangerous spirits and letting them get out of control. Someone might get hurt. It nearly happened once, you know that; you don't want it to happen again. The Gift is in your blood. You need to know how not to use it."

"Why couldn't we have done it in the summer, when the evenings were still light?" Hazel said. She was wishing she had stayed at home, watching *Neighbours* and annoying Franco.

"Dark for dark magic," Bartlemy said. "In summer, magic is all sparkle and fun, and the spirits come to us dressed in their best, scattering smiles and flowers. In the winter you get down to the bone, and the true nature of things is revealed."

Hazel said no more, remembering how she had summoned Lilliat, the Spirit of Flowers, to win her the love of a boy at school, and how Lilliat had turned into Nenufar the water demon and nearly drowned her rival.

Bartlemy gave her tea and cookies, and she sat for a while eating, insensibly reassured. Bartlemy made the best cookies in the world, cookies whose effect was almost magical, though he insisted there was no spell involved, just good baking. Anyone who ate those cookies felt immediately at home, even if they didn't want to, comforted if they needed comfort, relaxed if they needed to relax. Long ago another cook had tried to steal one for analysis, hoping to work out the ingredients, but he had eaten it before he got it home and the urge to commit the crime had vanished.

"I don't want to be like my great-grandmother," Hazel explained at last. "She lived for two hundred years, until she didn't care about anyone but herself and she'd curdled inside like sour milk. I don't think I want to live on when my friends are dead; it would be so lonely. And I don't want to be mean and bitter like her."

"Then learn from her mistakes," Bartlemy said equably. "You won't be mean and bitter unless you choose. I will teach you what you need to know for your safety and others', but how you use the knowledge—*if* you use it—is up to you. Tonight I think we will make the spellfire. That will do for a start."

He showed her how to seal the chimney and light the fire crystals, which cracked and hissed, shooting out sparks that bored into the carpet. Then he threw on a powder that smothered the flames, and the room grew smoky, and Hazel's eyes watered from the sting of it. Presently Bartlemy told her to speak certain words in Atlantean, the language of spellcraft, and the vapor seemed to draw together, hovering in a cloud above the hearth, and then the heart of the cloud opened up into a picture.

To her astonishment Hazel saw her mother with Franco, climbing the stairs to the bedroom, laughing and hurried. She was embarrassed and looked away. "Remember, the magic responds to *you*," Bartlemy said. "Magic is always personal. The pictures may have meaning for you, or they may not—sometimes their import won't become clear till long after—but it is something in your thought, in your mind, that engenders them. You are the magnet: they are the spell-fragments that are drawn to you. What do you see now?"

"The past," Hazel said. "At least, I think so."

She saw the Grimthorn Grail surrounded with a greenish nimbus: the snake spirals around the rim seemed to move, and a man with a dark alien face was gazing into it, speaking words she couldn't hear. In the background stood a woman with black hair bound up in a white veil or scarf, the ends of which hung down behind her in fluted creases. Her features, too, were somehow alien—her eyes too large, the proportions of her face elusively wrong—yet she was the most beautiful woman Hazel had ever seen. She held a tall yellow candle, and either they were indoors or the night was windless, because the flame burned absolutely still. Then Hazel saw the same man lifting a sword—the Traitor's Sword, which Nathan had brought back from Wilderslee—and there was a dim figure sprawled in front of him, on a kind of table or altar, and when the Sword fell blood jetted up, and as the woman proffered the Cup to catch it red spattered on the cloth that bound her hair. Both man and woman drank from the Cup, and she lifted a Crown from the thing on the table and put it on his head—a misshapen Crown of twisted metal spikes—and lightning stabbed up from the Crown, splitting the sky in half. For an instant Hazel glimpsed a symbol drawn in lightning, something she recognized, though she couldn't think from where: an arc bisected by a straight line, enclosed within a circle. Then the vision went dark, and she heard a voice crying out in an unknown language, words that seemed full of anguish or regret.

"What does it mean?" she asked Bartlemy, but he shook his head.

"This is Nathan's story," she said, "not mine," but her smoke-reddened eyes were wide, fixed on the changing images, and she no longer looked away.

"Keep in mind," he pointed out, "the pictures are relevant, but there may be no logic to them, and no chronology."

Now they were looking at a river—a slow lazy river, dimpled with sunlight, with the occasional overhanging willow, and little eddies scooping out pools under the bank, which vanished in a mudslide. A tidal river with hazardous currents beneath its dimpled surface, and lurking weeds that could entangle flailing limbs, and rafts of floating rubbish wedged here and there, hiding among the debris a child's shoe, a waterlogged teddy bear, an upturned hand. The River Glyde, which flowed through the village of Eade down the valley to the sea—the river where Effie Carlow, Hazel's great-grandmother, had been found drowned, though Hazel knew she had never left the attic of their house. She heard the voice of the spirit called the Child chanting an old doggerel, though the smoke-scene showed only the stream.

> "Cloud on the sunset,
> Wave on the tide,
> Death from the deep sea
> Swims up the Glyde."

And suddenly Hazel found herself wondering whose hand she had seen among the flotsam—whether it was her great-grandmother or some more recent victim, someone yet to be discovered . . .

A boat moved up the river, surely too large a boat for such a narrow waterway. It was all white, with white sails and a white-painted mast and a white prow without name or identification, and it looked faintly insubstantial, almost a ghost-ship. A woman stood in the bow wrapped in a long white cloak pulled tight around her body, with a drooping hood covering both hair and face. The picture shifted until Hazel thought she should be able to glimpse a profile—the tip of a nose, the jut of a chin—but under the hood there was only darkness. The boat drifted on, fading into mist, and then there was just a swan, wings half furled, floating on the water. Hazel had always hated swans, ever since one attacked her as a child; she thought they had mean little eyes.

She said: "That was *her*, wasn't it?"

Bartlemy said: "Perhaps. But remember: to come, she must be called. Nenufar is a spirit; there are laws she cannot evade. Have you called her?"

"Of course not!"

The vision dimmed, dissolving into smoke, and at a signal from Bartlemy she unblocked the flue. Gradually the air cleared, and she saw that the fire crystals had burned away; the room was ordinary again. An old room with heavy wooden beams, diamond-paned windows, lamplight soft as candle glow on the shabby Persian rugs and worn furniture. And in the middle Bartlemy, fat and placid and silver-haired, with eyes as blue as the sky. There were more cookies but Hazel didn't take one, not yet, though his dog sat looking hopefully at her—a huge shaggy dog of questionable ancestry, known as Hoover, whose age was as indeterminate as his master's. Suddenly it seemed to Hazel that the world was complex and baffling beyond her understanding, and magic and reality were no longer separate but part of the same puzzle, tiny fragments of a jigsaw so vast and intricate that its billion billion pieces could never be fit together, not though she had a hundred lifetimes. Her thought was too small, and infinity was too big, and she felt crushed into littleness by its immensity, its multiplicity, by the endless changing patterns of Chaos. Bartlemy asked her, "What troubles you?" and she tried to explain, groping for the words to express her diminishment, her confusion, her fear.

Bartlemy smiled faintly. "We all feel that way sometimes," he said, "if we have the gift of perception. Embrace your doubts: if there is such a thing as wisdom, they are part of it. I've had my doubts for more than a thousand years. Actually, I've always believed that the answer to everything must really be very simple." And he added, unconsciously echoing Annie on Irish history: "The problem is finding out the question."

"SO RIVERSIDE House is sold at last," Annie said to Lily Bagot in the deli. No one had lived in Riverside House since the tragedy, though rumors of new owners had circulated from time to time, only to fade as another sale fell through. "Do you know when they're moving in?"

"They're already there," Lily said. "Came down last week. Some family from London." All the newcomers in the village were from London these days, big-city types in search of a rural paradise, bringing with them their big-city lifestyle and their big-city needs—and their big-city income. "I daresay they'll be coming into the bookshop soon."

Annie managed a secondhand-book shop, owned by Bartlemy; she and Nathan lived in the adjacent house.

"I hope so," she said. She couldn't help being a little curious. She had been so closely involved in the events at Riverside, now two years past. She wondered what kind of people would buy a house with such a well-publicized history of disaster.

A few days later she found out.

A woman came in to browse among the books, a woman with a frizz of dark hair and a thin body that grew wide around the hips, dressed in antique shoulder pads, hand-printed scarves, carved jewelry from the remoter parts of Asia. She studied the shelves for a while, enthused over an early edition of Mrs. Henry Wood, then seemed to make up her mind and pounced.

"You're Annie Ward, aren't you? I know: I asked around. I'm Ursula Rayburn. We've just moved in to the oasthouse down by the river. Of course, I expect you've heard, haven't you?—gossip travels so fast in a village. Such an intimate little community—I can't wait to get to know everyone. Although Islington is really just a village enclosed in a city . . . Anyway, I've been dying to meet you. I hope you don't mind me introducing myself like this."

"Not at all—"

"You see, I did my homework. I know *you're the one who found the body* . . ."

Slightly at a loss, Annie said: "Yes."

"Was it awful? I gather she was there for months, slowly decaying, while her husband lived on in the house with his mistress, who was pretending to be her. I suppose he's in an asylum now . . . and they never caught the mistress, did they? I expect it was all her idea. Mind you, I don't really see the necessity—I mean, everyone gets divorced these days, it's as normal as eating your dinner. I've had two and Donny's had one and the kids are *totally* well adjusted. They say more parents mean more presents at Christmas and birthdays! Are you divorced?"

"Widowed," Annie said.

"Oh *dear*. And then to have to go through all that . . . you poor child. You must have been in therapy for *months*. Bereavement and then post-traumatic stress . . ."

"My husband died fifteen years ago," Annie said. She and Daniel hadn't been married, but she'd taken his name anyway. "And I don't have post-traumatic stress."

"But . . . you *did* find the corpse, didn't you? You found Rianna Sardou?"

"Oh, that." Annie was unable to resist lapsing into nonchalance. "Of course, it *was* rather unpleasant, but—"

"*Unpleasant?* I heard she was lying in the bed, little more than a skeleton, with her hair all spread out—it goes on growing, doesn't it?—and—"

"In a village," Annie said serenely, "you learn to take these things in your stride. Part of the great cycle of life and death, you know. I expect it's much the same in Islington."

"Well . . ." Disconcerted by Annie's composure, Ursula's gush of words ran down. "Not—not *exactly* . . ."

Annie took pity on her. "Would you like some coffee?"

While the contents of the cafetière were brewing, Ursula Rayburn filled in the details of her extended family. Her two exes, plus new wife/girlfriend/offspring, all on very good terms—"We wanted a big place where everyone could come and stay"—and Donny's ex and mother, "frightfully *bitter*, even after four years—they bossed him around all the time, and now they're like two cats without a kitten." There were five resident children, all Ursula's by previous partners: Jude, Liberty, Michael, Romany, and Gawain.

"Michael?" Annie queried before she could stop herself.

"His father insisted," Ursula explained, more in sorrow than in anger. "His first name is Xavier—I always called him that when he was little—but now he's a teenager he's gone so peculiar, he won't answer to anything but Michael. Or Micky, which is almost worse. And the psycho's name was Michael, wasn't it? I told him—I said it's ill omened—but he refuses to go back to Xavier, no matter what I say."

"I shouldn't worry," Annie said. "Lots of people are called Michael, and they don't go around committing murders."

"Of course not. But in this house, with the *atmosphere* . . ."

"Frankly," Annie said, "I never thought it had any. It's an old building, but the renovations made it so bland inside, all shiny new paint and unused furniture. Rianna was dead, her husband was so busy pretending to be normal his personality never made any impact, and the—the mistress was hardly ever there. I'm sure, with so many of you, you'll find it easy to change the feel of the place."

"Oh, but you can't wipe out the past," Ursula said. "I don't believe in the kind of ghosts that come with clanking chains, naturally, but there are *vibrations*. I won't use the tower room till it's been purified—I've got crystals hanging there now—and Melisande wouldn't even go through the door. She's my cat, pedigree Burmese, so *sensitive*. I know it's a cliché but animals do feel things, don't they? They're so much more telepathic than people."

Annie said something noncommittal and dispensed the coffee.

"They never found out her name, did they?" Ursula went on. "The mistress, I mean."

Nenufar, Annie thought. Nenufar the water spirit, the primitive goddess from the dark of the sea . . .

"No," she said.

"Strange, that. Nowadays they seem to have files on everyone—d'you know the police keep your personal details even if you were just caught smoking dope twenty years ago? It's an abuse of human rights. I'm a member of the campaign for civil liberties, of course . . . But it's curious they couldn't even find a *name* for her. Names are so significant, don't you think? We're not going to stay with *Riverside House.* It's really a bit *ordinary.* I thought Rivendell, but that's been done to death lately. Perhaps Hesperides . . . there are apple trees in the garden."

"Dundrownin'?" Annie hazarded. She wondered if she had overstepped the mark, but after a tiny pause Ursula burst out laughing.

"Still, Rianna didn't drown, did she?" she resumed. "It was some old woman who drowned."

Annie couldn't recall if they'd been able to prove how Rianna died, but she knew.

"You have to be careful of the river," she said. "It's not deep, but there are treacherous currents."

"Oh, I know," Ursula said. "I hoped the children would be able to play there—I had this mental picture before we came: rustic bliss, swimming in the river, maybe a boat. There's a mooring place, but everybody says boating's a bit chancy unless you've got experience."

"Why *did* you buy the house?" Annie said. "If you don't mind my asking. Since you know its history . . ."

"It was cheap," Ursula said candidly, "and it doesn't need work. Just repainting—like you said, it's white all through, very boring. We've been looking to move out of London for a while. And I thought the murders would give it *character* . . ."

Annie opened her mouth and shut it again, saying nothing.

"Actually, there is a bit of a problem," Ursula continued. "Do you know a good plumber? The inspector didn't pick up on it—he said everything was fine—but we keep getting leaks from somewhere. There was a puddle—really a *puddle*—in the living room only the other day. I don't know where it came from. No, of course it wasn't the cat—it was water, not pee. I said to Donny, if the inspector missed something major, we'll sue. Anyway, I need a plumber to come and check the pipes."

"Yellow pages?" Annie suggested.

"Isn't there—you know—a little man in the village? One of the natives who's brilliant and inexpensive and does all the jobs 'round here?"

"There's Kevin Bellews," Annie said. "He's brilliant but he charges the earth. He only works for city expats—none of the locals can afford him anymore. Besides, he's always on the golf course near Crowford."

"The country isn't what it used to be," Ursula mourned. "What happened to—to rural innocence and all those nice dumb yokels in stories?"

"They got smart," Annie said.

It was only after Ursula had gone that she found herself growing uneasy. There was never anything wrong with the plumbing at Riverside House before, she thought. Leaks . . . leaks meant water.

Water . . . ?

"JUDE's AT university," Hazel volunteered. "He's at least twenty. The next two are at the tertiary college up the road from Crowford Comp; Micky's seventeen, Liberty's sixteen. George fancies her, but she wouldn't look at him: she's far too grown-up. The point is, they're none of them our age, so nobody can expect us to be friends with them."

"Ageist," Nathan said. "What about the younger ones?"

"They're just kids." Hazel was dismissive. "They're still at primary school. They've got a different last name—Macaire—it sounds Scottish but I think their dad must be black. They've both got dark skin and fuzzy hair." Mixed-race children were still an innovation in Eade, though the villagers had finally gotten used to Nathan, with his Asiatic coloring and exotic features.

"Come to think of it, Mum said the little girl was adorable," Nathan commented, tolerant of maternal sentiment. "Anyway, you don't have to be so hostile." Hazel, he knew, was using the old-fashioned village mentality to shield her own space and the people she didn't want to share. "We should *try* to be friendly, at least to the two at tertiary. I can handle the age gap. They're our neighbors, after all."

"I suppose you fancy Liberty, too?" Hazel said.

"I haven't seen her. Is she pretty?"

Hazel shrugged. "Ask George." George Fawn had formed part of a threesome with them when they were younger, though they saw less of him now. "She's thin—long legs—tight jeans. She has this don't-care attitude, like she's way above anyone else. Probably 'cos they come from London. London people always think they're *so* cool."

"Maybe you'll live in London one day," Nathan remarked.

"*You* might; I won't. I'm not clever enough."

"You don't have to be *clever*—"

"You know what I mean!" Hazel flashed. "To live in London you need a good job, and to get a good job you need to pass exams, and everyone knows I'm going to eff up my GCSEs. So don't talk to me about living in London, okay?"

"I thought Uncle Barty was helping you with schoolwork and . . . stuff?"

"Sometimes," Hazel said. "When I can be bothered."

"Bother!" Nathan gave her a dig with his foot, almost a kick. Best friend's privilege. He didn't say *Do you want to be stupid?* because he knew that in a way she did: being stupid was her protest in the face of the world, her little rebellion against education and convention, her insurance against any expectations he or others might have of her. *I'll do nothing, I'll go nowhere, I'll be no one. I'm stupid. That's that.* He wanted to tell her it was childish but he knew it wouldn't do any good. "What about the witching?" he asked. "Have you done any of that?"

She hunched a shoulder, tugging her hair over her face in a gesture she had still to outgrow. "You know I don't like it."

"You tried it yourself last year," he pointed out, brutally. "You made a complete mess of it, too. Ellen Carver nearly got killed and so did I. Uncle Barty said—"

---

28 · Amanda Hemingway

"All right, all right, I'm learning it." She pushed her hair back again, and some of the sullenness left her face. "He taught me how to make the spellfire the other night."

"Wow . . . What did you see?"

"Smoke," Hazel said.

"Just smoke?"

"Pictures," Hazel conceded. "Smoke-pictures. The past, the future—it's all mixed up and you can't tell which is which, and Uncle Barty says there are so many possible futures, you don't know if any of it's true, so what's the point of looking? Magic is all shadows and lies: you can't trust it. Anyway, I saw scenes from your life, not mine—the Grail, and some kind of sacrifice, and people from another world."

"Our lives run together," Nathan said. "But . . . you're not supposed to see other worlds in the smoke. The magic can't look beyond the Gate. Uncle Barty's always told me that. Are you sure—"

"I'm not sure of anything," Hazel said irritably, "except that I'm hungry." They were in her bedroom, and her private store of chips had run out. "D'you think your mum would have anything to eat?"

They went around to Annie's, and although Nathan pressed her, Hazel wouldn't be any more specific about what she'd seen.

Annie supplied them with granola bars—"I don't like those," Hazel muttered, "they're *healthy*"—and the information that the Rayburns were having a Christmas party the following month, holding open house for anyone from the village.

"They're not the Rayburns," Hazel said, nitpicking. "I told Nathan, the two little ones are Macaires, and the husband's something else. Coleman, I think."

"Donny Collier," Annie said. "Boyfriend or husband. Let's keep it simple—just call them the Rayburns. Go with the majority. Anyway, it looks like they're planning a pretty lavish do. At least half the village disapproves of them, but I bet they'll go."

Hazel was surprised into a laugh.

"Stay for dinner," Annie went on. "It's cauliflower cheese."

"That's healthy, too," Hazel quibbled.

"Are you sure there's enough?" Nathan said. "I'm not going short—that's my favorite."

"I'll stay," said Hazel.

Annie allowed herself a secret smile.

ONCE IN a while Bartlemy had visitors not from the village, strangers whom few saw come or go and fewer still remembered. The man who hurried through the November dusk that year was one such, a tall, stooping figure as thin as a scarecrow, in a voluminous coat and hood that had seen better days, probably two or three centuries ago. Under the hood he had wispy hair and a wispy beard and a face crisscrossed with so many lines there was barely room for them all, but his eyes, amid all their wrinkles, were very bright and green as spring. A dog accompanied him, a wild-looking dog like a great she-wolf, who trotted at his heel and stopped when he stopped, without collar or lead or word of command. She never barked or panted, following him as silently as his own shadow. The man came striding along the lane through the woods on that chill winter's evening, too late to have come off a local bus, too far from the train, and the dead leaves stirred behind him, as if something woke and watched, and there was a patter of pursuing feet on the empty road.

Neither man nor dog looked back, though the hackles rose on the beast's nape and her ears lay flat against her skull. When Bartlemy opened the door, the visitor said: "*They* are out there. I fear I am not welcome."

"You're always welcome here," Bartlemy said, "though I could wish you would change that coat."

"It has traveled far with me," the visitor retorted. "It smells of the open road and open sky."

"Not quite how I would have put it," said Bartlemy. "Take it off for once and sit down."

"I expect," said the visitor, "you were just making tea."

"I am always just making tea," Bartlemy admitted.

In the living room the two dogs surveyed each other, acknowledging past acquaintance, exchanged a sniff, and lay down on opposite sides of the fire. The wolf-like dog was big, with a wolf's elegance and poise, but Hoover was bigger, shaggier, shambling, somehow more doggy. They both knew she would have deferred to him if he had made an issue of it, so he didn't.

"What brings you to my quiet corner of the world?" Bartlemy inquired over the tea tray.

"I heard it was not so quiet of late," said the stranger.

"You heard . . . from whom?"

"I am not too much an outcast to read the newspapers," the man said. "There was the reappearance of the Grimthorn Grail—a few murders—an arrest but not, I believe, a complete solution. These are matters of interest to people like us."

"Indeed," said Bartlemy, "but that was two years ago. Why come now?"

"It's a long walk from the north. I no longer have the power to put wings on my feet."

"Your power may be worn out," Bartlemy responded, "but you can still move swifter than any of us, at need. Don't fence with me, Ragginbone. You've always claimed to be a Watcher: what have you seen?"

"I saw a peacock with a fiery tail," Ragginbone quoted. "I saw a blazing comet drop down hail. I saw a cloud . . . There have been omens and portents, some too strange to be easily read. There is a pattern in the stars pointing to a time of great significance, but whether good or evil is unclear. And more than that, there are whispers among the werefolk, tales of a Gate that will open at last, a loophole in the Ultimate Laws—a chance to snatch at power unguessed. No one knows quite when, or where—or how—but I heard you named as a guardian, or an obstacle."

"Who—?"

"I cannot be sure. They were voices in a crowd, on a dark street, and it was not a place where I wished to linger. There are many streets in the city, some darker than others, and not all those who use them are as human as they look."

Ragginbone was not obviously a man of the city, even without his coat, but Bartlemy knew better than to categorize him.

"Your wanderings take you to strange places," he said.

"There are strange places around every corner, if you walk on the dark side," Ragginbone said. "Belief creates its own kingdoms, even in this world. As the legends change, so do the pathways, but the shadows linger as long as memory, and the shadow dwellers are always there. Some of them may be coming your way, or so rumor has it. Some may be already here."

"Nenufar," said Bartlemy.

"The name I heard was Nephthys, but it is the same. She is old, and cold, and forever angry. Once, men sought to soften her with worship, but she could not be softened, not she. Now she has been sailed and chartered, polluted and abused, netted and dragged and mined, and the tale of her grievances is the lullaby she sings to the storm. What she may hope for, should the Gate open for her, I do not know, but the drowning of all humanity is in her dearest dream."

"You're well informed," said Bartlemy. It was almost a question.

"I have heard her in the scream of the wind, in the roar of the waves," Ragginbone said. It was not an answer. "And there are those who flee from her, bringing word of her wrath."

"The word on the street," Bartlemy concluded. "Have you come to offer help?"

"I have no help," the other said. "My spells have all gone stale. I came to warn you—and to wish you well."

"Thank you," said Bartlemy. "I need all the well-wishing I can get. Or rather, Nathan does."

"Who's Nathan?"

"I think," said Bartlemy, "he's the key."

"I have experience of keys," said Ragginbone. "Perhaps I should have said, *what* is he?"

"A boy. A relatively normal boy, insofar as anyone is normal. Intelligent, resourceful, courageous—but a teenager."

"He'll grow out of that," said Ragginbone. "Is he Gifted?"

"Not in the accepted sense. The power of the Lodestone on which

Atlantis was founded has never touched his genes. But he has . . . ability. To be precise, the ability to move between worlds. There is a portal in his mind—he passes it in dreams—in extreme cases his sleeping form disappears altogether, materializing in another universe. He seems to have little or no control over the phenomenon, but I suspect that someone else may be controlling him—guiding him—even protecting him. Someone from beyond the Gate. He has dreamed of a dying world, of a few survivors on the last planet, one stop from extinction. The ruler there is trying to perform a Great Spell. Plainly, Nathan has a vital part to play, presumably as a gatherer of certain objects. He has already retrieved the Grail, as you have heard, along with a Sword."

"Extraordinary," said Ragginbone after a pause. For him, this was strong language. "Great Spells are perilous, and may be millennia in the preparation. Are you sure?"

"The necessary elements are there. The feminine principle, the masculine principle, the circle that binds. A Cup, a Sword, a Crown. The Crown appears to have been mislaid, but no doubt it will turn up in time. Whenever that time may be."

"A Cup . . . the Grimthorn Grail?"

Bartlemy nodded. "I have been wondering," he said—changing the subject, or so it seemed, but Ragginbone knew better—"about a theory of yours. The Gift, as we know, is not native to the human race: the Stone of Power in Atlantis warped those who lived in its vicinity, giving them the talents their descendants still possess. Longevity, spell-power, the various madnesses that they engender. You have always maintained that the Stone itself was the essence of another universe—a universe with a high level of magic—accidentally catapulted into our own. Supposing, instead, it was just a *part* of another universe—an entire galaxy, for example—and its presence in our world was no accident . . . ?"

"In infinity and eternity," Ragginbone said, "all things are possible. What are you suggesting?"

"Perhaps our universe was chosen—as a refuge or an escape route—many ages ago, at least in our Time. The Gift may have been given so that certain individuals could perform their part: Josevius Grimling Thorn, called Grimthorn, who accepted the Grail, and myself, as Nathan's protector when he was a baby. My role has been very minor; nonetheless—"

Ragginbone was frowning. "I don't like it," he said abruptly.

"It was merely a hypothesis," Bartlemy said. "I was looking for a pattern in Chaos, but—"

"You misunderstand me. The theory is viable. That's what I don't like."

"You mean—"

"I was thinking of the classics," Ragginbone said. *"Timeo Danaos et dona ferentes."*

"I fear Greeks bearing gifts. A reference to the Trojan Horse, a gift whose acceptance by the Trojans led to the downfall of their city."

"Exactly," Ragginbone said.

IT RAINED heavily that night. In the visitor's bedroom under the eaves the roof leaked, though it had never done so before. Ragginbone woke, or dreamed he woke, and saw the steady drip-drip from the ceiling, and the water spreading in a puddle on the floorboards. Presently, a hand emerged—a white cold hand with bluish nails, like the hand of someone who has drowned—and groped around the edge of the puddle, seeking for purchase. The wolf-dog approached and growled her soundless growl, snapping at the crawling fingers, and the hand withdrew, slipping back into the water. The puddle shrank and vanished. The dripping stopped.

"No spirit can enter here uninvited," Bartlemy said in the morning. "Are you sure it wasn't just a dream?"

"The time is out of joint," Ragginbone said. "The old spells are unraveling; even the Ultimate Laws may no longer hold. The future casts more than a shadow. Whatever is coming, it may change everything."

"Keep in touch," Bartlemy adjured, seeing his visitor to the door.

"I will," promised Ragginbone. He did not say how. He strode off under a drizzling sky with the she-wolf at his heels, and Bartlemy returned to the sanctum of his living room, looking more troubled than he had in a long, long while.

ANOTHER VISITOR came to Thornyhill Manor that week, but he came to the back door and would have been seen by no one, unless they had weresight. He was barely four feet high and bristled with tufts of hair and beard, sprouting in all directions as if the designer of his physiognomy had never quite sorted out which was which. His clothing was equally haphazard, rags of leather, Hessian, oilcloth tacked together more or less at random, covering his anatomy but unable to produce a recognizable garment. Yet the most noticeable thing about him was his smell—the stale, indescribable smell of someone who has slept in a foxhole for a hundred years and thinks bathing is bad for your health.

Bartlemy seemed oblivious to it. He made food for his guest, rather strange food, with ingredients from a jar that sat on an obscure little shelf in the corner of the kitchen all by itself. His cooking gave off the usual aroma of herbs and spices and general deliciousness, but Hoover sniffed suspiciously at a morsel that fell to the floor, and let it lie. While his guest was eating Bartlemy poured two tankards of something home-brewed and flavored with honey, then sat back, waiting with his customary patience.

The dwarf made appreciative noises as he cleared his plate.

"Ye can chafe up a mean dishy o' fatworms," he remarked in an accent whose origins were lost in the mists of time, "e'en though they were no fresh. Howsomedever . . ."

"You didn't come to talk of cooking, I imagine," Bartlemy supplied.

"Nay. Nay, I didna, but there's no saying I wouldna rather talk o' food and drink and the guid things in life, instead o' the dark time to come. Ye'll be knowing it, I daresay. Ye're one who would read the signs and listen to the whisperings. The magister, he used to say to me: There'll be one day, one hour—one hour o' magic and destiny—one hour to change the world. I didna care for that, ye ken. The world changes, all the time, but slow, slow. What kind o' change can ye be having in a wee hour? It canna be anything guid, not to be coming that quick. Aye, and the magister's face would light when he spoke of it, wi' the light o' greed and madness, though he were niver mad. He didna have that excuse."

Some time in the Dark Ages the dwarf had worked for Josevius Grimthorn, scion of the ancient Thorn family—once owners of Thornyhill—and a sorcerer rumored to have sold his soul to the Devil. What he had gained from the transaction no one knew, but he was said to have lived nearly seven hundred years and died in a fire in his own satanic chapel, leaving the Grimthorn Grail to the guardianship of his descendants. That guardianship, like the manor, had passed to Bartlemy. The dwarf had fallen out with his master and been imprisoned for centuries in a subterranean chamber in the Darkwood, until Nathan and Hazel inadvertently released him. The lingering dread of his old master's activities remained with him.

His name, when he remembered it, was Login Nambrok.

"Did he tell you exactly when this hour is due?" Bartlemy asked.

The dwarf heaved his shoulders in a shrug bigger than his whole body. "He said I would feel it," he offered, "i' the marrow o' my bones. I'm no siccar there's much marrow left—my bones are auld and dry— but there's an ache in me like a warning o' foul weather to come. And there are other signs than my auld bones. The sma' creatures i' the wood, they're leaving—aye, or scurrying 'round and 'round like they dinna ken where to go. And there's birds flying south wi' tidings o' darkness in the north, and birds flying north wi' rumors o' trouble in the south, and so it goes on. There's times I think the wind itself has a voice, and it's whispering among the leaves, but mebbe that's a' fancy. And there's *them*—the invisible ones—they'd gather down by the chapel ruin, under the leaves, muttering together in the auld tongue, though I doot they understood the words—muttering and muttering the charms that magicked them. But lately—" He broke off with something like a shudder.

Bartlemy looked a question.

"There was a hare I'd been following," Nambrok said. "I'd fancied him for my dinner, and I'd been stalking him awhile, quiet as a tree spider, and he went that way. *They* saw him. Time was, they wouldn't have troubled any beast, but they saw him and chased him, down the valley and up the valley, chased him till he couldna run farther, and then they were on him and crowding in his head, and now the puir creature is madder 'n March, and bites his own kind, and snarls like a dog when ye come near him. That's no honest end for a beastie. And ye canna eat a creature that's been so enspelled. There've been others, too . . . and one day it'll be man, not beast. It'll be some chile walking in the woods, or a dog that sets on his master. There's no reason to it—nothing to guard—no threat—but . . ."

"They're out of control," Bartlemy concluded. And he repeated, more to himself than his companion: "The old spells are unraveling. Things are beginning to fall apart."

"Aye," said the dwarf, "and there's little ye can be doing about it, or so I'm thinking."

"Maybe," said Bartlemy. "But we can try."

ABOVE NATHAN'S house a single star shone. The night was misty and the sky obscured, but that one star shone brightly, a steady pinpoint of light looking down on the bookshop, while Nathan sat on the edge of the rooflight, looking up. When the dreams were most intense—when half his life seemed to happen in worlds whose reality was still unproven—he would climb up to the roof and gaze at the star, and that kept him sane. Winter and summer, its position never altered. It had been there now for two years and more, a star that did not twinkle or move along the set pathways of the heavens—a star that could not be seen beyond the borders of Eade—fixed in its place like a lamp to guide him home. *His* star.

He went to bed, reaching in his mind for the portal that would once more let him through, and dreamed of the star.

It hung in a chamber of darkness at the top of a tower a mile high. Light streamed outward from its heart but seemed to go nowhere and illuminate nothing, absorbed into the gloom around it. Other stars were suspended around the periphery of the room, pale globes emitting a similar radiance, but it was his star at the center, turning slowly on its own axis, a crystalline eye of intercosmic space. A lens on another world. Here, *his* world was the otherworld, the alien country. This was Arkatron on Eos, a city at the end of Time. In this room with no visible walls or floor a ruler ten thousand years old—a ruler who had held a whole universe under his sway—gazed beyond the Gate to find a refuge for the last of his people, a way of escape from the Contamination that had eaten the numberless galaxies of his realm. By day, his subjects went robed and masked against the poisonous sun; by night, they slept uneasily, anticipating the End. But in this chamber it was always night. Nathan's thought floated in the darkness, waiting. Presently, the Grandir came.

If he had a name, no one knew it. Other Grandirs had come and gone, leaving their names behind them, but he was last, and nameless. In a universe with a high level of magic, to know someone's name is to have power over him: the power of summons, even of Command, if the summoner is strong enough. *Like knowing the prime minister's cell phone number,* Nathan reflected, smiling to himself in thought. *I bet he doesn't give that to just anybody.* But the Grandir didn't tell his name even to his nearest and dearest—if he had them—not even to his bride-sister, Halmé, Halmé the childless, whose beauty was a legend among her people, though few had ever looked on her face. She went unmasked only in private chambers, for the eyes of a privileged few. As for the Grandir, Nathan had seen his face naked just once, in a dream that plucked him from danger, and the memory of it still made him shiver, though he wasn't sure why.

The Grandir wore a mask now, a white mask with perfect sculpted features, lips slightly parted to allow for speech, eye slots covered with bulbs of black glass. He was tall even for a tall race, and his protective clothing either padded or emphasized the great width of his shoulders and the mass of what must be a muscular torso. A cowl concealed both head and hair; gauntlets were on his hands. In the gloom of the chamber Nathan could distinguish few details, but he knew the costume from many times before. He watched with the eyes of his dream as the Grandir moved among the star-globes, not touching them yet somehow controlling their rotation. It was strange to be intangible where he had once been solid, invisible where he had once been seen. He wanted to say something, but knew he would have no voice.

Every so often a picture was projected onto the ceiling from one of the globes, a glimpse into another world. Nathan saw a castle that looked familiar—not really a castle, more a house with castle trimmings—and with a sudden shock he recognized Carboneck, where he had found the Traitor's Sword. There were people crowding outside in a city that had once been empty, people with bright happy faces, and a girl came out onto the steps, arm in arm with a young man, a girl with a lot of hair falling in many waves almost to her waist. She wore a crown of white flowers like tiny stars and a white dress glittering with gems or embroidery. *Nell,* Nathan thought with a sudden stab in his heart. *Nell in her wedding gown* . . . Princess Nellwyn, who had been his friend and ally in the alien kingdom of Wilderslee, when he'd drawn the Sword it was forbidden to touch, the Sword possessed by a malevolent spirit and endorsed by legend . . . He'd kissed her in the Deepwoods under the many-colored trees—but that was ages ago, more than a year, in a dream long faded. And in her time many years must have passed, and her face was lit with love, and Carboneck of the shadows had put out all the flags and was garlanded for a party . . .

Another picture, another place. A world of sea—the world of Nathan's latest dream—a world he had visited, though only briefly, once or twice before. "Widewater," said the Grandir as if to himself, and though he spoke softly his voice was a shock, breaking the silence of that high chamber. A voice like the rasp of iron on velvet, like the whisper of thunder, like the caress of fire. "The realm of Nefanu the mer-goddess, who hates all things that breathe the air. But there is always land under the sea, under the blue deeps and the green shallows. One day the mountains will lift up their heads and touch the clouds once more."

The star-globe could not see beneath the waves, but the image showed several marine animals leaping and diving in a glitter of spray— seals? No: dolphins or porpoises. But there was one among them who looked different, a mercreature with arms that glowed like pearl and a purple tail, flying higher than the others, almost as if she would take wing. And when the school had moved on she remained, head above water, dark hair uncoiling like smoke in the wave pattern, gazing up into the sunlight, up at a star she could not see. *Denaero?* Nathan wondered, but the vision was too far off to tell.

Then Widewater vanished, and now it was *his* star upside down on the ceiling. *His* world. The patchwork of roofs and gardens that was Eade, little streets and twittens and paths, the meadows stretching down to the river. The mooring at Riverside House, with an inflatable tied up there, and children jumping on and off—presumably the Rayburns— under the casual supervision of their mother. One little girl—a brown- skinned elf with nubbly braids—slithered down the bank and fell in, disappearing immediately under the water. No one noticed. Nathan wanted to cry out, but he couldn't be heard in the dream, let alone be- yond. For what seemed like an age the river surface remained unbro- ken. Then her head bobbed up again, mouth open in a wail, as though she had been thrust up from below, and her family were snatching at her, too many rescuers tangling with one another in their haste, and she was plucked out of the water, onto the bank, and hugged and fussed over and dried.

The picture blinked out, and Nathan was just a thought in the dark. The Grandir was standing close to him, a huge physical presence where he had none—Nathan could hear the murmur of his breath through the mask, sense the steady motor of his pulse that seemed to make the air vibrate. And suddenly Nathan felt the Grandir was aware of him, lis- tening for his thought, reaching out with more-than-human senses for the ghost that hovered somewhere near, unseen but not unknown. An inexplicable panic flooded his spirit, violent as nausea, and the dream spun away, and he was pitched back into wakefulness on the heaving mattress of his own bed.

Gradually, the mattress stabilized and Nathan subsided into normal sleep. There were no more dream journeys to other worlds, but he was haunted by images of Princess Nell in her wedding dress, running and running through an endless network of corridors, while he tried in vain to follow. Her laughter woke him in the morning, fading into music as the alarm went off and his radio started to play.

Terror Firma

For a place where a murderer had lived, Riverside House seemed to Annie, as ever, curiously lacking in atmosphere. The round towers that had formerly been oasthouses were joined by a two-story building with all the mod cons, currently littered with boxes—boxes sealed or opened, half unpacked or collapsed into folds for reuse—and assorted furniture, often in the wrong place. There was a sofa in the kitchen and a double bed in the living room. Daubs of paint on the walls indicated experimentation with future color schemes. Much of the kitchen had turned lemon yellow, decorated with random stencils of art nouveau vegetables. The Rayburns were bringing their own atmosphere, Annie thought, but there was nothing underneath. Several murders and the residence of a dark enchantress had left little impression.

"Have a seat," said Ursula Rayburn. "No—not there! Sorry. That's Gawain's school project." She picked up a fragile construction that seemed to consist mostly of paper, feathers, and glue. "Isn't it wonderful? I think it's meant to be a phoenix."

"I'm sure it's just like one," Annie said obligingly.

"Those pink fluffy bits look awfully like Liberty's feather boa. She was wondering where it had gotten to. Oh well, it's such a tiny sacrifice for her to make for her brother's artistic development. All my children are *so* creative." She sighed happily. "Except Michael, but he's a sort of mathematical genius, so that's all right . . . I hear Nathan's frightfully brilliant?"

"He does okay," Annie said, feeling uncomfortable. She had no desire to boast of Nathan's genius or creativity. All she wanted was for him to be as normal as possible—and under the circumstances that was difficult enough.

"Did you get hold of a plumber?" she went on, changing the subject.

"Oh yes," Ursula said. "Some firm in Crowford—but he said he couldn't find anything wrong, and I said there's got to be. We keep finding water on the floor. So he said maybe the roof leaks—it *has* rained a lot lately—but I said then it would be on the *top* floor, and it isn't, it's downstairs. Anyway, he thinks it could be sort of funneled down somehow, but I don't believe it. I haven't found any damp patches on the walls or ceiling."

Annie asked, a little hesitantly: "Could I see where—?" She expected Ursula to find her curiosity bizarre, but her hostess clearly thought she was just trying to be helpful.

"Of course you can." She led Annie through into the ground-floor room in one of the towers, which had once been a study. "This is going to be a sitting room," she explained. "I *love* the shape. At the moment, Romany's sleeping here"—a vague gesture encompassed a mattress on the floor—"and Michael and Gawain are upstairs. Jude and Lib are too old to share so they have their own rooms. The *murder room*'s going to be a guest bedroom—but only when I feel it's been completely purged of bad vibes."

Annie grinned. "So when people come to stay you can tell them: *We've put you in the haunted room . . . ?*"

"Actually," Ursula said, "I haven't really sensed any ghosts. It's a bit disappointing. At least, not exactly *disappointing*, but when a house has a history like this—well, you'd expect more than just vibes, wouldn't you? It isn't that I want to see an apparition or anything, but I *did* think . . . You know, a bloodstain that won't scrub out, or—or perhaps moaning in the night. *Something*."

"And all you've got is a puddle on the floor," Annie said thoughtfully. In the middle of the room was a large damp patch where the carpet still hadn't dried out.

"There's nothing ghostly about *that*," Ursula retorted. "It's just a bloody nuisance. I suppose we'll have to get someone to look at the roof next. I tell you, I'm going to sue that inspector . . ."

They went back into the kitchen, and she poured coffee.

"We had an awful fright last weekend," she went on. "The kids wanted a boat so much, so Donny got them an inflatable—it's on the bank now, down by the jetty—and they were messing around with it, and Romany fell in. I don't know how it happened—that river *is* dodgy, isn't it? She must've gone right under, and then she popped up again, and we got her out somehow, and she was fine, but it absolutely terrified me. I mean, she's eight, she can swim a bit, but she kept saying how the weeds pulled her under. I told them all they're to stay away from the river, but of course they won't."

Absently, Annie found herself murmuring the familiar lines:

"Cloud on the sunset
Wave on the tide . . ."

"What's that?" Ursula asked.

"It's a sort of local folk-rhyme," Annie said. "About the river.

Cloud on the sunset
Wave on the tide
Fish from the deep sea
Swim up the Glyde.

The river's tidal, you see." She didn't go on with the poem.

"Does that mean you can get dolphins and things? Like in the Thames?" Ursula looked enthusiastic, then dubious. "Surely not—this river's far too small. I expect that's just fanciful."

"Yes," Annie said. "Fanciful." She gazed pensively into her coffee, unsure of her own thoughts—or fears. Unsure what to say, and what to leave out.

Water on the floor—in the room where Romany slept. And it was Romany who fell in the river . . .

"I think," she said, "you should keep an eye on her."

"On who?"

"Romany."

"I always do. Though in the main, she's such a good child. A bit solitary—always inventing her own games, making up imaginary friends, going off on adventures with them. Of course, she includes Gawain sometimes—he's her baby brother, after all. I expect she'll grow up to be a great novelist, or playwright, or something."

As long as she does grow up, Annie thought.

Or was she being paranoid?

She would have to discuss it with Bartlemy when the opportunity offered.

HAZEL THOUGHT too much of her time at Thornyhill Manor was spent on schoolwork. She didn't know quite how it had happened, but in the last few months she had begun redoing her lessons with Bartlemy, and although a tiny part of her was secretly pleased that her grades had gone up, the stubborn, awkward, *Hazelish* part still told her lessons weren't exactly her thing, and she would never do really well, so it was all a waste of effort. Besides, schoolwork was boring, and she was supposed to be there to learn about magic. Despite her stated aversion to it, magic wasn't boring.

"Could we try the spellfire again?" she said one day offhandedly. "I'm sick of math. I never get it right."

Bartlemy's mild gaze narrowed with a hint of amusement. "You're doing fine with that geometry," he pointed out. "Math teaches you to think. If you do magic without thought, you'll end up like your great-grandmother. Do you want that?"

"N-no. I've just done enough thinking for one day."

"As it happens," Bartlemy said, "there is something with which I need your help. But it could be dangerous. I want to be sure you won't lose your head."

"*Dangerous?*" Hazel brightened, doubted, dimmed. In her experience grown-ups didn't normally ask you to do dangerous things. But then Bartlemy was unlike any other grown-up.

She said: "It's usually Nathan who gets to do the dangerous stuff."

"This time it's you," Bartlemy said.

"What is it?"

"The behavior of the gnomons is becoming . . . unpredictable. Something needs to be done about them."

"I always carry iron when I walk in the woods," Hazel said, thinking of the number in her coat pocket—a number originally made to go on the door of a house, which Nathan had provided for her protection two years ago. "But I haven't seen—sensed—them around for ages. Anyway, I thought they only attacked when someone threatened the Grail—or Nathan."

"So did I," said Bartlemy. "But the rules seem to be changing. I am told they are getting out of control. Someone saw a hare pursued and sent mad. The next time it could be a dog that will turn on its owner— or a person. They have to be neutralized."

"How?" Hazel asked bluntly.

"If we can trap them in an iron cage, perhaps sealed with silphium— the smell is inimical to them."

"What's silphium?"

"An herb, generally extinct, but I grow a little of it in my garden. The Romans used it extensively in cooking: they made a rather pungent sauce with it, served with fish. It has a very powerful odor that gnomons cannot tolerate. Remember, they have little substance but are equipped with hypersenses, reacting abnormally not only to the magnetic field of iron but also to certain smells and sound levels inaudible to human ears. We should be able to use these elements to hold them, if they can be lured into the trap."

"Who does the luring?" Hazel said with misgiving, already knowing the answer.

"That would be your job. But I understand if you don't wish to do it. Geometry is much safer."

Hazel looked down at a diagram involving several interrelated angles, two triangles, and a rhomboid. "I'll do it," she said. "Whatever it is I have to do."

"I have a plan," said Bartlemy.

Afterward, when she had gone, he poured himself a drink from an ancient bottle—a drink as dark as a wolf's gullet and smelling like Christmas in a wine cellar. A wood fire burned in the hearth, an unmagical fire whose yellow flames danced their twisty dances above the crumbling emberglow and bark flaking into ash. The dog lay stretched out in front of it, pricking one ear to hear his master speak.

"You will take care of her," Bartlemy said. "I don't want her in real danger. But she needs to feel valued—that's the important thing. She needs to know she can make a difference, if only in a small way."

Hoover thumped his tail in agreement or approbation, or possibly in the hope of a morsel of cake from the plate at Bartlemy's side.

"There was a time when I thought nothing I did would change the world," Bartlemy continued, in a reminiscent vein. "I was too busy looking at what they call nowadays *the bigger picture*. But big things are made up of small things. Move one particle and you alter the shape of the universe. Perhaps Hazel will remember that as the decades go by and disillusionment sets in. Meanwhile, you and I will alter the shape of her universe just a little—if we can."

Hoover pricked the other ear and lifted a shaggy eyebrow.

"Cake is bad for dogs," Bartlemy said. "Even my cake."

NATHAN HAD the accident about a week later. He called it an accident but he knew, as soon as he was capable of knowing anything, that it was his own fault. He was by the indoor pool—Ffylde Abbey had both indoor and outdoor swimming pools—with a group of boys, and Ned Gable was vaunting their prowess at diving in Italy that summer. They had visited a little bay a few times and taught themselves to dive off a low promontory into the sea, turning a somersault in midair on the way down. One of the boys looked skeptical and made a casually snide remark that Nathan would have ignored, but Ned rose to the bait, asserting the truth of his boast.

"Okay, show us," challenged the skeptic. His name was Richard but he liked to call himself Rix. His father owned a merchant bank.

"I can't," Ned responded, looking both discomforted and angry. "Not with this ankle." He'd torn some ligaments in a rugger scrum and was banned from most sport for at least another fortnight. "You know that."

"Convenient," sneered Rix.

"Nathan could do it," said a supporter with a surge of misguided loyalty.

"I'm not sure about that," Nathan said. "The rocks in Italy were higher than this diving board, and the sea below was really deep. It would be a bit chancy here."

"The pool's six feet at this end," Rix said. "Tom Holland, who left last year, he did all sorts of fancy dives off that board. I saw him."

"Tom Holland was the Interschools Champion," someone else pointed out. "*And* he was dead short—about five foot nothing. He could've dived into a puddle."

"Of course," Rix said, a little smile tweaking at his mouth. A smile at once patronizing and faintly *knowing*. "Don't worry, Nat. I understand."

Nathan didn't like anyone calling him Nat.

"*What* do you understand?" Ned growled, picking up his cue while Nathan was still trying to let it pass.

"Oh, it's easy to be chicken when you're so tall people are too scared to tell you the truth."

There was a brief pause, then suddenly Nathan laughed. "Yeah," he said. "I'm the class bully. Everyone's *really* scared of me." Since he was notoriously tolerant and had never bullied anybody, most of the group laughed with him, and the tension of the preceding moment was defused.

Rix took the laughter personally. He was the sort of boy who would take it personally if it rained on his birthday or his favorite soccer team lost a match. "So what you're *saying*," he resumed, "is that Ned here is a bigmouthed liar."

Ned balled his fist. Nathan, who had thought the whole stupid exchange was over, said: "What?"

"*He* says you did the dive when you were in Italy. *You* say you can't do it now—the pool's too shallow and all that crap. Excuses. That means you're calling him a liar. Your best mate, right? Some friend you are."

One or two of the others laughed at this piece of sophistry—not a relaxed sort of laugh, the way they had laughed with Nathan, but the uncertain kind that tightens up the atmosphere. If the teacher had been around he might have noticed something amiss and put a stop to it, but he had gone to the infirmary when one of his pupils started a nosebleed. Nathan had no fallback position; he knew he should call a halt himself, but Ned was looking at him with absolute confidence that his friend wouldn't let him down, and Nathan couldn't fail him. The dive wasn't safe, but he had done many far more dangerous things, in the otherworlds of his dreams, and somehow he had always come through, protected by chance, by fate, by whoever watched over him—the Grandir, or the sinister forces that shielded the Grimthorn Grail. He had been plucked from the jaws of desert monster and marsh demon, from the spelltraps of Nenufar—he had lifted the forbidden Sword, defeated the unknown enemy. Perhaps, on some subconscious level, survival had made him complacent. He shrugged, not looking at Rix, only at Ned.

"I'll do it."

Then he climbed up the steps to the diving board, stood poised on the edge.

Dived.

He knew, immediately, that he'd miscalculated. Everything happened at once very fast and very slow—the world arced as he completed the somersault—he tried to straighten out, to cut the water cleanly—hit the surface at the wrong angle—felt the sting of the impact, the rush of bubbles as the pool engulfed him. He needed to tilt his arms, curve the dive upward, but there was no depth beneath him, no time to maneuver. He'd opened his eyes underwater and for a long slow millisecond he saw the bottom of the pool coming for him like a moving wall. Then it struck, knocking the air out of him, and he was breathing water—his lungs clenched—the world spun away into darkness and pain . . .

It was Ned who got him out, jumping in fully dressed in spite of his sprained ankle, heaving him out of the water while the other boys reached down to haul him over the edge. They'd done lifesaving techniques earlier that term, and someone managed to pump at his chest while someone else tried mouth-to-mouth. Ned said: "Get Mr. Niall," meaning the games master, but no one did and it seemed an incredibly long time before any adults appeared on the scene to take over. There was blood on Nathan's head, on his arm, blood fanning out across the wet floor tiles. Rix stood back from the rest of the group, looking pale and uncomfortable.

"This is your fault," Ned said, struggling to evade his own guilt, knowing Nathan would never have reacted to Rix's taunting if it hadn't been for him.

"He was sh-showing off," Rix stammered, determined to convince himself.

Later, in the headmaster's study, he said the same thing.

ANNIE WAS informed and drove to the school in her yellow Volkswagen Beetle, exercising all the self-control she possessed in order not to go too fast. By the time she got there they were able to tell her Nathan would be all right: he had a concussion, a dislocated shoulder, severe bruising, and what the doctor called "extensive physical trauma," but no broken bones or internal damage. His first words to her were: "Sorry, Mum." She sat by his bed in the infirmary, holding his hand until it occurred to her that might embarrass him, torn between standard maternal anxiety, pointless anger—*why is he always doing dangerous things, even when it isn't necessary?*—and the sneaking paranoia of other, deeper doubts. Romany Macaire, tumbling into the river . . .

Nathan, diving into a pool too shallow for him . . . *Water, water, every-where* . . . Was it mere coincidence, or some dark supernatural plot?

"Don't overreact," Bartlemy said when she confided in him. "We're surrounded by water all the time. It's essential to life. Don't start seeing demons in every raindrop. Teenage boys do rash and often stupid things. Children fall into rivers. Accidents happen. It's a very human weakness, needing someone to blame."

Ned blamed Rix, at least to his classmates. To Nathan, he blamed himself, saying awkwardly: "It was me. I made you do it. I shouldn't have—"

"Forget it," Nathan said. "It was my own stupid fault. I knew the dive wasn't possible there but I didn't want to admit I couldn't do it."

He, too, was blaming himself, not just for his recklessness but for the seed of unthinking arrogance that had made him believe that whatever he did, no matter how foolhardy, he would somehow get away with. His guardian angel—or devil—would take care of him.

But the devil had let him down, and now he knew he was vulnerable, and a tiny germ of fear grew at the back of his thought, not the fear of danger but the fear of fear itself. He could be hurt—he might be killed. Knowing that, would he be able to explore the otherworlds as boldly as before, doing whatever he needed to do, or would his newfound fear hold him back?

He couldn't talk to Ned about it, or any of his other classmates, because they knew nothing of the voyages he made in his dreams and would only think him nuts if they did. He couldn't talk to Annie, because she was his mother and worried about him too much already. He couldn't talk to Bartlemy, because although his uncle came to see him once he was back home, they had no privacy for confidences.

In the end, he talked to Hazel. Just as he always had.

"You think too much," Hazel said. "Like what's-his-name in Shakespeare who wanted to avenge his father's murder and kept messing it up and killing the wrong people." She'd been on a school trip to see *Hamlet* the previous term. "He got rid of nearly everyone in the play before he killed the right person, didn't he? The point is, he spent too much time agonizing and making long speeches to himself instead of just getting on with the job. You're starting to do that. Picking your feelings to bits and worrying about them. It's a waste of time."

"I don't make long speeches," Nathan objected.

"You'd better not," Hazel said grimly. "The play was quite good but the speeches were boring."

"They're famous," Nathan said, quoting: *"To be or not to be, that is the question—* and something about *to die, to sleep—to sleep perchance to dream . . . For in that sleep of death what dreams may come . . ."*

"Boring," Hazel said. "You're going all thoughtful on me. That's your problem. Thinking."

"Thinking is a sign of intelligence," Nathan said.

"No it isn't," Hazel argued. "Stupid people think, too. It's the thinking that *makes* them stupid. Like that guy in the play. He stuck his sword in a curtain and killed a harmless old man because he *thought* he was someone else. Hamfist, Prince of Denmark. Stupid."

"I don't go around sticking swords into people," Nathan said. "At least, only once." He had picked up the Traitor's Sword—the Sword of Straw—and slashed at the Urdemon of Carboneck, but killing a demon, he felt, wasn't the same as killing a person. "Anyhow, that was self-defense. I didn't have much of a choice. The point is, maybe I found it easy to be brave, because—subconsciously—I thought I was sort of *looked after*. And now I know I'm not . . . well . . ."

"You were brave from the start," Hazel responded. "You couldn't have felt looked after then. If you're more scared now, you'll just have to be braver. You'll manage it. You're a brave kind of person. As long as you don't start *thinking* about it."

She hadn't told him about the gnomons. Bartlemy had said he would set the trap that weekend. Hazel had already decided that if she didn't think about what she had to do she wouldn't worry, and if she didn't worry she wouldn't panic, but the effort of not thinking was taking its toll. She knew she wasn't as brave as Nathan, but that only meant she had to try harder. Nathan's self-doubts she regarded as trivial—yet it was strangely reassuring to find that he, too, was having to cope with the possibility of failure and fear. Somehow it made her feel better about her own secret terrors.

"No thinking," Nathan said. "Right. I'll—um—bear that in mind."

"And don't start being *clever*," Hazel added, throwing him a dark look. "I can't stand that, either."

"Sorry," Nathan said. "Am I treading on your inferiority complex?"

"I don't have one," Hazel snapped. "I don't do complexes and stuff."

"Oh really? Then why—"

But that was the moment when Annie put her head around the door with an offer of tea and cake, and the downhill run to a juvenile squabble was averted.

SINCE THE accident Nathan had been on painkillers to help him sleep at night, and his dreams had stayed inside his head. The drugs, he suspected, affected his sleep patterns, making it impossible for him to stray outside his own world, but because the concussion had made him sick and the bruising had left him too stiff to move, he had been feeling far from adventurous. Still, he was strong and resilient with quick powers of recovery, and that night he decided he could do without the acetaminophen, though he didn't mention it to Annie. It was hard to get comfortable—his shoulder still twinged at any awkward movement—but eventually he drifted into sleep, and through sleep into dream.

Only it wasn't a dream. It was a nightmare.

He was diving into deep water, hurtling down and down through an endless gulf of blue. The seabed rushed toward him like a moving wall. He couldn't breathe, couldn't scream. He tried to close his eyes, to brace himself for the impact—but there was none. No impact, no eyes. With an exquisite surge of relief he realized he was only an atom of thought, a bodiless observer whose horrifying plunge had speed but no substance. He slowed as the seafloor drew near and found himself gliding above the level sand that stretched away in every direction, featureless as a desert. He guessed the water couldn't actually be all that deep, since he could still see in the blue dimness, and high above there was the glimmer of the sun's rays reaching down. Something like a cloud passed overhead, a huge shadow blotting out the far-off daylight. A ship, he thought, gazing upward—but no, this was Widewater, it

must be, where the land had been devoured by sea and there were neither people nor ships. Yet it looked like a ship, a vast, deep-bellied
tanker hundreds of feet long. Others followed, five, six, eight, one far
smaller, another little more than a dinghy. Not ships: whales. A pod of
whales far larger than any in our world, sailing the ocean like a convoy
of giant galleons.

His thought floated up, passing among them, emerging into a world
of sky and sea. A golden void of sunlight hung all around him. The
backs of the whales arched out of the water, rising and falling like slow
waves on their way to the horizon. Below him he heard a strange echoing boom, like the music of sea trumpets blown in the deeps, and he
knew they were singing. He thought, on a note of revelation: *This is*
their *world. Nothing here can hurt them.* All of Widewater was their
kingdom.

Around the rim of the sky, clouds were piling up, great thunderheads swelling visibly, rank on rank of them, like mountain ranges
marching across the sea. The sun was swallowed up; a wind came scurrying before the storm, whipping the waves into restless peaks. But the
whales did not vary their pace, heaving and sinking to the same steady
beat. A dark rain came slanting down; thunder drums drowned out the
whalesong. Purple lightning stabbed at the wave caps, foiled by the salt
water. A stem of cloud came writhing downward, sucking the sea into
its vortex, until sea and sky were joined by a whirling cord as thick as a
giant's arm. The water seemed to be flowing up it, feeding the storm-
heart.

Then Nathan saw the Goddess.

He could not tell if she was solid or phantom, vapor or water, but it
made no difference: she was terrible. Her upper body seemed to spout
from the wavering column of the tornado, filling the sky, a pale cloudy
shape with billowing hair that mingled with the thunderheads and
lightning eyes. Her arms were stretched wide as if to draw the whole
ocean into her embrace; the storm flowed from her fingertips. This was
the Goddess who had eaten the islands, destroying all human life, who
had made Widewater into a sea without a shore—the Queen of the
Deep, ruler of maelstrom and tempest, an elemental with no soul and

no heart, made of rage, and power, and greed. Even as he was, without form or substance, Nathan feared her.

Not just because she was a goddess. Because he knew her . . .

She bent down over the whale pod; he seemed to hear her voice like a giant whisper on the wind. *Lungbreathers!* The whales dived, eluding her cold grasp—all save one, the larger of the two calves, who hung back from curiosity, or because his reflexes were too slow. Her long fingers spanned his back, and the sea plucked him away from the others—away and away—sucking him into the storm, rolling him in the waves, spinning him into the tumult of the tornado. Nathan followed, drawn in her wake, closing his mind against the nightmare of engulfing water . . .

Long after, or so it seemed, the sea was calm again. The morning sun shone down through the water onto a coral reef flickering with smallfish. The young whale was coasting along its border, now far from family and friends, seeking the currents that would lead him back to the north. Then Nathan saw the fin cutting the water, just one at first, then another, and another. Following him. Circling. Nathan didn't want to watch anymore, but the dream would not let him go, not till the sea exploded into a froth of lashing bodies, and the red came, pluming up through the foam. Then at last it was all over, and the sea was quiet, and the finned shadows flicked and circled, flicked and circled, while the stain thinned like smoke on the surface of the water, vanishing into a vastness of blue.

Nathan sank out of the dream, and once again he thought he was drowning, plunging into a darkness without air or breath. He struggled in a growing panic, fighting against the familiar asphyxiation—and then he was in bed, breathing normally, and there was a hand on his forehead. A hand that felt unnatural, cold and leather-smooth. A hand in a glove.

The hand was withdrawn, and when it returned it felt like skin. Nathan's eyes were shut, but a picture formed in his head: the Grandir in his protective clothing, with his white mask and black gauntlets. It was an oddly comforting image. He found himself thinking about skin, human skin, the softness of it, its coolness and its warmth, the intimacy of its touch. Only a flimsy layer between hand and brow, between sense and senses, between heart and heartbeat. Animals had hide and scales and fur, feathers and down, protection and insulation. But humans wrapped themselves in a tissue-thin covering so transparent the blood vessels showed through, so fragile it might puncture on a leaf edge or a blade of grass, so sensitive it could feel the lightest pressure, from the footstep of a fly to the breath of a zephyr. Yet humans in their vulnerable skin were the most deadly predators in all the worlds . . .

It occurred to him that these thoughts didn't come from him—they were unfamiliar, alien thoughts that seemed to stretch his mind into strange dimensions. The Grandir's thoughts, flowing from the touch of his fingers into Nathan's head . . .

He opened his eyes.

A face was bending over him, a face that he had seen only once before, yet he seemed to know it well. A dark curving face with a metallic sheen on the hooked cheekbones and the blade of the nose. Hooded eyes, and beneath the hoods the glimmer of hidden fires, like glints of light in a black opal. Behind the eyes, deeps of power and thought, a force of personality that could reshape the cosmos. But for now, it was all focused on Nathan. There was a tiny frown between the eyebrows that seemed to convey both anger and gentleness. The Grandir's spirit was larger than that of other men; he could feel many emotions at once.

He said: "You fear the water, don't you? It is waiting for you in your dreams, but you fear to go there, to be overwhelmed by it—smashed against the rocks, crushed into the seabed. I have read the fear in your heart where there was none before. You must face it, and face it down. There are things you have to do, even in the dark of the sea."

"What happens if I become solid?" Nathan said. "I won't be able to do it. Whatever it is. I won't be able to breathe."

"You must find a way. Your folly has made your fear—the risk you took, when no risk was necessary—and for what? For what?" The frown intensified; for a moment, anger supervened. "To impress your peers! To vindicate the one you call friend! They are nothing—less than nothing—but you *matter*. You have no idea how much you matter. And you might have been killed—for a *gesture*! An instant of bravado!"

The hand had left Nathan's forehead to stroke his hair. For all the Grandir's fury and frustration, his touch was soft as a caress.

Nathan said: "Everyone matters." He was trying to hang on to that.

"You don't understand. One day—but not yet, not yet. You *must* take care. No more folly. No more rashness." Voice and face changed. The hard curve of his mouth appeared to soften. Almost, he smiled. "You are just a boy—so young, so very young. It is long and long since I had contact with youth. I had forgotten how it shines—how valiant it is, and how defenseless. You have tasks to accomplish, but your youth will find a way. You will go back to Widewater. I will care for you— when I can. But I cannot always save you. Remember that."

Nathan said sharply: "Did you show me the whales? And the Goddess?"

"These are things you needed to see—"

"Who is she? I thought—I knew her."

"She is Nefanu, Thalassé, Queen of the Sea. You know her double, the witch from the river. But the spirit in your world is far less in power, though not in hunger. She would make earth her kingdom, a desert like Widewater, landless and bare. She seeks to open the Gate and draw power from her sister-spirit, her other self—but that is unimportant. She has no part in my plans. It is Nefanu who dominates your task."

"But how can I face a *goddess*?" Nathan demanded, trying to sit up. The hand restrained him.

"Only do what you must. Perform the task ordained for you; no more."

"*What* task?"

"You know what task. Enough questions. There may be a time later, but not now. Now, Time is running out. My world is running out. Do your part. All my trust is in you . . ."

The dream was receding, almost as if the Grandir was thrusting him away, back into sleep, into his own universe. He knew a sudden fever of urgency—if he could only find the right questions maybe he would learn the answers at last. *One day,* the Grandir had said. He was groping blindly between worlds, fulfilling some obscure destiny that no one would ever explain—a pawn in an inscrutable chess game, a puppet on detachable strings. He knew it had to do with the Great Spell—with the Grail relics that he alone could retrieve—but there was still no answer to the great *Why?* Why was he born with this bizarre ability to travel the multiverse—an ability he could not even control? Why was he sent on this unknown quest? Why *him?*

He tried to speak, to protest . . . but the Grandir's face was slipping away, curving into the swirl of the galaxy, glimmering into stars. Darkness followed, and a sleep without dreams, and he woke in the morning to the pain in his shoulder, and the ache in his head, and a tangle of thoughts to unravel.

Annie brought him tea in bed, a rare indulgence that, as she explained to him, would run out as soon as his bruises unstiffened.

"I'm not really stiff now," he said provocatively. "I could get up easily."

"No you don't." She scrutinized his face, noting the sallow tinge to his complexion and the shadows under his eyes. "You look as though you've slept badly. Did you take your painkillers?"

"I don't like taking pills all the time."

"Yes, but the doctor said you're supposed to take them at night for at least another week." She sat down on the bed, her exasperation changing to anxiety. "Have you—have you been dreaming again?" And, after a pause: "*Those* dreams?"

He shrugged. Nodded.

"For God's sake." Annie fumbled for the right words, not wanting to hear herself fussing—knowing fussing would do no good. "You're not fit enough yet . . ."

"I don't need to be fit. I wasn't there physically; just in thought."

"Something's scared you. You look done in."

He wasn't going to tell her about his fear of the water. "I'm okay," he assured her. "Just trying to figure out what's going on."

"Can I help?"

"Maybe." He hesitated. "How much do you know about the water spirit who was after the Grail?"

Annie tensed, her nebulous fears returning like bats to their cave. "Do you think she had something to do with your accident?"

"No. No, not that. But I've been to this place—Widewater—it's all sea, a whole planet with nothing but sea. There was land once but it was overwhelmed. *She* devoured it. She hates all creatures of the air—lungbreathers—even whales and selkies. They call her the Goddess, the Queen of the Sea—the Grandir said her name was Nefanu. She seems to have some connection with the water spirit here. Like an alter ego—a more powerful twin. And more evil."

"A doppelgänger," Annie said promptly. "I know. The theory is that we all have other selves in other worlds, living out alternative lives."

"It's something I've come across before, in a way," Nathan said. "Not exactly other selves but . . . parallels. The same stories running through every world, the same kind of people. Like, Nell always reminded me of Hazel—a medieval, princessly Hazel, much prettier and a bit spoiled—"

"Don't ever tell her that," Annie said hastily.

"D'you think she'd mind?" Nathan sounded a little surprised.

"The phrase *much prettier* isn't good. About this goddess—?"

"This is different. The link seems to be much closer—as if the spirit in this world *knows* her counterpart is out there, and wants to reach her, to bond with her. That's why she wants the Grail—and me. Or so the Grandir said."

"You've talked with him?" Belatedly, Annie was picking up on the implications. More bats came home to roost.

"Yes, but only briefly. He says he's helping me, or guiding me, but he never answers my questions. Not the really vital ones."

Annie asked, very carefully: "What kind of a—a *being* is he?"

"Human." Nathan was startled. "Like Eric, only taller. Big shoulders. He makes you feel . . . like he's huge, not so much physically but his personality, his mind. His aura. He has the kind of vibes that fill up all the available space. He could talk to a crowd of millions, and every single person there would think and feel exactly what he wanted them to think and feel. And he wouldn't even be trying: it would just happen. That's how he is. Huge *inside*. It's difficult to describe . . ." He was running out of metaphors, gazing intently at Annie in an attempt to convey some impression of the man who had ruled a cosmos—who had laid an ungloved hand on his forehead and stroked his hair. For a minute he thought his mother had gone deadly pale. The way she might have looked if a raven had flown into the room and perched on the bedstead, croaking: *Nevermore*—

And my soul from out that shadow that lies floating on the floor
Shall be lifted
Nevermore!

—but he concluded it was a mere quirk of fancy, a footstep on his grave; that was all. The bleak winter daylight made everyone look gray and cold.

He said: "Mum . . . ?"

"Sorry," Annie said. "I was . . . woolgathering. The goddess—what did you call her? Nefanu. Nefanu—and Nenufar. That's almost an anagram. It can't be coincidence."

"I hadn't thought of that. D'you suppose she's still around—Nenufar, I mean?"

"I don't know," Annie said, but her expression gave the lie to her words.

She knew.

AT FFYLDE, the blame chain had reached the headmaster. He had been in the job for less than a year, after his predecessor, the abbot, had left for higher things. Unlike Father Crowley, he was a layman who talked managementspeak and prided himself on his ability to bond with the boys, especially those with the wealthiest and most influential parents. Right now his main concern was that Nathan's accident had occurred in the absence of the games master, laying the school open to possible charges of negligence. It was therefore imperative that blame—like the baton in a relay race—was passed on to someone else. The only question was whom. After interviewing Rix, sympathetically and at length, he talked to the other witnesses.

"I gather Nathan was—hrmm!—showing off," he suggested.

Ned Gable said flatly: "No. Nathan never shows off. He isn't like that."

And, baring his chest for the knife: "It was my fault. I was the one who . . . I should've done the dive, but I couldn't because of my ankle. So Nathan had to."

"Very fine of you," the headmaster said indulgently, "standing up for your friend, but you can't take responsibility for his actions. That will be all."

"Sir—"

"That will be *all*."

The other boys received the headmaster's suggestion with variations on a blank gaze and stony silence. Father Crowley would have known how to elicit the true facts, but the new head had neither his piercing eye nor his uncanny omniscience, and was only too ready to take that silence for assent. In the classroom, *omertà* was the rule of the day: none of the boys would point the finger at Rix in front of an adult, whatever their private feelings—that would be the behavior of a super-snitch. However, many of them resolved secretly that on the rugger pitch they would make him pay.

All of which did Nathan no good at all.

"The boys shouldn't have been left unsupervised," the head told their form master, Brother Colvin. "That goes without saying. We can only hope the Ward woman won't get herself an unscrupulous lawyer—that could cause us a lot of trouble."

"*Mrs.* Ward," said Brother Colvin, laying some emphasis on the title, "is a very sweet person who would never dream of doing such a thing. A year or so ago Nathan had a problem with Damon Hackforth—he was a bit of a delinquent, we'd had a lot of problems with him—and Annie was quite amazingly kind and understanding about it. The whole business could have been very serious, both for the Hackforths and the school. If she hadn't shown truly Christian forbearance . . ."

"I see," said the headmaster. "I hadn't realized Nathan had a track record as a troublemaker."

"Nathan wasn't the one making trouble," Brother Colvin said. "I told you—"

"No, no, Brother, say no more. He never makes trouble, he's just caught up in it. That's the danger with these scholarship boys: we all feel obliged to bend over backward for them, no matter how badly they behave. They come to us from questionable homes—I gather Mrs. Ward is a single parent—no discipline, no moral standards, and they're thrown in the midst of decent kids from good families, and thanks to political correctness we have to make heroes of them. Well, I won't have it. I infer Nathan fancies himself as a 'tough guy'—he'd probably call himself street-smart—and that sets a very poor example to the others. And word gets around, believe me. Many parents of prospective pupils could be discouraged by that sort of thing. I intend to see that Nathan's scholarship entitlement for next year is going to be reconsidered."

"He's very bright," Brother Colvin pointed out with deceptive mildness. "His results make an important contribution to our position in the league tables."

"Well, well. We'll see. Perhaps Mrs. Ward may be offered some kind of subsidy, providing she can come up with the bulk of the fees. This is a prestige establishment, not a charity school. I see no reason why she should freeload when other parents are prepared to dig into their pockets—often to make sacrifices—for their children's welfare."

Brother Colvin blinked. He wondered fleetingly what sacrifices bankers, stockbrokers, and oil millionaires had to make to pay for their sons' education. Living half the year in a tax haven, perhaps?

He said, still fighting his corner: "Nathan's also an accomplished athlete. He's on the school team for both rugby and cricket."

"No doubt," said the head with a thin smile. "I don't believe in favoring a boy for such reasons. This isn't Cambridge, where they tolerate almost anything if a student can wield an oar." In his youth he had been turned down for Magdalen, and he still bore a grudge.

"Father Crowley had a very high opinion of Nathan," Brother Colvin persisted.

A tactical error.

"Father Crowley," said the head loftily, "was, I am sure, a naïve and trusting soul, as befits a man of the cloth. I, alas, am expected to take a more worldly view. The governors installed me as his successor since they needed someone with secular experience and the people skills that come from a life lived in the rough-and-tumble of the wider world." *He's quoting from the speech he made when he first came here,* Brother Colvin thought with a sinking heart. "Trust me: I understand these boys. I can sense a bad apple even before I bite into it. Besides," he added obscurely, "we have a good ethnic mix here." Belatedly, Brother Colvin realized this was a reference to Nathan's dark complexion. "Think of Aly al-Haroun O'Neill—Charles Mokkajee—just the sort of pupils we need."

"If the corruption charges against Mr. Mokkajee Senior stick," Brother Colvin said rather tartly, "he'll be spending a long time in a Bombay jail. Hardly the most desirable parent."

"Now, now," said the head with a tolerant smile. "He's innocent until proven guilty; we mustn't forget that. Anyhow, I gather the case will be bogged down in the Indian legal system for some years. And by the way, it's *Mumbai,* not *Bombay.* We don't want to offend Charles's ethnic sensibilities, do we?"

"No—of course not," said Brother Colvin. Seething with frustration and other, less Christian, emotions, he took his leave.

ON THURSDAY night Annie stood over Nathan while he took the painkillers. He tried not to be glad about it. He wasn't yet ready to face the sea again.

In Thornyhill woods, it was raining. Water drizzled out of the sky and dripped through the trees with the peculiar persistence of English rainfall. Hazel, peering out of a latticed window, thought the weather could keep it up all night and all the next day and probably right through the following week. It was that kind of rain. Although it was barely seven, she felt as if it had been dark for hours. Evening had set in midway through the afternoon with no real daylight to precede it, just the gray gloom of overcast skies and general Novemberitis. Bartlemy had cheered her up by allowing her to abandon math for supper—wild rabbit roasted in honey and chestnuts, creamed spinach, homegrown-apple tart—and now they were discussing the shortcomings of Hamlet and why too much thinking was bad for you.

"He was stupid, wasn't he?" Hazel insisted. "Not stupid like me, but clever-stupid, if you see what I mean."

"I see exactly what you mean," Bartlemy said. "He used thought as a substitute for action, and when he *did* act, it was in the wrong place at the wrong time. A common failing of highly strung, oversensitive adolescents. Of course, he was only sensitive to his own feelings, not other people's, or he would have been less prone to commit haphazard murders. As it was, *the native hue of resolution* got *sicklied o'er with the pale cast of thought.*"

"That's what I said," Hazel averred.

"However," Bartlemy resumed, "I didn't know *you* were stupid. This is hardly a stupid conversation."

"My teachers say I am," Hazel mumbled, caught off guard. "Anyway, my mum's not that smart—nor's my dad. To be clever, you have to have clever genes. That's right, isn't it?"

"Don't underrate your mother. Or your father, for that matter. Everyone has brains. The question is whether they choose to use them. How will you choose?" Hazel was silent, briefly nonplussed. "Pleading bad genes is a very poor excuse for unintelligence," Bartlemy concluded.

That was the point when she wandered over to the window, evading a response, staring darkly into the dark.

Neither of them saw the figure on the road nearby: little could be distinguished through the rain curtain and the November gloom. Only Hoover lifted his head, cocking an ear at the world beyond the manor walls.

The man on the road wore jeans that flapped wetly round his calves and a heavy-duty sheepskin jacket without a hood. Raindrops trickled down his hair inside his turned-up collar. His face was invisible in the dark, but if it hadn't been a passerby would have seen lean, tight features clenched into a lean tightness of expression, grimmer than the grim evening—grim with determination, or discomfort, or something of both. But there were no passersby. The road was empty and almost as grim as the man.

He had left his car more than a mile back, close to the Chizzledown turning, when the slow puncture became too hazardous for driving. No one would want to change a tire on such a night, but he was a chief inspector in the CID, on more or less official business: he could have called a subordinate to pick him up, or the AAA or a local garage whose owner owed him a favor after he had prevented a robbery there. Instead he chose to walk through the woods, wet and growing wetter, wearing his grimness like a mask under the water trickle from his hair.

It wasn't even the best route for him to take, on foot or by car, but he often drove that way, though this was the first time in over a year he had found a reason to stop. There was no light on the road and from time to time he stepped in a puddle, cursing under his breath as the water leaked into his shoes. The only sounds were the squelch of his own footfalls, the hiss of the occasional oath, and the murmur of the rain. He didn't know what made him turn around—instinct, perhaps, a sixth sense developed over years of seeing life from the dark side. He could make out little in the murk but had an impression of movement along the shoulder, a rustle beyond the rain—the sussuration of bending grasses, the shifting of a leaf. And then, light but unmistakable, the scurrying of many feet—small feet or paws running over the wet pavement. An animal, or more than one. Nothing human. Nothing dangerous. In an English wood at night, the only danger would be human. There were no panthers escaped from zoos, no wolves left over from ancient times—he didn't believe in such stories. No animal could threaten him . . .

He was not a nervous type but all his nerves tensed: Fear came out of the dark toward him. Fear without a name, without a shape, beyond reason or thought.

Fear with a hundred pattering feet, just out of rhythm with the rain . . .

He knew it was illogical, but instinct took over. He turned and ran. Ahead he saw the path through the trees, the gleam of a lighted window. He slipped in the wet and almost fell, lurching forward. Inside the house a dog barked once, sharp and imperative. The front door opened.

The man stumbled through the gap into Bartlemy's entrance hall.

"Chief Inspector Pobjoy," Bartlemy said. "What a pleasant surprise."

IN THE living room he found himself seated by the fire, sipping some dark, potent drink that was both sweet and spicy. Hazel surveyed him rather sullenly; after all, he had once treated her as a suspect in a crime. He said, "Hello," and, on a note of faint surprise, "You've grown up." He wondered if he should congratulate her on becoming a young lady, but decided she didn't look like an eager aspirant to young-lady-hood and he would do better to keep quiet. In any case, the Fear had shaken him—the violent, inexplicable Fear reaching out of the night to seize him. It wasn't even as if it was very late.

Bartlemy said, "There's some apple tart left," and threw Hazel an admonitory look when she muttered something about *waste*.

The tart was hot, blobbed with clotted cream. If Eve had prepared such a tart, the gods would have forgiven her the theft of the fruit.

Between mouthfuls Pobjoy said: "I had a flat."

"I'm surprised you didn't phone for help," Bartlemy remarked. "On a night like this."

"Battery needs recharging," Pobjoy explained.

Hazel thought with a flash of insight: *He's lying. Why? Has he come here to spy on us?*

She said: "Let's see."

Pobjoy stared at her but didn't answer.

"Hazel, don't be rude," Bartlemy said mildly. "I'm always happy to see the inspector. He helped save Annie from a psychopathic killer—or have you forgotten?"

"She saved herself," Hazel argued. "She's much tougher than she looks."

"I know," Pobjoy said. "She's a very brave woman." He was disconcerted by his own recent cowardice, by the strange panic that had held him in its grip. He hid uncertainty behind the leftovers of his former grimness.

Bartlemy looked faintly amused, as if he knew. "I think," he said, "you'd better tell us what happened out there before you fell through my door. You were running away from something, weren't you?"

"It was nothing," Pobjoy said. "Nothing I could see. The dark—some animal—I don't know what came over me. I'm not one to jump at spooks just because I'm on a lonely road."

It was Hazel's reaction that surprised him. *"Them,"* she said, and her voice was gruff. And to Bartlemy: "It is, isn't it?"

"I fear so."

"But why were they after *him?*"

"The rules have changed," Bartlemy reiterated. "They're out of control. You did well to run, my friend. Had they caught you, they would have entered your mind and driven you mad. Remember Michael Addison."

"This is nonsense," Pobjoy said, setting down his plate, fortified by the apple tart on its way to his stomach and the afterglow of the unknown drink. "I don't know what you're talking about, but I don't believe it. All that supernatural crap. I was just—spooked. That's all."

"Then go outside," Bartlemy said. "See for yourself."

Pobjoy got up, walked through the hall, opened the door.

They were there, he knew it immediately. Watching for him. Waiting. Just beyond the reach of the light. He saw shadows shifting in the darkness—heard the whisper of the rain on the leafmold, and behind it another whispering, as of voices without lips, wordless and soulless. Suddenly he found himself picturing Michael Addison's drooling mouth and empty eyes. Fear reached out in many whispers. The hairs crawled on his skin.

He drew back, closing the door. Against the night, against *Them.*

Back in the living room he said, trying to keep his voice even: "What are they?" And: "What do I do?"

"For the moment," said Bartlemy, "you stay. I think you need another drink."

A Touch of Death

Bartlemy sent Hazel home in a taxi that he paid for, even though she insisted she could perfectly well walk. "I have iron," she pointed out. "I'm not afraid." She was determined to put Pobjoy in his place, to show him that in a world of dark magic—a world where being a policeman counted for nothing—she was the one who could handle herself. But Bartlemy overruled her and Pobjoy barely noticed. He had more than enough to think about.

"What *are* those creatures?" he repeated when the two men were alone.

And in the subsequent silence: "I don't believe in ghosts."

"They are not ghosts," Bartlemy said. "Here, they might be called magical, but you must realize *magic* is merely a name for a force we don't understand. Once we can analyze it and see how it works, it becomes science."

"That's an old argument," Pobjoy said. "Television is magical unless you're a TV engineer. The *things* out there—how do they work?"

"They come from another universe," Bartlemy explained matter-of-factly. "They are made of fluid energy, with little or no solid form; partly because of this, some can migrate between worlds. The species has the generic name of *gnomons,* but those able to cross the barrier are called *Ozmosees.* I heard about them—read about them—once, but these are the first I have ever seen, since although they *did* exist in this universe, they died out here long ago. They are hypersensitive to sound, smell, light, but they have no intelligence and must be controlled. I am not sure how that is done; possibly by the dominion of a very powerful mind."

"What are you saying?" Pobjoy demanded, resolutely skeptical. "They got here through the back of a wardrobe?" He had read few of the right books but had once inadvertently watched a documentary on the making of *Narnia.*

"I doubt it." Bartlemy smiled. "Unfortunately, I know very little about them, and their behavior—as you must realize—is hard to study, though I have tried. The process may be assisted by attaching them to a person or object in *this* world, thus drawing them out of their place of origin. We cannot know for certain. However—"

"What object?" Pobjoy interrupted. He was a detective, and even on such unfamiliar territory he could work out which questions to ask.

"I imagine you can guess."

There was a short pause. "The cup?" Pobjoy said, as illumination dawned. "The Grimthorn Grail?"

"Precisely," Bartlemy replied, looking pleased, like a teacher with a pupil who, after a long struggle, has finally grasped the principles of calculus. "They appear to have been sent to guard it. There are also indications that their guardianship extended to Nathan and Annie—"

"*Nathan and Annie?* But—why?—how?"

"I don't know," Bartlemy admitted. "There is some connection between them and the Grail, too complicated to go into now. In any case, I am not yet sure exactly what it is, or how deep it goes."

"*Did* Nathan steal it that time?" Pobjoy asked sharply.

"Dear me, no. In fact, he got it back. It's a long story, too long for now. To return to the gnomons, the problem seems to be that they are no longer—focused. There was no reason for them to pursue you, yet they did. And there have been other incidents lately. Evidently they are getting out of hand. The power that manipulated them may be losing its grip, or merely losing interest. There could be other factors. At this time, we have no way of finding out."

"Are you saying someone here—some sort of *wizard*"—Pobjoy enunciated the word with hesitation and distaste—"is controlling these creatures? Some local bigwig with secret powers?" He didn't even try to keep the irony from his tone.

"Of course not," Bartlemy said mildly. He was always at his mildest in the face of scorn, anger, or threat. "Their controller is in the universe from which they came. That's why we know so little about him."

"*If* this is true," Pobjoy said, attempting to keep the world in its rightful place, "what's his interest in the Grail?"

"He placed it here," Bartlemy said. "Probably for safekeeping. A long time ago I had a teacher who contended there were many other-world artifacts secreted—or in some cases dumped—on this planet. He claimed they were responsible for almost all myths and legends, and several major religions. Apples of youth, rings of power, stone tablets falling out of the sky. That sort of thing. Of course, he may have exaggerated a little."

He's nuts, Pobjoy thought. *Clever, yes—harmless—but nuts. I wonder if Annie knows?*

Then he visualized the gnomons, waiting in the dark . . .

He spent the night in the guest room.

HE WAS woken in the small hours by someone tapping on the window. It was a gentle sound, barely louder than the rain, but it jerked him abruptly from sleep. Too abruptly. For a few seconds he didn't know where he was or what he was doing there. His bleary gaze made out a shape through the panes, behind the raindrops. A face. A pale blurred face with midnight eyes and a floating mist of hair. A face he had seen somewhere before, the same and yet different, but he couldn't quite catch hold of the memory. He got up and tried to make his way across the room, but he stumbled against the unfamiliar furniture and when he looked again the face was gone. Back in bed he returned gratefully to the realm of sleep.

It was only in the morning that it struck Pobjoy that his room was on the second floor. He opened the window, surveying the crime scene, but there was no convenient tree nearby, and the ivy on the wall would never support a climber. Downstairs, he slipped out into the garden, checking the earth for the imprint of a ladder, but there was none. Over the best breakfast he had ever eaten he called the AA for his car and the police station for a lift to work. For the moment, he wanted no further discussion with Bartlemy.

He needed some time to convince himself none of it had ever happened.

IT WAS a long time since Hazel had walked through the woods without the comfort of the iron door number in her pocket, and she was disturbed by how defenseless its loss made her feel. She had been in the habit of fingering the metal as she walked, fiddling with it like a worry bead, and now her hand was stuck in her pocket with nothing to do, clenching involuntarily from time to time, relaxing again when she noticed her nails digging into her palm. She was some distance from the road, on a track that wound its way toward the valley of the Darkwood, where it petered out. All tracks failed in the Darkwood, a deep fold in the countryside with a stream running through it that would change course in a shower of rain, where the trees tangled into thickets and the undergrowth grew into overgrowth and any sunlight got lost on its way to the ground. Long ago Josevius Grimthorn, first guardian of the Grail, had performed bizarre rites in a chapel there—a chapel buried for centuries under the leafmold and the choking tree roots. Nathan had stumbled into it once by accident, but there was a spell on the place that forbade him to speak of it, and it was long before he found it again. And Josevius's house had been there, too, burned down in the Dark Ages, where Login the dwarf had been imprisoned in a hole beneath the earth.

Hazel was thinking of that as she walked, wondering if he was watching her from some hidden hollow in the leaves, or perched furtively among the branches. She glanced around every so often, watchful and wary, but there was only the great stillness of the trees stretching in every direction. *That's the thing about woods,* she thought: *when you're inside one it seems much bigger than it really is, as if it goes on forever.* And they had their own special quiet, when they shut out the sounds of the free wind and the open sky, and you could hear a twig crack or an acorn drop a long way off. But that afternoon there was little to hear.

She knew this part of the wood well—she had come there as a child, when her father still lived at home and she wanted to be on her own. She would scramble up among the boughs and stay there for hours, watching mites creeping in the bark, or a caterpillar eating its way through a leaf, listening to the bird chatter and the insect murmur, and the great silence waiting behind it all. Later, when she was older, she had come to talk to the woodwose, Nathan's strange friend, with his stick limbs and sideways stare, till he went back to his own place. She had always felt at ease here, on familiar territory—until now. Now, when she knew the gnomons were lurking somewhere, no longer bound to their purpose but aimless and astray, ready to turn on anything that crossed their path. Hoover was trailing her, some twenty yards back, which gave her a little security, but nonetheless she jumped when a squirrel's tail whisked around a tree bole, froze into alertness at the tiniest rustle in the leafmold.

But they did not come. There were a hundred small warnings, a hundred false alarms. And nothing. The path ran out, and the woodland floor dipped toward the valley. *Don't go there,* Bartlemy had said. *There's no room to run, and you could easily get lost. If you reach the Darkwood, turn back.*

Hazel turned back. After a while, Hoover caught up with her, lolloping at her heel.

"No luck," Hazel said. If luck was what she was looking for.

"They inna there," said another voice close by—a voice with a brogue as old as the hills, and almost as incomprehensible.

"Hello," Hazel said, politely. "Have you seen them?"

"Nay," said the dwarf. "They'll be in the auld chapel, where the magister used to consort wi' the Devil when he popped up from hell for a chat. I've seen them there o' nights, a-heebying and a-jeebying, whispering thegither for hours, though I never heard they had aught to say."

"It's not night," Hazel pointed out.

"Night—day—at the runt end of the year, there's no muckle difference."

"Could you show me the place?" Hazel asked. "Not now—it's a bit late—but another day?"

"Aye," the dwarf said slowly. "But I'm thinking the goodman would not be wanting ye to go there."

"Then we won't tell him," Hazel said, doing her best to sound resolute. "We have to trap the gnomons. If they won't come to me, then I have to go to them."

"Ye're a bold lass," said the dwarf, but whether in approval or criticism she couldn't tell. "I'll be seeing ye."

He was gone, and ahead she saw Bartlemy emerging from the gloom of the fading daylight.

"They didn't come," Hazel said.

"So I gather. We'll try again tomorrow."

But on Sunday it rained too heavily for hunting phantoms, and during the week Hazel had school.

"I could skive off one afternoon," she offered, nobly.

"No," said Bartlemy. "We'll wait for the weekend."

"The weekend," Hazel echoed, thinking of the Darkwood and the chapel under the tree roots, and her stomach tightened in anticipation of terrors ahead.

NATHAN WENT back to school on Monday, still taking the painkillers each night, less to make him sleep than to keep him in his bed. It was always awkward wandering between worlds in the dormitory, since the more solid he appeared in his dreams, the more insubstantial his sleeping form would become. It was only when he was back home for the weekend, and assuring his mother he was restored to fitness, that he stopped taking the drugs.

That night, he lay for a while unsleeping, his body rigid at the thought of the planet undersea. The Grandir was right: he knew what he had to do. Find the third relic—the relic removed from Eos countless years ago by the Grandir himself, to shield it from the greedy and the misguided. The Iron Crown. The Crown of spikes forged originally by Romandos, first of the Grandirs, to form a part of the Great Spell to save their people—a plan laid over millennia, woven into the legends of a thousand worlds, hidden in a web of folklore and lies. Nathan still had no idea what the spell itself involved, or how it could engender salvation—he knew only that it had more power than a galaxy imploding and would shake the very multiverse to its core. Even the Grandir, he suspected, had yet to fill in all the gaps in his vision of destiny. The Grandir who thought he was a true-born descendant of Romandos and his bride-sister, Imagen, though Nathan had seen in his naked face the ghost of Imagen's lover Lugair.

Nathan lingered between sleep and waking, thoughts floating free in his mind. Lugair had betrayed Romandos—Romandos his friend—slaying him with the Traitor's Sword, to be slain in his turn . . . the Sword had been held in Carboneck for generations, a curse on the kings of Wilderslee and on their people . . . the Grail had been guarded by Josevius and the Thorns, the so-called luck of the family, its burden and its bane . . . and the Iron Crown must be in Widewater, somewhere in the deeps of the sea. The masculine principle, the feminine principle, and the circle that binds. Three elements that together might change a world, or all worlds . . . But Osskva the mage had told him it needed a sacrifice—it needed blood. Blood had begun it, Romandos's blood, and blood must finish it—the blood of his descendant. *It is expedient for us that one man should die for the people* . . . who had said that? Suddenly Nathan was sure the Grandir was ready for that, ready to make the ultimate sacrifice. Not out of love perhaps—it was hard to imagine him loving his people; he seemed above such sentiment—but from a supreme sense of duty, from pride, from his absolute commitment to his heritage and his world. And for Halmé, whom he loved indeed, Halmé the beautiful for whom he had said that world was made . . .

There must be another way, Nathan thought, knowing the thought was futile. He had no power to change things. He was caught up in this like a snowflake in a storm, a tiny component in a huge machine, and all he *could* do was whatever he *had* to do. *Only this, and nothing more.* Why did he keep thinking of that poem, and Annie's face when he talked of the Grandir, so pale and still? He had to find the Crown.

And then he remembered Keerye, talking of the Goddess, and how she had an iron crown that never rusted, kept in a cavern of air under the Dragon's Reef.

How could he have failed to pick up the clue? But he had been inside Ezroc's head, sharing his thoughts and feelings, no longer a boy but an albatross riding on the wind. Oh to fly again . . .

His mind turned to dragons—it *would* be dragons—great fire-breathing monsters, far more deadly than Urdemons or giant lizards. But no dragon could breathe fire underwater. He visualized a vast serpentine creature, winged and clawed and fanged, rising in a storm of bubbles, the sea boiling against its flanks. Its mouth opened on a gullet of flame, its red-hot tongue crackled like a lava flow in the alien element . . . The ocean erupted into steam as the dragon ascended, dripping wings driving it into the sky . . .

Somehow, in the midst of such visions, he fell asleep.

And *now* he was flying again, not the dragon but the bird. Soaring on the high air into a deep blue night. Southward and eastward there was a faint pallor along the horizon; light leaked into the sky. The sun's disk lifted above the rim of the globe and the light washed over the ocean, turning the waves to glitter. Ahead, Nathan saw a broken shoreline of crags and peaks and towers, rough-faceted, glimmering here and there with a glimpse of crystal. The Ice Cliffs. As he drew nearer he made out a vast colony of seabirds stretching along the escarpment: gannets, puffins, auks, gulls, terns—the squawking of their competing chatter was like the din of a whole city. On the highest part of the ridge there was a group of albatrosses, twenty or thirty pairs, far bigger than the other birds—bigger than the albatrosses Nathan had seen in nature shows—some, at a guess, nearly as tall as he was, or would have been if he had been solid. Ezroc, he realized, had grown, too: his wingspan seemed to reach halfway across the world. He gazed down at the mating pairs—Nathan remembered that albatrosses mate for life—and felt the sorrow in Ezroc's heart because he was alone, he had chosen loneliness to pursue his long voyages in search of Keerye who was dead and the islands that were no more.

In Ezroc's mind he heard a memory replaying, the voice of an older bird, a relative or mentor: *The islands are lost, young Stormrider, if they ever existed. You have journeyed many miles farther than your namesake— you have followed the great currents to the south—merfolk have hunted you, boiling spouts have singed your feathers, sea monsters have chased your shadow across the waves. You know the truth. The seas are empty. Stay here; settle down with your own kind. Until the Ice Cliffs melt, the northfolk will have a place to be.*

And Ezroc's reply: *It is not enough.* The words of a maverick, stubborn beyond reason, holding on to a vision no one else could see.

He passed over the colony, ignoring the birds that raised their heads to watch him, speeding along the floating shoreline. Below, Nathan glimpsed other creatures, refugees from the lost lands of long ago, surviving on the Great Ice. A troop of penguins waddling along a promontory, plopping into the sea—clumsy and comic on the ice, arrow-smooth in the water. A huddle of sea lions and trueseals, nursing their newborn pups. A great snowbear waiting at a borehole till its dinner came up for air. And an enormous walrus, tusked and bristled, heaving himself up onto a floe, who raised a flipper in greeting.

Ezroc wheeled and swooped down to land on the ice beside him.

"Greetings, Burgoss. May your mustache never grow less! I've been away awhile—what is the word along the Ice Cliffs?"

"Greetings, young'un," the walrus grunted. "What makes you think I have time for the jabber of chicks and pups? I don't listen to children's gossip, and when they're grown their talk is all of food and sex. Enough to deafen you with boredom. If that's the word you seek, ask elsewhere."

"You are the oldest and wisest creature in all the seas," Ezroc said, flattering shamelessly. "Except for the whales. If there is any news worth knowing, you will know it."

"Not so much the *oldest*." The walrus shook himself, feigning displeasure. "You have a beak on you, young Ezroc, you always did. I'd say you were getting too big for your wings if they weren't grown so wide I can barely see from tip to tip. What've you been eating down in the south? Hammerhead?"

"Too small," Ezroc said airily. "I feast only on sea monsters."

"All boast and no bulwarks," the walrus retorted. "Hrrmph! Well, I can guess the kind of news you need to hear, and it ain't good. A piece broke off the Great Ice away westward, maybe five longspans across. Perhaps Nefanu is bringing the sun north to melt us, though the days don't seem any longer to me. But I'm not as young as I was, and could be I'm out of my reckoning."

"She won't bring the sun," Ezroc said. "I don't think she has that power. Anyway, she doesn't need to. All she has to do is divert one of the warmer currents. If she hasn't tried that yet, it's only because she hasn't thought of it."

"Those old gods are as dumb as dugongs," Burgoss remarked. "How else did her queenship manage to wipe out the rest of them? Anyhow, ice breaks in the spring. It may not mean much. You've got other things to worry about. The Spotted One says he saw merfolk scouting below the cliffs last moondark. Says they took a snowbear, though there's no proof. The bears don't lair together; they wouldn't know if one's gone missing."

"The Spotted One . . ." The albatross might have frowned, if birds could frown. Nathan could sense his unease.

"The others don't listen to him," the walrus said. "Since old Shifka died they've grown complacent—complacent and careless. Apathy! Huh! The biggest killer of all time. Once that sets in, you're halfway to extinction. I'm old—though not as old as you seem to think—but I can still smell trouble coming. If the Great Ice were to break up—if the merfolk mounted a serious attack—"

"Do *you* believe him?" Ezroc interjected.

"Possibly. He's surly and solitary, but that don't make him a liar. Been an outcast since he was a pup, when they taunted him for his spots. Seal-brats can be cruel—cruel and stupid—just like any other

young'uns. He wasn't quick with words so as he got older he fought—
fought tough and fought dirty—teeth, flippers, fists, he didn't care
what shape he used as long as he won, and the odds were always against
him. Can't blame him for that."

"He killed someone," Ezroc said.

The walrus shrugged, a great rippling shrug that flowed right down
his massive body. "It happens. Don't think he set out to kill—he always
wanted the others to feel their bruises, or so I guess—but the brat got
his head smashed on the ice, and that did it for him. Skull too thin or
something."

"Brat?" Ezroc was appalled. "He killed a *pup?*"

"Nah. Just some half-grown flipperkin shooting his mouth off.
They're all brats to me. Point is, after that they avoided him, and he—
well, he'd have made himself an outcast even if they didn't. It suited his
mood. I thought you'd know the story."

"I was only a chick," Ezroc said. "Keerye never went into details.
He used to talk to Nokosha sometimes—he wasn't like the rest of them."

"Young Spots was the only one he couldn't best in a fight," Burgoss
said. "Strongest selkie on the cliffs. I daresay Keerye respected that."

"Nokosha still blames me for his death, I think," Ezroc said. "I've
never had anything from him but foul looks."

"When you've only got one friend, you'd want someone to blame
for losing him," the walrus said philosophically. "If you want to ask
Nokosha about the merfolk, you'll have to get past that."

"How?" Ezroc asked.

"Up to you."

"Where do I find him?"

"No idea. Wherever the others aren't. Those big wings of yours
must be good for something. Use 'em."

The albatross made a sound that Nathan knew for laughter—bird's
laughter, harsh as a cry. "Thanks, Burgoss," he said. "I owe you. You are
the wisest—and the fattest—creature in the sea, except for the whales—"

"Hrrmph! Be off with you, or you'll find I'm not the slowest, whatever you may have heard."

The albatross veered away, taking off in a few strong wingbeats, launching himself into a long glide out over the water. As he circled higher Nathan felt his doubts, the growing weight of fears still only half formed and founded on uncertainty. If he had learned one thing in all his travels it was that the hatred of the Goddess was unrelenting and her hunger insatiable. Once, she had hated the islands and all those who lived there, man, beast, or bird, drowning them in her tempests, driving out rival gods. Now she had turned her enmity on the last vestiges of the People of the Air—the lungbreathers whom she saw as aliens, dwelling in her kingdom but not of it, corrupting the purity of the great ocean. *And when we are gone,* Ezroc thought, *whom will she have left to hate? The rocks that hold up her reefs? The whales and dolphins who are not true fish—the crabs and sea scorpions because they have legs—any creature who ever tried to crawl or wriggle into the sun, when there was still something to crawl on?*

But as long as the Great Ice endured, the northfolk could withstand her. If they were careful—if they were watchful—if the merfolk stayed in the warm seas of the south . . .

He flew over a blue-green inlet, walled with ice, where a group of selkies were leaping and diving; Nathan could see them changing shape as they plunged beneath the surface, shedding their half-human form for the seal-fell native to the element. He knew from his bond with Ezroc that the selkies could transform themselves at will, though they rarely used their legs. A couple of them waved to the albatross, but although he dipped his head in acknowledgment he did not stop. A little farther on he came to a place where a great berg had broken away from the cliffs and was rocking gently on the swell. There was a figure on the lowest part of the berg, lying on its stomach, gazing into the depths below. Fishing, maybe. As Ezroc drew nearer Nathan saw it was a selkie, but unlike the others, his tail fur dappled with curious markings, black spots within gray, his thick hair, also somehow dappled, bristling like the mane on a bull seal. The bird lost height, and Nathan made out the ridged vertebrae along the selkie's back, and the bunched muscles in arm and shoulder. There was even a faint mottling under his skin, the ghost-markings of his dual self.

Ezroc circled the berg, calling out, "Nokosha!" but the selkie never raised his head.

The albatross landed on the water a little way off, sculling with his webbed feet to hold himself against the currents.

"Nokosha!" he repeated. "Can I talk to you?"

Still no response. What Nathan could see of the face, with its down-swept brows and brooding mouth, seemed to be shaped for scowl. The shadow spots spread across cheekbone and temple, making him look alien even among his own kind.

"I hear you saw merfolk," Ezroc persisted. "A raiding party, or— or scouts checking out the terrain. If that's true, we have to do something."

"What will *you* do?" For a swift moment Nokosha lifted his gaze. His eyes, too, were different, not velvet-dark like other selkies but pale and cold as ice. "Fly off 'round the world to gather tales from the small-fish of the reefs? Ask the sharks to tell us what their masters are doing? That will be a big help."

"Were these sharkriders?" Ezroc said, ignoring Nokosha's scorn.

"What if they were? No one listens to what they don't want to hear. It's easier to call me a liar than to face the truth. Soon or late, the fish-folk will come in numbers, and for war. The ice won't protect us. We're lazy and unprepared: we'll die like mackerel in a dolphin hunt."

"Did they really take a snowbear?" Ezroc said, keeping to the point. After all, he was getting information—of a kind.

"They dived under the ice and came up through the borehole to seize him. They had spears tipped with blood coral, and stone knives." The selkie also carried a knife, a short stabbing blade that he fingered as they spoke, jabbing it into the ice. "No doubt their leader now wears the skin. Impractical underwater, but he was that type. More ego than sense."

"Could you describe him? There are twelve merkings. If we knew which one he served—"

"You could do what? Fly off on a mission of complaint?"

"I have friends," Ezroc said, "even among the merfolk. They are not all *her* creatures. I might be able to find out more."

"Friends!" Nokosha mocked, and there was real hatred under the scorn: his voice shook with it. "Friends among the coldkin—the fish-eyed, the fish-hearted! Friends among the killers of the south! You're a traitor to your race, to all the People of the Ice. You abandoned Keerye—you led him to the killing seas and left him there to die. Come a little closer, birdling, and I will have you by the throat, and this will be your last flight."

There was no doubt he meant it. The albatross was bigger, far bigger, but the selkie was all knotted muscle and knotted rage. If he got his hands around Ezroc's neck, there would be no more to be said.

The bird kept his distance, paddling his feet in the water.

"I didn't abandon Keerye," he said. "He fell asleep on a Floater—I slept, too, but on the sea. We didn't know what it was. He thought . . . we'd found an island. When I woke, he was gone." And suddenly there was a memory in his head, a memory that didn't belong. A pale figure struggling against a web of tentacles, and a dozen mouths opening to feast . . . His mind reeled from the horror of it.

"I would never have abandoned him," he went on, struggling to suppress the unwanted vision. "He was my best friend."

"Keerye was everyone's best friend." This time Nokosha seemed to be mocking himself. "He was handsome and careless and beloved—the handsome and careless always are. You lost him. It's easy to plead innocence when there are no witnesses to give you the lie."

I'm a witness, Nathan thought. *A witness to the truth . . .*

"I have a witness," Ezroc said, and then flinched from his own assertion, the sudden certainty in his mind.

"Who?" Nokosha caught his bewilderment, staring at him with those ice-bright eyes.

"I . . . don't know. It doesn't matter." Ezroc shook his feathers, trying to pull his thoughts together. "Your hate . . . doesn't matter. The important thing is to find out what the merfolk are doing. If you could remember more about the ones you saw . . ."

"I remember everything." Nokosha was studying him, distracted by his lapse into strangeness.

"They were sharkriders?" Ezroc resumed.

"Yes. A dozen or so on blue sharks, but their leader rode a great white."

"Great whites cannot be ridden," Ezroc said.

"Do you doubt me? It was a great white. I saw the fragments of its last meal still caught between its teeth. He rode it with a bit that was metal, not bone, and it bucked beneath him once or twice like a spring wave."

"How come they didn't see you? You must have followed them for a while, and close."

"You should know better than to ask. I watched them from a berg—like this—and when I entered the water I used the drifting ice to screen my movements. They were wary of open attack but they weren't expecting to be stalked; they didn't look for me. I can dive without a ripple, or haven't you heard? If I came after you in earnest, you wouldn't know until it was too late."

Ezroc ignored the renewed threat. "Was there anything else about the leader?" he asked. "Insignia of any kind—something like that?"

"A tattoo on his chest. They do it with squid ink and the poison of the spiny tryphid. They say the pain of it will keep a strong warrior in torment for a week. I've never felt the need to prove my strength in such a way."

"I've heard of the process," Ezroc said. "Did you get a chance to see what it was?"

"A sea dragon."

"Rhadamu's emblem," Ezroc responded, and fell into silence, thinking his own thoughts.

The selkie dived so swiftly Nathan was barely aware he had moved before the outstretched hands came rushing upward, grasping at Ezroc's legs. Albatrosses are slow in takeoff but his long journeys had developed abnormal flight muscles, and close encounters with danger had accelerated his reflexes. His beak stabbed down—he rose in a flurry of wings, scudding across the water—the selkie sank back, bleeding red in the foam. Then the bird was airborne, already twenty yards away, veering into a turn to see Nokosha shaking the wet hair from his eyes, watching after him, apparently oblivious to his injured hand.

"You are vicious, albatross," he called out. "I will remember it."

Presently, he climbed back onto the berg and resumed his scrutiny of the depths, though Ezroc no longer thought he was looking for fish.

The brief northern daylight was already fading as the sun wrapped itself in a mantle of flame and slid back into the sea. The albatross headed for an eyrie on the top of a lonely crag and landed there, tucking his head beneath a folded wing. Only when Ezroc slept did Nathan, too, slip into unconsciousness, back to the slumberlands of his own world.

HAZEL FOUND Login awaiting her in the woods, close to the point where the path ran out.

"Follow me," he said.

Hoover, some way behind, gave an admonitory bark, but Hazel did not respond. The dog trotted after her as she descended into the valley, his intelligent eyes anxious under the sprouting whiskers of his eyebrows. If he had been human, he might have heaved a sigh; being canine, he merely panted.

Hazel picked her way downhill in Login's wake, moving slowly now that she had left the path, having to concentrate on every step. Perhaps because the dwarf had chosen his route well they made little noise: dead leaves swished about her feet, and every so often she slithered on a hidden patch of mud, but although she had to duck under low branches and step over knobbled roots there was no twig crackle at her passage, no tearing of cloth on briar. She paused frequently to look back, checking the way she would have to run, making sure the ascent was straightforward: she must not get lost before she found the path again, and a stumble could be fatal. She told herself she was being brave—brave and not foolhardy—but her heart shook within her, and her stomach, always the main part of her body to react to fear, seemed to have become one large collywobble. The recollection of Detective Chief Inspector Pobjoy staggering into Thornyhill Manor, his pale face paler than ever and his eyes haunted, gave her courage or at least encouragement. He was only a stupid policeman who didn't believe in ghosts. She knew better.

And then Nambrok stopped her with an outstretched hand, raising a finger to his lips. Hazel nodded and followed his example as he dropped into a crouch, peering down through a fork in the tree roots. She had been here before, she knew, but that had been in a summer storm, a freak of the weather or the backlash of old spells long gone rotten. The place looked different now, still but not peaceful, as if the very silence of the wood was tense with waiting. She could see the hole, ragged-rimmed with torn earth and hanging growths, and the dark beyond that suggested a hollow space, but nothing more. There was no spooklight to aid her vision, no eldritch glow in the blackness, and she lacked the weresight of the dwarf. *This is it,* she told herself, *this is the chapel;* yet all she could see was the dark.

She could hear, though. The sound was so faint at first she was barely aware of it, distant as the rumor of traffic on a road more than a mile away, insidious as the mutter of someone else's personal stereo. It was a sound with no shape, no definition; she knew it must come from the dark below but it seemed to be all around her, in the air, in the wood, inside her head. *Whispering.* There were no words, or none that she could hear, though Bartlemy had told her once that the gnomons whispered in the spelltongue of all the worlds, echoing the enchantments that bound them. Now the magic was fraying and their bonds had loosened, and their whispers had degenerated to a thread of noise, a menace without mind or purpose. Hazel listened, and felt her little store of courage draining away. The collywobble in her stomach crept down her legs. She knew she had to do something before terror immobilized her, and she straightened up, stepping backward from the hole, checking out her escape route one last time.

"What about you?" she whispered to the dwarf.

"I rub the herb on me," he said. "The herb from the goodman's garden. They'll leave me be." His own odor was so strong, Hazel hadn't even noticed the smell of the silphium.

I wish I'd done that, she thought, but Bartlemy had said they might not come after her if she used any deterrent.

She called out "Hoy!" in the direction of the hole, feeling stupid and terrified all at once. It wasn't the most dramatic summons, but it was all she could think of. "Hoy!"

Then she ran.

Don't look back! Bartlemy had warned her. *Looking back slows you down; you could miss your footing, miss your way.* She didn't look back. The whispering grew, becoming a stream of Fear that poured out of the hole behind her and came skimming over the ground, flowing uphill like a river in reverse. She leapt the tree roots, snapped through branches. She needed no incentive to run: Fear was on her heels. An invisible pursuit that tore through the wood like a swarm. Leaves she hadn't disturbed whirled far in her wake.

She was gasping when she issued from the valley but she had tried harder at sports that year, taking up karate—a year-eleven option—and so far neither her legs nor her lungs had let her down. And *now* she was on the path, following the track she had worked out with Bartlemy, and the ground was level, and running easier. But the hunt was catching up. She could feel their nearness, hear the dreadful whispering that, if she faltered or fell, would be on her in seconds, pouring into her thought, blanking her mind forever. Somewhere close by Hoover howled, a skin-crawling, hackle-raising sound, unfamiliar as a wolf on your hearth rug.

Hazel careered left, into a thicket of winter briars. Her knees buckled—she pitched forward and fell—

The iron grille dropped down behind her.

The gnomons recoiled, spinning the dead leaves into a maelstrom. A net of twisted wires came out of the sky, encasing them in a fragile cage, but its strength did not matter—it was iron, and it held them. There were wires even beneath the leafmold, embedded in the ground. The smell of silphium, coating the metal, impacted on their hypersenses, stinging them into a frenzy. Bartlemy came out of the bushes to see the very air boiling as if with a miniature sandstorm: earth crumbs, leaf fragments, twig fragments whirled into a living knot of fury. The whispering had ceased; in this world, their pain was voiceless. He stood for a moment, his bland face more expressionless than usual, then went to help Hazel to her feet. She was trembling with reaction and the after-math of effort. Hoover came loping through the briars to his master's side; some sort of wordless communication passed between dog and man.

Bartlemy said: "I see."

Hazel gazed in horror at the tumult within the mesh. "Will they stay there?" she demanded.

"They must. Iron emanates a magnetic field that contains them; there is insufficient space for them to pass between the wires. And the smell of silphium torments them. I made the cage too small: they will be in agony as long as I keep them there."

Hazel said: "Are you *sorry* for them?"

"They cannot help what they are," Bartlemy responded. "Nature—or werenature—made them, who knows for what purpose. Like the wasp that lays its eggs inside a living grub, or the mantis that eats its mate's head during intercourse. They have no intelligence to be held respon-sible for the suffering they inflict. Responsibility is for us. We *know* what we do."

"Will they die?" Hazel asked in a lower voice.

"I don't know," Bartlemy said. "I've never captured such creatures before."

The sandstorm showed no sign of abating.

"Let's go home," Bartlemy went on. "You need food."

"Yes, please."

"And *then* you can tell me why you disobeyed my orders and went into the Darkwood."

THE FOLLOWING morning Bartlemy went to check on the cage. He had used his influence to steer dog walkers—and their dogs—away from the place, and he saw immediately that it had not been disturbed. But the occupants were gone. He walked long and far that day, watching and listening, but there was no feel of them anywhere in the wood.

At last he came to the chapel on the slopes of the valley, though he had never found it before. The dwarf was there waiting.

"They're gone," he said. "Would ye be wanting to look inside? I'm thinking you're a mickle too broad to be crawling into rat holes."

"And I'm thinking," Bartlemy said, "you're a mickle too bold, leading a young girl into danger. I'd permitted her to take a little risk; I hadn't intended it to be a big one. Or was that your idea of help?"

"I didna suggest it," Login said. "She was the one who was so set on it. I warned her you wouldna be any too keen, but she—"

"Warnings like that seldom deter teenagers," Bartlemy said. "Between Josevius and me, you've spent too much time with very old men. The young are more reckless, and more—perishable. *Rose-white youth, passionate, pale.*"

"That maidy o' yourn," Login said, "isn't the sort I'd be comparing to roses, white or red. Too many thorns."

"It depends on the rose," Bartlemy said.

NATHAN SPENT Saturday with his friend George Fawn, playing games on the computer—George's brother David had Grand Theft Auto: San Andreas—talking about music and television and school, and hearing how Jason Wicks, the village tough guy, had stolen his cousin's motorbike to go joyriding over the fields, been charged by Farmer Dawson's bull, and fallen off into a bog.

"There aren't any bogs," Nathan quibbled.

"Well, it was *like* a bog," George said. "A big patch of mud. Very muddy mud. A bog sounds better, though."

"Mm. I bet he got filthy."

"He looked like the swamp monster. It was *wicked*. Mike Rayburn saw him, he said he couldn't stop laughing. Libby was there—Jace fancies her, so he couldn't do anything, and he was, like, *seriously* embarrassed. It was the best thing ever."

"I wish I'd been there," Nathan said.

"You must be as tall as him now," George remarked. "Maybe taller."

Nathan grinned. "You make me sound like a freak."

"No way. Girls like tall." George was on the short side. "I bet you could have lots of girls."

"Not much chance of that at Ffylde."

"No, but—here. There's Hazel—she likes you. She's not the prettiest girl in town, exactly—her tits are too small, for one thing—but she's a *girl,* isn't she? And you like her . . ."

"Hazel is Hazel," Nathan said sharply. "She's my best friend—only that—and don't you ever sneer at her again."

"I wasn't sn—"

"Ever!"

George subsided, mumbling an apology, and they changed the subject for the rest of the afternoon.

The night Nathan was back in the dream. Not the same dream—the wonder of flying with the albatross, sharing his feelings and his fears—but one of the dark. He was falling through a hole in the world—through the faint lights and faraway stars of another universe—falling into a narrowing chimney of blackness, far beyond the reach of sun or supernova. He remembered the prison pits of Arkatron where he had once met Kwanji Ley—but there had been light there, the soft unchanging light of Deep Confinement. And then he struck the bottom, thrown into his own body with a jarring sensation like a blow, and he saw the darkness was less dark, and there was a door in front of him that he had seen before. A door marked DANGER.

It wasn't locked—it never had been—though surely such a door should have been secured with secret codes, retinal scans, digital palm-print readers. Nathan pushed it ajar—cautiously, he was always cautious in that place—and slipped through. Inside, there was a strange mixture of low lighting and high technology. There were the benches stacked with scientific paraphernalia, with snarls of tubing like glass intestines, and pulsating metallic sacs, and cylinders glowing eerily at top or base, and jars where deformed *things* floated in preserving fluid, hopefully dead, and hunks of ominous machinery glistening in the dimness. And let into the walls were the cages, the cages that made Nathan both frightened and sad, mostly empty, but not all. In one a snake reared up, striking at the glass; globules of pale mauve venom spattered the surface and ran down in snail tracks that smoked wispily. In another, there were what appeared to be giant locusts, until Nathan looked more closely and saw they had human faces and forelimbs ending in tiny hands. And in a third was the familiar cat, stiff and dead with its paws in the air, and yet, from a different angle, somehow alive, tail twitching, watching Nathan through slitted eyes.

It was the Grandir's laboratory, deep underground, the laboratory where he had bred the gnomons to protect the Grail and imprisoned a primitive elemental, potent and savage, in the Traitor's Sword. And there he was, leaning over a separate cage at the far end, accompanied by a man in a purple cowl. Nathan recognized the cowl if not the man; it might have been a symbol of office.

He thought: *Am I in the past—the past of Eos? Is the Grandir doing something to the Iron Crown—magicking some awful spirit into it, like he did with the Sword?*

There was a noise in the background that hadn't been there before, a sort of faint cacophony, remote but persistent, as if a group of people with acute laryngitis were screaming in agony. It seemed to Nathan to be a long way off yet at the same time inside his head. He didn't like it at all—it was too familiar—but he ducked under a bench and crept nearer, bent double, trying to hear what the two men were saying. He might have shown himself to the Grandir but not in front of Purple Cowl; instinct told him that would be a mistake.

"It must be a spell," the Grandir said. "Nothing else would cause so much pain. Iron repels but does not torture them."

"What will you do?" asked the other. "They should be killed. Some things are too deadly to be allowed to live."

"They are what they are," said the Grandir, sounding, had Nathan but known it, a little like Bartlemy. "They have served their purpose. I will call them back."

"But can you—"

"They are bound to my edict, to my very thought. I can call them, even across the worlds. They ozmose."

He straightened, raising his head, speaking a few words in the universal language of magic—a language Nathan could recognize but not understand. Purple Cowl drew back, perhaps afraid of fallout, but the words, though commanding, were quiet, creating scarcely a ripple in the atmosphere. Nathan thought the summons was as insistent as a tug on a noose, as compelling as hypnosis, but almost gentle, almost kind. As if the Grandir were saying: *Come home. Come home to me.*

And they came. There was no lightning flash, no crackling rent in the dimensions. They were simply *there,* in the cage at the end; Nathan could see them through the glass sides, though not in detail—for which he was grateful. They were visible in this world, their fluid bodies quaking in the aftermath of pain—homunculi about a foot high, with triangular faces all eyes and ears, hardly any mouth, bat-like wing growths stretched between arm and torso, skin dull as shadow. Their substance was unstable, blurring and solidifying at random as they climbed over one another and scuttered up the sides of the cage.

"You cannot keep them here!" Purple Cowl exclaimed, forgetting the deference due to his leader. "If they should escape—"

"They will not escape." The Grandir's tone was repressive. "But you are right, there is no sense in prolonging their captivity. I have no more use for them, after all." He went to a cupboard in the wall, stamped with symbols in red. It opened at a finger touch, and he lifted something from inside. It looked like a box, oval in shape and about the size of a fist.

The Grandir pressed a button to release the lid.

"What's that?" asked Purple Cowl, echoing the question in Nathan's mind.

"Photokromaton," the Grandir replied. "Also called the Eye of God. You would do well not to look when I open it."

Nathan almost thought the warning was addressed to him. He crouched right down, shutting his eyes tight, covering them with his hands . . .

The light, when it came, seared through hand and eyelid, filling his head with a white dazzle brighter than a hundred suns. The scream returned, no longer remote, soaring to a crescendo in a fraction of a second—and in a fraction of a second it was gone. Nathan felt a sort of twist in his gut, a tug of nausea that he could not explain. The Grandir's voice fell softly on his ears, like a spool of darkness against the fading of that terrible light.

"There is a bond among all living things, from the greatest to the smallest. The same subatomic motes—the same specks of infinity and eternity—make up us all. Death always touches us, even the death of such as these. If we are strong we can go beyond that, but we must not lose the ability to feel, nor forget the common source from which we spring."

He spoke as if to Purple Cowl, but this time Nathan was sure the words were for him. The Grandir knew he was there, recognizing his presence with senses far beyond those of the gnomons, acknowledging him while telling him to remain hidden. Those words of reassurance—of insight—were for Nathan and Nathan alone. He dropped his hands, opened his eyes.

The Grandir and his companion were standing side by side, their backs silhouetted against the leftover light. Behind them, the cage was empty.

"Thank the Powers," said Purple Cowl. "I could not have slept easily, knowing those things were around."

"Be careful," the Grandir said, very gently. "They were my creatures, to use or destroy, but all my creatures are dear to me, after a fashion. You would do well to keep that in mind."

The other man appeared to quail, his silhouette shrinking, but Nathan's dream was growing dim, subsiding into sleep, and a cold little voice at the back of his thought, on the edge of the dream, was telling him: *That was important. What the Grandir said was important. Remember it . . .* And then the dream was gone, receding down the chimney of the dark, and all the stars of the universe glittered past him into oblivion.

On Sunday, Hazel told Nathan about catching the gnomons, and he told her about his dream.

"You could hear them screaming?" Hazel said, hoping he'd noticed how brave she'd been—brave enough to be told off by Bartlemy—though he didn't seem to have considered it. "All I could hear was that hideous whispering noise while they were coming after me. And then, when they were trapped—nothing."

"They screamed in a different world," Nathan said. "They seem to be more audible there—and more visible. I must say, you did really well luring them out like that, but I think Uncle Barty could have asked me. I mean . . ." *You're a girl*. But he didn't say it.

"I do dangerous stuff, too," Hazel said. She could have done with more appreciation, but at least she had made her point. "So what's this important thing the Grandir said?"

"I can't recall the exact words. He was sorry for the gnomons . . ."

"So was Uncle Barty."

"He said . . . they were his creatures, to use or destroy, but he still cared about them. He felt their death—*I* felt it—a sort of sick sensation inside, like I'd witnessed a massacre. They were *gnomons* . . . they were mindless and evil . . . but he had compassion for them. That must be the important thing. Compassion . . ."

"Uncle Barty had compassion," Hazel reiterated. "Anyone can. Compassion's cheap. It's what you *do* that counts, not what you feel. I think the Grandir's a supervillain, the sort you always get running a whole universe. A coldhearted, ruthless megalomaniac, just like in all the movies."

"He's ruthless," Nathan conceded, "but not coldhearted. He only kills when he has to. He's trying to save his whole world—or what's left of it. Life isn't like the movies. Even in this world, rulers have to make decisions that get people killed, if the survival of their country is at stake."

"Like George Bush and the Americans invading Iraq?" Hazel said with heavy sarcasm.

Annie, who had just walked in, listened with the warm glow of an adult eavesdropping on Concerned Youth.

"I was thinking more of England resisting Hitler in the Second World War," Nathan said. "Hitler was a supervillain, if you like—a much more successful one than Saddam Hussein. He was a real megalomaniac."

"Yes," Annie said, "but did you know he loved dogs?"

"See!" Hazel said triumphantly. "The compassion thing again. Anyone can do it. It doesn't mean squat. Saddam Hussein's probably kind to . . . camels, or something. Your Grandir—"

"He isn't my Grandir," Nathan said. "But he isn't a supervillain. I'm sure of it. You're making snap judgments the way you always do. I'm trying to be fair."

Annie asked, with difficulty: "What about the Grandir?"

And once again, Nathan saw that look of *Nevermore* on her face.

Eye
of
Newt

Annie was stock taking when Chief Inspector Pobjoy came around, standing on a stool cataloging the higher shelves. It was her private theory that the books up there had a secret life of their own, reshuffling themselves unobtrusively during the night and hatching new titles that she had never acquired, things like *Dandelion Walks of Southern England*, *A Collector's Guide to Bedsteads*, and children's fiction from a duller past—*Helen's Midnight Pony*, *Alice Pulls It Off*. She really must scale the heights more often and see what the books were up to. She was talking to them in an exasperated tone when Pobjoy entered the shop, and because she had never bothered to have a bell installed and he closed the door very quietly, she didn't immediately hear him.

"What do you think *you're* doing? *Fifty Top Golfing Holidays*! Not on my watch. *Crochet for Beginners*—that's so boring it's almost a style statement. Oh no—it's *Croquet*. Even worse. *Rhoda Rides to Glory*—not another pony book? Good heavens, no, I do believe it's vintage porn . . ."

"Hello," said the inspector.

Annie dropped the book.

There was a brief period of adjustment while Annie scrambled down from the stool slowly enough to dilute her blush and Pobjoy retrieved *Rhoda Rides to Glory*, trying very hard not to look as if he was looking at the pictures.

"I didn't buy that," Annie said abruptly. "At least, if I *did*, I thought it was something else. I don't stock porn—not unless it's really *classic*, like Casanova's journals or de Sade . . ." Realizing she was digging herself deeper and deeper in, she shut up.

Pobjoy handed her *Rhoda* with an air of suppressed embarrassment. Annie accepted it, holding it with her fingertips as if it were a piece of very hot toast, and stuffed it hastily onto a lower shelf.

Pobjoy said hesitantly: "You were talking to . . . talking to . . . ?"

"The books?" Annie's voice was bright and brittle. "Of course. I often talk to books. It's an early sign of insanity, but don't worry, it's not at all criminal."

Pobjoy, recognizing humor, permitted himself a smile. He was drawn to Annie's company, often against his better judgment, although he found much of what she said and did completely incomprehensible. He hoped she would offer him coffee—with Annie, offering coffee was almost a reflex—since the problem he wished to discuss with her was rather delicate, and a relaxed atmosphere would help. But she didn't. She was too shaken by being caught in the act of a conversation with a pornographic book, and having done her best to brazen it out, she took refuge in formality.

"What can I do for you?"

"Well, I . . . it's a little difficult."

"Is it?" Annie decided to be unencouraging.

"I was visiting your uncle, Bartlemy Goodman, the other week. At least, not exactly *visiting*—I got a flat tire, and I had to walk, so I stopped off at Thornyhill. It was a wet night, you see, and . . ."

"Of course." Bewildered by his faltering manner, Annie found her tone softening. "Uncle Barty's very hospitable when people are in trouble. What happened that's worrying you?"

"We had a conversation." Now that he was getting to the point, Pobjoy tiptoed around it. "I've always liked talking to the old man—

not that he's very old, when you come to think of it. He can't be much more than sixty. He—"

"Oh, he's old," Annie said. "Much older than he looks. But he's not at all gaga, I promise you."

"No indeed. Of course not. A bit eccentric, perhaps . . . He was going on about otherworlds, and creatures—aliens—who can cross the dimensions. Like a science-fiction novel, only he seemed to believe it. *Really* believe it. I was a little concerned—I know you're very close to him. He definitely seemed—well, two hard-boiled eggs short of a picnic, as they say."

Annie walked over to her desk, sat down on the swivel chair. Swiveled. Stopped. She said very deliberately: "Bartlemy has all his hard-boiled eggs, I can assure you. He has the full picnic. Where some people have a soggy sandwich and a can of beer, he's got the smoked salmon canapés and the bottle of champagne. His picnic is as picnicky as it gets."

"I'm sure he's very clever—"

"Don't you believe in otherworlds? I'm not brilliant at particle physics, but I understand scientists have proved they exist, though I don't know how."

"It isn't the kind of proof that would stand up in a court of law," Pobjoy said dismissively. "I can accept that there are alternative universes out there *in theory,* but to claim there are people regularly popping across the dimensions for tea—that's ridiculous."

"Not *regularly,*" Annie said.

For a minute the implication of her response passed him by. Then slow light dawned.

"You . . . you think . . . ?"

"It isn't what I *think,*" Annie said, "it's what I *know*. Look, I can see you're going to make up your mind I'm—I'm several paperbacks short of a bookstore, but that can't be helped. Supposing you tell me what got this whole conversation with Bartlemy started?"

Pobjoy began to look uncomfortable. "It was nothing, really. I'd been walking along the road through the woods—it was dark—lonely— I got spooked, that's all. It was nothing."

"What spooked you?"

"I thought I was being followed—heard footsteps—animal, not human. Probably just a fox."

"You wouldn't get spooked by a fox," Annie said positively. "What aren't you telling me?"

"It's the police who're supposed to ask questions like that," Pobjoy pointed out. "Anyway, there really isn't anything else. My imagination was on overtime, that's all."

"I shouldn't have thought you had much imagination," Annie said absentmindedly.

"Thank you!"

"I mean," she fumbled, "you're not the sort of person to scare *yourself*. If you were scared, there'd be a reason."

"Who said I was scared?"

"You did. Well, you said you were spooked. Same thing."

"All right, I was scared," Pobjoy admitted. "I was scared shitless. I don't know why. It was almost as if the fear was something tangible, like a smell—as if it had an identity of its own. But that's insane."

"Yes it is," Annie said somberly. "That's what *they* do to you. If they catch you—if they get inside your head—you go mad. They sort of suck out your mind, till you're left an imbecile. They're called gnomons. But I don't see why they would come after *you* . . ."

"Goodman said they were out of control," Pobjoy said. "Hell, I'm doing it now. Talking as if they're real—as if all this stuff exists. It's all nonsense. Fairy tales and fantasy. Look, I came here to warn you about Goodman, to tell you he's—slightly potty. Harmless, I'm sure, but—"

"And instead you found out I'm potty, too," Annie said. "Disappointing for you, isn't it?"

She knew she was being unfair to him but just then she didn't care. She found his willful mind-closing idiotic and his warning pompous. Worst of all, he was good looking in a grim-faced, police-inspectorial way, and somehow that compounded the offense. There are few things as annoying to a woman as a good-looking man who tries to patronize her.

Pobjoy stood in silence, at a loss for a response.

Annie took pity on him, after a fashion. "You're a detective, aren't you?" she said. "You might try believing the evidence of your eyes and ears, just for once."

"I didn't see anything!" Pobjoy retorted.

"Of course not," Annie said. "Gnomons are invisible. If you don't see them, that's how you know they're there."

Pobjoy gave up and left, succumbing to the onset of a huff.

There are few things more annoying to a man than a woman who attracts and intrigues him against his will, particularly when she doesn't appear to be attracted—or intrigued—in return.

AT SCHOOL, with GCSEs due the following summer, Nathan knew he should be concentrating on work rather than distracted by his dreams. But the dreams still came, invading his sleep and snatching him away into the multiple universes of his mind. Fortunately, in most of them he seemed—so far—to remain incorporeal, thus avoiding the embarrassment of his dormitory companions wondering where he had gone during the night. His ability to dematerialize in sleep was always potentially awkward. With luck, he thought, it would be Christmas vacation before things progressed that far—and then he would have to deal with the problem of being solid on a planet entirely covered in water, spending all his time in the sea when he couldn't even bring himself to get back in the pool.

Worrying about it brought no solutions but he still worried, often far into the night. His injuries were mending but they gave him an excuse to keep out of the pool; on Widewater, he would need more than an excuse to keep out of the sea. He found himself speculating, idiotically, on whether he could go to bed with an Aqua-Lung, and if he would ever be able to cope with the terror of total immersion. When the worrying wore him out he slept, and then he was on Eos or some other planet of that cosmos, whirled through different fragments of time, watching once more as Romandos forged the Crown of spikes, as the Grandir ascended his solitary tower to gaze across the worlds, as Halmé the beautiful walked the empty chambers with her face unmasked, though no one dared come to gaze on her. Once, he saw Romandos in some palace of long ago, with a woman whom Nathan guessed to be Imagen, a woman both like and unlike Halmé, serene, aloof, yet far more alive, far more passionate. She wore a long green mantle embroidered with flowers that seemed to open and close, and bees that flew from blossom to blossom, and butterflies fanning themselves with jeweled wings. She and Romandos were talking, though Nathan couldn't hear what they said. Then another man entered the room—Lugair the traitor—Lugair the handsome with a hint of cruelty about his mouth—only here he was still young and his mouth was not yet cruel. Imagen looked up at him, and it was as if a light came on behind her face. She loved him, Nathan thought, but she had to marry Romandos. It was custom—it was tradition—it was *greed,* keeping the genes of power in one family, one bloodline, so that family might rule forever. She wasn't allowed to choose for herself. And somehow he felt that the seeds of destruction were sown, for the bloodline and for the world, when Imagen was forced to marry according to custom, and against her heart.

Time spun around him, and he was in another somewhere, another somewhen. He saw the Grandir—the last Grandir—placing the Iron Crown on a plinth in a darkened room, possibly a cave; Nathan could distinguish few details. The only light came from the object itself, or the plinth, a cone of faint radiance that showed the many spikes of the Crown, coiled and twisted and warped into a shape like a thorny wreath, and the Grandir's hands, encased in gloves of what looked like silver mesh. Little of his face was visible beyond the light, but Nathan knew him now, knew him so well that he thought he would have been able to identify that presence, that aura, even in complete darkness. Something about the Crown itself struck him disagreeably: it appeared deformed, inexplicably sinister, the metal gray and lusterless, the spiked points dagger-sharp. Many of them curved inward as if they would impale anyone attempting to wear it. Nathan recalled seeing Romandos, long ago, place it on his head, and the blood running down his face . . .

The Grandir was speaking, or chanting, an incantation of some kind. Even as Nathan watched it reach a climax on a single word, plainly a Command, and the world changed. It was as if the darkness turned inside out; for a timeless instant—a millisecond, a millennium—there was no plinth, no cave, no universe, only the Crown, suspended in light. Insubstantial as he was, merely a thought floating in the ether, Nathan felt *squashed,* as if his awareness were being compressed to the size of a single molecule and forced through the eye of a needle only wide enough to admit an atom. Then the world opened up again—a different world, all blue—and there was water rushing past him, and an explosion of bubbles. For a terrible moment he thought he was solid, and he tried to breathe, to hold his breath—thought he was struggling, drowning—then he realized the bubbles came from the Crown, and he was still bodiless, and thankfully breathing was unnecessary. In front of him the Crown reeled down through the water, gases streaming from its plunge like a comet's tail. Light had been transmuted into heat, boiling the sea, enfolding the falling object in a vortex of spinning currents. Gradually, it came to rest hooked on a point of rock, and the sea cooled until only a few slow bubbles spiraled around it before drifting lazily upward toward the air.

Eyes watched from a crevice below. Fish finned past indifferently. Darkness slid over the reef, the storm shadow of Nefanu's hair. Long webby fingers with nails like talons of pearl reached toward it and drew back, repelled by the magnetic force of the iron. She was a werespirit; she could tolerate the proximity of iron, but for all her strength she could not touch it. Still, she sensed the power emanating from it, not just the power of iron but the spellpower of the Crown itself, and she knew this was something she could use.

Presently, a huge octopus came slithering over the rocks, its mottled colors shifting and changing as it moved. It probed the Crown with its tentacles, turning blood scarlet at the contact. Somewhere Nathan heard Nefanu's voice, like the sound of the wind far off, echoing strangely through the water. *Bring it! Bring it to me!* Tentacles wrapped the lethal spikes; ink belched out in a cloud, enclosing everything in blackness . . .

When the vapor cleared the dream had changed, and Nathan was somewhere else. Out of the water, low in the air, skimming the wave crests as the breakers heaved and tumbled over the spine of a reef. The rocks were so near, their highest points almost broke the surface—almost, but not quite. Beyond, the water was still and green, translucent as a lagoon. Something dark thrust upward, a small oval silhouette with a shadow puddled behind it like more octopus ink. Then Nathan saw a pale arm extended, the wave of a hand, and the shape acquired meaning. Denaero. Her head emerging from the sea, with the long purple hair fanning out around her.

"Ezroc!" she called.

The albatross came to rest on the water beside her.

Nathan thought: *She's older. Not a child anymore.*

Ezroc, confused by the intruder in his head, said: "You've grown."

"It's been six moons since you came by," she said, "but I don't think so. My cousin Semeele says I'm stunted—she's two handspans longer head-to-tail—but if I grew any more you might not be able to carry me, and I couldn't bear that. You don't think I'm too big now, do you?"

"Of course not," Ezroc said. "I don't know why I— There's something odd happening to me lately. Almost as if . . . as if I have someone else's thoughts inside my head."

"Don't say that!" The mermaid looked alarmed, glancing quickly from side to side. "The shamans can do that. They put a hex on you, and mutter spells, and wherever you are you hear them, like voices in your mind, and you have to do what they say. If the shamans are after you it's because they know about us—our friendship and the flying and everything. And if *they* know, then Father knows, and—"

"Don't panic," said Ezroc. "It isn't shamans, I'm sure it isn't. It's a thought, not a voice." In his head Nathan was trying to convey reassurance. "It may be nothing. Anyway, I don't *think* it's dangerous, just . . . strange. Sometimes I remember things—only they're things I didn't know."

"Like what?"

"About Keerye . . ." He didn't want to explore the horror of his friend's death.

"Keerye was fun," the mermaid said. "I'm sure I would've liked him a lot, if I'd had the chance to know him better. Are all selkies like him?"

"No," said Ezroc. "He was special. There are selkies who hate your people as much as you hate ours. Northfolk, southfolk—lungbreathers, coldkin—we're supposed to hate each other. Stupid, but true."

"Why do you call us coldkin?" Denaero asked. "You're the ones who live on the Great Ice. We live here, where it's warm."

"Yes, but your blood is cold, like that of a fish," the albatross explained. "Lungbreathers are warm-blooded."

"It's not a reason to hate each other," Denaero said. "Sometimes I think people *like* to hate. It gives them somewhere to put all their anger, all their cruelty. They say, *Northfolk are our enemies, we must hunt and kill them, or they will hunt and kill us,* and that makes it all right to be angry and cruel. My father talks like that when he gets worked up, and some of his captains are worse. One of them came back from the north recently with the skin of an ice monster. It was hairy all over, like a seal-skin I saw once, and huge, and it had four legs with claws, and big teeth. Uraki said it was the selkies' creature, trained to kill merfolk, and it *did* look terrifying, but all the same I wished I could have seen it alive. Uraki said it *walks* on its four legs, walks across the solid ice—it must have been amazing. I couldn't help wondering . . . if it really had to be killed."

"It didn't," Ezroc said. "It was a snowbear. They kill trueseals, not merfolk, and they don't serve the selkies any more than sea scorpions and giant crabs and crested serpents serve your people. The raiders waited for it at a borehole in the ice and took it with spears."

"I am sorry," Denaero whispered. "It's true what I said, isn't it? Hate makes people cruel, and then they think they've been brave, and they boast of it, as if it were a great deed. But . . . how did you know? About the bear, I mean."

"The raiders were seen," Ezroc explained. "There was a selkie—"

"One like Keerye?" Denaero looked hopeful.

"No. There are none like Keerye. One of the others, as full of hate as your friend Uraki, though he doesn't boast of it."

"Uraki isn't my friend!" Denaero said indignantly. "He talks to me sometimes, because I'm the princess, but that doesn't mean I have to like him. Who is this selkie?"

"They call him the Spotted One," Ezroc said. "He's not popular—even his own people avoid him—but he's clever. He thinks the raid was a scouting party—that one day the merfolk will come north in force to make war on us. I fear he may be right. Do you know anything about your father's plans?"

Denaero shook her head, looking bewildered. "I can't believe it. It's one thing to hate, but—*war*? It would be pointless. The ocean is a big place; there's room for all of us. And it's not as if merfolk could live in the north: it's far too cold."

"But the Goddess," Ezroc said, "hates lungbreathers more than any of your people. It could be her hatred driving the merkings. If there's a war, many will die on both sides, but she won't care."

Denaero's little face scrunched into a scowl. "She may be my goddess," she said, "but *I* hate *her*. She ate the islands and the creatures who walk on legs. I could have learned to walk—I could have climbed up onto the land and seen the legwalkers and the weeds that grew there. My father said the islands were all dry and empty, because nothing grows out of water, but my grandmother told me the weeds there were different—as tall as the sky, waving and bending in the wind, and there were birds like you, but smaller and many-colored, and all kinds of landfish, and people who couldn't change, who had legs *all the time*. Now we aren't even supposed to change, except to mate; my father says legs are no good in the sea. If he found out I changed when I sit on your back he would be even angrier than about the flying."

"He mustn't find out," Ezroc said anxiously. "I don't want to get you into trouble."

But Denaero was still smoldering away to herself. "It's all *her* fault," she went on. "It's all Nefanu. She hates lungbreathers, and legwalkers, and anything to do with land and air. She doesn't even love *us*, although we're meant to be her own people. Her shaman-priestesses made my brother have the tattoo, even though he didn't really want to.

He screamed for a week, the pain was so bad, and then he was ill for two moons with tryphid poisoning. The shamans said he wasn't brave enough—he had to be brave to please her. How could a god be happy because people are in pain? She's evil . . . evil . . . I don't care what anyone says. When I have to go to the rituals I shut my mouth tight, I won't say the liturgies anymore."

"Be careful," Ezroc warned her. "If your father notices—"

"I pull my hair over my face," Denaero said. "Anyway, I don't see why gods need praise so much. They must be incredibly vain, wanting people to tell them all the time how wonderful they are. Why should I praise a goddess who doesn't even care if her people die, as long as she gets more power, and more prayer, and wider realms to rule?"

Ezroc didn't even try to answer. "Denaero," he said, "if she's going to get the merkings to start a war, I have to know. Can you find out for me?"

"You mean," she said, "so the selkies can be warned, so they can fight back, wait in ambush—kill my people?"

Ezroc's beak dropped; he made a confused squawking noise, more like a chicken than an albatross.

"It's all right," she said quietly. "I'll find out. Otherwise . . . it's playing *her* game, isn't it? I won't play her game. I don't want the merfolk to be massacred. I don't want anyone to be killed at all."

"If we knew war was coming," Ezroc suggested, "maybe we could try to stop it."

"You and me?"

"Er—"

"Just you and me?"

There was a short, hopeless silence.

Then Denaero said with a sudden change of tone: "Can we fly now? When I fly with you, I feel I can do anything."

Her face had brightened; Nathan noticed how quickly her moods switched. Like a child who stops crying at the offer of chocolate cake—only she was an adult now, with an adult's concerns. Yet her indifference to danger, too, was curiously childlike.

"Not in daylight," Ezroc replied. "You could be seen—the risk is too great. Just meeting is chancy enough. I'll come back when it's dark."

"At sunset," she begged. "No later. Promise me."

"After dark," Ezroc amended. "I promise."

He rose, splashing across the water, mounting skyward while the mermaid gazed after him, receding into the distance, a small black dot against the gold-green shadow of the sunken reef.

URSULA RAYBURN came into the bookshop the day after DCI Pobjoy, with the object of giving Annie a formal invitation to her Christmas party.

"We've finally set a date," she said. "The second Saturday in December. I want to ask *everyone* in the village, to say thank you for making us so welcome. My friends in London told me I'd loathe village life: hostile natives, snooty county types, yokels with accents you could cut with a knife . . . Anyway, it hasn't been like that at all—everyone's been lovely. Oh, and if there's anybody you'd like to bring, that's fine, too. I'm sure there are loads more people 'round here whom I'd adore, even though I haven't met them yet. There's your uncle who lives in that gorgeous house in the woods—I've heard a bit about him. Would he like to come, do you think? Or is he too old and doddery? I'm not at all ageist, honestly—I don't mind old people if they don't *act* old, if you see what I mean."

Annie suppressed a grin. "Uncle Barty isn't at all doddery," she said. "I'll ask him—thank you—but I don't know if he'll come. He's not really a party person."

"Is he a recluse? How exciting! I've never met a real recluse. It's such a social coup if you can get them to venture out."

"I'll try," Annie promised. "What about Nathan? You *did* say you'd be having all the children."

"Heavens yes. That way no one has to worry about babysitters—and lots of kids rushing about always make a party *sound* lively even if it isn't. My best friend Sharia's coming down from Camden: she's still breast-feeding her little boy, she does it in the pub and everywhere. It really gets the men going seeing that sumptuous brown boob popping out of her dress!"

"I expect it does," Annie said, blanching slightly. She had always done any public breast-feeding in the ladies' room. "I've been meaning to ask you, how's Romany? After her fall in the river—"

"That was *ages* ago." Ursula waved the incident away, dismissing it into the remote past. "*Now* she's got the flu—or a cold—one of those fluey, coldy things kids get all the time, though I must say it's not like her. Gawain's usually the sickly one. She has these shivering fits, and every morning when she wakes up the sheets are soaked. I got really panicky and called the doctor, but he says there's nothing much wrong with her. If you ask me, it's that room. There's damp getting in some-where; I don't care what anyone says. I'd like to move her upstairs but I'm still worried about the vibes."

"That's where you hung the crystals, isn't it?" Annie said. "Ri-anna's bedroom. Isn't it purified yet?"

She was troubled by Romany's illness but didn't want to show it. She didn't need Ursula, too, thinking she was nuts.

"I'm not opening it to the public till the party," Ursula declared rather grandly. "I want to show people up there—you know—*This is the room where the body lay, a rotting corpse, for six months* or whatever it was. Donny wants to get a mock skeleton with a wig and lay it out in the bed, just for a laugh. It would give people a hell of a shock, wouldn't it? By candlelight, like when you found it."

"It was daytime," Annie said.

"Dramatic license," said Ursula. "You don't *mind*, do you? I wouldn't expect you to go up there—too traumatic—that's why I'm telling you about it. Only don't mention it to anyone else—that would spoil the surprise."

"I won't," Annie assured her. "About Romany—my uncle's pretty knowledgeable about herbs and stuff. I could ask him to prepare a tonic for her, if you like. Just natural ingredients. It can't do harm and it might do good, as they say."

"Fantastic! I bet he knows all sorts of ancient mystical recipes . . ."

"Probably," Annie concurred.

"Will it taste all right? She's not very good with nasty medicines, I'm afraid."

"Oh yes, it'll taste fine," Annie said with quiet confidence. "Which reminds me, what are you doing about food for the party? Would you like me to bring something?"

"That's awfully kind. I'm doing soup and sausages and things—I thought, *not* salads, not midwinter, though I know people *do*. It's just, salad in cold weather is so depressing . . ."

The conversation became technical.

When Ursula had gone Annie sat for some time gnawing on her secret worries, wondering what, if anything, she could do, about Romany and other matters, and how much of it was her imagination, and whether evil, once let into your life, could ever be completely exorcised.

"Could you draw the circle?" Annie asked Bartlemy over the phone, later that day. "It might tell us if Romany is in danger."

"And it might not," Bartlemy said. "Even if I conjured Nenufar—"

"No, don't do that," Annie said hurriedly. "But the other spirits—"

"—may not know. Still, it would give Hazel a chance to try her skills, under the proper supervision."

"*No!* Not Hazel. I—I don't want the kids to know . . ." Annie's voice faltered, petered out.

Bartlemy said calmly: "If they are aware of a potential threat, they can be on their guard. That's no bad thing."

"Yes, but . . ."

"What is it you really want?"

"I *am* worried about Romany—we've talked about it before—it's just . . ."

"Nathan?" Bartlemy said.

"I want to *know*." Annie's tone went suddenly harsh. "His father— *I want to know*. All his life I've wondered, doubted . . . Now I need the truth."

"You mean, you suspect—"

"Suspicion isn't enough. I want to be *sure*. Then I'll deal with it. I'll—I'll tell him, if I have to. If it's important . . ."

"You know it's important. But Annie—"

"Please don't *but* me. I've made up my mind. I want to ask the spirits—the powers—whatever you call them. The usual suspects. The seeress, the Hunter, the Child. Then—"

"They won't be able to tell you much," Bartlemy reminded her. "We are fairly certain Nathan's father is from another universe. In the moment of Daniel's death you passed the Gate and became pregnant—that's a matter beyond the scope of the spirits of *this* world. As I've said before, the magic circle has its limitations."

"I know, but—what if he's interfering? What if he's been interfering *here*—in our world—for hundreds of years? That would put him within their scope, wouldn't it? We have to ask them. Please. There's no one else to ask, after all."

Bartlemy sighed softly. "Very well. Come tomorrow. But don't hope for too much. Spirits, like oracles, prefer to talk in riddles, if only to make things more complicated. And riddles can conceal ignorance as well as truth."

The following evening Annie walked over to Thornyhill. There was a wind seething in the treetops, sending the last of the leaves scurrying down the road. Even without the gnomons, the wood seemed to be full of spirits—not the sinister phantoms of the Grail but strange, wild spirits with strange, wild purposes of their own. A restlessness crept over her, as if she was infected with some of that wildness, a feeling unlike any she had ever known. All her life she had run with fate, fighting the small battles that came her way, bracing herself for the bigger ones. Accepting, coping, but never challenging, never defying. Loving Nathan completely, she had rarely thought about her emotions for his true father, the being who had taken her without her permission, in some dimension beyond her will—taken not just her body but a piece of her soul, giving her a child not in love but for some goal too obscure to comprehend. Yet the seed of emotion was there, long dormant, perhaps not a seed but an ember, a smolder; she could feel the flicker of it kindling inside her, waking another Annie, an Annie who was everything she wasn't. An Annie who would burn down the barriers between worlds, who would find him if it took a thousand lives, a thousand deaths, who would find him and face him and make him pay. *He had no right!* The words scorched across her heart. She fought down the flame and the fury, but the other Annie remained, just under the skin, changing her—changing her for all time. *I love Nathan,* she thought, *I would give my life for him. But it isn't for him I want to know. It's for me.*

It's for me . . .

Opening the door to her at Thornyhill, Bartlemy felt that a little of the night came in with her—a breath of the wind's wildness, a sense of lost seasons blowing away like leaves. She had always seemed such a gentle creature, slight and soft, with her heart-shaped face, her wispy mouse-brown curls, the secret strength barely visible in the set of her mouth, the openness of her gaze. But now she appeared suddenly lit up, both pale and glowing, a hint of glitter in her eyes. *She looks almost beautiful,* Bartlemy thought, *almost dangerous . . .* And he was troubled, because he loved her as if she were indeed his niece, and although he had lived fifteen hundred years he still had everything to learn about women.

He said, "Do you want some tea?" but she declined, accepting a drink instead, the dark strong drink that she guessed he brewed himself. She swallowed it quickly, out of not bravado but impatience, scarcely feeling the heat of it in her throat.

In the living room Bartlemy had already drawn the curtains, rolled back the rug. The blackening of former circles showed like a brand on the boards. He had sprinkled the powder around the perimeter, traced the Runes of Protection outside. Annie sat in a chair safely out of range, with Hoover beside her. Bartlemy lit the spellfire on the hearth and extinguished the electrical lamps, so the light was blue and flickering. Then he spoke the word and the powder ignited, etching both circle and runes in thin lines of flame. Annie had seen the routine before, finding it both fearful and curiously banal, since Bartlemy's attitude remained efficient and matter-of-fact, devoid of melodrama. But now the urgency of her need consumed all other feelings. She sat tautly, leaning forward, unconscious of Hoover's body pressed against her legs, offering protection—or restraint.

Bartlemy spoke briefly in the language of the Stone—the same language the Grandir used for spell and sorcery—the language of power throughout the multiverse. A faint mist appeared at the hub of the circle, shaping itself into a seated figure, ghost-pale but veiled in red. It lifted a transparent hand where the tracery of bone showed through phantom flesh and drew back the veil. The face beneath was equally dim, skull and skin melding one into the other, the eyes empty. But the apparition held in its other hand a small orb that it placed in one eye socket; the orb glowed into definition and color, focusing on some remote point far beyond the borders of both spell and circle.

Bartlemy said: "Greeting, Ragnlech."

"Who disturbs our meditation?" As ever, the voice of the seeress echoed strangely, as if many voices blended into one. "We are the sisterhood; we are not to be summoned lightly. We are watching for the hour of Doom."

"Will it be soon?" Bartlemy asked with the hint of a frown.

"The portents are unclear. But the old spells are disintegrating; new spells must take their place. There is a break in the Pattern, the Balance begins to fail. We have no time for lesser matters."

"Yet the lesser matters, too, have their part," Bartlemy said. "You know me, Ragnlech. I have been involved in these things for some while." The seeress bowed her head as if in affirmation. "There is a child who may be in peril, Romany Macaire. She lives at Riverside House, where Nenufar the water spirit once dwelled in the form of a mortal woman. I believe Nenufar still hopes to obtain one of the Grail relics for her own purposes. She could be using this child. What can you see of all this?"

"The Three are shielded," the sibyl said. "I have told you before. We cannot see them—it hurts our Eye. It hurts . . . it hurts . . ." Red tears ran down her cheek from the socket that was occupied, dripping into nothingness. "We will not look farther. We are watching the Pattern . . . There is a child, but she is not significant. The werespirit uses what she can. They are too close to the breakpoint—the point of power. We will not look!"

"So as the hour of Doom approaches you will watch the Pattern, not the flaw," Bartlemy mused. "A useful task for a seeress."

"We have given warning—"

"But few details."

"It is enough." The form of Ragnlech started to fade. "I *will* go—"

"One more question." Something in Bartlemy's tone, a note of spell-power or Command, called her back. "Nothing to do with the Three. There is a boy living here, now fifteen. Nathan Ward. Tell me the name of his father."

There was a silence. The Eye glowed brighter: red veins stood out on its surface, like cracks in marble. Annie thought she could see it beginning to pulsate.

"Forgive me," Bartlemy said. "It is such a simple question. One for a streetwitch or a reader of tea leaves, not for the sisterhood."

"We cannot—see!" The wraith-hands flexed and clenched. "The doom is in him—in *him*. Nathan Ward . . . the child of two worlds! His father's name is beyond the Gate—beyond the Veil of Being. It is written in the stars of another world. We cannot see—we cannot look—"

Bartlemy murmured a word, made a gesture of dismissal. The sibyl faded, taking her Eye with her.

Annie whispered: "The doom . . . is in *Nathan*?"

"Riddles," said Bartlemy. "Empty riddles. She told us nothing we don't already know. But she is a seeress; she has a reputation to protect. The sisterhood know how to elaborate on blindness. Do you want to go on?"

"Yes," Annie said. She was shaking, but her resolution was unchanged.

Bartlemy turned back to the circle, resumed the summons. The old crone whom Annie had seen once before appeared, half bald and mumbling on her single tooth.

"Hexaté," said Bartlemy. "You were not called."

"There was talk of a child," the crone said with unexpected clarity. "And Nephthys—my sister Nephthys. We shared the ceremonies, binding earth and water. We drank the blood together—wine and blood—blood and wine. We danced in the moondark. They brought us children for the sacrifice, always girls, no more than six or eight years old, plump and sweet. Plump and sweet! We roasted them in the spellfire and ate their flesh. Are the ceremonies to begin again? Have they brought a fresh young child for us to share? I cannot smell the roasting flesh . . . Where is Nephthys?"

"Go back to sleep," Bartlemy said. "The fires you speak of are long cold. This is another spellfire, one not used for roasting children. Go back to sleep!"

"Nephthys . . . my sister in kind, my sister in kin . . . She will need me, or the rites will not be complete . . ."

"She has other fish to fry. Literally, I suspect. Begone!" The archaic order seemed to penetrate the fog of the werewoman's mind: she glanced around with extraordinary speed, as if someone had tapped on her shoulder, then vanished in a trail of yellowish smoke and a smell of decay.

"She still hangs around," Bartlemy remarked, "clinging to her memories. Senility in a mortal is a disease of the mind and the body, but not the soul. Senility in a spirit is something else. A turning inward, a clutching at the past—almost self-indulgence. She may malinger for centuries. There is, I'm afraid, nothing to be done."

Annie said only: "Go on."

She wondered briefly what had happened to the good guys, the fairy godmothers who would bless the princess in her cradle, send the kitchen maid to the ball, find the loophole in every wicked enchantment. Gone back to the children's books from which they came, she thought. And even in children's books, all the oldest stories were about blood. The Ugly Sisters cutting off their toes to fit their feet into the crystal slipper—the old witch in her gingerbread house who tried to push Hansel and Gretel into the oven . . . In the end, there was always blood.

Children like stories about blood. Grown-ups know better.

Bartlemy had switched back to Atlantean, repeating the incantation. The air thickened within the circle; another figure materialized. A tall figure with the antlers of a stag and a savage, swarthy, slant-eyed face, not quite human, not quite animal. He wore only a few ragged skins, and the hair on his chest and arms was as dense as a pelt.

"Cerne," said Bartlemy.

"Wizard," said the Hunter.

"You are the Lord of the Wood," Bartlemy continued. "The lord of all woods, or so they say. What do you know of the water spirit who trespasses on your territory?"

"I do not fear her," Cerne replied, in something close to a growl.

"I never asked if you did," Bartlemy murmured. "So she is to be feared, even by such as you? Well, well. I asked what you knew of her."

"She comes rarely to my domain; she dare not. The sea is her kingdom and her retreat. But there is a word on the wind and in the chatter of the streams, a word in the whispers of the night. They say a portal will open, or be opened—a key has been found to a Gate without any keyhole. A time is drawing near that will change all things. Werespirits may no longer be bound to this world; there may yet be a way through. I heard of a region where the trees go on forever. I would give much to see it."

"I believe I know the place you mean," Bartlemy said. "You might be disappointed. The Deepwoods of Wilderslee stretch far, but not forever. There are realms of men there, too."

"There would be," Cerne snarled. "Mankind is a plague that rages through all the worlds. Nonetheless, she whom we spoke of thinks to find a place without Men, a dimension of the Sea. Maybe she would draw a storm from it to wreak havoc in the shorelands here. She wants worship and power again—she is not content with her exile in the dark."

"Is she using a child as her instrument?"

"Perhaps. I do not know. The fate of mortals does not concern me."

"It should," said Bartlemy. "In the world Nenufar wants to reach, men and trees drowned together. No matter. What do you know of the boy whom the sisterhood say is born of two worlds? Can you tell me his father's name?"

The Hunter's whiteless eyes became twin pits of flame. "What is this? Am I a servant to be summoned thus for questioning? Or do you mock me?"

"I would not—"

"You call him *boy*—you flatter him! The bastard brat born of two kinds—the witch's brat with his father's seed, a seed that could never germinate, never endow him with life! You know the story—who does not? Why taunt me with it?"

"Ah," said Bartlemy with sudden comprehension. *"Him."*

"I took her body and she took mine—my impress, my heritage, flesh of my flesh. She made him—an infant botched together from witch woman and wood god, animated by a spirit plucked from who-knew-what infernal region—a monster of neither her world nor mine. What would you want with *him*? As for his father's name—who is there who does not know my shame?"

"You misunderstood me," Bartlemy said. "I did not allude to the witch's child, nor wish to offend you. If I have done so, I ask your pardon."

"If—!" Cerne laughed bitterly. "Be careful how you talk to me, wizard. It is not well to offend one of the Oldest—especially for a fat soup stirrer who prefers to remain out of trouble."

Bartlemy ignored both insult and menace, as he invariably did. Maybe he had heard it too often before.

"The boy I spoke of is all human," he said, coming back to the point, "but his father is from another universe. It is *his* name I seek."

"That would be impossible," Cerne said contemptuously. "No child could be so fathered, human or otherwise. The Gate does not open for a moment of lust. When mortals pass through, they do not return."

"Yet you said the portal *will* open, for mortal and immortal alike. If it *will*, then maybe it already has."

"Mere speculation." Cerne shrugged. "If small talk is all you want of me—"

"The seeress said the hour of Doom was approaching," Bartlemy said. "Whose doom?"

"I do not know." A sudden dark smile curved the Hunter's mouth, changing his face into a diabolical mask. "But we may yet hope it is the Doom of Man!"

Bartlemy let him go without further questions.

"What was all that about his son?" Annie asked.

"I touched a nerve I did not intend," Bartlemy said. "Old Spirits cannot procreate; it is the usual price of immortality. They have no need to pass on their genes. But once, a very long time ago, Cerne had a liaison with a young witch who used her power to make his seed grow inside her. The thing in her womb had no life, no glimmer of a soul to animate it, so she took a spirit from some unearthly plane and bound it in the fetus for all time. She hoped, I think, to create something superhuman—mortal and werespirit combined—but instead she made a monster. Cerne hated her for her betrayal of him, and hated the son as the symbol of that betrayal. The witch, too, hated her failure—the aberration of her power. And the monster child hated them both."

"Poor monster," Annie said.

And then: "That wouldn't be . . . *the* Child, would it? The one who—"

"No," said Bartlemy. "You would know the monster by his human side. Eriost is all spirit. Shall I call him?"

Annie nodded.

"We are not learning much," Bartlemy said.

"Keep asking. Please."

Presently, the Child appeared in the circle. He looked as Annie remembered, with his flax-pale curls, and the innocent beauty of his face, and his demon's eyes. Werefolk, she knew, cannot change. It had always disturbed her that she could not tell what sex he was; *he* was the pronoun of convenience.

He favored riddletalk even more than the others.

"The hour draws near," he said. "The mouse runs. The clock strikes. Hickory—dickory—*Dock!* There was a prophecy once, or a rumor, that one day a babe would be born who would hold the fate of the world in his hands."

"Ah, but which world?" Bartlemy countered wearily. "It sounds like all the other prophecies since Time began. Do you know who the prophet was?"

"There was a magician in the Darkwood," said the Child. "But he was no prophet, so maybe it was only a rumor. It was whispered on the wind, written on water."

"I know the routine," said Bartlemy.

"Then why ask, Omniscient One? Why ask the question if you already have the answer, O Wisest and Fattest of Wizards?"

"I know only a few of the answers," Bartlemy said patiently, "and there are many questions. This prophecy of a baby born to save the world, is it different from the others?"

"No," said the Child, and laughed his silvery laugh. "The tales are always the same. Slugs and snails and nursery tales . . .

What are little boys made of?
Eye of newt and toe of frog
Mandrake root and hair of dog
Finger of birth-strangled brat
Tailor's thumb and tail of rat
Gossip's tongue and eye of cat
Tooth of this and nail of that—
That's what little boys are made of!

It was a prophecy—a rumor—a murmur—a grape on the grapevine, an ear in the cornfield. Babes are born every day, every hour. What of it?"

"It is as I feared," Bartlemy said, as if speaking to Annie, or the dog, or himself. "The Child knows less than the Lord of the Wood, less even than the Hag with all her jabbering. We will finish it."

"The Hag?" The high clear voice grew sharper. "What does *she* know? Age has made her stupid: her mind has turned to jelly and her mouth to dust. Talk to the worms in the graveyard; they would make more sense. The magician spoke of a babe, but the tale came from elsewhere. From an oracle, maybe, the source of prophecy—or from his master."

"Which master?" Bartlemy asked.

"He sold his soul to the Devil," Eriost replied lightly. "There is only one who wears that crown. Would you dare to question *him*?"

"I heard that his master came from beyond the Gate," Bartlemy said. "The Devil you speak of has no mandate there."

"I cannot see that far," said the Child. "You know that. Unless the Gate should open to the werekind at last . . .

Sing hey nonny nonny, and hip hip hooray!
The Day of Doom is coming, and it might just be today!
Summer is icumen, loudly sing cuckoo!
The Knell of Doom is tolling, and it might just be for you!"

"Your rhymes are getting worse," Bartlemy said. "I think I've had enough of them."

The spirit vanished slowly from the feet up, still laughing and chanting—*"The Day of Doom is coming!"*—until only his head remained, floating in a nimbus of pale light, lips parted in song. Then, like the Cheshire cat, everything was gone except the mouth. It hung around for a while, singing in a faint, faraway voice, till Bartlemy disposed of it with a word.

"That's that," he said, turning to Annie. "I could call up lesser spirits, or greater, but the former would know nothing, and the latter—well, they would probably know nothing, either, besides being extremely dangerous. I think we should leave it for tonight."

"The Child—Eriost—mentioned someone he called the Devil," Annie said. "Is there really a Devil, like they tell you in church?"

"There are hundreds," Bartlemy said cheerfully. "Or rather, there are hundreds of spirits who have assumed that role. There is one in particular, however, who has always been at his best in the part. That was the one to whom Eriost referred."

"Can you question him?" Annie asked abruptly. "If he had dealings with Josevius . . . "

"That is not proven."

"The seeresses said . . . the doom is *in* Nathan. I have to know more. For his sake." *And for mine.* "Is it too—too risky, calling up the Devil?"

"We will see," Bartlemy said with resignation. "It is certainly too risky, and probably a waste of time, but . . . we will see. Wait here. There is something I need. Don't go near the boundary."

He went out, and Annie was left alone, except for the dog—alone with the magic circle. The circumference hissed softly as the flameline sputtered and sparked; behind it, the spellfire still flickered, its light shrunken to a dancing glimmer that barely reached beyond the hearth. The room seemed very dark. Although the circle was empty, Annie found herself increasingly aware of its potential; it appeared somehow *alive,* expectant, as if awaiting an occupant. Without Bartlemy's comforting presence Annie felt the magic was not on hold, but running on by itself, and something not conjured—an intruder, unwanted, perhaps deadly—might yet come through. She was suddenly very glad Hoover was there, his warm strong body between her and the spellring, ears pricked as he stared fixedly into the gloom.

Bartlemy was gone several minutes. At the heart of the circle, the darkness grew a little darker. Annie thought at first it was her imagination; then she was sure there was something there, a black shape crouching or hunched up, obscuring the far side of the perimeter. She felt Hoover stiffen and rise to his feet; her fingers tightened on a handful of his fur. He was making a noise in his throat, a distant rumble like the beginning of a growl. She gazed and gazed into the spellring, trying to see, trying not to see, still unable to distinguish anything clearly. There was a pulse in her neck pounding so hard she felt slightly sick.

At last she heard Bartlemy's footsteps returning, the opening of the door. For an instant from the shadow in the circle two red eyes stared back at her—then Bartlemy came in, and the shadow was gone.

"There was something there," Annie said. Her voice was unsteady. Hoover had ceased growling and made a sound like a canine grunt.

"It is possible," Bartlemy said. "A magic circle, once opened, draws many things. There are primitive elementals specifically attracted to acts of sorcery. Don't worry: whatever it was, it's no longer there."

"But . . . but . . . it *saw* me," Annie stammered. "You told me, spirits summoned to the circle only see the Questioner, and then not clearly. But this . . . thing . . . saw *me*."

"I doubt it," said Bartlemy. "It may have been trying to peer outside the boundary, and you got in the way. However, if you're serious, we should call a halt now."

Annie struggled to pull herself together. "No," she said. "It—it was nothing. I don't want to stop now."

"As you wish. But move your chair back; you are too close. From now on, whatever happens, don't speak, don't get up. Hoover will look after you. The spirit I am about to summon is one to whom the usual rules don't apply. I will do what I can to restrict the manifestation—without limitations, calling him would be far too hazardous. But be wary, stay silent, don't interfere. All right?"

Annie said "Yes" and pushed back her chair. Bartlemy was making a break in the spellring, stepping through in order to place some small object at the center. His movements were careful and very deliberate but even so, as he bent to set it down on the floor, Annie thought a wisp of shadow slipped through the gap behind him. The impression was so fleeting she could not be certain of it, and although Hoover turned his head he made no noise. Bartlemy withdrew, sealing the perimeter again, and began an incantation longer than any he had uttered before. The firelines burned brighter; smoke rose from the rim of the circle, and here and there tiny tongues of flame probed upward. Now Annie could make out the object in the center, a wooden figurine about a foot and a half high, sun-scorched, weather-cracked, age-blackened, its original shape all but lost after the battering of Time. It seemed to have a suggestion of goaty legs tucked under its belly and a broad head on top, with worn stumps for horns and the remnants of a malevolent grin cut into its cheeks. One arm was broken off, the other folded across its chest. It must once have been crudely carved but erosion had given it an air of mystery; the very blurring of its features made them somehow more evil. Nonetheless, Annie didn't find it really frightening.

Not till it spoke.

"Bale," Bartlemy said—he pronounced it as in *hay bale,* though she wondered later if it was a corruption of *Baal.*

And the statue answered. Its wooden mouth moved stiffly; a voice scraped from the harshness of its throat.

"It is seven hundred years since any called me in that name. Let the summoner identify himself!"

"Who I am does not matter," Bartlemy said prudently. He had told Annie long before that the spellmaster should never give his name to the spirit he summons. In the world of magic, names have power, and if the spirit does not know him it is safest to leave it in ignorance. "But I recall something of your history—seven hundred years ago. The people of the village offered to bind themselves to you for all time, them and their descendants, if you would keep the Roses from their door. But the Roses came anyway, and they all died, and the priest in his last hours called you accursed and burned the chapel around your image. Now even the ruins are gone."

"I ordered them to build a barrier and let no one out, no one in," the statue said, in a reminiscent vein. "But there was a woman whose husband returned from somewhere far to the south; she stole secretly to meet him and came secretly back, and he gave her the Roses in recompense. They called me faithless among demons, but it was they who broke faith. The woman betrayed them, betrayed *me*."

"There's always one," Bartlemy said.

"Bale was a collector of villages, a god of the common people. But I am Azmordis, Utzmord, Babbaloukis, Ingré Manu! I have collected whole cities and kingdoms, and the great and the good have bowed down before me!"

"Not the good," Bartlemy said gently. "And it is Bale whom I invoke. As Bale I summoned you, as Bale I bind you, in this image and this circle. It is as Bale I address you, and only Bale."

"What bargain do you seek with Bale, mortal? The Roses will not come again. What is the price on your soul?"

"No bargain," Bartlemy said. "Only a few questions."

"Questions!" A shudder ran through the idol; its wooden eyelids opened on cracks of livid radiance. "You called me here for *questions*? What am I—some Greek pythoness or gypsy soothsayer? I, Azmordis—"

"Bale," Bartlemy said. "You are Bale."

"Do not trifle with me, charlatan, lest your simple magics falter. The circle will not hold me long!"

"Long enough. And my question is not trifling, though it might appear so. The sisterhood tell me the hour of Doom draws near. No doubt you will know of it."

"I have seen many hours of Doom come and go. What is one more?"

"This could be the climax of an old, old spell, a spell that may have been set in motion by one Josevius Grimling Thorn, called Grimthorn. Rumor has it he sold his soul to the Devil. Did you have him in your keeping?"

There was a pause before the idol answered. "I remember him," it said at last. "A petty wizard whose ambition far outreached his powers. He sought me once, but I turned him away. What would I want with the soul of such as he—a soiled, shopworn thing without fire or fury? He wanted to be elevated to the Seraphain, to fly with my Fellangels . . . *Athamis! Incarnu!* My highest servants! . . . I spurned him with the scorn he deserved. He had nothing to offer me. He was already bought and sold."

"By whom?" Bartlemy said softly.

"What matter? Some minor spirit of no account. He hinted at a connection beyond the Gate, and called on the Ultimate Powers, but they did not hear him. He talked big and thought small. There are many such, especially now. The men the world calls great are no longer heroes and villains, only overblown egos with little substance behind the celluloid mask. They sell themselves for mere money when once they would have asked for the hand of Helen and half the kingdom. And now I must wear a suit, and sit in the Dark Tower dealing with corporations, where in other times I dealt with warriors and kings."

"Depressing for you," Bartlemy murmured.

"You are soft-spoken, wizard, quiet and cunning. No doubt we have met before, in the days of lime and Roses; perhaps we will meet hereafter. I will remember you. But you will not conjure me in this form again. Bale was a little god for the little folk; his time is done—his time and theirs. This idol is old and rotten. Your circle fails. It takes more than deadwood and spellpowder to hold *me*—"

The statue began to swell and split; a glow brighter than magnesium shone through the cracks. Instinctively, Annie shut her eyes. She heard Bartlemy's cry of warning—*"Cover your face!"*—his desperate rush of Atlantean—a report like cannon fire as the idol burst. Flying splinters sprayed the room; one embedded itself in her hand. When she opened her eyes again Bartlemy had switched on the lights; there was blood running down her arm. His hands, too, were bloodied, and the circle was broken and scattered. A ceramic vase had fallen to the floor and rolled intact on the folded rug; books were tumbled across the table; all the pictures hung akimbo.

"Has he gone?" Annie said.

"Yes. I called him as Bale, and as Bale he had to stay—or go, in the end. At least he was sufficiently curious to talk to me first. Not that your question was answered, but it tied up the loose ends." He took her hand, extracting the splinter, which was over an inch long. "I have a salve for this, then we'll clear up. After that, I think we both need a drink."

ANNIE WALKED home. Bartlemy had tried to call a taxi for her but there was none available for more than an hour and after a couple of drinks his alcohol level was too high to drive.

"I could cheat the Breathalyzer," he pointed out with a twinkle in his eyes. "I am a wizard, after all—in a small way."

"I know, but you shouldn't," she replied. "It's dangerous to drive even a little bit drunk, and we've had enough danger for one night. The gnomons are gone; I'll be fine."

It was cold, and she wound her scarf around her neck up to her chin. Her coat was several winters old and growing shabby but it never bothered her; fashion was not one of Annie's priorities. She walked down the road in the dark, knowing her way, no longer the wild strange Annie of earlier that evening but herself again, quiet and sure. Somewhere inside her a decision had been made, without conscious reflection, a result or side effect of all the questions, the riddles, the inadequate answers—a result that had less to do with what was said than what was not. *I'll tell Nathan*, she resolved, *on his sixteenth birthday. I'll tell him everything I know, and everything I don't know. The rest he can work out for himself. At sixteen, he can handle it.*

It was time to be done with childhood fairy tales and let him grow up on his own.

I don't believe all that stuff about doom, she concluded. *That's seer-talk. They would probably say we're all doomed, given half a chance—and they'd be right. We're all going to die. What of it? That really is yesterday's news.* And she smiled to herself on the dark lonely road, a little smile making curvy lines in her cheek, indifferent to the rush-and-tumble of the wind as it worried at the treetops.

It was then she heard the footfalls.

For a second her heart jumped into her throat—but no, the gnomons were gone, and anyhow their footsteps were many and light, whereas these belonged to a much larger creature, soft-shod or barefoot, two-legged, human or nearly so. And her imagination pictured a following shape blacker than the shadows, watching her with ruby eyes.

She swung around but did not call out. She couldn't see it, though she knew it was there. Then she strode off, quickening her pace, hearing the soft, heavy footfalls some distance behind her, neither too fast nor too slow, pursuing her like an echo all the way back to Eade.

The Visitor

It was Friday night before Nathan found himself back on Widewater. He was at home—sometimes his mother picked him up on Friday evening, sometimes Saturday morning, depending on his school commitments—and as things turned out, that was a relief. In the otherworld, flying with the albatross over the endless curve of the sea, he realized very quickly that hardly any time had passed since they'd left Denaero. Increasingly he thought of himself and Ezroc as a single unit, *we*, a kind of gestalt, rather than two separate entities. Time in different universes does not run concurrently; although there was in every cosmos a period to which Nathan returned most frequently, and which he thought of as "the present," he might find himself turning up a couple of millennia too early, or a day too late, and a week, a year, or a minute might pass in a few hours of earth time. Now he sensed they were going back to find the mermaid, keeping a promise. The sun was setting, and the reflected light stretched across the water like a track of beaten gold, rippling with countless waves. Nathan was beginning to find the vast sameness of the seascape wearying, with not even a rock to break the monotony, nothing but the empty ocean from sky to sky. He found himself thinking wistfully, not of green shores and white beaches, but the Ice Cliffs of home, and knew his emotions were melding with the bird's until he had trouble recollecting which was whom, and whom was which.

Dusk was almost welcome, softening the vacancy, wrapping the vastness in twilight and stars. A thin moon floated away westward (Nathan had lost his sense of direction, but the albatross never did); beyond, a few long strands of cloud cruised like basking sharks above the horizon. Soon they saw the gleam of whitecaps along the spine of the reef, and as Ezroc dipped low Nathan made out the pallor of Denaero's head and shoulders rising from the water, and the dark pool of her hair.

"You're late," she accused as the great bird settled on the sea swell. "We said sunset."

"We said after dark. At sunset we could be seen too easily."

"No one is watching me," Denaero said. "In my father's hall they are banqueting by the light of electric eels and sea stars that glow in the deep, eating a whole coelacanth that Uraki and his sharkriders caught two days ago. There is the music of tritons and conch shells, aqualyres and terpsichords, and my sisters wear garlands of pearls and glitter-worms and will dance till dawn. My favorite brother is there nursing his sore tattoo, trying not to look bored, but I told them I had a head-ache and would eat balmweed and sleep the night away. In the caverns below the shaman-priestesses chant their dreary chants while their gardens flower with living eyes and tiny mouths that open and close, open and close as the tide flows over them. One brought me the balmweed to chew, but I tucked it into my cheek and spat it out when she had gone. Who cares for dancing and feasts and shaman-cures? I'm going to fly—to fly—to fly—"

She flung her arms around the bird's neck, and he laughed his croaking laugh and told her to climb up, and as she did so Nathan felt her tail change, dividing into soft slim legs that curled around his body.

"Hold on tight!" Ezroc said, and reared up, wings pounding, skid-ding across the water in a trail of spray. Denaero shrieked with glee, clutching his neck feathers, and then they were rising up . . . and up . . . wheeling into a great spiral that left the sea far below and bore them ever higher toward the stars. The mermaid seemed to be leaning forward to gaze down at the moonglimmer on the distant water, and Nathan found himself wanting to share her experience, to feel what she felt, to see what she saw. Somehow he wrenched his mind free of the albatross and then he, too, was straddling the bird's back, just behind Denaero, ducking to one side to avoid the web of her hair, which whipped in long wet strands across his face. He was so eager to be part of it— the flight, the stars, Denaero's excitement and happiness—that he forgot all caution, pouring himself into the moment as he had done in other dreamworlds when the thrill of *being* lured him on.

And suddenly, he was solid.

Ezroc felt the extra weight and his ascent faltered; he tilted and reeled. Denaero looked around and screamed. Nathan didn't know quite how it happened, but in that instant of panic she lost her balance. His thighs gripped the albatross's body as Ezroc lurched to the left, but Denaero, unfamiliar with legs, had no grip, or none that she knew how to use. She keeled over, snatching at air—and then she was gone. Nathan flung himself forward onto the bird's neck, staring after her— saw her limbs flailing as she plunged headfirst toward the sea, the streaming plume of her hair. The drop was a hundred feet or more. Ezroc swooped after her, but he could not match the speed of her fall. And then somehow her body streamlined—even in the growing dark Nathan could make it out—arms outstretched, legs flowing together into a tail—and she was an arrow-shape streaking smoothly downward, cleaving the water in a perfect dive. Nathan caught his breath at the transformation, at her grace and instinctive skill. And Ezroc, relieved of anxiety for her, terrified by the sudden stranger on his back, folded his wings and plummeted seaward. Nathan tried to hang on but the bird shook himself, rolling sideways—and he dropped like a stone into the water.

There was no time to dematerialize—even if he had known how— no time to correct his position. The impact stung like a whole-body slap, then the sea opened and swallowed him. He was sinking, struggling, drowning in the choking horror of the water—it was his every nightmare revisited. He tried to swim, to kick back toward the surface, but he seemed to have no control over body or mind, and in the frenzy of the moment all he knew was panic and the dark. He felt something tugging him—felt small strong hands under his arms—he lashed out in confusion but whoever it was didn't let go. He was already gulping water, fighting not to breathe while his chest tightened into a fist—

Then he broke the surface, gasped thankfully at the rush of air into his lungs. Denaero released him; the albatross paddled on a ripple close by. He was treading water but felt that any second he might sink. He said: "Don't let go. Please—"

Denaero caught him underarm again, supporting him with little effort. "Why don't you change?" she said.

"I can't," he said. "I'm not merfolk—not seafolk. My legs don't—"

"What are you?" the albatross demanded. "Where did you come from?"

And Denaero, doubtfully: "You must be . . . some kind of selkie . . ."

Her night vision was far better than his and she could see the unfamiliar darkness of his skin against her own pale hands.

"No," Nathan said. "I'm human. I came"—he looked at Ezroc—"from your head."

"It was *you* . . ."

"You were in his head—in his thought—and now you're *solid*?" Denaero was trying to work it out. "That's serious magic. Even the shamans can't do anything like that."

"Were you spying on us?" Ezroc asked.

"Of course not. At least, not in a bad way."

"Who sent you?"

"No one." *Possibly the supreme ruler of another universe, but let's not complicate things.* "It's a bit difficult to explain. I come from—from a different world . . ."

He had had these conversations before, but never while trying to keep his head above water. He thought now would be a good time to wake up, but of course he couldn't.

"What world?" Ezroc said with evident skepticism.

Nathan spoke the thought foremost in his mind. "One with land."

"*Land!*" said Denaero. "You mean—you're a legwalker? A *real* legwalker?"

"Yes."

"You get up and walk about—on legs?"

"Yes."

"But how do you stay up without the water to support you?"

"It isn't that hard," Ezroc said. "Selkies do it sometimes. And snowbears—but they have four legs. Birds do it, too, when we land on the Great Ice."

"Yes, but he's so *tall*. And he has no wings. How can you balance?"

"Practice," Nathan said. "Firm ground is a big help." In the north, he reflected, he could have climbed out onto the ice, but he would probably have died of hypothermia. Here in the tropics, the sea was as warm as a bath.

"Why don't you stay still?" Denaero asked, as he accidentally kicked her tail.

"Because I'll sink."

"*I* don't sink. Unless I want to."

"You're a mermaid."

"You don't belong here," Ezroc said slowly. "I've flown all over Widewater, and I've never seen anything like you. Why is your skin that color?"

"My ancestors lived in the sun a lot. It's the practical color for people who live in the sun. In my world some people are much darker, almost black."

"And they don't dry up?" Denaero said. "Walking around—on legs—in the sun . . . How much time do they spend out of the water?"

"All the time," Nathan said.

"I don't believe you!"

"I do," Ezroc said unexpectedly. "You were in my head—I felt you. I'd have known if you were evil, or a liar. But I don't understand *how*—or why—"

"I'll try to explain," Nathan said. "But it may take some time. Couldn't we go somewhere—rest—?"

"We *are* resting," said Denaero, puzzled. "If you'd only stop fidgeting . . ."

"I don't *fidget*!"

Eventually, they decided Nathan could climb onto Ezroc's back and sit there while they talked—Denaero complained she was bored trying to support him—though it meant the bird had to turn his head right around in order to see whom he was talking to. For all the avian suppleness of his neck, it was not a comfortable solution. "You're twice as heavy as Denaero," he objected. "It was easier when you were in my mind."

"What's this funny loose skin 'round your legs?" Denaero asked, tugging at his tracksuit trousers. Annie, who felt the cold, always kept the heating on high in the winter months, and Nathan had gone to bed without a top on.

"It isn't skin," he said. "It's clothes."

"What are *clothes*?"

Neither merfolk nor selkies went in much for clothing. Rhadamu's warriors wore battle armor made from the carapace of giant crab, horned lobster, or sea scorpion, and both males and females favored elaborate jewelry, with necklaces at throat and waist, bracelets, rings, hair ornaments. Disney mermaids, Nathan reflected, invariably sported C-cup scallop shells, but Denaero was completely topless. When her tail had split into legs, he had noticed she was bottomless as well. Her breasts were small, shallow mounds that barely broke the eel-smoothness of her body, but they were still breasts, and as a normal fifteen-year-old boy he couldn't help being aware of them. He decided the one advantage of the underwater situation was that, since she was more or less covered to the throat, it did minimize the embarrassment factor. If they had both been seated on the albatross, with him behind her—the idea made his brain spin . . .

"I need to keep warm," he said briefly.

"But it's not cold!" Denaero protested. "How can *this* keep you warm?"

"Well, it would if it wasn't wet—if I was out of the water." He definitely wasn't going to go into issues of modesty.

Denaero seemed unconvinced. She was obviously intrigued by his strangeness, but it was plain she was not much impressed by Nathan himself. In Wilderslee, he had found it easy to impress Nellwyn after saving her three times from an Urdemon, even if a large amount of luck had been involved. Here, he had knocked Denaero off her perch on Ezroc, fallen into the sea after her, nearly drowned in panic, shown himself awkward and cowardly in water, and generally failed in the hero stakes. Although Nathan didn't expect girls—princess, mermaid, or otherwise—to be automatically impressed with him, he wasn't used to looking a complete fool, and in view of what he had to accomplish it wasn't an ideal starting point.

"If you come from another world, how did you get here?" Ezroc asked. "And what are you here *for?*"

"I dream myself here," Nathan said. This was never an easy thing to explain. "It's like there's a portal in my mind that opens when I'm asleep, and I go through into otherworlds. And I'm always—sort of—*integrated*. I can speak the language and everything. Only I never found myself in someone's head before. I'm sorry: I don't do it deliberately. It just . . . happens. I think . . . it's part of something. A quest. There are things I have to do . . ."

"You mean—you've been to *lots* of worlds?" Denaero said, uninterested in quests.

"A few."

Her eyes widened; she turned to Ezroc.

"Is he telling the truth? The shaman-priestesses can leave their bodies in dreams, but they can't move between worlds. How could that happen? It must take big magic."

"Not magic," Nathan said. "Physics. We're all made up of these tiny particles, too small to see, and they can move in and out of reality. With me, it's like—the same thing, only scaled up." He had no idea if this was correct, but that was how he rationalized things to himself.

"Particles of what?" said Ezroc.

"Stuff," Nathan said helplessly.

"I'm not made of particles!" Denaero declared. "The First Gods made us when the God-King killed his wicked father with the Sickle of the Moon, and the blood dripped into the sea, mixing with the moonlight on the foam, and so the merfolk were born. Everyone knows that."

"But you and the sea and all things are made up of these particles," Nathan said. "Particles of . . . of energy."

"Magic particles?" Denaero asked.

"In a way." He left it at that.

"What about this quest?" Ezroc persisted.

"I was coming to that." Nathan began to explain about the Iron Crown, and how it was part of a spell to save another universe, and he had to get it back, but suddenly he felt dizzy, and the sundazzle on the water was blinding him, and the sea started to revolve like a huge flat disk—and then he was falling, falling into deep water, out of the dream into the dark.

NATHAN AWOKE almost immediately feeling very uncomfortable and realized it was because he was still wet. He got up, toweled himself down, and swapped his dripping trousers for a dry pair. The bed where he had lain was sodden, and after a minute's thought he crept into the bathroom to borrow Annie's hair dryer. It was around three A.M. and he didn't want to disturb her but he supposed, by the morning, her sensitive maternal antennae would have detected the problem and she would be requiring an explanation. That was the thing about mothers, he reflected. They always knew when you were in some kind of trouble even if they couldn't tell precisely *what* kind. He thought of saying his hot-water bottle had leaked but that might be worse; Annie was well aware he only went to bed with a hot-water bottle when he was ill. No, he would have to tell her the truth. She had always been pretty good about such things in the past, but he knew she worried, and he would have done almost anything to prevent that.

He found himself wondering if fathers were the same. Did they have twitchy paternal antennae and lie awake agonizing over the behavior of their sons? He didn't know, and it seemed to him odd that he had never thought about it before. And why should such thoughts occur to him now, when he was nearly sixteen, long past the age—in his opinion—of needing fatherly care? It wasn't as if his childhood had been lacking in male guardianship. There had been Bartlemy, less than

a father but more than an uncle, a large, reassuring figure in spite of—
or because of—his wizardly skills, cooking wonderful food, listening
to his problems, helping and guiding him, *being there*. And the Grandir,
a remote but inexplicably caring presence, gazing down from the star
that wasn't a star, clearly exercising some influence over his otherworld
adventures, watching over him, for all his other concerns, from beyond
the world. What father could have done more?

He snuggled down into his blow-dried bed and slid back into sleep
feeling curiously comforted, as if there were a mantle of protection
wrapped around him thicker and warmer than any duvet.

In the morning Annie scooped up the damp trousers and said
philosophically: "At least it isn't demonspit. I thought I would *never* get
that out. And it didn't do the washing machine any good, either. I had
to have the man 'round a month later: he said it had gummed up the
filter."

She kept her tone light and turned her head away so Nathan wouldn't
see the anxiety in her eyes.

Later that day Nathan caught the bus to Chizzledown to visit the
Thorns. Rowena was the last surviving member of the ancient family
who had owned Thornyhill Manor since time out of mind, the only le-
gitimate descendant of Josevius Grimthorn. Despite two marriages
locals still called her Rowena Thorn, and since her second husband
seemed to have no particular surname, or none of distinction, he had
become Mr. Thorn willy-nilly, though he didn't appear to object. His
real name was Errek Moy Rhindon, an exile from Eos whom Nathan
had yanked into this world largely by mistake, dumping him on the
beach at Pevensey Bay as an illegal immigrant with no papers and
nowhere to return to. It had taken Nathan some while to catch up with
him again, by which time he had begun to learn the language and as-
similate an alien and—to him—backward culture. Unfortunately, he
had seen the original *Star Wars* trilogy at the house of a charity worker
not long after his arrival, giving him a view of our universe that he had
never lost. In the Grandir's world, fiction was banned, since it was said
to be founded on corruption and lies, and accordingly Eric had believed the films constituted an account of our history, detailing a high

point of civilization from which we had subsequently declined. Even now that he was married to Rowena and had learned rather more about the world that had adopted him, he was still prone to greet people with *May the Force be with you!* and to bracket the fall of the Republic and the Emperor's seizure of power with later events in Rome or revolutionary France.

Rowena ran an antiques shop, with a two-story apartment above where she and Eric lived. She was on the phone when Nathan arrived, what sounded like a business call about something whose provenance she clearly doubted, so Eric took him into the small kitchen at the back and made coffee. Since he came to this world, he had developed a passion for it. Nathan accepted a cup with plenty of milk and sugar and sat down on a rickety chair.

"So," Eric said, "you have been on Eos again, in a dream?"

"Mm."

"The Contamination has not yet reached Arkatron?"

"Not yet," Nathan said. The Contamination was a form of magical pollution, probably the fallout from a war that had gotten out of hand, which had poisoned the entire cosmos, destroying all living things. Eos was the last surviving planet, and even there only a few regions were still free.

"Do you miss your home?" Nathan asked diffidently.

"Only a little. It seems so far away—so long ago. Another world! This is my home now." *Integration,* Nathan thought. *Like in my dreams. You find yourself in a different universe, you start to belong to it. It must be some form of survival trait.*

He said: "But on Eos, you lived for ages. Thousands of years." The Eosians used their magic to prolong life, resulting in a population so sterile, no children had been born there for centuries. "Here—you'll grow older." He didn't say, *You'll die,* but Eric knew what he meant.

"Everyone grow old, in the end," Eric said largely. "Is nature. Here, maybe it happen faster, but life better. Also, I not wish to outlive Rowena. Is good we pass the Gate together. Who know what lies beyond? Perhaps we are reborn in new universe, have another life, another youth. In winter leaves wither, fall from tree, but in spring they grow again.

Perhaps the same with people. Death part of a cycle, then there is room to regrow."

Eric had a decidedly philosophical streak, Nathan reflected, but that was a possible side effect of intercosmic travel. He himself showed a tendency to philosophize from time to time, and he was a teenager.

He said, "I suppose so," and took a chocolate cookie from a package Eric had thoughtfully placed by his elbow.

"You find the Crown yet?" Eric inquired.

"Sort of. I know where it is, but it's going to be difficult to get. You know so much about the Grail relics—they're a major legend in your world. What kind of protection does the Crown have? Is there a spirit trapped inside, like there was in the Sword?"

"I don't know. Maybe . . . but I never hear of one. Power of iron protect the Crown. Iron very strong in my world, stronger than here. Makes magical field to keep all evil away. Where is Crown now?"

"In a place called Widewater. It's a world—a planet—entirely covered by sea. The Crown's in a cavern under a reef—this sea goddess has it, Nefanu, only she's a werespirit and I think she can't actually touch it."

"Crown cannot be undersea," Eric said positively. "Iron and water make rust. Rust not good for sacred relic."

"It's supposed to be a cavern of air," Nathan said, "even though it's underwater. I'm not quite sure how that works, but that's what I've been told. Could the power of the Crown somehow expel the water?"

Eric shrugged one of his flamboyant shrugs. "Maybe. I not know."

"Perhaps it was Nefanu," Nathan said, thinking aloud. "Perhaps *she's* the guardian of the Crown, like the gnomons for the Grail and the elemental in the Sword. Only the Grandir didn't have to conjure her, he just made use of her. He knew she would want the Crown—she would recognize its power—it's like a kind of trophy for her. I can't see how she could use it, if she can't touch it or wear it, but—"

"Crown is not Sword," Eric said. "Sword is for use. Crown just *is*."

Nathan thought about that for a minute.

"Until the Great Spell," he said. "Then someone—the Grandir—will use it."

"Crown is . . . circle that binds." Eric was trying to explain something, but Nathan wasn't sure he knew himself what it was. "We have old saying: hand on the Sword, blood in the Cup, Crown on the head. Three rules of king making from ancient days. Great Spell bring together many things. But king is also sacrifice. So . . . blood in the Cup, Crown on the head. But whose head? To save a world, whose head?"

"The Grandir's," Nathan said.

"Maybe. But none wear crown since Romandos's day. Too heavy. Weight of iron, weight of power, weight of doom." And he repeated: "Crown just *is*. To wear it, death. So they say."

"If it's part of the spell," Nathan said, "then the Grandir will wear it. Whatever the cost."

THAT EVENING Nathan, Hazel, and George went to the sixteenth-birthday party of an old friend from primary school. Annie stayed at home watching Saturday-night TV and wondering if she was becoming middle-aged, lapsing into completely irrelevant thoughts about what DCI Pobjoy might be doing now and how he spent his Saturdays. Investigating crime, probably. She was just picturing him leaning over a corpse in some exotic location, like Crowford or Crawley, when she heard a noise from the bookshop. She couldn't be sure against the sound of the television but she thought it was a door closing. As if someone had come in very stealthily, taking care not to let the handle rattle. Access to the house was through the back door from the garden or through the entrance to the shop; she had left the latter unlocked for Nathan, only putting up a CLOSED sign, in case anybody wanted to buy a secondhand book in the middle of a Saturday night. Eade was the kind of place where people still left doors unlocked, a sleepy little village where apart from the odd robbery and serial murder nothing untoward ever happened. Nathan had a key, but he had left it in his gym bag at school.

And now there was someone in the shop. Annie switched off the television and waited for a knock on the adjoining door, a familiar voice—*any* familiar voice—demanding her attention. Lily Bagot, or

Ursula Rayburn, or . . . Silence. The hairs rose on the nape of her neck. Long ago, Bartlemy had told her that werefolk and wizards could not enter a house uninvited, but a bookshop, she knew, was different. Anyone could enter a shop; that was what it was about. She walked to the door, laid a hand on the knob. Telling herself fear was idiotic, irrational, she pushed it open.

"Is anybody there?"

No answer. The interior was very dark, only a glimmer of light filtering through the front window from a nearby street lamp. Annie flicked the light switch and stepped through the door.

Everything seemed to be as usual, the books snuggled together on the shelves, spine leaning against spine, dreaming of the otherworlds between their covers. Annie always fancied there were more universes here than Nathan's mind could ever encompass, a portal on every title page, countless voyages, adventures, sagas, endings both happy and sad. She found it strangely reassuring to think of them all coming together in the small secret environment of her little bookstore, a between-world place from which, simply by opening a book, travelers could set out across the multiverse. It made it easier to deal with the concept of Nathan's dream journeys, knowing that, in a sense, otherworlds were part of her everyday life. She looked around her, saw that nothing was disturbed, started to relax. Noises could be deceptive sometimes, especially at night. It must have been something next door.

She turned back to her living room—her work desk was beside the door, just inside the shop—and there he was.

She didn't know how she could have failed to see him, by what power or chance the alien presence had escaped her. He was sitting behind the desk, in her swivel chair, apparently at ease, a big, ugly man—so ugly he was almost handsome—in a peeling leather jacket and jeans so worn and faded, they barely had shape or color anymore. His hair was thick and ragged, framing his face like the mane of an animal; under the matted bangs his forehead seemed to be puckered by an old scar. His skin was either pockmarked or merely rough-textured, like granite, his cheekbones were crooked, his shoulders hunched, his deep-set eyes so narrowed she could not see any whites. She knew instantly he was werefolk—inside her, alarm systems shrieked in warning—yet there was something about him that was unmistakably human, though she couldn't quite define what it was. She thought afterward that he carried his humanity like a flag of defiance in a losing war.

His eyes widened very slightly as she stared at him, and she saw that as she had suspected they were whiteless, dark as rubies from edge to edge, with pupils like black slits.

For a long moment neither of them said anything at all.

He looked very large, and very strong, and very dangerous. Wild phrases ran through Annie's head—*Avaunt thee, witch!* or, in this case, *warlock*—*Begone, foul dwimmerlaik,* whatever a dwimmerlaik was— and there was bound to be something appropriate in *Macbeth,* if only she could remember it. But the man just sat there, unmoving, watching her with his demon's eyes.

In the end, she said: "Do you—do you want to buy a book? Because I'm afraid we're closed."

He smiled. It wasn't a nice smile—it didn't, for instance, make dimples in his cheeks or friendly lines around his dark red eyes—and it exposed a motley collection of teeth that included one chipped molar and two very sharp canines. But it indicated humor, and humor is a human thing. *Almost the same word,* Annie thought, wondering why she'd never noticed that before. *Humor . . . human . . .*

"I didn't come to buy," he said. "I came to sell."

His voice, like his eyes, was dark red, with gravelly undertones.

"To sell me a book?" Annie said, surprised, baffled, and intrigued all at once.

Now that they were talking, she wasn't *quite* so scared.

"Not exactly," he said. "Books come my way from time to time, but I doubt they would interest you." He tapped with one finger on the volume lying on the desk. It was a big finger with a nail that jutted like a claw, but what Annie chiefly noticed was that the book—of course— was *Rhoda Rides to Glory*. It would be. She had put it there after Pobjoy had gone, intending to file it somewhere unobtrusive, and hadn't gotten around to it. The edges of the demon's smile still lingered.

Annie temporarily forgot her fear in the upsurge of annoyance and embarrassment. How he knew what was in the book—since he hadn't had time to open it—she couldn't guess, but obviously he did.

"I sell lots of books," she said. "Not just ones . . . like that. I mean, there are none like that really—except the classics . . ." She wouldn't go down that route again. "Look around you. Anyhow, if you don't want to sell me a book, what *are* you selling?" With eyes like that, she thought, it could be anything. A ring of power, a vial of poison, a gorgon's head. "I don't have much money. Even if I want whatever it is— which I probably won't."

"It's information," he said. "You want it."

And then she knew. A darkness in the circle . . . footsteps on the road . . .

"*Who are you?*"

"You can call me Kal," he said.

"Is it your name?"

"Sometimes." Werefolk, she had learned, were like that. They had a name for every form they took. She wondered what he really looked like. And yet there was that trace element of humanity about him. Laughter—and a capacity for pain . . .

"Don't do that!" he snarled. His kind often snarled.

"Do . . . what?"

"Reach out. Try to . . . *understand* me. No one does that. I don't permit it. If you try any more of that insight bollocks, I'll leave now."

Demons rarely used human swear words. They had their own, in an assortment of strange languages. Puzzling over it, Annie was about to say he was welcome to leave when she checked herself. He had come to the circle unasked—and he had information.

About Nathan's father . . . ?

"I'm sorry," she said. "I didn't mean to be nosy, honestly. You came to the circle that night, didn't you? When Bartlemy left the room. Do you know something about—do you know the answer to—?"

"I knew Grimthorn." The red gaze shifted, focusing on some point far in the past. "Briefly. He crisped in his skin like a boar on a spit. Well for him. If he hadn't, I might have torn his head off—slowly. Your friend the wizard was asking about him—him and other matters. But I prefer to talk to you."

"You said you were *selling*," Annie said guardedly, trying to ignore the part about tearing heads off. "I told you, I haven't much money. Or—or anything that would interest you. Just books."

"I've eaten books," the demon said conversationally. "When I couldn't get something better. Betimes, the leather still tastes of the flesh it once clung to. But these are mostly paper—wood pulp—vegetarian stuff. Not on my menu."

"Everyone needs their greens," Annie found herself saying.

"So they say in the rhyme.

A roast pig a day
keeps the fart tucked away
but cabbage and sprout
will soon let it out."

"I don't believe there's any such rhyme," Annie accused. "You made that up."

Part of the smile crept back. It was a wolfish smile—the smile of a predator at its prey—but not, Annie hoped, completely evil.

"So will you pay my price?"

"You haven't told me what it is."

"It is high," he said. "But you can afford it—if you choose."

"What is it?"

"Invite me in."

"You *are* in," Annie pointed out.

"I am in the shop. Invite me into your home."

Ah. Silence fell again, the silence of comprehension and returning fear. Annie struggled to consider the implications, her thought scurrying around in circles like a rat in a box. She didn't want to do it—she *really* didn't want to do it—her home was her haven—but . . . *If he was going to kill me,* she assured herself, *he'd have done it already. And why give me information if he intends to tear my head off afterward?* Of course, she was assuming he was a rational being, which wasn't always the case with humans, let alone werefolk. Instinct warned her to beware of him—but instinct wasn't always right. Was it?

She said: "This information—how do I know it's worth it?"

"You don't. I don't. Your wizard friend didn't say why he was asking. There's only one way to find out."

Annie thought—hesitated—nibbled her lip. Laid a hand on the doorknob.

And then she remembered to ask the missing question.

"Why? Why d'you want to come in? There's only me here. My son'll be back later, only . . ." Her tone sharpened. "Is it him? Is it him you want?"

"I know nothing of your son."

"Then—why?"

"Invite me in," said the demon called Kal. "It's like the information. You have to invite me in and then—maybe—you'll find out."

She looked directly into the ruby-dark eyes. It wasn't encouraging.

"All right," she said, opening the door. "Come in."

He got up, slowly, padded after her into the house. He wore sneakers that sounded like paws on the wood floor. Annie led him into the small living room and indicated a chair.

"A fire," he said, glancing at the logs smoldering happily in the grate. "I like that. So many houses nowadays don't have fires. They keep the heat in metal boxes and the light in bubbles of glass. Stupid, when a fire gives you both. Yet they call it progress." Werefolk are even more prone to nostalgia than mortals; living practically forever, they have a lot to be nostalgic about.

Annie said nothing, merely switching on a lamp—a bubble of glass—giving her a clearer view of his face.

"Who *are* you? I know your name's Kal, but—are you one of the Old Spirits, like the Hag and the Child?"

"Yes," he said, "and no. You may have heard of me. My mother was a mortal witch, my father a werespirit. Such lusts are common enough, but should not have issue—only my mother thought she could outwit the Ultimate Laws, and she used spellpower to make the fetus grow, and bound a stray sprite inside it. She was ill prepared for what she got."

Annie remembered Cerne's rage and shame when he spoke of his son, but she knew it would be fatal to show pity.

"I've heard of you," she said.

He looked at her with a sneer on his mouth and a flame brightening his red, red eyes, but she sensed the pain beneath. *You would know the monster by his human side,* Bartlemy had said.

And suddenly she thought she knew why he had wanted to come in.

"I am Kaliban," he said, "the witch's demon child. The sword with the twisted blade—an abortion of both nature and werenature. You have invited me into your home. Isn't it customary, under these circumstances, to offer me a drink?"

"Certainly," Annie said. "I've got whiskey, and vodka, and there's some cheap wine I was using for cooking, but that's awful, and—"

"I'll take whiskey."

She poured him the whiskey and one for herself, then sat down, facing him, feeling very slightly more comfortable in his company.

"Well?" she said by way of a prompt.

"Well?" he mocked her.

"You said you knew Josevius Grimthorn."

"So I did. May he burn in hell—only he already has. One of fate's better decisions. I met him . . . I forget the year. Too many have gone past. It was when I was still young and couldn't alter my demon form. So they hunted me, the men who called themselves nobles—not that the peasants were any kinder. They hunted me with arrows, they hunted me with dogs, but I plucked the arrows from my flesh and tore out the throat of the leading hound with my teeth. Then I ran into the woods. They were deeper and thicker then, and the Darkwood down in the valley had a bad name: few went in, fewer still came out. But I had no fear of rumors and tales. The pursuit became tangled in briars and frightened of shadows, but I went on into the valley until I came to the house. It was in a clearing, but the trees clustered close behind it, and Grimthorn stood in the doorway calling me in. I didn't trust him—I trusted no one, noble or villein, wizard or werefolk—but my wounds hurt, and I was tired. He invited me in, gave me water to wash my injuries as well as salves and bandages. He broke bread with me. Do you understand?"

Annie nodded. She knew that traditionally a guest who has shared food and drink with his host was sacred.

"We had wine—not much; it must have been drugged. I slept. When I awoke I was shackled hand and foot and half a dozen of my erstwhile hunters were standing beside me, gloating over their captive. Grimthorn was smirking and pocketing gold." Kal's mouth twisted at the recollection. "He didn't smirk for long. He had forgotten my history, if he ever knew it. Iron does not weaken me. And I am . . . *very* strong. I burst the bands on wrist and ankle and swung the chains that had weighted me so fast the air thrummed. I took two men's heads off through steel collars with the force of it. The rest fled—they were lightly armed and had no dogs—but it was Grimthorn I followed. He was only a footstep ahead when he entered the chapel, but I could not cross the threshold. The ward-spells sealed it from me. Once inside, he called on powers I had never heard of—powers from beyond the world—and the air split, and the accursed Cup was there, glowing green as decay. I watched from the door, forgotten, and then I slunk away into the night. Grimthorn I did not fear, but the power he summoned . . ."

"The Devil?" Annie asked.

"Hardly." Kal laughed. "I have known *him* for a thousand years. This power was something else—I felt it. Something so much greater—something that might have crushed the most potent werespirit as I would crush an ant. It nudged at the fabric of our world like the fist of a god brushing a spider's web. The darkness cracked like an eggshell—the ground shook. I had always known when to fight, when to run, when to hide. I ran and hid. I sensed Josevius was doomed, and soon. No man could meddle with such power and live."

"It fits with what we know," Annie said. "Someone—presumably the Grandir—used spells to send the Grail and the other relics across the barrier of the worlds. After that Bartlemy says they became unstable and would travel easily between universes. But . . . what of the other question? Do you remember—Bartlemy asked for a name? The name of—of Nathan's father?"

"I know nothing of his father," said the demon. "But I saw the boy Nei-thun, and his mother. That was what I came to tell you."

"His *mother?*" Annie stared at him, startled into blankness. For a minute she thought Kal was taunting her, until she saw his gaze lowered, preoccupied with memory.

"It was long after," he said. "Three, four hundred years, maybe more. By then I had learned to live secretly; I was the hunter, not the hunted, killing in the dark. There was a witch in these parts, some descendant of Josevius—she had a lust for a demon lover, and she summoned me to the circle, and stepped within the perimeter, thinking to lie with me there. But I remembered the witch who was my mother, and I broke her neck. The spell failed, and the circle was open, and I walked away into the night. It was Halloween, or Beltane, or Lammas—one of those nights when witches are abroad and there is magic in the air. The priest hid in his chapel, the peasant in his cottage. In the churchyard, the Whistlers were out, whistling the dead from their graves. That sort of night."

Annie started to ask *Who are the Whistlers?* but she didn't want to slow down the story. "What happened?" she said.

"The woman was on the road through the woods. There was a road by then, though not such as you see now; this was just a track cleared of trees, so farm carts and wains could pass through. The woman had a dozen servants with her, all dressed like princes, and a boy of about sixteen. That was why I watched—because of the boy. He was deformed, his legs so twisted he could barely walk, or so I guessed—he and his mother rode in a phaeton drawn by two white llamas. The servants were on foot. I heard the woman call him Nei-thun, though what language they spoke I didn't know. I told myself if opportunity offered I would spook both the servants and the llamas, and when the phaeton broke on the rough ground I would take the cripple, because he could not run away."

"You don't mean—you would have *eaten* him?" Annie demanded, horrified.

He flashed her a smile without humor, his assorted teeth gleaming in the lamplight.

"They came from the East, I knew that," he went on. "They smelled of the spices they ate, and the hot dust of the Eastern deserts. She must have been a queen, a sorceress—either or both. You could tell by her jewels and her pride. Her skin was golden and her hair crimson and her eyes were those of a cat. Oh, she was mortal enough, but the mark of the Gift was on her. I knew I would be hard-pressed to take the boy when she was near. Still, I watched her. I've always hated witches. All save one."

"Which one?" Annie queried, but he didn't answer.

"After the woods she turned aside and made her way to the Scarbarrow. She couldn't have known the country but she must have had directions, or maybe she'd seen her way in a spell. On Scarbarrow she stood in the circle, and the symbols flamed around her, and her servants hid their faces in terror. I might have taken any one of them, they were so unwary, but I wanted to see what she did. There was a storm on the hill, a witch's storm, with lightning that crackled from sky to circle and the clouds sucked into a vortex of power. In the woods below, small things crept under the leaves and stayed there, trembling."

"How do you know?" Annie said.

Kal flashed her a scorching look from narrowed eyes. "Because I'm telling the story. Had I been small enough, I would have crept under a leaf, and I do not scare easily. Are you answered?"

"Sorry."

"It was a night like no other. The woman stood in the circle with her arms raised and her face to the lightning, and the boy sat at her feet, hugging her legs. He did not seem to be afraid, not while she was there. Not till the end. Then I heard her call on the powers of another world— the powers Grimthorn had summoned to the chapel centuries before— and the grass died on the hill, and the servants fled, and there was a stillness at the heart of the spell like the eye of a hurricane. She took a jeweled knife from her belt and brandished it, and the edge of the curved blade shone like balefire. *Then* the boy was afraid, weeping and calling her *Mother,* but she seized him by the hair and cut his throat, and his lifeblood ran down her legs into the dead grass."

"No," Annie whispered. "You're making it up. No mother could do that to her child. You're making it up."

"She killed him," Kal said, "as the priest kills the prize bull, the pick of the herd, to please the gods. Thus the burden of tradition. Even the sickly Christians have such tales. My mother might have killed me, if she had valued me more highly."

"No mother *could* . . ."

"She stood in the circle with the body at her feet, and drank the blood from a cup of obsidian, and the storm hung over Scarbarrow like a black crown spiked with lightnings. But the Other Powers made no answer, and the fabric of the world did not stir. The woman screamed in the language of the Stone, as though mere fury would open the forbidden Gate—screamed until her voice failed, and she sank to the ground, weeping for her son, or herself, or the end of her hopes. I had no hunger anymore; I left her to her wretchedness. In the dawn I saw the servants creeping back, and later in the day there was nothing left but the blood, already grown cold. And that was the end of it."

"Is that all true?" Annie demanded. "I still think no mother could . . . Is it really true?"

"I've drunk your drink, and warmed myself at your hearth," the demon said. "I could lie to you, but for what purpose?"

"Why did you come to me—not Bartlemy?"

"I like wizards no more than witches. And you were the one who wanted to know. I did not hear the name of either mother or father, but the boy was Nei-thun, and he is dead. Does that answer your questions?"

"No," Annie said frankly. "It just makes things more complicated." She found she was shaking, perhaps from the proximity of the demon, more likely from the impact of the story. She believed him, whether she wanted to or not, and the horror of it seemed to taint her life, like a bloodstain in a familiar room.

She glanced at the clock and saw it was midnight precisely; it would be. "N—my son will be coming home soon," she said. "I don't want to be unfriendly, but please would you go now? I don't think he should meet you."

The ruby eyes darkened. "You love your son," Kal said. "Still, mortal love is a fragile thing, the emotion of the moment. Only werefolk know what it is to love forever."

"You're wrong," Annie said. "Our lives may be short, but they are not empty. Werefolk endure; they do not know what it is to truly live, or truly love."

The demon rose, and looked down at her, his alien features enigmatic. "I am werefolk," he reminded her. "Do you think I cannot feel? If I bit your throat out and drank your blood, do you think I would not taste your pain?"

Annie made herself breathe slow and deep.

"You have a mortal soul," she said with sudden certainty, "though I don't know where you keep it."

Kal drew back a little, and the corner of a smile came and went. "I am growing one," he said. "In a pot of basil."

He stepped into the kitchen, heading for the garden door, though she hadn't told him where it was. "Thank you for your hospitality. I will not forget it." For a second, watching him go, she thought she saw lion's paws below the hem of his jeans, and the twitch of a tail that protruded somehow, flickering across the floor. As he went into the garden she heard him singing a ballad she knew well, though one word sounded wrong. His voice was deep and unexpectedly musical.

"Are you going to Scarbarrow Fayr?
Parsley, sage, rosemary, and thyme.
Remember me to one who died there
He once was a true love of mine."

And then the shop door clanged, and she knew Nathan was back.

THAT NIGHT, the little house was full of dreams. Annie saw the Eastern witch standing in a circle far larger than the one Bartlemy had made.

Flames played along the perimeter. Her hennaed hair hung down to her knees, and at her feet sat the boy, his arms clasped around her legs, his head bent. She raised the knife; the curve of the blade gleamed with wicked light. Then the boy looked up with Nathan's face, Nathan's eyes, and Annie was the witch, and the knife was in her hand, and she couldn't help it, she couldn't stop, though the tears ran down her cheek she was pulling back his head and drawing the blade across his neck . . .

She woke up screaming.

She got up and trod lightly into Nathan's room to tell him it was all right, she had had a nightmare, that was all, nothing to fear. But he still slept, and when she laid a hand on his shoulder he didn't stir, and she knew he wasn't there.

NATHAN WAS in Widewater, no longer solid, a thought drifting in a submarine world. Through the blue dimness he saw tall chimneys of rock bubbling with noxious gases; the surrounding water was cloudy with nutrients and flickered with tiny creatures that had come there to feed, ghost-shrimps and spiny stars and gulping mouths that swam without tentacle or fin. Nathan could make out little through the mist of plankton, but gradually he realized it was growing darker, the darkness not of night but of depth. He knew he was descending farther than ever before, and panic set in at the idea of it—the weight of water above him, the terrible pressure that would crush his lungs if he should materialize. He didn't know how the merfolk survived it, magic perhaps, but he remembered that even in our world there are many fish and other marine animals that can endure such pressures, though scientists still do not fully understand how. He had left the stone chimneys behind now; ahead of him there was a wall of utter blackness. As he drew nearer he realized it was a vast cliff, the roots of the reef. Things wriggled past him in the dark; he was aware of their passage as a trembling in the water and was glad he could not really feel or see them.

Presently, he made out a kind of glow somewhere in front, and as his vision improved he saw there were phosphorescent growths adhering to the rock like deep-sea fungus, quivering in the current. Beyond was something that looked like a garden, a garden on the ocean floor in the endless midnight of the deep, with sea shrubs whose every stem was tipped with a lidless eye, and writhing clumps of spaghetti-grass, and flowers like a frill of lip sucking at the water. He floated above it, invisible and intangible, but a bush of glittering eyes swayed toward him as though half aware of his presence, and tentacles of spaghetti groped at his nothingness, and flower-mouths gaped as he passed. He remembered Denaero saying something about the gardens of the shaman-priestesses, and assumed that was where he must be. Then in front there was a break in the wall, and the cliff opened to engulf him.

Nathan's dream carried him along the tunnel—he tried not to think of being trapped there, solid, with air and sunlight hundreds, perhaps thousands, of yards above—until it widened out into a huge cavern. It was roughly circular, ribbed and vaulted like a natural cathedral, lit with the pale mauve radiance of sea stars and the reflected glimmer of quartz and crystal veining the rock. In the center around a species of altar a group of merwomen were chanting. Their tails and bodies undulated with fluorescent stripes; their fins were barbed and their faces skull-thin, shrunken-cheeked, and lipless like beings halfway to starvation or decay. Their closed eyes bulged in hollow sockets as though straining to split their lids.

The chant climaxed; the eyes opened. They were not whiteless like those of most werefolk but all white save for the elongated pupils, glowing with a luminescence of their own. They spoke in voices blended and distorted by the water, lilting without music, moaning without the wind.

"The Goddess calls to her people. The time has come."

Come . . . come . . . Watery echoes rippled around the cave.

For the first time Nathan noticed the listeners—they must have been waiting in a shallow chamber in the cavern wall, and now they moved forward, approaching the altar. The foremost was a merman whose massive torso was laden with chains of coral chips and pearl shells; he wore a coronet of uncut quartz on his head, surely too heavy to sustain without the support of water. Mermen are beardless, smooth-skinned, and virtually unwrinkled unless they live to extreme old age, their bodies kept moist by the element in which they live, their faces slightly androgynous, but this one looked unmistakably masculine, older by his build and a certain authority in his carriage. His mouth was a stern line, his rather flattened nose—typical of his kind—very broad, his sharp-cut nostrils flaring and shrinking visibly as he drew in the water that was filtered out through the gill slits in his neck. In the glow of the sea stars, his long hair looked more purple than Denaero's, and his skin had a sullen tinge that might in another light have been subtly green. Nathan guessed this must be Rhadamu.

Two others flanked him, both with the sea dragon tattoo on their chests, one clearly a warrior, with spiked shoulder plates and arm-bands, and an assortment of knives on a belt at his hip. Possibly Uraki, the sharkrider Denaero had spoken of. The other had the slender mus-cles of youth and wore a small circlet of red coral that suggested he might be the king's eldest son.

"We are the chosen of Nefanu, the children of the Sea."

Sea . . . Sea . . . , murmured the echoes.

"The time has come. You must destroy the lungbreathers, the mon-sters who live on the northern ice. They are traitors who dream of the land and live half their lives in the air, eating our fish to stoke the heat of their blood—the fish that Nefanu gave us to protect and to feed on. If they are not stopped, they will eat all the fish in the sea to perpetuate their unnatural warmth. They despise us, calling us coldkin, wormkind, mackerel to be hunted and slain. They have dreadful weapons hidden on the ice: swordfish lances that can travel for miles, and poisons to be-foul our water. You must attack first and destroy them ere they destroy us. Unite the merkings! Summon an army! Purify the ocean for the true children of the Sea!"

Sea . . . Sea . . . Sea . . . The cavern threw back the word in a wash of mingled reverberations.

Why does this sound familiar? Nathan wondered. Was the call to war always the same?

They are different—they are dangerous—we fear them—kill—kill— KILL . . .

"The Goddess is all-powerful," Rhadamu said. "Can she not melt the Great Ice so the northfolk perish without their sanctuary?"

A shiver ran through the priestesses; the rhythm of their exhortation faltered.

Nathan thought: *They don't like the question. They don't like* any *questions . . .*

Nefanu wants obedience, without awkward objections.

"The Ice melts!" said the priestesses, but their voices were no longer in unison. *Melts . . . melts . . . melts . . . ,* said the echoes. "The Ice melts—and refreezes! The cold of the utter north cannot be changed. The Goddess could tilt the world on its axis, but she must refrain, lest the balance of life be overthrown."

I bet she can't do it, Nathan said to himself. *She doesn't give a damn about the balance of life.*

"The Poles are the anchors of the globe. To move them would bring death to more than the northfolk. The currents of the world would shift—the seas would boil—the stars would weep blood . . ."

Rhadamu's face remained as expressionless as a shark. Possibly he had heard it all before. "The Goddess is all-powerful," he responded. "Could she not melt the ice for just a brief time—a day, a night, an hour? Then the northfolk would drown or panic, and fall easily to our spears."

"The meltwater would flow south and chill the reefs." One of the shamans spoke alone, her voice quavering in isolation.

"Has the merking no stomach for the fight?" asked the others. "He is the regent of the Goddess, foremost of the twelve kings, protector of the Death Crown. Is such a being to show himself craven before the ultimate battle?"

Battle . . . tattle . . . rattle . . . , said the echoes.

They mean the Iron Crown, Nathan thought. *The Death Crown. It must be.*

"I have no stomach for the slaughter of my people," said the king. "I hate the northfolk with a deep and bitter hatred, but they are many, and strong, and will fight long and hard for survival. They will be in home waters, familiar with every riptide, every ripple. They can retreat onto the ice where we cannot follow—our legs have been unused for too long—and use their hidden weapons against us. In such a conflict, the outcome is far from certain. The Goddess loves her children; she must share my concern."

"The Goddess expects her people to die—" *Die . . . die . . .* "—die bravely, die gladly, in a great cause. The heart is strong, the spear is sharp. Let none cry *Hold!* until the last of the lungbreathers breathe their last. Trueseal and selkie, pinwing and snowbeast—all must be slain. To war! To war! The northfolk are many—the merfolk are more! Summon the twelve hosts, mount the sharkriders, arm the spearslingers, poison-tip both javelin and lance! Nefanu will send the monsters of the deep for the laggard and the latecomer, the wounded and the weak. Let none cry *Hold!*—let none hold back. To war!"

War . . . war . . .

"We are ready!" said the warrior whom Nathan thought might be Uraki. "We will dye the northern seas red with their blood and ours—the cliffs will drip with icicles of scarlet—Nefanu's pets will make such a feast as has never been seen. If they flee from us over the floes we will raise the Leviathan who crunches whole icebergs in its jaws—"

"No!" No . . . no . . . , sang the echoes, rebounding almost before the priestesses had spoken. "Not the Leviathan! Let him sleep—sleep in the deep—deepest sleep—never to wake—never to rise. Better the last merman die than the Leviathan should stir . . ."

"I know the peril," said Rhadamu, not even glancing at the warrior. "My captains are sometimes foolhardy, but not I. We will prepare. I will call the merkings to a council of war—the twelve hosts will be gathered—we will go north with the moontide when all is ready. The Goddess has my word. I will not fail her."

"Be swift!" said the shamans. "Speed is of the essence. The foe must have no warning. There are spies and traitors even among your own people—at the very heart of the kingdom. The tale of their perfidy is a murmur in the ear of a shell, a bubble in the mouth of a smallfish—but we have heard it. We hear everything. Treachery slips like an eel between the cracks of your defenses. It may yet undermine all our plans."

With any luck, thought Nathan.

"Use your magic!" said the king. "Find the traitors. Are you not the elected priestesses of Nefanu? Do you not see as well as hear? Find the traitors, and I will chain them to the Dragon's Reef, and crabs will nibble their flesh while they still live."

"The spells are brewing," said the priestesses. "Soon we will know. But the magic cannot be hurried."

"Be swift," the king adjured. "Speed is of the essence. I will not go to war with treachery at my back."

I must warn Denaero, Nathan thought, feeling the dream pulling him away—away from the priestesses with their white eyes, and the talk of war and blood, and the cathedral echoes repeating and repeating it in a murmuring liturgy. Away from the dark of the ocean into the safer darkness of a dreamless sleep.

Denaero . . . warn Denaero . . .

Then his thought was extinguished, and when he woke he was back in his own world.

AT BREAKFAST Annie looked pale and tired, but Nathan was too preoccupied to notice. He was desperate to return to Widewater and contact Ezroc and the mermaid, but he knew from previous experience that sleep would not come at will, and any attempt to force the portal would either fail or land him in the wrong universe. The day stretched ahead, a space to be filled—he needed action, diversion, discussion, anything to get him through.

"I'm going out," he told Annie.

"Where?" Even her voice sounded pale, though he didn't pick up on the tone. The horror of her dream and Kaliban's story clung to her like a shadow that could not be brushed off.

"Hazel," he said, almost at random. "I—I need to talk to her."

"But you saw her last night?"

Last night . . . A vague recollection of the party came to him, reduced to insignificance by subsequent events. "We didn't talk. You can't talk properly at parties. 'Bye, Mum—see you later."

She let him go, wondering where he'd been in his sleep to make Hazel's company so imperative, wishing he would talk to her—but he was a teenager, and teenagers rarely choose their mothers for the role of first confidante. She poured herself more coffee, and let it grow cold. Some time later, she picked up the phone and dialed Bartlemy's number.

At the Bagots' house, Nathan found Lily in the kitchen with Franco experimenting with a new cappuccino machine and Hazel in her room making a figure out of pipe cleaners. It had a curl of black hair glued on top that might have been Franco's and a snarl of red wool around its neck in imitation of a scarf he favored.

"What are you doing?" Nathan demanded.

"Sympathetic magic." The short end of a pipe cleaner protruded between its legs. Hazel bent it until it was pointing downward, murmuring what might have been a magic word.

Then again, it might not.

"That's not funny," Nathan said. "I bet Uncle Barty didn't teach you that."

"No, he didn't. It was in one of great-grandmother's books."

"You know what happens if you use magic to harm people. You tried that once before."

"Stop lecturing me." She looked up at him, pushing her hair back off her face—the tangle of hair she had always used to hide herself. "You don't think there's anything of Franco in *this*? It's a bunch of pipe cleaners and a piece of wool." She didn't go into details about the hair. "Even Great-Grandma wouldn't have been that stupid. It takes more than that to make a simulacrum. I was just doing—transference."

"Transference?"

"Something Uncle Barty *did* teach me. You make an image for your hate, and you torture it, or burn it, or just make it look stupid, and the hate transfers into the image, and then it's gone. Burned up—laughed out of court. Transference."

"*Un*sympathetic magic." Nathan relaxed a little, letting himself smile at her. "Are you sure you didn't—do anything more?"

"Almost sure," Hazel said airily. "You're all knotted up: I can feel it. What's happened?"

Nathan poured out the whole story—about Widewater, and Denaero, and the priestesses of Nefanu, and the imminent conflict between merfolk and selkies.

"I thought you were meant to find the Crown," Hazel said, "not stop a war."

"I don't suppose I *can* stop it," Nathan admitted. "I don't think anyone can. But I can't let Denaero be hurt."

"You said the king was her father," Hazel recalled. "She's his youngest daughter, right? She's bound to be his favorite—it's like that in all the stories. He wouldn't hurt her."

"I don't know. The Goddess makes them all mad. She's like Nenufar, only worse. I'm afraid Denaero's in real danger."

"You like her, don't you?" Hazel said gruffly.

"Yes, of course."

"The same as that princess you were so hooked on?"

"Oh no. No, not at all. She's very pretty, but . . . sort of cold and fishy." He wasn't going to mention the lack of scallop shells.

"Does she wear one of those seashell bras like in films?" Hazel asked with an unnerving flash of perception.

"N-no. But she's awfully flat-chested, so it doesn't really matter."

Hazel said nothing, brooding on her own lack of development in that area.

"Anyway, she thinks I'm stupid," Nathan went on. "I know it's pretty feeble, but I'm still scared of the water after the accident—and even if I wasn't, it's not as if I can go under for ages like she does, or cope with the pressures when you get down really deep. If you want to do something useful, instead of fiddling about with pipe cleaners you could find a spell to help me."

"Useful?" Her face reddened with anger. "Of course, I never do anything *useful*, do I? You're the one who does the *useful* stuff, popping between worlds and rescuing people all the time. I just get to—to sit around and clap 'cos you're such a hero. And now I can make myself *useful* by finding you a spell so you can go swimming with a topless mermaid! That would be really *useful*, would it? That would help to save the world?"

"You're overreacting," Nathan said, vaguely surprised by her outburst. "I didn't mean it seriously. I shouldn't think there *is* any such spell—and if there was, it would take a very powerful witch to pull it off. I only meant—"

"Thank you! So I can't possibly be *useful* because—because I'm not even much good as a witch?"

"But you never wanted to be," Nathan pointed out, reasonably. "You always hated the idea of doing magic—you were afraid you'd end up like Effie Carlow, lonely and sly and sour inside. You only got into the magic thing when you fell for that creep Jonas Tyler, and he wasn't exactly worth it, was he?"

"Whereas you're hanging out with a half-naked mermaid!" Hazel fumed. "At least Jonas kept his trousers on!"

"Actually," Nathan said scrupulously, "she isn't so much half naked, more, sort of, whole naked. Only her bottom bit is usually tail. Except when it turns into legs . . ."

"I don't want to hear this!"

"Look, I have to warn her about the priestesses. I keep telling you, she's in danger—"

"I bet she's in danger," Hazel said savagely, "going around with no clothes on! Go and save her, why don't you? You're always doing it. First it was that stupid princess, now it's a mermaid with no knickers. Why don't you just whiz off and—and do your superman stunt? You don't need my help for that."

"For heaven's sake, calm down," Nathan said. "You're acting really weird lately. Anyway, you're in no position to criticize the company I keep—you spent the best part of last night talking to Damian Wicks. I mean, Jason's kid brother—and they say he's just like Jace only shorter and not so tough. Do you really like hanging around with a failed school bully who wants to be a thug when he grows up?"

"Damian is *nothing* like Jason," Hazel protested. "He's really sweet and—"

At that point there was a knock on the door. Hostilities were suspended for a breathless minute. The door opened a few cautious inches, and Lily Bagot peered through the gap, flushed with the triumph of culinary achievement. "Would anyone like a cappuccino?" she offered.

Pooping the Party

On that Sunday afternoon, Bartlemy came to tea with Annie, driving into the village in his old Jowett Javelin, a car so retro most people had never heard of it, let alone seen one. It was already dark when they sat down by the fire, with the teapot keeping warm on the hearth and the coffee cake Bartlemy had bought on a plate on the table. Coffee cake was Annie's favorite, and he sensed she needed a treat. Nathan was with George, in theory helping with his history homework, in practice playing World Domination on the computer. Annie wanted to talk about her visitor of the previous night, but not in front of her son.

"He sat right where you are now," Annie said. "It's funny, you'd think I'd be used to that sort of thing, but I'm not. Even after being attacked by the water spirit, and finding Rianna's corpse, and the things I've seen in the circle, and that time Nathan went missing, or when he was kidnapped, or turned up covered in slime from a giant man-eating slug . . . anyway, I still found it hard to take. Maybe it was because I felt he wasn't just a demon, there was a human inside somewhere."

"Possibly," said Bartlemy. "That doesn't mean it was a good human. Werespirits have their own loyalties but no moral sense, only appetites and needs. Whatever humanity he might have had has long been distorted out of shape. Don't be tempted to pity him. In such dealings, pity can be terminal."

"I know," Annie said. "Still, he told me—what were his words?—he was *growing* a soul."

"A strange way of putting it," Bartlemy commented. "I must take more interest in your friend Kaliban—particularly if he is taking an interest in you. What did you say he called himself?—the sword with the twisted blade. A reference to his name. *Caliburn* is what he was christened, if christening came into it: a variant of *Excalibur*. His mother wanted a weapon, not a child. The name was changed later, becoming *Kaliban,* or *Chalyban*—from *Caulborn,* I believe, one born in a caul. Shakespeare must have heard it somewhere, heard tales of the name and its owner, when he used it for Sycorax's son in *The Tempest*. And so the legend grew. A name to live down to."

"What does he really look like?" Annie asked. "I thought, when he was leaving, he had paws, maybe a tail . . ."

"What does any of us really look like?" Bartlemy said. "If there was a true mirror to show us the shape of the soul . . . I have never seen him—either his mortal seeming or his demon self—but I am told he is a patchwork creature like so many werespirits, a bit of this, a bit of that. The horns of a ram, the muscles of a bull, clawed feet, tufted tail. Why do you think so many of the ancient gods had scales or feathers, animal heads, eagle's wings? Werenature could never resist the chance to experiment, to make something bigger and better, nastier and scarier than anything mere biology could achieve. Most spirits create their own forms, but I fear Kaliban was stuck with his. I didn't know he could assume a more acceptable shape. That must be a recent development."

"His hair hung forward," Annie volunteered, "but his forehead was sort of scarred, as if it had been burned."

"Scars," Bartlemy mused. "Yes. Those cannot be altered. I don't know the story of his."

"Was I right," Annie went on, "inviting him in?"

"Had I been there, I would have advised against it. But I was not there. You behaved with generosity and trust, as I would expect of you, and you have lived to tell the tale. So perhaps my advice would have been wrong. I am more concerned with the story he told you. That is . . . potentially disturbing."

"He said the boy was about sixteen," Annie reiterated, "and his name was Nei-thun. That must be coincidence—mustn't it?"

"I don't know," Bartlemy admitted. "I feel—we have a glimpse of a pattern, a pattern that must mean something, but only a few details are illuminated, and the outline is still unclear. Which is a fancy way of saying that I have no idea what's going on, and at this stage I can only guess."

Annie managed a smile, but it was a halfhearted effort. "Why did he sing that verse from 'Scarborough Fair'?" she said. "Only he said *Scarbarrow*—the place where the woman . . . did it. D'you suppose *that* meant something, or was he just playing with rhymes like the other spirits in the circle?"

"Oh, that means something sure enough," Bartlemy said. " 'Scarbarrow Fayr' was the original name of the ballad. It changed over the years the way songs do, as the Scarbarrow was forgotten and the town slipped in instead. There was a story behind it, an old, old story. The Scarbarrow was a hill somewhere around here, supposedly the burial place of a primitive king. Some said he was a mortal man, others the king of Elfland, and inside the hill were the gates to Faerie. Of course, the gates to Faerie have often been equated with the Gate of Death . . . Anyway, legend had it that on certain nights of the year the hill would open, and the fairyfolk would come out and dance with the souls of the dead, seeking to lure them through the gates beyond the reach of church or god. People would place special herbs on the graves to shield their inmates from the charms of the fae—parsley, sage, rosemary, and thyme."

"Like the song," Annie said, relaxing sufficiently to take a bite of coffee cake. "I see."

"The ballad springs from one particular incident. Myth or truth, we don't know, and it hardly matters. A beautiful girl—a young man—true love. The usual thing. But she was sought after by a local lordling—the youth challenged him—they fought—he died. The lordling was a skilled swordsman, the youth a peasant with no skills at all. The girl

mourned him, spurning her noble admirer, so he decreed in his jeal-
ousy and rage that the youth could not be buried, but must lie un-
coffined till after Halloween, with neither herb nor prayer to save his
soul. The girl kept vigil over him, determined to protect him at any
cost. It was the night when the hill would open—the night of Scarbarrow Fayr—and she knelt in the churchyard beside his corpse, watching
and waiting, while the moon sailed the cloudwrack and the fairyfolk
came dancing down the hillside, carrying their little green candles and
whistling, whistling for the souls of the dead."

"The Whistlers!" Annie exclaimed with a flash of revelation. "He
talked about the Whistlers. *That* was what he meant."

"Folk thought it bad luck to name the people of Faerie," Bartlemy
said, "so they gave them other names. The Little People, the Good
People, will-o'-the-wisps, starsprites, the Whistlers. They would call
up the spirits of the dead with a whistling noise like the piping of some
unearthly bird. It was an eerie sound to hear on a wild night, a sound to
chill the blood."

"But you can't have heard it," Annie protested. "It's just a story. It
isn't *true*."

"Stories change," Bartlemy said. "Truths change. The gates to the
hill are shut, and the hill itself is forgotten, and even the location of the
Scarbarrow is lost forever. I heard the Whistlers once, on a night such
as I described, but maybe it was only a bird."

Annie felt a shiver like a cold draft on her nape. She said: "What
happened to the girl?"

"She knelt in the graveyard, and she heard the Whistlers, and her
hand clutched the cross about her neck. Presently, she saw the souls rising like smoke from those graves where no herbs were laid, and the
dancing lights came to her lover's corpse, though she could see no
shapes carrying them, and the spirit rose from his body and reached for
her with glimmering arms. But the werelights spun around them, and
invisible hands drew him into the dance, and shadow fingers plucked at
her dress and pulled her hair, tugging her, turning her, harrying her
into their mad fandango, over grave mound and tombstone, out of the
cemetery and up the hill, to where the gates of Faerie stood open

wide—the gates to eternal damnation. She could not resist, for her cross was torn off in the hedgerow, and the magic had gotten into her feet, and the face of her lover was ever before her, though she could not make him hear her nor catch his hand. But even as they reached the gates his voice came to her, urgent and low: 'Go back! Go back! It is too late for me, but not for you. I will give my soul for yours. Go back!' Then he called on Jesus, and immediately the whistling ceased, and all the lights went out, and the hillside was dark and empty. She walked slowly homeward and told no one what had chanced, and the next day they buried him, and she prayed beside his coffin for the soul that was gone. And on afternights when there was magic in the air she would linger on the hill singing her song, but the gates never opened, and the Whistlers did not return, and she knew she would not find him again on earth or in heaven."

"That's so sad," Annie said. "Beautiful and sad. But I don't believe in damnation."

"It happens," Bartlemy said. "But people make their own hell, usually this side of the Gate. They need no gods for that. As for the story, it's one of those pagan folktales that Christianity adopted when they set themselves up as the good guys. A little truth, a little fantasy, a moral at the end. Who knows what really happened—if anything?"

"Then what does the story have to do with us?" Annie said. "And the woman whom Kal saw—who sacrificed her own child—did she think that would open the gates to Faerie? Did she think the Whistlers would come for him and let her through?"

"That is the question," said Bartlemy. "And as ever, we are short of answers. But I wouldn't trouble yourself too much. I don't see you as the sacrificial type." He smiled his gentle smile, and she found herself responding, comforted by his mere presence, his quiet common sense. "Have some more cake."

"So now Hazel and I aren't speaking," Nathan said. "It's idiotic. Just because I made a stupid joke . . . She's being completely unreasonable."

"You didn't tell her so, did you?" Annie said with foreboding.

"I—I might have. I mean, she was *so* overreacting—"

"Did you tell her *that*?"

"Yes."

"What else did you tell her?" Bartlemy inquired with an air of clinical interest. "You didn't suggest she should calm down, I suppose?"

"Actually . . ."

"Actually?" Bartlemy prompted.

"Yes, I did."

"Good God," his uncle said faintly.

"What did I do wrong?" Nathan demanded, slightly aggrieved.

"Telling an angry woman she's overreacting and ought to calm down," Annie explained, "is on a par with stuffing a lighted firework into a bottle and waiting for it to blow up in your face."

"But Hazel and I aren't, like, a man and a woman," Nathan protested. "Not in *that* way. We're best mates. We always have been. After all, we've known each other since we were kids."

"You aren't kids anymore," Annie said patiently. "You're not kids and you're not adults. You're stuck in the in-between zone of teenagerdom. Basically you're just two giant hormones. It changes things—you have to start learning to *think* before you speak on occasion."

"Not with *Hazel*!"

"You said she was behaving stupidly at the party," Bartlemy remarked. "What exactly did you mean by that?"

"Nothing really. It's just . . . she was talking to Damian Wicks. You know. For ages. Damian as in brother-of-Jason-Wicks. He's a complete prat. All that family are. And she said he was *sweet*," Nathan made a face. "I sort of worry about her. She really does have awful taste in boys."

Annie and Bartlemy exchanged glances.

"I think," Annie said with resignation, "I need to teach you some of the dos and don'ts about dealing with the opposite sex. Before you get yourself horribly murdered and some poor girl pleads justifiable homicide."

"I'm not *that* bad with girls," Nathan objected. "Nell thought I was all right."

"You kept saving her life," Bartlemy pointed out. "That tends to create a good impression."

"Besides," Annie added, "you didn't spend that much time with her, did you? Your dream probably whisked you away before you had a chance to put your foot in it."

"You seem to think I'm a dead loss," Nathan said a shade sulkily. "Thanks very much."

"You're fifteen," Annie said gently. "The fifteen-year-old boy who is good with girls doesn't exist. In fact, nor does the sixteen-, seventeen-, or eighteen-year-old, and so on ad infinitum. The thing is, as girls grow older they suss out how to deal with boys. That's kept relations between the sexes going so far."

Nathan managed a grin.

Bartlemy said: "Fortunately for you, you have a wise and sympathetic mother who will undoubtedly offer you a few tips. Pay attention. That will give you a head start. Probably ahead of me—I've been around fifteen hundred years, and I still haven't worked women out."

Nathan eyed his uncle dubiously, unsure how to react. He found the thought of Bartlemy having any interest in women, or vice versa, deeply unnatural, but he was too polite to say so.

His family read his mind without difficulty.

"We'll talk about it some more over vacation," Annie said. Nathan, being at private school, was due to start a break shortly. "You'd better go to bed now. School tomorrow."

In bed Nathan brooded on his argument with Hazel for a while, puzzling over the general incomprehensibility of female behavior, then his thoughts switched to Denaero and his need to get back to Widewater. He wondered if the same rules applied to mermaids, even though they were part fish, and had a grim suspicion they did. For all he knew, they applied to fish, too. But he still felt somehow cheated by Hazel's attitude. After all, this was *Hazel*. His best friend. She wasn't supposed to be like the other girls.

She wasn't supposed to be so easily impressed by a prat like Damian Wicks . . .

He fell asleep without realizing it and slid into a muddle of ordinary dreams. He was marrying Denaero, only she still had her tail, and Bartlemy was pushing her into the church in a wheelchair. She had a veil on but kept refusing to wear the scallop shells he'd provided. Then Hazel swept past in a white wedding dress with her hair up in a butter-fly clip the way she'd taken to wearing it lately. "It's all right, Nathan," she said. "It doesn't matter about the scallops. I'm going to marry Damian." She went inside with the prospective groom, and all the church bells were ringing, and Nathan was left alone among the tomb-stones. Suddenly it was dark, and nearby someone was whistling, or maybe it was a bird, and there was fear all around him . . .

Dream faded into oblivion. Much, much later, when he opened his eyes, he was Elsewhere.

Not Widewater—the lack of sea was a dead giveaway—nor Eos, nor Wilderslee. In fact, it was nowhere he recognized. He seemed to be on a broad curving platform encircling a cylindrical tower, with different-sized tiers set one on top of another like a stack of irregular plates. It continued upward for many stories, alternately widening and tapering, until it terminated in a conical roof tipped with a spire of gold. The whole edifice was constructed from some pale yellow stone, polished and gleaming like marble. Nathan allowed his thought to float toward the edge of the terrace; beyond the balustrade, he could see only a rose-pink sky dimpled with cloud like a drift of apple blossom. He peered over the stone rail, and although he was weightless and bod-iless he felt his mind reel. There was no ground below that he could see, only more sky, and the tower, broadening toward what he hoped was its base. Perhaps a thousand feet down the cloud thickened and pressed against the building, obliterating the view. Nathan pulled him-self away, his dream turning back to the tower, where two lines of peo-ple had emerged from a double doorway and were ranging themselves across the terrace. They wore deep-purple-black robes, perhaps denot-ing religion, or rank, or any combination, and under the hoods they had the lean, curved, long-boned faces of Eosians. Nathan was evi-dently somewhere in the same cosmos, if not on the same planet. He re-membered the Grandir's purple-cowled henchman, and wondered if these men fulfilled a similar role—whatever that was.

The doors opened again, and three more people came out, one of them a woman. Imagen. She wore a long violet gown and her hair was piled on her head in a complex arrangement of loops and whorls and wound with a strip of silk. She carried a cup in both hands—*the* Cup, the Grimthorn Grail. It looked dull and lusterless in the roseate light. Beside her was Lugair, Lugair the traitor, holding the Sword. Nathan knew it at once. And in front of both walked Romandos, dressed in what looked like cloth of gold, wearing the Crown. Some of the spikes turned inward, pressing his brow, but he did not seem to bleed.

At the very edge of the platform he stopped, facing the sky, and commenced a slow incantation. Nathan knew this was the beginning of the spell, the Great Spell whose long binding was still unfinished. The purple-robed figures echoed the chant in a chorus like the wailing of distant winds. He was reminded of the shaman-priestesses of Nefanu, or the sisterhood of seeresses whom he had once seen in Bartlemy's magic circle, speaking with many voices though a single mouth. Perhaps there was a special potency in numbers, in the synchronicity of mind and word. As the incantation progressed he lost track of time; he thought hours or even days might have passed, and the blossom-clouds gathered together and mushroomed into a storm, and the towering vapors formed into shapes like great wings sweeping across the sky, and galloping horses with tossing manes blended into billows like waves on the sea. Then the billows dissolved into faces, a thousand faces shifting and changing, men and women, heroes and demons, until at last they all flowed together into one huge face filling half the sky. Romandos. And the chorus called out his name, and the sound of it seemed to be carried across all the worlds, and the pink daylight darkened into night, and lamps flared along the parapet, and meteors streamed past the tower like silver rain. Romandos turned to Lugair and held out his bare arm, and the other man drew his Sword across the bare skin, and Imagen knelt holding the Cup to catch the blood. Nathan felt the emotion seizing on his heart like a clamp, though his heart was in bed at home, and with it came knowledge, and horror.

This is it, he thought. *This is where it all goes wrong . . .*

And then it happened. The rhythm of the ritual broke. Lugair raised the Sword and plunged it into Romandos's breast, and the blood ran down into the Cup and overflowed, splashing Imagen's arms, her dress, her face. "So be it," said the first of the Grandirs, and his dying whisper was the loudest thing in all that world. "Not just my blood but my lifeblood. Heart's blood. The Sword takes what it must . . . the Cup drinks what it needs. The power has spoken. The spell is sealed. So . . . be . . . it." From the spikes of the Crown, more blood ran down his face in red streams. He gasped a little, coughed, and died. The chorus gave a great wail, no longer like the wind. The clouds opened and rain poured down, extinguishing the lamps. In the dark Lugair let fall the Sword—Nathan heard the clatter as it struck the marble—and one of the purple-robed figures picked it up and thrust it toward him, but somehow Imagen got in the way, and she collapsed into his arms, and the robed attacker was slipping in the wet, and everything was blood and rain.

Nathan's mind spun away into the dark, thinking: *It was the spell. The spell needed Romandos—it needed his life—so it used Lugair. Maybe he was chosen long before the magic was made . . .*

Later, the darkness cleared. How much later he didn't know; sleep distorts time. This was another terrace, another palace. Beyond stretched a garden where carved dragons wrestled in a dazzle of fountain spray and the sky was eggshell blue. Nearby in a curtained pavilion a woman was admiring the view. Not the view of the garden but the view of her own face, the most beautiful face in the world, shining out of an oval mirror like a vision of Helen. Halmé, Nathan realized, but not the Halmé he had known. This was a girl, young and fresh and radiant with vitality and hope.

"Beauty is truth, truth beauty," she said. "Am I the truth? Am I the one and only truth for you?"

"The one and only," said the man on the couch beside her. He was naked under the embroidered coverlet, and the interplay of his muscles might have belonged to the statue of an athlete or a god.

The Grandir—the last Grandir—the one with no name.

He looked unnervingly like Lugair, save that there was neither cruelty nor treachery in his face, only passion and the intensity of his secret will.

"We will have children," Halmé said. "We will have children now, before it's too late. A daughter and a son. Beauty and strength." She stroked his arm, admiring their joined reflections, his arm laced around the slenderness of her waist, the shadow of his face behind hers.

"Maybe," he said.

"We will," she insisted. "I feel the fruit swelling inside me, the ripeness and the readiness. Don't fear for my fertility—there will be children!" She laughed and stood up, wrapping herself in a silken garment that trailed along the ground behind her. Then she stepped out between the curtains and walked along the terrace, lifting her face to the sunset.

Now they have the sundeath, Nathan thought. *She cannot look at the light except through a mask.*

In the pavilion, the Grandir withdrew his other hand from beneath the coverlet. He was holding a vial so bright it might have been cut from diamond, full of a milky liquid. The air glittered faintly around it, the afterglow of magical transition.

"Alas, my love," he said, "there will be no children. My seed is precious; I cannot spare it. I need it for other things. One day, when this world is old and dying, I will give you another, but the price is high. Your price. You are paying now, though you know it not. Our son will never be. Your sorrow will outlast Time, and there will be no remedy. But the choice is mine, and I have chosen. So be it."

The same words Romandos used, when his dying sealed the Great Spell. *So be it.* Nathan knew that this time the Grandir was unaware of him; this dream journey formed no part of any plan. Yet he sensed a pattern that grew clearer, though he still couldn't see what it was. He tried to concentrate, to bring the blur of his thoughts into focus, but before he could grasp detail or meaning the dream drifted away, and he was sinking back into sleep.

THE TERM was over, and Nathan still couldn't get back to Widewater. Hazel came around to the bookshop, asking Annie to ask Nathan something, and Nathan told Annie to tell Hazel something else, and in the end Annie lost her temper and ordered them both to start speaking to each other or she would not be answerable for the consequences. The flare-up made her feel marginally better, as though her pent-up anxieties had found a brief outlet, and afterward, when normal service had been resumed, she gave them some of Bartlemy's almond ice cream and reflected, a little sadly, that soon the day would come when they were too old for ice cream to melt their differences. Although with Bartlemy's ice cream, anything was possible.

It was the tenth of December, the day of the Rayburns' party. Annie went around early with her contribution to the festivities: cocktail sausages from the local butcher cooked in honey and mustard—"You just need to heat them up a bit at the last minute and stick the toothpicks in"—and what she called all-vegetable soup, made with a pint of the liquid from Bartlemy's mysterious stockpot, which had been simmering quietly for the past several centuries and might contain almost anything.

"It's probably not for vegetarians," Annie told Ursula. "Barty says he last remembers putting meat into it in 1973, but he might have added something since and forgotten about it."

Ursula laughed, on the assumption that it was a joke. "That's so long ago it doesn't count," she declared largely. "After all, when you bury people they turn into grass eventually, don't they? So whatever it was would have died naturally by now and been transformed into vegetation anyway."

Annie didn't attempt to follow her reasoning. The house was in a state of chaos, with assorted children running up- and downstairs in the persistent way children do, Donny and a friend trying to set up a beer barrel in the drawing room, some enterprising teenagers mulling wine on the Aga, and Sharia from London changing diapers in what Ursula had christened the Room of Death. "I decided it would be really good for the vibes to put her in here. New life, you know, sort of *burgeoning*, which should completely override the negative impact of having a corpse hanging around all that time. Sharia! This is Annie. She *found* it, only she's incredibly cool and just takes dead bodies in her stride. They have lots of murders here: it's exactly like Miss Marple's village in Agatha Christie."

"So you didn't do a skeleton in the bed after all?" Annie said.

"No: isn't it a shame? It was such a great idea, but the only one we could get is a plastic model three feet high, so it's hanging in the kitchen instead with a piece of tinsel 'round its neck. Which reminds me, I must go and see to the mince pies. I'm never sure how long they're meant to bake."

"Nor me," Annie said, thinking how the house was cheered up by all the people and the noise and the mess. "I'm going home to get changed. See you later."

"Are you *sure* your reclusive uncle won't come? I'm longing to meet him. That tonic he made for Romany was so good, we all drank it."

" 'Fraid not."

Back at home she put on a skirt with an uneven hemline that owed less to fashion than erratic shrinkage after washing, a glittery top from one of the posher charity shops, and the leaf pendant Daniel had given her, set with a smoky green stone that Bartlemy said was an emerald cabochon. She tried to recall when she had last been to a party, and couldn't. Once you got past twenty, parties were not a big feature of life in Eade. Nathan emerged from his room wearing a newish sweater as a concession to the occasion and said: "Hazel's coming with us. She says it would be too embarrassing arriving with Lily and Franco."

Annie grinned.

While they were waiting, they had a glass of wine in the kitchen. Nathan felt suddenly very grown-up, taking his mum to a party, having a drink together first like sophisticated adults, and Annie felt grown-up, looking at her tall, handsome son, who had somehow turned into a man she could rely on—when he was in the right universe. She remembered coming to Eade all those years ago, a very young girl clutching a baby, running from phantoms, and thought, not for the first time, how lucky she was, and tried not to be afraid, because luck is a fragile thing. This was a moment to savor, a memory to hold on to, both of them being grown-up, sharing a drink, sharing their lives, before he went his own way for good. *They always go their own way,* she thought. *That's how it's meant to be*—but a sudden cold fear came to her, out of the future, and she closed her mind on the moment, holding it tight, tight, to keep it safe in her heart forever.

Then Hazel arrived, and they went to the party.

At Riverside chaos had evolved along haphazard lines, following one of those creation theories that say everything happens by accident, and order is achieved by a series of fortuitous mutations. Different kinds of music were playing at either end of the house and colliding in the middle. People whose normal idea of fun was the local darts tournament stood around drinking steadily and looking slightly baffled. Other people—like Annie—said how long it was since they'd been to a party, and what a good thing it was to have one, and how they must do it themselves sometime soon. Annie foresaw a wave of parties hitting Eade the following year, causing a boom in the sales of cocktail sausages and cheap glassware. Children hurtled through the crowd at a subterranean level while higher up food floated on platters and trays, which teetered from group to group before returning to the kitchen empty of everything but the toothpicks. Adolescents clustered in knots to deplore the behavior of their elders—"Oh God, Dad's dancing! It's *sooo* cringe making"—and plotting an ambush to change the music to something, like, *bearable.* Several aging hippies were smoking pot. The mulled wine had evolved into a hellbrew potent enough to send rockets to Mars, but fortunately it tasted so vile even the hardiest underaged drinker could manage very little of it. Locals swapped gossip and bemoaned the advent of too many city types; city types admired the Room of Death and said, really, country life was so exciting. Lily Bagot shocked older residents by turning up in a strapless dress and crimson lipstick and wrapping herself around Franco at regular intervals.

The Wickses hadn't been invited so Hazel was unable to spend half the evening talking to Damian, which Nathan considered an extremely good thing. Jason gate-crashed later with a couple of henchmates, presumably with the intention of causing trouble, but by then the party was booming and nobody noticed.

Ursula introduced Annie as if she were a minor celebrity, and various Islingtonians expressed sympathy for the trauma she must have suffered after finding the body, and understood that she couldn't bear to talk about it, but was it true she'd known the murderer really well, and what was he—you know—*like*, and was he different from other sociopaths she might have known? Annie said he was just a perfectly normal murderer, as far as she could tell.

"Anyhow," she concluded, "the police think that the actual killing was probably done by his female partner, the woman who pretended to be Rianna Sardou." In fact, she wasn't sure what the police thought, but was prepared to give them credit for inside information they didn't possess. The recollection of Nenufar sent a brief chill through her thoughts, but at a party it is difficult to believe in demons, even when you know they exist, and ghosts and terrors do not thrive in an atmosphere of celebration. She even allowed herself to be persuaded into a dance, and then tried to recall how long it was since she had last danced with someone, and realized it was entirely possible she hadn't had a dance with a man since Daniel died . . .

Hazel, gazing at Lily and Franco with revulsion, decided she didn't do the mixed-generation thing, and parties should be reserved for people under twenty-five, who were supposed to behave like that, while their elders should be forced to stay home and watch television and generally be saved from themselves. She nudged Nathan, pointing out that Annie was now in a clinch with a man whose green sweatshirt seemed bent on Saving the Rain Forest, but Nathan had fallen into conversation with Liberty Rayburn and didn't appear to mind. In desperation, Hazel went to look for the loo.

She wasn't familiar with Riverside House so although there were several bathrooms it took her some time to find one that was unoccupied. When she emerged she overheard Ursula extolling the thrill of the Room of Death and leading a gang of friends up the spiral stair in Rianna Sardou's tower, so she followed, out of mild curiosity, but there was nothing of interest to see and she came back downstairs without waiting to hear a story the true version of which she knew well already.

The room below was obviously being used as a cross between a bed-room and temporary storage space: there was a bed with several stuffed animals in residence, and a stack of cardboard boxes, opened but not unpacked, evidently full of books. Hazel climbed onto the bed to check her face in an adjacent mirror—she was sure she had a pimple com-ing—and saw that behind the boxes there was a pool of water on the floor. Toddler's accident, she thought, but no, there was too much of it for that, and the corner of a piece of paper caught her eye, sticking out from under the duvet, and when she pulled it out she saw a few words on it written in a language that was not in everyday use. The language of the Stone.

She glanced up into the mirror, and the face that looked back at her was not her own.

"Well, well," said the reflection. "It's been quite awhile."

For an instant, it was beautiful, with silver-blond hair and petals falling around it like spring snow—Lilliat, the Spirit of Flowers, whom Hazel had conjured more than a year before when she wanted to becharm a boy in her class. Then it changed into the pale drowned vis-age of Nenufar the water spirit, its hair a streaming darkness and its eyes black, completely black, with no whites or visible pupils, like a glimpse into the ocean deeps.

"*Vardé!*" Hazel cried, trying to keep her head. "*Néfia!*"

The reflection slid across the mirror, flickered briefly in the water pool on the floor, and was gone.

"What was that?" Ursula said, descending the stairs. "Did you call out?"

"Whose room is this?" Hazel demanded, forgetting her usual shy-ness.

"Romany's—just for now, though I wasn't planning to leave her here. There's a problem with damp—" Her gaze fell on the puddle. "Oh God no, not *again*. It's got to be the plumbing, but I don't know how—"

"Where is she?" Hazel interrupted. "Shouldn't she be in bed?"

"Heavens no. I always let the kids stay up for parties—it's not like there's school tomorrow, and it would be so mean to send them to bed

when everyone's having fun. Gawain's given up—Jude tucked him up
in the other tower about half an hour ago—but I think Romany's still
going strong. She'll be around somewhere. Who—?"

"Where did she get this?" Hazel held out the piece of paper.

"What is it?" Ursula glanced idly at the unfamiliar words. "Is that
Basque or something? I haven't seen it before. I suppose it must have
been with the stuff we found here when we moved in, books and so on.
I seem to remember Romany going through some of them—she reads
way above her age—"

"I think we should find her," Hazel said. "Like, now."

"I told you, she's around somewhere. There's nothing to worry
about."

Hazel snatched the piece of paper from Ursula's slackened grip and
ran back to the focus of the party. She couldn't recollect seeing a little
girl around who might have been Romany Macaire, or not for some
time, but you didn't really notice children at parties, they were just
there, interchangeable small beings rushing around and getting under
everyone's feet, hazards to be stepped over or avoided. At least Romany with her chocolate skin and nubbly braids couldn't be mixed up
with the others. *She's almost certainly all right,* Hazel thought. *I just want
to see her—ask her—*

She found first Annie, then Nathan, showing them the piece of paper,
explaining about seeing Nenufar. Annie responded instantly, shedding
the ginger beard, saying: "I was afraid of something like this." Nathan
took longer, distracted by Liberty, who was clearly a little scornful of
what she saw as a panic reaction to nothing of importance.

"Romany's okay. She's probably curled up somewhere with a book.
What's the fuss about? Mum doesn't keep her on a leash, you know."

But once Nathan had grasped what was happening he joined Hazel
in a search that instinct told her was fruitless. They found half a dozen
younger children in the other tower, playing Nintendo or lapsed into
slumber. None of them had seen Romany for some while. Jude Rayburn asked what was going on and, since it was obvious by then that
Romany was actually missing, roped in his brother and sister to help.
They peered into every corner, turned over every cushion, lifted up

every blanket, but Romany was nowhere about. Annie fetched Ursula, who said she was sure there was no need to get upset, and then remembered the river and sat down very quickly and had to be restrained from running down to the bank and jumping in the water immediately.

Donny Collier called the police.

The party, infected by the creeping shadow of disaster, began to disintegrate. Guests offered to help organize search parties but Annie sent most of them home, saying they would be contacted if it was necessary. In a momentary lull she called Bartlemy.

"I'll be there," he said.

Jude led a group of people to check the garden and the riverbank, slightly inhibited by being able to only find two flashlights, and they came across one of Romany's mittens under a bush, but, as Annie said, that didn't really mean anything, since she could have lost it days ago.

Hazel said: "We must *think*. Nenufar wouldn't kill her . . . what would be the point? She's using her as a way in, a way to—"

Liberty said: "Who's Nenufar?"

A couple of police officers arrived, clearly feeling panic was premature. Children weren't kidnapped at parties, merely mislaid. The little girl had obviously wandered off and fallen asleep somewhere, she would turn up presently none the worse for wear, Mrs. Rayburn wasn't to worry . . .

"Of course I'm worried!" Ursula retorted. "What about the river?"

One of the officers said they couldn't get divers till morning, which had Ursula screaming for spotlights and where was modern technology when you needed it.

At some point Bartlemy appeared, inserting himself into the scene with his usual unobtrusive authority. "The recluse," Ursula said. "Not *now*," but he persuaded her to drink an herbal tea he had brought with him, which smelled, and presumably tasted, far more interesting than ordinary herbal tea, and which calmed her down and made her drowsy.

"He's much too fat and kindly to be a recluse," she told Annie. "He ought to have a lean and hungry look." And then, with a sudden resurgence of anxiety: "Maybe he's a pedophile. Pedophiles often look kindly—to reassure the children. Oh my God . . ."

"He's not a pedophile," Annie said. "Anyway, *they're* the ones with the lean and hungry look. I've seen them on TV cop shows."

Ursula accepted this—a tribute to the side effects of the tea—and presently allowed Donny to put her to bed on the sofa, since that wasn't the same as really going to bed, and she was still there if they needed her, ready to do something, if there was something to be done. Her eyes closed—"What *was* in that tea?" Annie asked Bartlemy—while those guests who were staying over sat around feeling awkward, since it was far too late for them to find alternative accommodation, and some of them started clearing up the party debris, and others went with Jude and Donny to search the water meadows, and got very muddy, and found nothing, and Nathan and Hazel joined Annie and Bartlemy in a discreet huddle to discuss what *they* could do, fighting a rising sense of futility, and frustration, and fear.

"Couldn't we find her by magic?" Hazel said. "After all, she's lost by magic, isn't she? If we drew the circle . . ."

"Possibly," said Bartlemy. "But not here, and not now. The best thing is for you all to go home and leave it to me."

"No," said Hazel, forcefully—Nathan, resolutely—Annie, quietly.

"What about Hoover?" Nathan suggested. "He could track Romany by smell. He's better than any bloodhound."

"You'd think that the police would have brought dogs," Hazel grumbled.

"They're sending some over," Annie said. "I heard one of the officers on the phone."

"Hoover's already out looking," said Bartlemy.

"Isn't he supposed to sniff something of hers first?" Nathan said. "So he's got a scent to follow."

"As you said," Bartlemy murmured, "he's better than a bloodhound."

It was about two in the morning when DCI Pobjoy walked in, just before the advent of the dogs and their handlers. Annie felt a rush of relief at seeing him, even though she knew he couldn't make everything all right.

Hazel said disagreeably: "It's *him*. D'you think he believes in ghosts yet?"

Bartlemy said: "I thought they might contact you for this."

"They always call me when it's Eade," Pobjoy said. "This place has become my specialty. But a missing child's a new one. What's your involvement?"

"I called him," Annie explained. "I was at the party when Romany disappeared."

"D'you think she's really missing," Pobjoy asked, "or just hiding somewhere?"

"She's missing," Bartlemy said.

"Is there anyone in the village who might have taken her? A stranger—a newcomer—someone who might be concealing a secret perversion?"

"There are always strangers and newcomers," Bartlemy said. "This isn't the nineteenth century. People move around. But there's nobody of that type—not that I know of. We think Romany may have stumbled across some connection with the Michael Addison affair."

"That was my next question," said the chief inspector. "I thought it was straining coincidence that this was his house." He had clearly forgotten his assertion that Bartlemy was mildly insane and was prepared to rely on his judgment again.

"Actually," Hazel said, a shade defiantly, "we believe Romany's being controlled by the same water spirit who pretended to be Michael's wife. Her name's Nenufar. She's probably still after the Grimthorn Grail."

"This is no time for fairy tales," Pobjoy snapped. "We have a lost child here."

"If you don't listen to the fairy tales," Nathan said, "you won't know where to look for her."

"I think we should go," Bartlemy intervened. "We'll leave the detectives to their detecting. We have our own resources. Come along."

Annie told Liberty to call if Ursula needed her and they went out, piling into the Jowett Javelin, which was parked up the lane. "I could take you all home," Bartlemy said.

"No," said Nathan, and Hazel, and Annie.

They drove to Thornyhill.

THE BASIN seemed to be made of brass, tarnished and green with age. Bartlemy half filled it at the tap in the kitchen sink and placed it on the table, adding a few drops from a dark bottle of what looked like oil. There was a smell similar to patchouli, only stronger and sharper, stinging the sinuses. The oil spread across the surface of the water in a widening smear.

"Great-Grandma did something like this," Hazel said, "only she used more ingredients."

"Unnecessary," said Bartlemy. "The magic is very simple, if you do it right. Watch and learn."

He spoke a few words in a soft, ordinary voice, and the ripple of oil broadened and disappeared. Presently, the basin began to glow with a dim yellow radiance: the glimmer of Aladdin's lamp, or candlelight reflected in an ancient mirror. Nathan and Annie peered into the water but could see nothing; the surface had become cloudy and opaque. Then Hazel leaned over, and for her there were shapes in the cloud, faint faraway shapes that gradually grew nearer and clearer.

"What do you see?" Bartlemy asked.

"Hands," Hazel said. "Holding hands—Romany and *her*—Nenufar. They're on a boat, an old-fashioned boat with lots of sails. No . . . no, that was a memory, it's different now. More like a motor launch, the kind millionaires have, all long and sleek and gleamy."

"The white ship," Nathan said. "I thought that had gone long ago."

"It's a legend she uses," Bartlemy said. "Werefolk, like serial killers, tend to repeat the same patterns of behavior." And to Hazel: "Is there anything more?"

"I don't think so. Romany seems to be sleeping now, on a sort of cushioned bench at the back."

"Aft," Nathan murmured.

"Whatever. I can't make out where they are—it's all kind of misty—but I think there's too much water for the Glyde. Anyhow, you'd never get a boat that big up the river."

"Nonetheless, the river is where you'll find her," Bartlemy said. The glow faded from the basin, and he tipped its contents down the sink. Annie wondered fleetingly what went on in his drains, and whether strange life-forms were evolving there in an atmosphere of magical pollution. "As I said, Nenufar is always predictable. And clearly she *wants* to be found. That's why she took the child—so you would come and find her."

"Me?" Nathan said.

"Us?" said Hazel.

"Romany is only a hostage. It's you she wants." He nodded to Nathan.

"But we're going, too," Annie insisted. "Nathan can't deal with Nenufar on his own. He'll need your help."

"No," said Bartlemy. "If she even senses me in the vicinity, she may flee, or kill the child out of pure spite. With Nathan and Hazel she won't feel threatened. Hazel's magical skills have grown, but Nenufar doesn't know that. She won't be wary. They must find a way to deal with this together."

"Well, *I'm* going—"

"*No.*" Bartlemy laid a hand on her arm, speaking to her very gently. "What can you do other than be one more person they have to protect? This one is for the children. They are, after all, hardly children anymore. Nathan must go because he is the one Nenufar hopes to trap—to trap, not to injure, if worse comes to worst—and Hazel has a little power, a little skill, a little foreknowledge of the enemy. She will be more use to him than you. A girl's life is at stake. We have to take risks, but not with that."

Annie made a tiny whimper of protest, knowing she couldn't really object. Nathan and Hazel swapped a glance that said: *We're in this together. What the hell do we do?*—then turned to Bartlemy with an air of mutual resolution that didn't convince him for a second, though he made no comment.

"We'll head for the river," Nathan said. "If Nenufar wants to be found, I expect we'll find her."

He was remembering a verse heard once before.

The white ship waits on the river shore
for one who cannot stay.
The ship will wait a sennight more
to steal your soul away!

He couldn't recall much of how it had felt on board, except for the cold. The white empty chill that ate into your bones and your heart . . .

"Hoover will go with you," Bartlemy said. "Nenufar knows only the creatures of the sea. She has little understanding of land animals— she will think him of no account. Rukush!"

After a long moment the back door opened at the nudge of a nose and the dog trotted in. Annie ruffled his head, whispering: "Look after them."

Bartlemy said, to Hoover, perhaps, more than the others: "Bring Romany back."

He took a flashlight from the shelf and passed it to Nathan.

"You'll need this. Good luck. There is always luck, if you are bold enough to look for it."

Nathan didn't feel at all bold, but he had no intention of saying so. Hazel zipped her jacket and the two of them stepped out into the night with the dog at their heels. Left in the kitchen, Annie said: "Will they be all right?"

"I hope so," said Bartlemy.

THEY WALKED along the road a short way, back toward Eade, till they came to the edge of the woods, then they turned left, taking a path through the fields down to the river. The flashlight beam danced on the ground before them, a pale irregular oblong that leapt and flickered over root and tussock; it would have been little help if they had not known their way. All around stretched the huge dimness of the night;

clouds hid the stars; a ragged half-moon peered briefly between torn edges of cumulus. Hazel stared ahead to where a pale mist lay along the riverbank, but Nathan kept glancing from side to side, and once or twice Hoover stopped altogether, turning to gaze back along the path where they had come. In the silence while they halted Nathan thought he heard a footstep, the murmur of the grass, but he couldn't be sure.

"There's someone following us," he said. "Look at Hoover." The dog's ears were cocked; a faint rumble swelled in his throat, almost a growl.

"Login Nambrok," Hazel said. "That's all right. He's on our side."

"Would Hoover growl at him? He must be used to him by now."

"Shouldn't think he'd get used to the smell."

"Maybe." Nathan raised his voice, called: "Nambrok! Hello!"

No answer.

"Hello?"

The grasses were still; the night didn't stir.

"He'll show himself when he's ready," Hazel said. "You can't order him. He may have reasons for keeping a low profile."

"Or it may not be him."

"The gnomons are gone. Who else would it be? No human could move that quietly. Could be a fox, I suppose."

Nathan said: "Hoover wouldn't growl at a fox."

After a minute, they went on. Nathan heard no sound of a footpad, but there was a prickle in his neck as if he sensed watching eyes, and the dog continued warily. As they drew near to the river the mist enveloped them, making even the darkness pale and shapeless. Without the light they might too easily have missed the path and stumbled into the water.

"Do we have a plan?" Hazel asked in a low voice.

"No," said Nathan, baldly.

"Well . . . well, we need one."

"I'm open to suggestions."

"It's you who does all the rescuing. You're meant to think of things."

"Your turn," Nathan said nastily, feeling he had a score to settle.

Hazel took the point, but felt this was not the moment to make an issue of it. "You talk to Nenufar," she said. "Barty says it's you she wants. Then maybe I could . . . I could . . . sneak onto the boat and get Romany."

"I don't think it's the kind of boat you can sneak onto," Nathan said.

"You have a better idea?"

"No," he conceded. "I'll talk to her, anyway. You stay out of sight with Hoover. The mist will help with that. And Nenufar's awfully single-minded—with luck it won't even occur to her to look for you. Perhaps you could put a spell on her."

"I don't know any spells," Hazel said. "Not proper ones, anyway."

"You should have brought your pipe cleaners."

"As it happens . . ." Hazel pulled a couple out of her jacket pocket—possibly the remnants of a Franco figure. "But I need something of hers to make it work. If it works at all. I'm not that certain about my success rate. Besides, she's werefolk."

"She's a magical being," Nathan said, "so she should be susceptible to magic."

"Did Uncle Barty say that?"

"No, I did. Just now."

"Smart-arse."

"Sssh."

"What?"

"*Sssh!*"

"*What?*"

"There's something coming . . ."

They caught the rumor of an engine, an engine so quiet you could barely hear it, blending with the hush-hush of the water against the riverbank. The veil of mist shifted and the white gleaming shape of the boat appeared, its prow as sharp and streamlined as a spaceship in a science-fiction film. The demoness stood in the bows, wrapped in a pale cloak and hood that flared behind her in slow billows, as though lifted on a wind no one else could feel. Hazel shrank back into the bushes, tripping over something in the dark, but Hoover's body was there to brace her and she made little noise. Nathan moved forward to draw attention away from her, shining the flashlight across the water.

"You don't need that."

Nenufar turned toward him, pushing back her hood. Her long hair spilled over her shoulders, mingling with the darkness, making her one with it. Her face was a white oval, shining like the boat, her eyes twin almonds of blackness. The launch drifted closer to the bank, though no one was steering it; the engine cut. It was surely too large for the Glyde, but in the misty night the river seemed to have broadened and the farther shore was lost to view. Now Nathan was only a few yards from her. The aura of her power reached out to him, like a magnet drawing him toward the water. He had forgotten how strong she was, how effortlessly she had once controlled his mind.

She said: "You left me last time. We were going to sail away to my kingdom beneath the sea, but you left me. That was ill done of you. Who was it who stole you away? That fat wizard who thinks he's protecting you?"

"No," Nathan said. "It was someone you cannot touch." He didn't mention the Grandir, but the thought of him was like a touchstone in his heart, giving him courage and the will to resist. "Someone who has a power far beyond yours."

"There's no such person!"

"You think so?"

"I would feel power like that, I would feel its immanence . . . There's no power here now. Only the night, and me. And you have come back . . ."

"I came for the child."

"I knew you would!" She laughed a soft, triumphant laugh. "Mortals are so sentimental about their children. She's such a sweet, serious little girl. I will take her away with me and show her the deep places undersea, the fish that light up in the dark, the giant squid, the Kraken—the coral groves where mermaids used to play. I promised her, you see. Werefolk keep our promises."

"When it suits you," Nathan said. "Anyway, there are no mermaids anymore. Not in this world."

Then he had her. He could feel the change in her focus, the sharpening of her attention. Her whole thought veered toward him, oblivious to all else.

He wondered what Hazel was doing.

"Which world then?" Nenufar demanded. "Tell me where the mermaids are."

Hazel was inching down the bank in the lee of a willow, her bottom in the mud, her best skirt filthy and rucked up around her hips. Hoover's teeth gripped the back of her jacket to stop her from sliding into the river. She could see the stern of the boat perhaps five yards from the bank, but although the distance was no problem she knew the river was weed-choked and treacherous, and the sides of the launch looked too high for her to climb, and she was quite sure she could never make it in silence. *What do I do, Hoover?* she mouthed, but the dog, his jaws full of jacket, did not make a sound. She took out the pipe cleaners and managed to twist them into a new shape, but she had neither hair nor wisp of cloth to invoke the original. *Even if I had something of hers,* Hazel thought, *it's all water, it would probably just run away. She's* made *of water.* River water . . .

"Hold on," she whispered to Hoover. "I just have to get a bit closer."

Nathan was talking about Rhadamu, and the twelve tribes of merfolk, and the sea where no island dared raise its head.

"Leave the child," he said, "and I will go with you in her place. We'll sail to that otherworld, a world where the Sea is all-powerful, and your sister-goddess, your other self, reigns alone. Together you can create a—a duality, twin rulers with a single mind, a single purpose. She is your destiny." He was groping for words, sounding—he thought—like the script from *Star Wars,* but Nenufar in her eagerness was beyond noticing, even had she been able to recognize the source.

"I knew it!" she cried. "I knew she was out there somewhere— somewhere in all the worlds—spirit of my spirit, heart of my heart. I will join her and become her, and together we will raise such a wave as to wash away the Gate itself, and sweep back across the lands of this world until all—*all* are drowned forever. Come with me—come with me *now*—"

The darkness by the willow moved very cautiously as Hazel dipped the pipe-cleaner figure in the water. Then she wedged herself securely against the tree and began murmuring the spell. *"Fia simulé, fia im-laure, fiasse Nenufar, esti verular . . ."* She repeated it over and over, stroking the figurine, willing it to become the werewoman, to borrow a little of her substance, a little of her self. She was concentrating so hard she scarcely noticed a slight noise behind her. Hoover stirred and stiffened; she laid a hand on his neck and felt the bristling of his fur. Something slid into the river a little way away, quieter than an otter; a ripple moved in the darkness. Hazel ceased her charm, staring across the water. An arm stretched up, black against the white hulk of the boat, grasping the gunwale; then another. Very slowly, so the tilt of the deck might seem hardly more than the natural motion of the river, something pulled itself up onto the rail in a single fluid movement—something human-shaped but unhuman, a shadow made of muscle, a darkness all strength and control. It balanced on the rail, crouching, its massive head swaying from side to side. Hazel could distinguish little in the murk but she thought it looked more ape than man, a monster half seen, half imagined, its prehensile tail anchoring it to the stern, its head bulky with horns, or helmet, or mane. Finding what it sought, it slipped down onto the deck, reappearing almost immediately with a bundle in its arms.

"Romany!" Hazel muttered, her grip tightening unconsciously on Hoover's neck, pinching a fold of his coat.

Tucking the bundle under one arm, the shadow slid back into the river.

Hazel glanced toward Nathan—Nathan on the very edge of the bank, with Nenufar reaching toward him—then down at her crude pipe-cleaner doll. She fumbled hastily in her pockets, but she had no pin, no knife—only the cigarettes she had been smoking on the quiet, and a cheap throwaway lighter that might have run out of fuel. "Pray it works," she said to Hoover, meaning the lighter, or the spell, or both. The shadow was out of the water and up the bank; a dark voice close to her ear said: *"Run."*

"Nathan!" Hazel cried. "We've got Romany! Get away from her! Get away! *Now!*"

Nenufar seized his hand in a grip as strong as the ocean currents, somehow managing to pull him toward her, onto the launch. Hazel clicked the lighter—once—twice—a tiny flame sprang up, and she held it against the doll. There was a smell of singed pipe cleaner.

Nenufar screamed.

It was a scream that tore the night like the screech of a hundred seabirds, sudden and shocking. She doubled up, releasing Nathan, who fell forward toward the river. But Hoover was behind him, tugging at his clothes, and he was back on his feet, clutching the flashlight, following Hazel's voice, and they were stumbling along the path toward the meadows.

"Romany!" he panted. "You said—Romany?"

"Ahead, I think—"

"You *think*?"

"We had help."

A little farther on, Nathan demanded: "Whose?"

"I don't know . . ."

"Here," said the dark voice somewhere in front of them. They stopped short. The soft not-quite-growl grumbled around in Hoover's throat.

"Who are you?" Nathan asked, pointing the flashlight.

The beam showed a man—a man in a leather jacket stiff with water, shaggy hair dripping down his face. His forehead was creased with old scars, his cheekbones were crooked, his eyes shone red in the torchlight. This was not the shape Hazel had seen climbing over the stern of the boat, but she knew somehow it was the same. In his arms he held Romany, also wet, one hand over her mouth.

"Take her," he told Nathan. "She's frightened of me."

Nathan thrust the flashlight at Hazel and took Romany, who gave a little gasp when her mouth was freed and clung to him, shuddering with cold. But she did not cry.

"*Who are you?*"

"It doesn't matter. Just—an old friend of your mother's."

"*What?*"

"So your name is Nathan. I didn't know. I wish I could stay around to find out what happens next, but I have other commitments. Beware of the werewoman: she won't give up." He turned to Hazel. "That was clever. The simple charms work the best, after all."

"Why did you help us?" Hazel said. "You're not—not—"

"Not human? No. This was . . . my good deed for the century. I'm growing a soul. Maybe, after tonight, it will put forward a new shoot." His eyes narrowed, gazing back toward the river. "Go quickly now. No doubt the dog will take care of you. And tell him not to bark at me—I eat dogs."

Hoover gave a low-key *ruff*, just to show his indifference.

Nathan said: "Thank you. But—"

The shadow had gone, vanishing into the night from whence he came.

They took Romany to Thornyhill, though Riverside House was probably nearer; both of them thought she would be the better for one of Bartlemy's tisanes. Annie called Ursula as soon as they arrived to give her the good news, and Romany revived sufficiently to complain she wanted to go with the lady even though she had funny eyes, and learn to swim like a mermaid. Bartlemy gave her chocolate in various forms, possibly enhanced with a natural soporific, and by the time they got her home she was warm and dry and almost asleep. Ursula sobbed over her daughter, over Annie, over Nathan and Hazel—heroes of the hour—and swore undying gratitude. When Pobjoy insisted on hearing the whole story Bartlemy suggested he come back to Thornyhill and they left the Rayburns in peace.

"We could all do with a restorative," he said. "Annie and I haven't heard what happened yet, either. Come to breakfast. We can sleep in the morning."

"He won't believe us," Hazel said, eyeing the inspector scornfully. "He never does."

"He's learning," Bartlemy said.

How to Start a War

When you have spent half the night partying, and the other half in a potentially disastrous confrontation with the forces of evil, there is nothing like the prospect of a good breakfast. They sat down about six in the dining room at Thornyhill—a long room with a big oak table that Bartlemy, who preferred small-scale entertainment, rarely used—to eggs fried and scrambled, buttered mushrooms, sausages, bacon, tomatoes. On the side there was toast and honey, toast and marmalade, porridge and cream, coffee, tea, fruit juice, beer. They ate, talked, ate some more. "Now," said Pobjoy, unavoidably mellowed, "I want the whole story. From the beginning."

"Ah, but where is the beginning?" said Bartlemy. "The entire life of mankind is only a tiny part of the history of this planet, and this planet is only one of millions in a vast universe, and this universe is merely a handful of atoms spinning through the endless wastes of infinity."

"Never mind that," said Pobjoy. "Start with the party."

"It was a good party," Annie offered. "You should have come."

"I don't go to parties."

"Get in the habit," Annie said. "Then you can be on the spot for all the crimes that invariably happen when people get together in large numbers to have fun and drink too much."

"Can we keep to the point? When did you first realize Romany was missing?"

"I didn't," Annie said. "It was Hazel."

Pobjoy duly turned his interrogation technique onto Hazel, who launched into an account of everything that had occurred from the moment she saw Nenufar in the mirror, culminating in the appearance of the mystery rescuer to save Romany. Pobjoy's expression grew increasingly skeptical as the story progressed, but his accusatory questions— "How could you have seen her reflection if she wasn't standing behind you?"—ran down, as if he felt himself defeated by her matter-of-fact tone and the others' equally matter-of-fact acceptance of all she said. He knew much of the tale was preposterous, perhaps not a direct lie but some sort of bizarre juvenile exaggeration; Harry Potter syndrome, perhaps—there was bound to be one—a condition where children imagined they were living in a magical world populated by wizards and monsters. At the same time he, too, had seen the white ship, more than a year ago—he had run from the gnomons—he had felt the fear of that which is beyond science, beyond reason. He didn't want to believe because it would overthrow his whole view of the world—a world he saw as dark and disorderly but at least rational, subject to fixed laws, the laws of physics, the laws of nature, the laws of men. That was a world where he had some control, if not much. But in a world of magic and demons a policeman was as helpless as anyone else.

"This . . . person," Annie was saying as Romany's rescuer entered the story. "Describe him."

"I didn't see much," Hazel said. "It was too dark. He had a long tail, maybe horns. He moved a bit like an ape. But after we got away, when Nathan shone the flashlight on him, he just looked human. Except for his eyes."

"What sort of human?" Bartlemy asked. "Tall? Short? Skin color— hair color?"

"Quite tall." Nathan frowned with the effort of memory. "Not short, anyway. Dark hair, brown skin. Not actually brown like mine, more sort of tanned and roughened and weathered. There was something wrong with his forehead, like scarring: the flesh looked all red and kind of scrunched up. And he had a really cool jacket, leather, very worn and wrinkled."

"And his eyes?" said Pobjoy, like someone probing a wound.

"They were red," Hazel said with a certain malicious satisfaction. "Not bloodshot, before you ask. Just red. Dark red. No whites at all."

"Kal." Annie was looking at Bartlemy. "I knew it."

"He said he was an old friend of yours," Nathan recalled. "I thought he must be joking. Do you—do you really know him?" He stared at his mother as if she had just revealed a previous association with a leading Mafioso or international terrorist.

Pobjoy's face wore a curiously similar expression.

"He came to see me the other night," Annie said. For once, her son's reaction had passed her by. "He's kind of part demon, part human—which is meant to be impossible. He says he's growing a soul."

"He said that to us," Hazel averred. "Like it was a plant. Weird."

"*Why* did he come to see you?" Nathan demanded.

"It's a bit complicated," Annie said. "Bartlemy drew the circle—to find out something—and Kal showed up unasked, and disappeared, and then came to see me later at the shop. I don't know why. He wanted me to invite him in."

Nathan understood the dangers of that. "You didn't, did you?"

"Yes, I did. So he told me some things—"

"What things?"

"It's not important now. He told me things, he left, and now he's helped us by saving Romany. Which proves that inviting him in wasn't a bad idea."

"Do you often invite strangers into your home?" Pobjoy said, back in accusatory mode.

"Only if they're very sinister," Annie retorted. "Getting friendly with demons and murderers is my specialty."

"You're all living on Planet Zog," Pobjoy declared, desperate to hold on to what he hoped was reality. "All this crap about spells and monsters—it's a delusion. Did you take Romany yourselves"—he meant Nathan and Hazel—"then pretend to search for her and bring her back?"

Annie gave a cry of protest, but Nathan responded with unexpected coolness. "We never left the party till long after she went missing," he said. "You can check that. It's called an alibi."

"Up yours," said Hazel. "Why can't we get rid of him? He's so stupid he's no use to anyone."

"We may need his help in the future," said Bartlemy. "I suggest we call a halt to this conversation—before it implodes. We've had a long night. Unless you wish to arrest someone, Chief Inspector, I think we should all go home to bed."

"Not right now," said Pobjoy, trying for menacing, and only succeeding in sounding grumpy.

"Can I make a pipe-cleaner figure of *him*?" Hazel muttered.

Bartlemy called a taxi and sent her, Nathan, and Annie back to Eade. To Pobjoy, he said: "Have some more coffee. Another piece of toast?"

The inspector, who lived alone and rarely ate a proper meal, succumbed with little hesitation. After all, a crime had happened, or might have happened, or was probably happening somewhere, and after a fashion he was investigating. Sitting at the table with more toast, all oozy with honey from the beehives in the garden, he struggled to convince himself that Bartlemy was a lunatic, but it was no good. His host looked peculiarly and disturbingly sane. So sane, Pobjoy found himself wondering if the world was inside out, and he was the one going quietly around the bend.

"Do *you* believe it?" he asked abruptly.

"Believe what?"

"The kids' story."

"Oh, that. Yes, of course. It's so much easier believing things than doubting them. And it was very coherent; I'm sure you noticed. All the bits fit together. Successful liars—and there are very few—have to construct such elaborate structures to support their deceits. They always make a few minor mistakes, and only get away with it because the generality of people are amazingly inobservant. But you are a trained observer; you would always be difficult to fool."

"They haven't fooled me," Pobjoy said stubbornly. "I know that rigmarole can't be true."

"Naturally. You're a policeman: you believe in the evidence. The evidence of your own eyes, your own ears. You have seen the white ship and the woman on board. You have—er—failed to see the gnomons. Do you believe *your* story, James?"

Pobjoy had forgotten telling Bartlemy his Christian name. He said: "Not really."

"I see. I've always understood that as well as evidence, policemen go in for hunches. Do you have a hunch about all this?"

"Yeah, I have a hunch. I have a hunch as big as"—he groped for literary parallels with the uncertainty of someone who hasn't read enough of the right books—"as the phantom of the opera."

"Quasimodo," Bartlemy supplied. "The hunchback of Notre Dame."

"Yep. Him. I have a hunch about this village. It's a quiet, sleepy little place with robberies and murders and kidnappings and serial killings, strange disappearances—stranger reappearances. I have a hunch there's something *big* going on here, some crime so huge that nobody can see it, and all these bits and pieces are just the proverbial tip of the iceberg, the tiny visible part of this major unseen crime. But whenever I try to get a closer look, it all turns into fantasy, wisps of magic— ghosts—dreams. Like snatching at smoke. You can't arrest smoke."

"You're doing pretty well," Bartlemy said. "There is indeed something going on here, something big—it may even be a crime, though I doubt if you'll ever get to charge anyone."

"It's a crime," Pobjoy insisted. "I can *feel* it."

Bartlemy smiled the smile of someone with superior knowledge; he was to remember this moment, much later. He said: "Maybe. Whatever happens, trust to hunches. And when you see the smoke, don't snatch— just watch where it goes. And try not to inhale."

Pobjoy didn't laugh. "What do I say to Annie?" he asked.

"Well," Bartlemy said, judiciously, "it would be a good idea not to tell her she's delusional. The rest is up to you."

"But . . ."

"But?"

"What if she *is* delusional?"

"What if she isn't?" Bartlemy said.

BACK IN Eade, Nathan and his mother headed straight for bed. Although she was exhausted, Annie found she had passed the point where she could sleep easily; her brain was still in overdrive, the events of the night running and rerunning in her mind as she struggled to work out what it all meant. Pobjoy's attitude—*He quite liked me once,* she realized, too late for the knowledge to do any good, *but now he just thinks I'm a total fruitcake*—and the behavior of Nenufar, and above all, Kal. Was he good? Was he evil? Whose side was he on? Werefolk, Bartlemy had told her, were mostly neither all good nor all evil, and took no side but their own, yet she felt Kal was different, or trying to be different, though she didn't know why. Sleep crept up on her in the middle of her deliberations, and when she awoke it was lunchtime.

She went downstairs, looking in on Nathan, who was still dead to the world, if not to all worlds, sprawled on his bed fully dressed as he had been when they came in. In the kitchen she set about making coffee. And suddenly there was a footstep behind her, the draft from the opening of the garden door.

She knew who it was even before she turned around.

"Kal," she said.

In daylight his battered face looked paler and even more battered, like a sculpture in rough concrete. His eyes were no longer rubies but had darkened to the color of burgundy. There was mud on his clothes.

"Would you like some coffee?" Annie asked. She was still frightened of him, but it was a reflex of her nervous system rather than her mind.

He said "Thank you" after a long pause, as if unfamiliar with the word.

She meant to say *You saved Romany,* but instead she found herself remarking: "I gather we're old friends."

"By my standards," said Kal. "I daresay you measure your friends by the years you have known them, but you're wrong. Friendship is not measured in years."

"Fair enough," Annie conceded. "But *old* is."

"I *am* old," Kal said with something like a grin. "I'm the oldest person you know."

"I doubt it," Annie said tranquilly. "Bartlemy was born in Byzantium in the latter days of the Roman Empire, or so he once told me."

"I date from King Arthur's times," Kal said. "I've no idea which came first. History never interested me, unless I was part of it. Do you deny our friendship?"

"No," Annie said. "Of course not."

"That makes you almost unique. I have very few friends. In fact, I'm not sure I have any."

"Your habit of tearing people's heads off might have something to do with that," Annie said, a little rashly.

He laughed—a real laugh, without mockery. *Human . . . humor*, Annie thought.

She said: "Do you take sugar?"

He looked confused. Clearly coffee was something new and strange in his life. "Should I?"

"Probably." She added two teaspoons with cream, not milk. He sipped the resultant mixture doubtfully.

"I had another friend once," he said presently. "She gave me a soul to grow—and then she forgot about me. Humans are so fickle." Curiously, he didn't sound bitter about it.

"I won't forget you," Annie said. "You saved Romany. Why—why did you do that, if you don't mind my asking? Was it because of your soul?"

"No," he said, looking at her very steadily over the coffee cup. "It was because you invited me in."

Annie smiled the smile that lit her face, making her suddenly beautiful, though she didn't know it. "You are always welcome," she said, even more rashly, not completely sure if she meant it, but feeling it should be said.

Kal swallowed the coffee hastily, hissing at the heat in his throat. "I am leaving now," he explained. "I came to say farewell. But maybe I'll come back, ten, twenty, fifty years from now. Your door is open to me for as long as you live. Will you still call me welcome when you are old and frail, if I stumble in here with bloodstained feet, seeking sanctuary?"

"Couldn't you just come for coffee?" Annie said.

"I will . . . bear that in mind." He set down the cup, turned to the door.

"Goodbye," Annie said. "And good luck, wherever you go."

"You, too. I fear you may need it. There is trouble in the air. You hadn't told me your son's name. Still, he is not like the other. Nor are you."

"No, I'm not," Annie said.

And then he was gone.

He could've shut the door, Annie thought prosaically, shivering in the icy air. Presumably werefolk didn't feel the cold.

She closed the door herself and took her coffee into the bookshop, switching on a small radiator by the desk and settling down with her laptop for a while.

Upstairs, Nathan was no longer there.

HE WOKE up conscious of cold, a cold far colder than December in the south of England. An open-air cold, ice-tipped and dagger-sharp. He had dropped off in his sweater and quilted jacket, and happily was still wearing his shoes; otherwise he thought he would have frozen to death in minutes. He was lying on snow—powder snow mantling a surface of ice. A pale winter sun had evidently just lifted over the horizon, hollowing blue shadows in the snow and making a diamond glitter on the nearby sea. A few yards away a huge gray-brown hump shifted slightly, making the snorting, bubbling noise of someone who has half woken and is determined to go back to sleep. The walrus, Nathan thought. What was his name? Burgoss . . . He walked over to the big sea mammal and sat down beside him. He smelled of the sea, a salty, wet-fur smell with a tang of fish. It wasn't something that, under normal circumstances, Nathan would have wanted to smell from close up, but he realized immediately that the walrus was warm, or at least warmer than his surroundings, and sharing his body heat seemed like a very good idea. He leaned his back against Burgoss's sunward flank and decided that, like this, he might not die of cold just yet.

"I know you're there," the walrus mumbled from the other side of his huge bulk. "Impertinent cub! Lost your mother?"

"Not exactly," Nathan said. "But I suppose I *am* lost. And it's too cold for me here."

"Too *cold*?" The walrus started to roll over—Nathan had to move quickly in order not to get squashed. "What is he talking about?" And then, as the boy came into view: "Who *are* you? Come from the south, did you? Spy of the merfolk?"

"No, of course not. I'm not a merman. I'm human."

"Human, eh? *Human.* I never heard of such a thing. No human has been seen on this planet for two hundred years. Some say they're a myth. You don't look like a myth."

"I'm not," Nathan said. "I come from another world."

"Hrrmph! My great-aunt told me about other worlds. Said they would break off ours like bergs off an ice floe, float away, and evolve all by themselves. Can't say I ever believed her—she was mad as a puffin, poor old dear. So what's this world you're from?"

"Warmer," said Nathan. "A l-lot warmer."

The walrus lowered his big head, peering into Nathan's face. "You *are* a chilly little thing, aren't you? No fur at all. What's all this?"

"Clothes," said Nathan shortly, determined not to get sidetracked. "That's not important. P-please—"

"Lean against me," Burgoss said grudgingly. "Before you freeze to death. If you're a spy, you're a bloody inefficient one."

"I told you, I'm not a spy. I'm a friend of Ezroc's." The walrus's body generated enough heat to stop Nathan's shivering, and the smell, like all such smells, disappeared when you got used to it.

"Are you indeed? That I *can* believe. Ezroc would make friends

with a two-headed shrimp if it told him there was a land beyond the
sun. Where did you meet him?"

"I have to see him," Nathan said, ignoring the question, since the
answer was too complicated. "Rhadamu's shaman-priestesses are telling
him to go to war. I don't think he's that keen—it's all Nefanu—but
he'll do it. If we don't stop it there'll be a bloodbath. And Denaero's in
terrible danger."

"Sounds like you're a spy of *ours*," the walrus said. "Didn't know
we had any. Where d'you get all this? You seem pretty well informed
for someone from another world. And who's Denaero?"

"She's a mermaid," Nathan explained. "Rhadamu's daughter. She's
a friend of Ezroc's, too. Where is he? I *really* have to find him."

"You don't find him," Burgoss grunted. "He finds you. You should
know that, if you know anything. It's been two full moons since I saw
him, and albatrosses fly swift and far. He could be halfway 'round the
world by now."

Nathan was silent, wondering what to do. His dreams were usually
more helpful than this.

"So he's friendly with the coldkin, too, is he?" Burgoss mused.
"That figures. Like I said, a two-headed shrimp . . . All this about the
war—is it true?"

"Yes."

"You better talk to the selkies, young'un. If there's an attack coming, we need to prepare."

"Will they listen?" Nathan asked. "You said they were complacent
and apathetic."

"*I* said? *I* said, did I? Who—"

"Ezroc told me," Nathan said desperately, taking shortcuts to avoid
awkward explanations. "Nokosha's the only one who really believes in
the threat, and he's so hostile he wouldn't be any use."

"Knock me down with a sea lion's whisker! You really *are* telling
the truth, aren't you? All right, cub, I'll talk to the selkies. You—well,
you'd better talk to the Spotted One. He won't like you at all, but then,
he doesn't like anyone. And he'll listen—*if* he believes you."

"He won't," Nathan said gloomily. "He'll probably kill me, too—just for the hell of it. He's obviously psychotic."

"Sy—what?"

"Never mind. Look, I can't—"

"If you've come all the way from another world to help us," Burgoss said, "it's pretty stupid to chicken out now. You don't look like you'd be much good swimming in these seas, so I'll go find Nokosha. He'll be curious if nothing else. I'll see to that. Wait here. And try not to freeze over."

"I'll do my best," Nathan said. In fact, he seemed to be acclimatizing, though he had no desire to go near the sea. The temperature, he reckoned, would kill him in seconds, long before he had time to be afraid of drowning.

Burgoss was gone a long while. The sun traveled a little farther on its low arc across the sky, its rays blinking off ice and snow in a dazzle of almost unbearable whiteness. Nathan wished he'd thought to go to sleep in dark glasses. He got up and walked about, determined to keep warm, slithering once or twice on the treacherous surface. *No wonder they don't use their legs much*, he thought after his feet shot out from under him and he sat down hard. *Easier to start where you'll finish—on your bottom or your stomach*. He struggled to get up again and resumed his pacing, taking more care this time.

The voice behind him took him by surprise. Nokosha's voice. "Burgoss was right. You *are* a legwalker."

Nathan turned to face him. He was sitting on the edge of the floe, his tail dipping in the water, his spotted features as inscrutable as those of a cat. A leopard, Nathan decided, a sea leopard, ghost-gray and deadly, his feral eyes not white like those of the shamans but silver, glittering as though chipped from ice.

"Yes," Nathan said, "but legs aren't much good on this surface. It's easy to fall over. I wouldn't want to try running." He was determined to preserve his coolth, if at all possible. After all, he was in the right place for it. His coolth had rarely been cooler.

Nokosha said: "Running?"

"Moving fast. One foot in front of the other." He kept his distance from the selkie, an instinctive precaution, realizing that on terra firma he had a slight advantage. Selkies evidently used their legs for walking purposes little more than merfolk. "Where's Burgoss?"

"Gone to try to rouse the northfolk. It'll take a season or more—and Burgoss isn't a rouser by nature. More a grumbler."

"Maybe he'll grumble them into action," Nathan said.

"When penguins fly. He believes your story—merfolk massing for war. I don't. Not because war isn't coming—I know it is, soon or late. But I don't make a habit of believing strangers who pop out of nowhere and try to stir things into a maelstrom for their own ends. What was the idea? Get us all into a group and lure us into a trap? Or wear us out with false alarms, so when the real attack comes we're exhausted and off guard?"

"You're off guard already," Nathan said. "And I don't know when the attack is coming, or where, so I can't do any luring. You'll believe me when there's a spear in your gut, though it won't do you much good." He didn't feel like being diplomatic. Besides, he was sure it wouldn't work.

"So who are you? *What* are you? And why are you here?"

"My name is Nathan, I'm human, and I'm here to get the Iron Crown. What Nefanu calls the Crown of Death. It came from another world; it has to go back. Getting mixed up with your lot is just incidental."

The selkie was silent for a minute. "That sounds almost convincing," he said at last. "I like it. There are many strange stories about the Crown. Easy to add one more."

"What stories?"

"Don't you know?" Nokosha sneered.

"I know Nefanu can't wear it or touch it," Nathan said wearily. His patience was growing thin. "She's a werespirit: iron is anathema to her. And it would rust in water, so she keeps it in a cavern of air under the Dragon's Reef. Wherever that is. I'd still like to know how she got the water out of the cavern."

"I heard the story from the whales," Nokosha said, watching Nathan with cold concentration. "They have long memories. They say she closed every exit save one. Then she made a great whirlpool and drew the air down through the vortex into the hole, forcing the water out, until all the caves were filled with air. She sealed the entrance with a boulder, so no one could go in or out, and the Crown was shut inside. There's supposed to be a secret door where she gets in sometimes to gloat over it. Apparently, it's an object of power, though what the power is for remains a mystery. She collects such things, the sunken treasures of civilizations long gone—broken, useless, lifeless artifacts. The caves are said to be full of them."

"That must have raised the sea level," Nathan said, diverted by his own speculations. "That's why the lands drowned. If you could open the caves—move the boulder—it would be like pulling the plug out. The seas would sink again. The islands would reappear."

"Why should we want that?" Nokosha demanded.

"*You* wouldn't," Nathan said. "You'd prefer to massacre all the merfolk and live on the Great Ice forever. Alone. That's the way your brain works—or rather, doesn't work. Burgoss once said you were clever, but I haven't seen much sign of it. The selkies need a leader. They probably wouldn't have you, but from what I've heard there isn't anyone else. Yet you don't even try. You're too busy not caring."

"They hate me," Nokosha said. "Why should I care?"

"Because they're your people. Because this is your world. Because—because caring is part of being alive. They only hate you because you want them to. When you were a child—a cub—they mocked you for your spots, didn't they? So now you have to be a pariah by way of revenge. I think that's so idiotic it's unreal." He was getting angrier, knowing there was no way to get through to a closed mind, kicking at the door in frustration. "Everyone you care for—everyone you *ought* to care for—is going to be killed, but that's all right as long as you can go on being an outcast and telling yourself it's all their own fault."

"They don't listen to me," Nokosha said. "Why should *I* listen to *you*?"

"No reason. No reason at all. I didn't come to talk to you. I wanted to find Ezroc. At least he's trying to save people, even if they don't want saving."

"You know Ezroc?"

"Didn't Burgoss tell you?"

"No, he didn't. It isn't a recommendation. The albatross killed my only friend—or left him to die."

"Oh, grollocks," Nathan said—a vulgarism unique to Widewater. "Ezroc told you what happened. You just want someone to blame. Keerye was taken by the Floater, even though Ezroc told him to be careful. I saw it."

"The witness . . ." The selkie drew himself up onto the ice, moving nearer to Nathan, the sweep of his seal body reshaping itself into legs that wormed across the floe.

"I was in his mind. You wouldn't understand—or believe me. You're so obsessed with not believing in anything—"

"I certainly don't believe in you. Otherworlds are fairy tales for chicks and cubs. I believe—" He sprang so fast Nathan had hardly any time to react. He jumped back, but his feet skidded and even as he fell the selkie was on top of him, pinning him down, a hand around his throat. Fingers pressed on his windpipe, squeezed the vein beneath his ear. The bloodbeat grew loud in his head.

"I believe in *this*," the selkie said with vicious satisfaction. "*Now* you'll tell me the truth. What are you really after?"

"The Crown." Nathan's voice was reduced to a croak. "I—told you. Stupid . . ."

Nokosha's grip tightened. Nathan saw the spots detach themselves from his face and spread through the air, turning vision into a blur. "The truth!"

"Told you." The croak had become a whisper. "I come—from—another world . . ."

And then everything went black.

NATHAN WOKE up in his own room to find his throat bruised and tender and snow melting on his clothes. Even so, he was half smiling. He lay for some time picturing Nokosha's face when his victim vanished from his chokehold into the empty air.

At tea he said to Annie: "Doesn't it make you furious when you're telling the truth and people don't believe you?"

"Definitely," Annie said, thinking of Pobjoy. "But there's no point in losing your temper. You just have to convince them."

I hope Nokosha found my disappearance convincing, Nathan thought. And then, with a pang of guilt: *I still haven't been able to warn Denaero . . .*

"He thinks I'm potty," Annie said, more to herself than her audience. "He thinks we're all potty."

"Sorry?"

"Nothing. What do you want for supper? After last night, I don't feel much like proper cooking. And we did have a big breakfast."

"Toasted cheese?" Nathan suggested.

"Good idea."

ON MONDAY morning Annie was in the bookshop when she got the letter. The headmaster of Ffylde had picked his moment, giving her the holidays to adjust to Nathan's changed circumstances and, since he would be away, preventing, or at least postponing, her storming his office in an outburst of maternal rage. He informed her that although Nathan's academic record was satisfactory—"Satisfactory!" Annie expostulated—the school had decided to terminate his scholarship after GCSEs, feeling such preferential treatment was unfair both to other pupils and their parents. His predecessor, Father Crowley, had been prone to favor those students with family problems—"What family problems?"—or other personal difficulties, sometimes forgetting that boys from a more stable environment were equally deserving. Under the new regime the idea was to create a level playing field where no such favoritism would be allowed. If Ms. Ward was unable or unwilling to pay the fees—perhaps she might consider extending her mortgage— no doubt Nathan would be perfectly happy in state education, where he would have the opportunity to make friends more suited to his outlook and lifestyle. The headmaster might even venture to suggest that such a change would be beneficial to Nathan, since it would demonstrate to him that in the real world there was no such thing as a free pass to the future.

He was hers faithfully, et cetera.

Annie finished reading the letter, set it down on the desk, checked that the shop was empty, and screamed.

It provided her only a modicum of relief. When she had finished screaming she read the letter all over again, fuming at every sentence, every phrase—"*Ms.* Ward! I've always been Mrs., even though I'm not. How dare he call me Ms.? He's talking like I'm a bimbo who shags around and doesn't even know who Nathan's father is. Family problems, indeed! All right, I *don't* know who Nathan's father is, but he doesn't know I don't know, and the school doesn't know I don't know, and they have no *right*—*Friends more suited to his outlook*—*No such thing as a free pass*—anyone would think Nathan had done something *wrong* instead of being the best pupil they've ever had. His English teacher, his history teacher, they all agree . . ." She reached for the telephone with a hand trembling with fury and distress, and dialed Bartlemy.

"Would you like me to pay his fees?" Bartlemy said. "I would be happy to do so, if that's what you want."

"Oh no—no—I didn't mean—I wouldn't ask—"

"You're my family," Bartlemy said. "And I can afford it, I assure you."

"Thank you," Annie said. "Thank you so much. You've been better than family, to both of us. But that wasn't why I called. I wanted to—"

"To get things off your chest?"

"Absolutely. It's such a horrible letter, so condescending and—and *superior,* as if Nathan were the sort of boy who collected Anti-Social Behavior Orders in his spare time and was going to grow up to be a hooligan—and even if he *was* like that, no headmaster worthy of the name should ever dismiss him in that way. Sorry, our school is only for the rich and the privileged; your son may have brains but he should stay in the gutter where he belongs."

"Is that what he said?" Bartlemy remarked. "Dear me."

"It's what he *meant*. And since it's an abbey school, I assume he's supposed to be a Christian. I don't want Nathan to go there anymore if that's how they feel about him, but . . . but . . ."

"*He* may want to stay," Bartlemy supplied. "His friends are there, after all. Apart from Hazel and George he's not close to the children in the village, not anymore. You'll have to discuss this with him. But don't rush at it. Calm down first. You've got the whole of the Christmas vacation."

"Of course," Annie said gratefully. "I'll do that. It's just—I got so *angry* . . ."

"Naturally," Bartlemy said. "I suspect the new headmaster has his own agenda. He sees the school as a business that is intended to make money—he's probably going to increase the fees as soon as he can, and put all sorts of expensive extras into the curriculum. His motto is presumably that you get what you pay for, and the more people pay, the more they will think they get. Much of modern society subscribes to that sort of logic. And as the school revenues expand, so the headmaster's reputation will expand with them, carrying him on to other, more highly paid headmasterships at still more expensive and expansive schools, with a possible knighthood somewhere at the end of it. Not to mention seats on various prestigious committees and a life of general prestigiousness. I'm sure he has convinced himself that although Nathan is a bright pupil, he's a disruptive element whose departure would benefit his classmates—and there are always other bright pupils, preferably with wealthier parents. Can I make a suggestion?"

"Go on."

"Write back in the next week or so. There's no hurry, but it will do you good to be taking action. Say you have consulted with Nathan's uncle, who is happy to pay the school fees for a nephew so talented and promising. Mention me by name, and give this address. However, explain that the aforesaid uncle feels Nathan might perhaps be better off at another private school with rather higher academic standards, and in view of that you would like some time to consider the position. Conclude that you trust this will not be inconvenient, and so on and so on. Be very dignified and polite: that should put him in his place."

Annie laughed aloud.

"That ought to make you feel a bit better."

"Oh yes, it will. *Thank* you. You're a genius."

She hung up with a final *thank you* and was in the process of composing her dignified and polite reply when Pobjoy came in. The shop door, which seemed to have a peculiar affinity with her more questionable or unwelcome visitors, failed to clang, but she had already been distracted from her task by the entry of another customer—"Just browsing"—and she mouthed a greeting. In view of his attitude the previous weekend, she didn't feel a smile was appropriate.

He didn't even pretend to look at the books, approaching her desk with a brusque "Hello" and eyeing the intrusive customer resentfully.

In due course the customer selected a book, paid for it, and left.

"Who was that?" Pobjoy demanded unreasonably.

"Someone who wanted to buy a book," Annie said. "This is a bookshop, remember? Although far too many of my visitors don't, especially lately." She added, setting him at a distance: "What can I do for you?"

"Nothing," he said. "I'm the one who—look, I wanted to apologize. Things were very strained the other night, and some of us weren't completely sober."

"Are you suggesting *I* was drunk?" Annie said, mustering all her native hauteur, which wasn't very much.

"Of course not. Not drunk, perhaps, but—"

"Not exactly sober?"

"You *were* at a party . . ."

"I was sober," Annie perjured herself, "and before you ask, the children were sober, and Bartlemy was sober. We were all incredibly sober. I thought you said you came to apologize."

"I did, but you're not giving me a chance. I can't believe that story the kids told—not the way they told it—in a court of law they'd be charged with contempt, but I shouldn't have expressed myself quite so . . . I know you're not nuts, and you can't possibly be a criminal, though there's obviously something criminal going on. I'm sorry if I

204 · Amanda Hemingway

gave offense. Perhaps we could just agree to look at things differently. What you call a demon, I call a psychopath—"

"I wouldn't if I were you," Annie said. "He might just tear your head off."

"See what I mean?"

To his surprise, she laughed. "If Kal's growing a soul," she said, "you seem to be growing a sense of humor. Maybe you should put it in a pot and water it regularly."

"I'll try," he said seriously. And then: "I could use some help. Perhaps you'd have lunch with me?"

"All right," Annie said, caught off guard. "I mean—thank you."

NATHAN HAD gone to Chizzledown to see if Rowena Thorn could give him a job for a couple of weeks. He'd worked for her the previous year—she was always busy in the run-up to Christmas—and although the money was not particularly good he enjoyed learning about cleaning and restoration, and between them he and Eric were strong enough to move everything but a grand piano. Rowena, with whom he was something of a favorite, agreed immediately and said if he liked he could start now. He sent Annie a text, spent the rest of the day happily polishing chairs, and in the evening dropped in to see Hazel on his way home.

"You're so lucky," she said enviously. "I don't have enough vacation to get a job. Anyway, Uncle Barty wants me to spend all of it working on stuff for school. He says we're going to do some magic, too, only I know what he's really up to. He'll tell me I need to sharpen my brain first, like it was a blunt pencil, and then we'll have to go through French grammar or something for the next two hours. It's a plot to make me pass my exams, only it's a complete waste, because I won't." She had evidently decided to relapse into self-doubt again.

"Well, if you're sure . . ."

"Of course I'm sure."

"Okay," Nathan said. "Don't then. It's up to you."

"Stop it," Hazel snapped.

"Stop what?"

"Trying to persuade me to—to make more effort, and be *motivated*, and all that crap."

"I never said a word to persuade you. I was just *agreeing*—"

"It's the *way* you agree. I know you're being devious."

"If you know, then it isn't working, is it?" Nathan pointed out. "I've been meaning to tell you, you were awfully clever last weekend—the pipe-cleaner trick. I shouldn't have made fun of it. Only please don't do it on anyone else."

"It was pretty good, wasn't it?" Hazel said, gratified. "Actually, I didn't think it would come off. It never seemed to have any effect on Franco."

"How would you know?"

"He and Mum should look unhappy."

"D'you really want to make your mother miserable? Honestly, Hazel . . ."

Fortunately for their mutual accord, they left the subject, reverting to the events of the weekend, discussing them thoroughly and at length before Nathan moved on to Widewater and his encounter with the Spotted One. *I may not be able to get into other worlds,* Hazel thought when he'd gone, *but at least I'm involved now, I can* do *something.* And she remembered what Nathan had said about needing a spell so he could survive underwater. There must be such a spell, somewhere in the annals of magic; she could always ask Bartlemy about it. Only it would be so much better if she could find it herself . . .

She started reading through her great-grandmother's notebooks.

NATHAN SLEPT on top of his bed, fully clothed, on Sunday night and for the three nights following, but he didn't return to the Great Ice and eventually, reasoning that he was hoping for warmer waters anyway, he went back to tracksuit bottoms and a T-shirt. He didn't really need the T-shirt but the recollection of Denaero's topless condition made him opt for it, although he couldn't have analyzed the rationale behind his thought processes. It simply made him feel more secure, imagining himself face-to-face with her, modestly T-shirted. He wasn't, he thought, exactly prudish; he just didn't want to put his body on show.

But the next time he found himself on Widewater, he had left his body behind.

He was looking down on the Great Ice, at a vast crowd that seemed to cover the floe in all directions: selkies, trueseals, sea lions, penguins, a score of great albatrosses and flocks of lesser seabirds—gannets, puffins, auks, terns, and others he didn't recognize. The occasional walrus loomed up, tusked and whiskered; snowbears hung around the northward edge, far larger than our polar bears, shag-haired and saber-toothed. In the middle there was a clear space, and Nathan could see Burgoss, his head moving from side to side as he scrutinized the audience, a couple of selkies with weather-lined faces and an air of age if not wisdom, and Ezroc, biggest of the albatrosses, perched on a pinnacle of ice where he could look down on the scene. But at the very center on a hummock of snow stood Nokosha, the Spotted One—Nokosha the outcast—the ghost-spots mottling his naked legs, haranguing the crowd in a voice that carried effortlessly in the cold clear air. He talked of the coming attack, the greed of the merfolk who wanted the seas all to themselves, the wrath of Nefanu who hated all creatures that walk on legs—and Nathan knew that was why he had changed into his human form, he alone among all the selkies there, as an act of defiance, a gesture, a challenge. He talked to the crowd, and they listened, doubted, rallied; once in a while there was a clamor of approval. As an outcast he had hunted alone, as a leader he stood alone—always alone, whether rejecting his people or stepping forward to call them to battle. Ezroc and Burgoss, the two elders, were behind him but a little way off, as though whatever was driving him—the fire of his heart, the need of a desperate hour—was somehow contagious and might yet destroy them all.

Great, thought Nathan. *We've started the war on both sides. Now we have to stop it*—and with that thought the crowded floe fell away beneath him, and the ocean wheeled, and he was floating above the turquoise waters of the tropics, with the steams of the Reef Wall far to the south, and the westering sun flashing sparks from every wavelet. And there was Denaero, her dark head rising from the lagoon, watching the empty sky, looking for the albatross, maybe even for *him*—believing, perhaps, that now that he had learned what he needed, Ezroc had abandoned her. Nathan wanted to materialize, to reassure her that Ezroc would never willingly fail her, to warn her of the shaman-priestesses and their probing spells—but he could not. He was trapped in his nothingness, voiceless and powerless, able only to observe.

Presently, another head emerged beside Denaero, a mermaid with greenish brown hair threaded with yellow pearls and looped around speckled cowries. "Come away," she said. "Father calls for you at the banquet. The eleven kings are all there; he says he is dishonored by your absence. Why do you linger here?"

"Banquets bore me," said Denaero. "I came to see the sunset."

"The sun does not set northward. What are you looking for? Is it the talk of war that troubles you?—are you afraid the selkies will come south from their cold seas to harry us? Don't worry: I heard Uraki say that he has set guards all along the reef. Not a smallfish passes but he will know of it. There is nothing to fear."

"I am not afraid," Denaero said, and her voice was aloof and very cold. "Go back to the feast, Semeele. When the sun sets, I will come."

"Father will not be pleased," Semeele said.

"He will forgive me, in the end," Denaero said hopefully. "He always does."

Her sister sank out of sight, and Denaero waited while the sun dipped beneath the waves, and the blue dusk arched across the sky, and the stars came out, singly, then in clusters, like flowers opening to welcome the dark. In the east the husk of the old moon floated like the belly of a sail running before the wind. Now Nathan could barely see the mermaid, but he sensed her tension and the ache in her heart. At last she, too, disappeared from view—he saw the white curve of her back as she dived, the ridge of her vertebrae, the dorsal fin unfurling for the plunge. Then they were both descending into the night beneath the sea, and for a long while all he could make out were dim blue shadows that seemed to melt and change as they drew near, and the occasional silver flicker of a fish, caught in an errant ray of moonlight or starlight that found its way down from above.

Then suddenly he heard music, the rippling notes of terpsichords and spindlestrings, the throbbing boom of the gongs, the plaintive chime of dead-men's-bells. Ahead, the reef was lit up with a million points of light: glitterworms, bubble-globes, sparklefish, luminous shrimps and sea stars, all glinting and gleaming, illuminating the coral fans that waved in the current, the prowling shoals of nocturnal hunters, the claws of crab or lobster snapping from a crevasse. They came to a cave mouth sculpted into a triple arch; beyond was what seemed to be a great hall, carved with twining eels and sea dragons, decked with mother-of-pearl shells, shimmering with living lights. It was full of merfolk, some eating and talking, others going to and fro carrying clams and abalones piled with strange delicacies, all many-colored and many of them wriggling. The musicians were playing, mermen and other creatures; Nathan saw a large squid plucking at the spindlestrings with its multiple arms, and a lobster clashing its pincers like maracas and tapping the gongs with the tip of its tail.

At the far end Rhadamu sat on a throne surmounted with the skull of some long-dead sea monster and set with uncut gemstones, wave-smoothed into huge clear pebbles as bright as eyes. There were guards on either side of him, merkings and warrior-captains seated nearby, but he paid them no attention, beckoning Denaero as soon as he saw her, indicating a seat to his left.

"Where have you been?" he demanded. "I told your sister you were to come immediately."

"I wanted to see the stars," Denaero said.

"There are more stars in my halls than ever shone in the sky. If you cannot come when I send for you, I will have you shut in your chambers, with guards to see you do not leave."

"I would escape," Denaero said, making a face at Semeele, who sat a little way off. "I always do."

"You are the most wayward and tiresome of all my children," the king complained. *Hazel was right,* Nathan thought. *She's his favorite.* "I shall be only too glad to see you married to some poor unfortunate, and be rid of you."

"I'm too young to marry," Denaero objected.

"You are too young only till I say you are old enough," the king retorted. "Your sister Miyara is to marry this moon, Seppopo of the Western Reef. It will cement his allegiance to my house."

"Politics!" Denaero sniffed. Merfolk cannot actually sniff underwater, but her tone was sniffy. "Seppopo is fat, and he has three wives already."

"I have seven," Rhadamu reminded her without enthusiasm.

"You're the High King. He's only a low king. He isn't allowed more than three."

"In time of crisis," Rhadamu said, "it pays to be flexible. He has a great admiration for Miyara—"

"She's the prettiest of us," Denaero said. "Everybody admires her. She shouldn't have to marry a fat old porpoise like Seppopo. What is the crisis? Is it a new one, or just the same old crisis we always have?"

"Same old," said Rhadamu, his expression unchanging, but Nathan heard the trace of a smile in his voice. "A little more urgent this time."

"Are we going to war?" Denaero asked.

The king was silent.

"It's the Goddess, isn't it? She wants us to kill the northfolk—the selkies and the seabirds and the monsters on the Great Ice. Why does she hate them, Father? Why do *we* hate them?"

"They are lungbreathers and fish stealers," said the king. "Their blood is hot. If we do not destroy them, they will destroy us. This is a war to save our people. We are fighting for our lives and our livelihoods."

"The seas are wide," said Denaero, "and there is room for everyone. Why can't we all just live together?"

"You are such a child." Rhadamu sighed.

Denaero turned away, her small face very still. When she was offered food she took a sliver of yellow sea urchin but did not eat, flicking it to a crab that lurked under her seat.

Her father said irritably: "Don't do that. I've told you before not to give tidbits to your pets during a formal banquet. Eat your food instead of playing with it. You're too thin."

He began to talk to the captain on his right, the javelin-happy warrior whom Nathan had guessed must be Uraki. Denaero let her hand trail beside her so the crab could nip her finger and gazed at nothing in particular with eyes narrowed to slots of emerald.

The shaman-priestesses entered in a group, moving as a single entity, many-armed and multi-tailed, their hair writhing about them, the livid stripes rippling on fin and scale. At the sight of them, the music ceased, and the bubble of conversation slowly deflated. Servers retreated from their path; diners stopped with dainties halfway to their lips, abandoning the feast. Some of it swam away. Those skull faces and undulating ribs were not conducive to appetite. One of the shaman-women reached out with skeletal fingers, snatching at a passing smallfish—not part of the menu—and crammed it into her mouth. The tail tweaked for a moment, then it was sucked in. Nathan thought he could see the lump traveling down her throat into her meager body.

He knew what they were there for, but he could not stop it, could not speak. Could not even whisper a warning.

They approached the throne, gliding over the rock. As ever, they spoke in unison.

"Hail Rhadamu, High King of the Twelve Tribes."

"Hail," said the king, mechanically.

"There's a traitor in your midst. The spells have spoken. We have looked in the All-Seeing Mirror, noted her discontent even as she obeys your word. She has a lover who is not the one you have chosen for her. And at night she goes to the surface and meets with one of our enemies, an albatross, a windbringer from the Great Ice. She *changes,* not to mate with a merman but to ride the evil bird, letting him carry her up into the high air. She becomes as a lungbreather, a legwalker, alien to her own kind."

"You say—*she,*" murmured the king. "You speak as if she is one I know well."

"She is your own kin. Your daughter." Denaero's hand was clenched on the shell carving of her chair; the gill slits flexed in her neck. "Your daughter Miyara, whom you betrothed to your brother-king Seppopo— Miyara who rebels against your orders, preferring another, consorting with our enemies in a desperate attempt to evade your commands and have her own will. Let the guards take her! She must be punished. Who knows what secrets she has already betrayed?"

Denaero's mouth made the shape of a protest, but her voice was very soft. Another mermaid was dragged from her place by the guards— a mermaid whose long dull-bronze hair was only a shade away from Denaero's—at night, Nathan guessed, in a spell-mirror, it might look the same. Her face was a perfect oval, her eyes the green-gold of shallows in the sun. She cried: "No, Father—please! It's not true! I don't love Seppopo—there's someone else—but I never met the bird, I swear it. I never betrayed you!"

"She lies," said the shamans. "The All-Seeing Mirror cannot err. It showed her in the twilight, waiting at the rendezvous, until the bird flew down to join her."

"It wasn't me!" Miyara protested.

"Then who?" The king's voice was leaden. "People may lie, but the spells do not. They can only misconstrue. Who met the albatross?"

Miyara shook her head.

He knows, Nathan thought with a sudden flash of insight. *They all know. Not the shamans but her sisters, her father, her kin. They knew from the moment the priestesses spoke of the albatross. She had always been the problem child, the one who came late to the feast or not at all, wayward in her worship of the Goddess, doubting, questioning, gazing up at the forbidden stars.*

"It was me," Denaero whispered, and then, louder: "It was me."

Miyara bowed her head. The king looked at his youngest daughter with an expression that was set in stone. It occurred to Nathan that merfolk could not cry; the ocean swallowed their tears.

"Why?" Rhadamu asked. "Why do this terrible thing?"

"It wasn't terrible," Denaero said. "I told no secrets." *No, that was me,* Nathan thought. "I just wanted to fly. You don't know what it's like, being high above the world, riding the air like a wave . . . Ezroc isn't evil; he's my friend. Why do we have to kill people, just because they're different? Why can't we live in peace? Why *can't* we be friends?"

"Traitress!" chorused the priestesses. "Let her tongue be torn out for saying such things! Cut off her tail—she is no longer one of us! Pluck out her eyes and we will plant them in our garden! Her very thoughts blaspheme the Goddess."

"Good," said Denaero with a last flare of defiance. "I hate the Goddess!"

A gasp of shock rippled around the hall.

"Sacrilege!" said the shamans, jolted out of unison by their fury. "May she die slowly and in pain! Nefanu demands atonement. Give her to us, and we will—"

"You misread the spells," said the king, his tone sharpening. "Neither I nor the Goddess tolerate incompetence. Begone! I am the ruler here, and I alone mete out punishment to my subjects. Go back to your caves in the deep. When I have need of you, I know where to find you."

"High King—"

"*Go!*"

They slunk away with extraordinary speed, melting into a nest of groping limbs and snaking hair that traveled over the rock like a monstrous octopus. When they were gone the king turned to Denaero, though his gaze avoided hers. The guards had released Miyara and now held her sister, but she didn't struggle. Her small, solemn face was white and unchanging.

"Take her away," said Rhadamu. "Her punishment is already ordained. Chain her to the rocks on the Dragon's Bridge; there the eaters of carrion, big and little, will have their way with her. It is the traditional fate of traitors."

"Father!" Denaero's voice seemed to burst out of her. "I didn't betray you! I just wanted to fly—to fly to the stars—"

"Take her!"

The guards took her. The king sat on his throne of jewels and bones, silent as death. All around the hall the visiting dignitaries waited, caught between schadenfreude and social embarrassment, unsure whether to continue their meal or to depart. Presently, the king said softly: "Uraki?"

The warrior drew nearer. As if picking up a cue, the musicians resumed their play. The guests began to talk again, if not to eat. Under cover of the noise, the king said to his captain: "When this is over, go to her. See to it that the end is swift and painless. I could not bear that my Denaero should suffer. Do you understand?"

"Yes, sire."

"I shall ask of you nothing more dreadful, nor nearer to my heart, though the forthcoming war should last a dozen seasons. Give me your word you will not fail."

"You have my word," Uraki said.

The dream was going dim. *I have to save her,* Nathan thought, but there was no time, no time, and Widewater was slipping away, and he was sucked into the blackness of sleep like someone sinking into a bog.

He woke to the dark of a winter morning, and the fear that Denaero's time had already run out.

The Dragon's Reef

Hazel sat on the bed in her room to go through her great-grandmother's things, if only because there was no space on the floor. The carpet was buried beneath the inevitable litter of empty chip packets, discarded shoes, crumpled clothing, CD cases without CDs, CDs without CD cases, uncompleted homework, magazines, half-read books—Hazel started books all the time, but with a low boredom threshold and a short attention span she often failed to finish them. Her desk had disappeared under computer and iPod, files and makeup. Even duvet space was running out beneath the advancing tide of jacket and scarf, notebook, pipe cleaners, the singed remnants of the Nenufar doll, and the contents of Effie Carlow's bag, emptied out in a heap on top of a stuffed animal dating from Hazel's infancy that no one was supposed to see. She ran through the various bottles until she found the one she wanted, holding it up to the light to be sure. It was a vial about four inches high, cut into facets, with the dregs of some dark brownish liquid in the bottom that, upon removal of the cork, smelled like rotting vegetables.

"It's crystal," Hazel said aloud, wrinkling her nose at the odor.

Bartlemy had taught her that crystal, if pure, passed easily between the dimensions, and she had concluded that was almost the same thing as crossing between worlds. The brownish stuff looked sticky and too old to be important; she would have to clean it out.

She put the bottle down and turned to a sheet of thick yellow paper on her left. It was blank except for the heading—ALTERNATIVE ELEMENTS: HOW TO SURVIVE IN FIRE AND WATER—but she murmured something in Atlantean and words began to write themselves across the page, slanting black words that rippled into being like snake tracks on the surface of the desert. Even as Hazel read the instructions they began to fade—she was scribbling frantically in her notebook, rummaging through the bottles and jars again in search of the more obscure ingredients, copying down Runes of Power. "*Someone* liked to make things difficult," she muttered to herself. When the writing reached the foot of the page the magic ran out; the last words vanished, leaving only the empty sheet with its tantalizing title. Hazel knew from previous efforts that it would have to be left for a while, as if it needed to cool down, and when she reactivated the spell the writing might tell her something entirely different. It wasn't Effie's hand; she was almost sure about that. Besides, her great-grandmother's powers had been limited: she had been a village witch in the old style, a spinner of little charms for little things, removing warts—or, knowing Effie, inducing them—cursing her petty curses, spying and scrying. Hazel had always sworn she would never be like that.

But this was something else. This was serious magic. She found the calligraphy pen that she had bought specially, nicked her finger with a kitchen knife, and dipped the nib in her own blood. Then, clutching a tissue in her left hand to stanch the bleeding, she carefully wrote out the runes on an adhesive label. It took her awhile to get them right, and there were a couple of red smudges in the background when she had finished, but she decided it would do. She would stick the label onto the crystal bottle only when it was clean and ready for the potion she had to make.

She spoke in Atlantean again, and the words recommenced their snake-like wriggle across the empty paper. Hazel was concentrating so hard, she didn't see the slight twitch of the burned pipe-cleaner doll as it turned to watch what she was doing.

DREAMS DO not come to order. Although Nathan knew from experience that time in this world and time in Widewater did not run concurrently, nonetheless he lived two days with urgency and fear, hoping each night to return, unable to find a way through. He was desperately grateful for the distraction of his job, talking events over with Eric while cleaning a Georgian silver cruet or daubing centuries of dirt from a painting that might—or might not—prove valueless.

"If you are meant to save her, you will," Eric said philosophically. "Look how you save me. Is purpose in all things."

"Do you think so?" Nathan said. "I know the Grandir sort of controls my dreams, sometimes—at least, not exactly *controls*, but nudges things in certain directions, so I can find the Grail relics, do whatever it is I have to do. He protects *me;* he's saved my life more than once. But he isn't really concerned with the problems of other worlds—he's got his own world to save, I expect that's problem enough. If I want to— to try and help, I have to work that out myself. Once or twice, I've managed to open the portal without falling asleep, but I never end up where I want to go. It all happens in my head, but *I* have no control at all."

"But it work out, in the end," Eric said. "Last time, you save the princess, cure the sick king. All end well."

"I couldn't save Kwanji Ley," Nathan said somberly.

"She was of my world. She went to do Great Spell not meant for her. Maybe best to die."

"Was it?" Nathan said without conviction. "I messed up. I left her out in the desert. I'll never, never forget that."

"You should not forget. But move on, as you say here. In my world, no one move on for a long, long time. Many thousand years. All things should move—people, time, history. Not good to look back so much you never see forward. But on Eos, we run out of history. We just wait."

"I know," Nathan said. "But right now, I just want to get to Denaero. She may not be part of the purpose—part of the Grandir's purpose— but I can't bear it if she dies."

"You get there," Eric assured him. "You save princess, like last time. Is *your* purpose."

"I wish I was sure of that. Funny, I suppose she *is* a princess. She's the king's daughter. I seem to spend a lot of time hanging out with princesses. Only merfolk don't use the title—or not that I've ever heard."

"Is your fate," Eric declared, "saving princesses. Hazel is princess, too. Maybe one day you save her."

Nathan laughed. "I can't see *Hazel* as a princess," he said.

"Why not? She is princess at heart. The heart is what matters."

"She wouldn't have any truck with princessness. She's a natural republican."

"Perhaps. But you save her, yes?"

"She's more likely to save me."

AND NOW at last he was back—back on Widewater, back in the dream, back in the sea. There was a rush of confused images: Denaero struggling as the guards bound her to the rock above a wave-worn arch, barracuda finning silently beneath; Uraki, saddling his great white while it twisted and snapped viciously at his fingers; a long defile of lobsters, marching in pairs across the seabed. And then very briefly a glimpse of the albatross flying southward with someone on his back, chasing his own shadow across the wrinkled surface of the ocean. Nathan thought how visible he was in a world where few birds remained. And then the images fled away and there he was, solid, floundering in water up to his neck, trying to stay afloat, to survive, and all around him in every direction there was nothing but the sea.

Afterward, he didn't think it lasted very long, but it *felt* long as he paddled with legs and arms, fighting panic, thinking of the depth of water below him and the things that might be lurking there, picking up the vibration from his threshing limbs. Yet somehow the emptiness above was even more frightening—the arching void of the sky, the unbroken expanse of sea stretching from horizon to horizon. He took a breath and dipped his face beneath the surface, opening his eyes on blue, but there was nothing to be seen, though he knew it was merely a matter of time.

He thought, with the small part of his brain not occupied by fear: *I'm no good to Denaero here.*

So much for a rescue . . .

And then he saw the speck in the sky, a speck that drew swiftly nearer, broadening into wings, great wings that swept the air with scarcely a beat, and a figure leaning on the bird's stooping neck. A closed, intent face, shadow-dappled hair blown back in the wind.

Nathan waved, but the albatross had evidently seen him already. His flight dipped; he landed on the water a short distance away. Nokosha slid from his back, legs melding into tail even as he dived.

"You'd better hold him up," Ezroc said. "He doesn't swim very well."

"Good," said the selkie. "Let him drown. I don't trust someone who disappears when I strangle him."

"He's been in my mind," Ezroc said. "He doesn't lie. I felt it."

"You're going to have to—start trusting people," Nathan said, rather breathlessly, "if you want to save your world."

"Save the world?" The selkie caught Nathan underarm, his grip a little too tight, a little too strong. But still, it was support. "Save my people, maybe. The world can take care of itself."

Nathan let it go—for the moment. "Does he know about Denaero?" he asked Ezroc. "She's in danger—her father found out—"

"He knows. I told him we had to contact her, only—"

"I don't like traitors," said Nokosha. "But I'll use them."

"She's not a traitor, *stupid*!" Despite the hazards of his position, Nathan felt the familiar surge of anger and frustration. Was it always like this, in every world—closed minds, labels, prejudice, hate? "She just wants your people and hers to get along. She helped Ezroc and Keerye, ages ago. Now you've got to help her, whether you like it or not. She's chained to somewhere called the Dragon's Bridge, and she's going to be eaten by crabs and things—"

"Sounds good to me," said Nokosha, his fingers tensing, digging into Nathan's flesh. "May all the merfolk end that way."

"I know the place," Ezroc interrupted. And to Nokosha: "Lift him onto my back. We'll get her. You wait here. She was a friend to me, and to Keerye. You should understand that, if nothing else."

"You told me. I agreed to see her only because of that. I'm coming with you."

"I can't carry two—"

"Then leave *him*. He's no more use than a dead herring."

Nathan was already scrambling onto the albatross, with little assistance from Nokosha, hoping he wasn't hurting Ezroc as he grasped a handful of feathers. The selkie seized his wrist to pull him back into the sea, but Ezroc croaked a warning.

"Let him go! You can follow by water if you want. The bridge is at the eastern end of the reef, close to the bend of the current . . ."

"There could be guards," Nathan said, remembering Semeele's words.

"Hope they are unwary," Nokosha said, "for their sake."

The albatross took off in a trail of spray, and when Nathan looked back the selkie was gone.

The sea wheeled and sped beneath them; the sundazzle blinked in his eyes. "How do you know the way?" he asked Ezroc. "Don't you ever get lost?"

"Lost?" The bird sounded baffled at the concept. "How could I be lost? I see the reefs beneath the waves, the flow of the currents, the tides of the moon. I feel the winds that circle the globe. There are patterns in the air that do not change: the pull of the Poles, the turn of the world through night and day, the great cycles of cold and heat, of storm and calm. I know where hurricanes are born, where all weathers die. I hear the song of the whales and the heartbeat of the sea. I always know where I am. Don't you?"

"If I know what world I'm in," Nathan said, "that's the best I can do."

He could make out the reef now, a shadow beneath the sea. The water lightened to turquoise and green as the sand floor neared the surface, darkened with the outline of submerged rocks. Far to the south there were the ascending vapors of the wall. *If there are guards,* Nathan thought, *they'll see us.* The albatross was the only thing in the sky.

"Where's the Dragon's Bridge?" he asked.

"There."

Ahead, the rock shadow narrowed to an isthmus joining two sections of the reef; the water on either side was ultramarine with depth.

"We must be quick," Ezroc said. "The Great South March passes beneath the bridge, and it is the season of their migration. If they scent her, they will climb up the rocks to feast."

"What's the Great South March?"

"The march of the lobsters. They live in large numbers along the Midwater Mountains 'round Cape Hook, and every spring they come south to feed in the rich waters near the Reef Wall. They march in a long winding line, two by two; it may go on for miles. No one knows why. They will eat anything in their path."

"I saw them," Nathan said, remembering the brief visions in the early stages of his dream. Beyond the image of the marching lobsters, Ezroc's words—the Midwater Mountains, Cape Hook—opened new vistas in his mind: suddenly he saw that Widewater was more than just a vast flatness of sea. There were valleys and mountain ranges, deserts and forests—a whole world of submarine geography lying just below the waves. *And if I could pull the plug out,* he told himself, thinking of the huge boulder sealing the caverns of air, *then the ocean would sink, if only a few yards, and some of it would become land. Land where seabirds could nest, and seals could bask, and merfolk and selkies could walk together on legs . . .*

Land for people to fight over, because where there is land, there is war.

One problem at a time, Nathan thought. He had problems enough.

"Everyone knows of the Great South March," Ezroc was saying. "That's the trouble. Bigger predators follow them—predators who eat lobster. And anything else they can find."

"Sharks?" Nathan said.

"No. There are worse things in the sea than sharks."

The albatross was descending in a wide spiral, scanning the surrounding waters. Peering past his shoulder, Nathan found he could see far down into the glass-clear depths. There was the rock bridge, a natural arch six yards wide and perhaps fifty long, spanning the chasm that split the reef in two. Halfway along he made out the mermaid—the pale gleam of her body, the smoke of her hair. She seemed to be seated, plainly bound, on the very edge of the reef; her tail twisted from side to side as if she was struggling to be free. Far below he glimpsed a long line of movement on the seabed. The march of the lobsters.

He could not see the guards or any other merfolk in the vicinity.

Ezroc settled on the water, dipping his head to look down. Denearo's face was upturned, marked with desperation and fear.

"You came!" Nathan heard her cry. "You came for me!"

Ezroc said to him: "I can't release her. I could dive down there, but I have no hands to loose her bonds. You must do it."

"But—"

"You *must*."

Nathan slid off the albatross's back and hesitated, treading water, one hand on the feathered neck. He couldn't say *I'm afraid*, but the terror that filled him seemed to drain him of both breath and nerve. His stomach churned, his heart thudded. All the clichés of fear, but knowing that didn't make it any easier. In other dreams, other worlds, he had had to make choices—choices forced upon him by circumstance and danger, hopeless, last-minute choices whose outcome might be uncertain or fatal. To leave the safety of the cave in the Eosian desert, eluding its dreadful guardian—to confront the Urdemon in the marshes of Wilderslee, which picked him up in its toothless jaws and tried to swallow him—to lift the Traitor's Sword, which would maim or slay anyone who dared lay a hand on it. He had chosen, not in courage or bravado but desperation and despair, opting for the last resort, the forlorn hope. Now he had to choose again. But the desperation and despair were Denaero's, not his. All he could think of was crushing pressure and blackness engulfing his mind . . .

For what seemed like a century he paused, gazing down through the water.

Then he filled his lungs, and dived.

The first few strokes were the worst. The water dragged as he fought his way down; fortunately, the bridge was close to the surface. Then he reached Denaero, clutching at a hunk of coral to keep himself from floating back up again, almost cutting his palm on the hardened polyps. He saw there were stone manacles around her wrists—merfolk have no way to work metal—connected with bindings of what looked like thongs that were lashed through holes bored in the rock of the bridge itself. After a minute's thought, he picked up a piece of broken coral and began to saw at them.

"No!" said Denaero. "You can't cut through leatherwrack. You have to untie the knots. Hurry—please hurry—"

The knots had been pulled tight. As he strove to unhitch them he noticed for the first time that there was webbing between the mermaid's fingers. He thought: *My hands are more efficient than a merman's. I should be able to do this*—but he could not get even a fingertip through the loop. His chest felt squeezed, and he realized belatedly that he needed to breathe. With a vague gesture to Denaero he pushed himself up to the surface for air.

Going down was easier the second time. And the third. Eventually, he managed to thrust a coral chip under the thong, wriggling it to and fro to loosen the knot. He had forgotten about the approaching lobsters until Denaero screamed.

"Behind you! Behind you!"

He turned just in time. Huge pincers snapped within inches of his face. He kicked out, dislodging the creature from the bridge—it pitched backward and floated off into the deep. But there were many more mounting the cliff from below, giant crustaceans three or four feet long, armor-plated, with stalk-eyes and groping antennae, half crawling, half swimming up the rock face. Flailing his legs to keep himself submerged, he looked for a boulder to roll down on top of them, but all the available boulders appeared to be fixed in place. He returned to wrestling with the leatherwrack, winkling a strand free at last, glancing around every other instant until Denaero said: "I'll keep watch. *Hurry . . .*"

He had to go up for air again, dive again, anchor himself to the bridge while he tugged and strained at her bonds. And then just as he released her wrist—one wrist, the other was still in its shackle—he saw the claws advancing from the far side, not just one pair but several, a phalanx of lobsters rising over the rocks, relentless and hungry. He fumbled for a weapon, lobbed a stone at them, but the water slowed its trajectory and it fell short. The pounding in his ears told him he had to breathe, though his fear of the water had vanished in other fears. Denaero clutched at him with a whimper of terror.

And then something swooped in front of him, a gray shape shadow-spotted, part seal, part man. The saw-edged pincers drew blood—he saw the thread of it thinning to a mist in the water—but the foremost lobster was smashed against the bridge, and the corpse became a weapon to turn on the rest, knocking them off the rock.

"You free—the fish-girl!" called Nokosha. "I'll keep these—at bay!"

Nathan surfaced, breathed, plunged. The second knot was harder, a tangle of thongs snarled together. He lost count of how often he had to go up for air. Nokosha said "Can't you get a move on?" and came to look, but his fingers were thicker than Nathan's and less agile, and after a brief attempt he returned to his fight with the marauding lobsters, still wielding his first victim like a club. Now he was having to dart from one end of the bridge to the other as more and more of the creatures swarmed up from the deep. He couldn't maintain the defense on both flanks: they were too many for him. Nathan was forced to abandon the second knot, lunging out with a chunk of broken coral that cracked instantly between crushing pincers. He drew back, weaponless, tried another kick, and nearly lost a toe. Denaero gripped him with her free arm, gasped: "Don't leave me!"

Darkness rushed up from below—jaws champed—the attacking lobster was bisected in a single bite. Nathan glimpsed the sweep of a body as long as a barge, a reptilian maw lavishly trimmed with teeth, the flat glare of a fish. Giant flippers propelled it through the water; a whiplash tail flicked against the rock, dislodging more lobsters. Glancing down, he saw it was not alone. Beneath the bridge another similar shape was dive-bombing the march. He might have been relieved, but for the horror in Denaero's voice.

"Icthauryon!" she cried.

The enormous head came around again—an alligator head, only several sizes larger, with eyes like dinner plates. Nokosha leapt in front of them, flourishing his lobster-club—there was a crunch, and most of the lobster was gone. Nathan realized he had to breathe and kicked up to the surface, hoping nothing took his legs off in transit.

"What's happening?" Ezroc demanded. "I thought I saw—"

"Don't ask."

Back down again. Nathan tried to focus on the snaggle of leather-wrack but it was impossible. The icthauryon dived under the bridge: he saw its hide, crusted with barnacles, ridged and pitted like old armor, discolored with parasitic growths. He thought, fleetingly: *It doesn't have any arrangement with cleaner fish*—then its tail lashed the cliff, and the rocks shook. It made a U-turn, scooped up a lobster, spitting out shell fragments like bits of pottery, returning to Denaero out of curiosity, or irritation, or greed. Nokosha had drawn his knife and hacked off a branch of coral—most selkies go unarmed, since their whole-body change makes carrying weapons impractical, but he kept the knife in a sheath strapped beneath arm or flipper. As the alligator gape rushed toward him he rammed the branch down its throat. *He may be a pain in the butt, but he's brave,* Nathan thought appreciatively. The head twisted from side to side—blood seeped from cuts in the tongue and palate. It appeared to be choking—but its bite was too strong, the branch crumbled, it returned to the attack. Nokosha was running out of ideas. Denaero wrenched at the remaining shackle as if trying to tear her own hand off.

Then Nathan saw the shark. A great white, seven yards from nose to tail, speeding out of the blue like a torpedo. He could make out the saddle lashed to its back, the bit clamped in its jaws. Its rider was leaning forward, his tail looped over its flank, his torso covered in jointed plates, his face visored with scorpion shell. He held the reins in one hand, a javelin in the other. As the icthauryon veered toward him he threw; the blood-coral tip plunged deep into its eye. Almost before the shaft left his grip he had plucked another from behind the saddle and was ready to throw again. The shark swung aside even as the alligator head flinched—the fish's mouth snapped like a gin trap, taking a piece from the monster's flipper.

"Raagu!" Denaero said. "Uraki on Raagu!"

Nathan had never thought he'd be happy to see a great white.

Nokosha—he suspected—had never thought he'd be happy to see a merman. He shot upward for air—selkies need to breathe roughly every twenty minutes—while Nathan yanked at the leatherwrack with renewed energy, breaking off only to glance at the conflict beyond the bridge. Maddened by its injuries, the icthauryon arced and writhed, teeth clashing on nothing, just missing the flick of Raagu's tail, the out-stretched arm of the warrior. A second javelin was embedded in its neck, but it seemed to have done little damage. Then its mate surged up from below, abandoning the lobster hunt, coming in for the kill. The sharkrider darted aside at the last moment, almost trapped against the cliff—the two monsters thudded into the rocks again and again, shaking the bridge to its foundations. Nathan finally felt the knot begin to give, but he was nearly out of breath and time. He couldn't hang on any longer—he would have to go up again—

The selkie was back, a gray seal-streak diving straight down onto the injured icthauryon. Somehow, he latched on behind the head, jerking the javelin free. Then he thrust it deep into the neck at the base of the skull, sawing the shaft from side to side, working it inward—severing the spinal cord, shutting down its nervous system, blanking out its brain . . . A red cloud billowed upward, obscuring the selkie from view. The thrashing body grew still, drifting into the abyss. The other icthauryon turned aside from its prey to follow; nature allows little loyalty to the dead, and this was an easier meal. The lobsters, Nathan guessed, would take their share. He went up for a mouthful of air, returned to his task.

Nokosha had emerged from the blood-cloud and crouched close to Denaero; the sharkrider hovered beyond the bridge.

"You saved my life," Uraki said. "When we meet in the battle, I will remember it."

"Ditto and ditto," said the selkie.

They ought to have a beer, and bond, Nathan thought wryly. But Widewater was a beer-free zone.

"The king ordered me to kill her," Uraki went on, with a jerk of his head at Denaero.

"My father ordered you——? He *can't* have——"

"He asked me to make it quick and painless. He didn't want you to suffer."

"I'm not suffering!" raged Denaero. "I just want to get out of *this*——" She tugged at the manacle. "Why didn't he order you to set me free? Why do people have to be so *tragic* about everything?"

"What will you tell him?" Nokosha had moved between Uraki and the mermaid, as if prepared to protect her. Nathan wondered if the gesture was instinctive.

"I will tell him . . . she didn't suffer. Take her north with you. See to it she eats fireflowers to warm her blood or the cold will kill her."

"Is that what you did on the raid?"

How Uraki might have responded Nathan never knew. That was the point when the knot unraveled, and he and Denaero headed for the surface. And now at last he could breathe again—breathe at leisure in the bliss of his own element—gulping the air like wine, hanging on to the albatross for support. Ezroc had seen most of the battle, but the action had taken place too far down for him to help. Denaero hugged him, then hugged Nathan, her small naked breasts squeezed against his chest. Nathan felt a flicker of relief—slightly tinged with regret—that he had worn his T-shirt: at least they weren't skin to skin.

Then Nokosha emerged, without Uraki.

"Where did he go?" Denaero asked.

"He went," the selkie said curtly. "Back to his people. His war. I'm stuck with you. A spoiled child who's betrayed her kin and her kind—oh, and the legwalker, who's no use to anyone."

"He freed Denaero," Ezroc snapped. "His fingers are nimbler than yours."

"Very well," Nokosha said with what might have been a shrug if it had been above the water. "But now they're both just baggage. This whole expedition has been a waste of time. I need to get home. I, too, have a war to fight."

"Wrong," said Nathan.

"What?"

"You're not going to fight the war, you're going to stop it."

"How?" asked Denaero.

"I'm not exactly sure—"

"That's a surprise," said Nokosha. "If you want to stop the war, don't talk to me. It's the merfolk who are attacking us. You're the one who brought news of it—and I've no intention of calling off the defense."

"Why did you bring *him*?" Denaero asked Ezroc. "He's not as nice as Keerye. Or as handsome."

Nathan gave her hair a yank in the hope she would take the hint and shut up.

"Nefanu is the one starting the war," he reminded them. "Without her shamans to stir things up, the king would never have made a move. So it's Nefanu we have to target."

"You want to challenge the Queen of the Sea?" For once, Nokosha was taken aback. "You can't even swim properly."

"He's doing fine," Ezroc said. "Go on, Nathan. What's your plan?"

"I haven't got one yet," Nathan conceded. "But I need to get the Iron Crown—the Crown of Death—from the caverns of air. Suppose we could unblock the entrance somehow? Then the air would rush out, and the sea would sink, and the islands would return."

"How would that stop the war?" Nokosha said.

"It would create one hell of a diversion. Nefanu would have a lot more to worry about than destroying the northfolk, and the upheaval would throw everyone off their stride. I know it's a long shot, but have you got a better idea?"

"Fight!" the selkie snarled.

"Only if we have to," Ezroc said. "If there's another way—"

"You're psychotic," Nathan told Nokosha. "You and Uraki both. Two of a bloodthirsty kind. You could have been friends back there—

you nearly were—but you'll grab any excuse to butcher each other, because that's the way you are. It's the human in you—seals and fish manage to exist side by side. Only people kill."

"We're going north," the selkie said, as if concluding the debate. "You can come, or vanish back to your own world—I really don't care. With any luck you'll drown here and we'll be rid of you."

"I can't carry three," Ezroc pointed out.

"I'm not going," said Denaero. "It's too cold up on the Great Ice. There are places here I can hide. Anyway, Nathan will need me to find the caverns of air."

"Do you know how to get in?" Nathan asked her.

"Of course. It's meant to be a secret, but it's the sort of secret that everyone knows. Only it'll be far too deep for you."

"Drown him," Nokosha repeated grimly, swinging himself onto the albatross's back. Insofar as a bird can assume a facial expression, Ezroc looked annoyed. "We're going home. I have a battle to plan."

"Any fool can start a war," Nathan said with contempt. "It takes brains to stop one."

"*I'm not starting it*. Drown him!" He kicked Ezroc, who twisted his head and clipped his beak within an inch of the selkie's face.

"I'll be back," said the albatross, beating his wings against the water. "This one's no help to us. Keerye would've tried . . ."

"Don't talk about Keerye!"

They took off in mid-argument, describing a wide circle around Nathan and the mermaid. "I'll—be back!" Ezroc called.

"Be careful!" cried Denaero, who was evidently learning caution from recent disaster. "I'll send you a message by smallfish!"

"Don't thank me for saving your skin!" said Nokosha.

"I won't!" Denaero retorted.

Then the bird swung northward, racing away on a single wingbeat, darkening to a silhouette that dwindled and vanished into the huge blue of the sky. Nathan was left treading water beside the mermaid, wondering what to do next.

"I'm getting awfully tired," he said.

"I'll hold you up," Denaero promised, swimming closer.

Nathan experienced a brief panic at the proximity of her nakedness, but the twinge was lost in his general exhaustion. All the diving down, and holding his breath, and fighting his fear of being underwater—a fear now gone forever—had worn him out. He felt sleep washing over him, drawing him down into the sea. He tried to say, *I'll be back* as Ezroc had, but he never knew if he managed it. The dark took him, bearing him back to his own world, leaving Denaero alone on the borders of the reef.

IT TOOK some time for Hazel to be satisfied with the potion; she knew she could not afford to get it wrong. According to her phantom instructor, the final result should be clear, with a slight greenish tinge, and her first two attempts were both cloudy and murky, one of them a sinister tint of purple. She tipped them down the loo, hoping there was nothing living in the sewers that would be affected by drinking them, murmuring a deactivating spell as she tugged the handle to flush. Then, back in her room, she started again. It would have been simpler to work in the attic, as Effie Carlow had—there was more space—but she was slightly superstitious about it. Effie had told her she had inherited the Gift, the witchcraft gene, her words malevolent as a curse, as if she were illwishing her own great-grandchild, condemning her to a future of solitude and madness. Working in what had been Effie's spellroom would, Hazel felt, somehow compound the curse, turning her into everything she feared to become. In her bedroom, whatever magic she did was hers, and hers alone.

Besides, it was in the attic she had once seen Nenufar's head emerge from a basin of river water, and the horror of that moment had stayed with her, so she could not even enter there without a chill in her heart.

She mixed the ingredients of the potion in a glass bowl she had borrowed from the kitchen, murmuring the spellwords, thinking it would have been better, or at least more dramatic, if she'd had a cauldron. Fortunately, the mixture didn't require heating, though she knew when she got it right the bowl would grow warm toward the end. She had raided Bartlemy's garden for a couple of the less well-known herbs, waiting till he was busy elsewhere, not wanting to tell him what she was up to. When the charm was completed—when she knew it had worked—*then* she would tell him. If she was going to fail, she preferred to keep it to herself.

This time she concentrated harder, making sure she spoke the incantation at the appropriate moment, watching for color changes as each new ingredient was added. At one point the contents of the bowl turned black and smelled like a whole harbor full of dead fish; then it went bright green, and there was a far-off ripple of music, very fluid in tone, as if the instrument was playing underwater. And then at the last the liquid changed to a sparkling clarity, and she knew this was it.

As the spell climaxed, Hazel did not see the pipe-cleaner doll charring and crumbling into a few flakes of ash—did not notice, while she turned to retrieve the crystal vial, how those flakes drifted into the bowl, swirling around in the potion, congealing at the bottom. But when she looked again, there was the pearl. She poured the liquid through a funnel into the bottle and it rolled out, caught in her palm, a tiny, perfect sphere of rainbow gray, its sheen like oil pollution on a puddle. Hazel had never really liked pearls. She associated them with middle-aged dowdiness, with women in cashmere twinsets and country accents, running fêtes for charity and talking about hunting. But this pearl was different. Not just because it was gray—the color of smoke and shadows—but because it looked, somehow, magical. *Never trust anything that looks magical*, Bartlemy had told her, *because it probably is*. But finding a magical object in a magic potion was to be expected, even if it hadn't featured in the original specification. Finding an unmagical object there—that would have been weird.

"What do I do with it?" Hazel wondered aloud, glaring at the sheet of paper from which her latest instructions had already faded.

After a moment's thought, she repeated the question in Atlantean.

Place the pearl in the bottle, the writing told her, rippling its way across the page. *Without the pearl, the potion will not be viable. The bottle with the pearl must be carried at all times. It is a talisman.*

And then, when the page had cleared, two more words wrote themselves emphatically across it.

Tell Nathan.

The words stayed there for a long time before they began to dissipate.

Something about that final edict made Hazel uncomfortable. She put the pearl in the bottle, corked it, sealed the cork with a magical Command. Then she sent Nathan a text telling him to come and see her as soon as possible, it was important, she had a surprise for him—but all the while there was a niggle at the back of her mind, a dim consciousness that something was not quite right. She went over what she had done from her own notes—*Check,* Bartlemy always said. *Check, double-check, triple-check. The precise wording of a spell may vary, but the elements never do. A tiny error can be catastrophic*—but she didn't think she'd made any mistakes this time. She failed to register the absence of the Nenufar doll from the clutter in her room. After all, it was leftovers from a charm long worn out; she had no more use for it.

Some spell-debris is like radioactive waste, Bartlemy had said, tipping the contents of his brass basin down the sink. *Be very careful how you dispose of it.*

The next morning Hazel had school, and the niggle was pushed even farther back in her thoughts.

In the evening Nathan came around.

He asked Lily for another cappuccino, earning himself a glare from Hazel.

"You're being charming to my mother," she accused. "You know I hate it when you're charming. Anyway, you don't need to. She's known you all your life."

"I like cappuccino," Nathan said. "Especially the froth on the top. Your mum remembers the chocolate powder, too. She's better than Café Nero." Eade didn't have one, but there was a Café Nero in Chizzledown, which he and Eric frequented from time to time.

"Charm!" Hazel reiterated. "You do it much too often. Like chocolate powder on top of everything."

"I have to compensate for you," Nathan said.

"You should be yourself. Nothing more."

"What if my self is charming?" Nathan suggested provocatively. "Sometimes, anyhow."

"Nobody's self is charming," Hazel declared. "Charm is . . . is . . . an acquired virtue. It doesn't grow by itself."

"You can't know that."

At least it was a friendly dispute, Nathan reflected, accepting his cappuccino from a gratified Lily. Franco wasn't around that night, and she had already appalled her daughter by painting her toenails, an activity only allowable in the summer months to go with sandals. In winter it hinted at decadence, and private orgies.

"Next she'll be buying her underwear from Agent Provocator," Hazel grumbled.

Nathan thought about correcting her pronunciation but decided she was doing it deliberately.

"Why not?" he asked.

"How would you feel if Annie bought Provocator underwear?"

"Why're we always talking about underwear these days? You've got a fixation." As a retort, Nathan knew it was probably a mistake, but he couldn't be bothered to be diplomatic with *Hazel*.

"Actually," she said in an arctic voice, "*actually*, I got you 'round here about something *far* more important. But if you're only interested in conversations about knickers—"

"You started the subject," he said. "Not me."

"You went on with it," she said unfairly. She had learned long ago that Nathan could always out-argue her, and being unreasonable was her best policy. Especially since—like Nathan's charm—it came naturally.

"No, I—never mind. Just tell me what's so important."

"I've solved your problem for you, that's all."

"Which problem?" Nathan queried. He could think of a dozen for starters.

"The Widewater one. I've found a spell that will mean you can swim underwater like your mermaid friend, even right down deep where the pressure gets bad. You told me to make myself useful, so I did." She produced the vial, holding it out to him. "The bottle's crystal: you should be able to take it with you. You drink the potion when you get there, but keep the bottle on you because of the pearl. I'm not quite sure how it works but it's a kind of talisman. You could hang it 'round your neck on a piece of string—something like that." She waited expectantly, enjoying the look on Nathan's face.

"Wow," he said faintly. "That's—that's amazing. I didn't mean . . . I didn't think you could do anything like that. The pipe-cleaner trick was brilliant but this—this is the big league. Did . . . did Uncle Barty help?"

"No," Hazel said. "It was just me."

"Wow," Nathan said again. There was a trace element of doubt in his appreciation. "Are you sure . . . it's all right? I mean . . ."

"I haven't tested it," Hazel said. "How could I? Anyway, it took me ages to get the bloody potion right, and there's just enough for one. I don't know how long the effects last: I think it's twelve hours, but it might be twenty-four, the small print wasn't clear. Swallow it and see."

"Drink me," Nathan quoted, holding the vial rather gingerly. "Like Alice in Wonderland. Maybe I'll shrink to the size of a plankton . . . I suppose that would mean it had worked, in a way. Where did you find the spell?"

"In Great-Grandma's stuff." Hazel didn't mention the blank page that had fallen out of one of the books, and the handwriting that wrote itself. She had a feeling Nathan wouldn't like that part.

"It's not that I don't have faith in you," he went on, after a pause. "It's just . . . things like this don't happen. I need a spell to make me swim like a mermaid and hey, presto! one turns up, just in the nick of time. It's too—too pat. Too good to be true."

"It didn't just turn up," Hazel said. "I had to find it—I had to get the ingredients—I had to make it come out right. I burned the midnight oil—at both ends. It was worse than math homework. Now you're acting like I'm trying to con you—or d'you think I messed up?"

"No—no, of course not . . ." *You've messed up before,* he thought. But he didn't say it.

"Look," Hazel said, lapsing unexpectedly into tolerance, "just give it a go. You've got nothing to lose. If it doesn't work, then it doesn't. You're in the same situation you were before. If it *does*—then you come back and grovel to me. Deal?"

"Deal." Nathan grinned suddenly. "You know, whether it works or not, I really am grateful. It was a wonderful thing to do for me. And you always said you didn't like witching."

"I don't," Hazel declared, retreating abruptly into her hair. "It's a bore. But I do lots of things I don't like."

She cleared some space on the duvet, and they sat down while Nathan finished the cappuccino.

"You know your trouble?" Hazel said.

"Mm?"

"You don't believe in magic."

"I suppose I don't," Nathan admitted. "Not the kind that makes everything work out perfectly, anyway."

"You were able to pick up the Traitor's Sword," Hazel reminded him, "even though no one was meant to touch it. You were the right guy in the right place at the right time. Mr. Destiny."

"I know," Nathan said. "It's always bothered me. I didn't *feel* chosen by fate or anything. Just scared. I'm scared a lot, in my dreams."

"How *do* people feel when they're chosen by fate?" Hazel asked.

"Calm and confident?" Nathan hazarded. "Anyway, you don't believe in magic, either. You've always made a point of it."

"No," she said, "but I believe in science."

"In what way is this science?"

"Probability Theory," Hazel stated. "Uncle Barty says that as we have infinity and eternity, everything—*everything*—must happen somewhere. Probably. So maybe, just for once, this is somewhere."

"It's a theory," Nathan said, "even if it isn't very probable."

Hazel felt that tiny vestige of doubt at the back of her mind, but she saw no need to take it out and look at it. After all, as she had said, if the spell didn't work Nathan had lost nothing.

"You could always take an Aqua-Lung as backup," she suggested.

. . .

NATHAN SAW the war-host in his dreams, camped along the western end of the Dragon's Reef. There were no tents—they had no need of them—but their banners of fishskins streamed in the current. They had swordfish lances and spears tipped with narwhal horn, knives and swords of volcanic glass, glinting where the sun penetrated, shields made from the carapace of long-dead turtles, limpet-studded armor, helms decked with teeth and tusks, plumed with colored weeds. Some rode blue sharks, tiger sharks, hammerheads, others huge seahorses with spiny manes or manta rays that glided through the water like stealth bombers. A few came in war-chariots made of giant clams, drawn by teams of dolphins, or reptilian creatures like distant cousins of the icthauryon, with long narrow snouts and snake-thin bodies. Nathan saw Uraki several times, swimming to and fro among the battalions; he always stood out, for Raagu his mount was the only great white, and even the reptiles flinched when he passed. A wisp of a dreamer watching from anywhere and nowhere, Nathan could not interfere, merely spectate.

"We will kill them all," said a dark-haired merman who wore a coronet of white coral around his helm, like icing on a wedding cake. "We will spill their hot blood into the northern seas until the ocean boils and the Great Ice melts in the steam. We will give them no quarter, no mercy—neither warrior nor seal-woman, neither saber-toothed monster nor puling cub. We will—"

"You will find it less easy than you think," Uraki said coldly. "There are brave fighters even among the selkies."

Aha, Nathan thought. Nokosha made an impression.

"Bubbletalk!" said the merking, evidently one of the lesser monarchs. "We will go through them like tuna through a shoal of sardines. They don't even know we're coming."

"They know," said Uraki, and his lips flexed in something like a smile. "Believe me, they know."

Another time—another dream—Nathan saw him talking with the High King. Though their features were humanoid, neither face wore much expression, perhaps because of their piscine genetics. In that they resembled the selkies, whose animal heritage also gave them a certain impassivity, less from the desire to hide their feelings, Nathan thought, than the inability to reveal them. Expression was a human trait, and their humanity was still only half formed. Adequate for killing, Nathan reflected bitterly, but not for showing laughter or compassion.

"The men grow restless," Uraki was saying. "We must move soon."

"Do you think I don't know?" said the king. "Already they begin to eat the reef bare. But I must wait on the shamans—they are harvesting the fireflowers from along the wall, and it will take very many to ensure that every rider and his mount is supplied. The fireflowers must be enspelled so they release their core of heat into the blood. I infer the charms are complex and slow to mature. I dislike the delay—but privily, I am not eager for the battle. Many will die, on both sides."

"Must we kill them all?" Uraki asked reluctantly—almost as if the question was wrenched from his tongue.

"You are less battle-hungry than of yore," said Rhadamu. "Is this the advent of fear?"

"I fear nothing," Uraki insisted. "But—"

"You are fortunate. I fear all the time. I fear for my people—for all peoples—though not for myself. I have few feelings left anymore. Since you executed my last commission . . ."

Nathan sensed Uraki faltering on the verge of speech.

"You did well," Rhadamu continued heavily. "Now there is nothing left to hold me back." *Except the fear.*

"She did not suffer." Uraki spoke as if with difficulty.

"It is well," Rhadamu reiterated. "Soon, we will have suffering enough. I hope to go with the next new moon. The tides then will be with us. Perhaps we may yet take them by surprise."

"No, sire," said Uraki, giving him a very direct look. "They are waiting for us."

"I see," said the king. He did not ask his captain where he had obtained the information. "Ah well. At least it will be a fair fight."

"We have the advantage of numbers," Uraki reminded him. "The odds are many times in our favor."

"That is the kind of fair fight all generals wish for," said the king.

The dream shifted—for a brief moment Nathan glimpsed the shamans, no longer wound together in a single entity but strung out along the wall, plucking the red-tentacled flowers, like living chrysan-themums, that flourished in the sulfurous water. Then they were back in their cave, poured into a huddle by the light of a solitary sea star, whispering together. In their midst on a flat-topped rock was a mirror made from a solid disc of mother-of-pearl. Dim shapes moved in its depths, not reflections but visions. But they were hazy and ill defined; Nathan thought it would be difficult to identify an individual or do more than guess at their activities. The priestesses spread their choppy fingers above the mirror as if trying to draw out the magic, muttering incantations, but the pictures grew no clearer.

One said: "It is Denaero. She is not dead—"

"How can you be sure? The image is blurred."

"I am sure. It must be her. Look! She is somewhere on the reef, hid-ing, waiting to betray us."

"You were sure last time. It could be another."

"If she had been devoured there would be signs. Leftovers."

"The warrior said there were icthauryon hunting, close by the Dragon's Bridge. They leave nothing. One was slain . . ."

"Slain! By whom? Nefanu's pets must not be slain."

Nefanu . . . Nefanu . . .

"We cannot see what happened. Maybe the monster died. All things die in the end."

"Except the Goddess . . ."

Nefanu . . . NEFANU . . .

One said: "Denaero is dead. She had the king's heart. Now it is ours."

"The king's heart should belong only to the queen—the Queen of the Sea!"

NEFANU . . .

"The All-Seeing Mirror cannot lie. Show us the traitors! Show us the ones we must seek out and punish!"

*"Mirror mirror undersea
in shadows whence the demons flee
who is the traitor? who the spy?
Whence the Sight can fill thine Eye?*

Mirror mirror of the night
who is Evil in thy Sight?"

In the sheet of pearl the images melted—changed. For an instant Nathan saw his own face, clear as truth, gasping for air, drowning—bubbles burst from his mouth. It could have been a vision from the future, or almost anytime in the recent past. The priestesses cried out, pulling back in horror, then clustering forward—"Lungbreather!—Legwalker!—*Human, all human*—" But the phantom slipped between their fingers, and the mirror blurred, and the merwomen muttered their charms in vain.

Nathan's dream darkened, and he moved on.

He was on another part of the reef, far from the assembled war-hosts. Ahead was a rocky overhang bearded with swaying weeds, jowled with sea anemones; the darkness beneath might hide the lair of a moray eel or giant octopus. As he approached he saw something moving in the sea gloom—something pale, something dark, shade welling from the shadows like squid ink, spilling out in a cloud. For a second, bodiless though he was, he felt afraid—until he had identified it. Not ink but silk, a million threads unfurling through the water. Mermaid's hair—Denaero's hair. Her hands followed, parting her own tresses to gaze cautiously around her, then the white shape of her face with its questing eyes. Presently, her attention was caught—Nathan turned and saw another mermaid finning toward her, slipping around a shoulder of rock.

"Miyara!"

"Little sister! I knew you were not dead, even before you sent the crab to tell me. I felt it *here*." She touched her stomach. "I taxed Uraki with it: he said the icthauryon took you, but I didn't believe him. He's a very bad liar. How did you get away?"

"My friends saved me—my friend the albatross, and a boy from another world. There was a selkie there, too, but I didn't like *him*."

"A boy from another world? What are you talking about? Mixing with northfolk is bad enough. Denaero, are you in *more* trouble?"

"I'm dead," Denaero pointed out. "How can I be in worse trouble than dead? What's happening at home? Does Father grieve for me?"

"You know Father. He won't allow any of us to mention your name."

"Good," said Denaero. "He grieves. I hope the pain eats his heart."

"He acts like he has no heart," Miyara said. "I am to marry Seppopo, in spite of everything. The wedding is three days from now. I told Father I couldn't do it—I love Jaino—but he said his children were all willful and disobedient, and I could choose between doing my duty or being fed to the sharks. So you see—"

"He's ridiculous!" Denaero declared passionately. "Does he plan to chain all his daughters to the Dragon's Bridge until some monster shows up to devour them? Why does everything have to be about killing?"

"Men are like that," Miyara said fatalistically.

"All except Ezroc," said Denaero, "and Nathan. But Ezroc's a bird, and Nathan's from another world, so I don't suppose they count."

"What is this otherworld nonsense?"

"Nathan's a legwalker," Denaero said. "A real one. Human. He comes from a world with lots of land, where people walk about on legs *all the time.*"

"I don't believe it," said Miyara. "They'd get tired. You need sea to support you. Anyway, how does he get to Widewater?"

"He dreams himself here," Denaero answered. "The shamans can do it—their spirits travel in dreams, or so they claim. Well, Nathan can travel not just in spirit but sometimes with his whole body. He'll come back soon, I know he will."

"He must be a very powerful magician," Miyara said doubtfully.

In a pig's eye, Nathan thought.

"He is," Denaero asserted with conviction. "Except he calls it something else. Physics. He's really clever. He's got a plan to stop the war."

"Stop the war? You're mad. You always had your head in the foam. The war can't be stopped—the killing can't be stopped—and you have to live in hiding, and I have to marry fat old Seppopo, and Jaino will be killed in the battle, and in the end I'll probably die of a broken heart—"

"Don't be so *dry*!" Denaero retorted. "You're as useless as a fish out of water. It would serve you right if you *did* have to marry Seppopo. You know what happens with people like you? You say: *It can't be done, it can't be done,* so you don't try to do it—whatever it is—and then of course it doesn't get done. At least I'm trying. I might get eaten by icthauryon or—or blasted in the wrath of the Goddess, but that's better than just wringing my hands and moaning *It can't be done* all the time. And I'd rather be eaten by icthauryon than married to Seppopo any day."

"You don't know what you're talking about."

"Yes I do," Denaero said. "I've looked into the mouth of an icthauryon. Have you?"

"I've looked into the mouth of Seppopo," Miyara said gloomily.

There was a moment when their hands twined, and the argument was over as quickly as it had begun.

Then Denaero said in an altered voice, "Something's coming," and dragged her sister into the shadow under the rock.

A turtle was cruising along the borders of the reef, a very large turtle. Nathan was visited by the notion that it was the same one Ezroc and Keerye had met way back in Widewater time. All turtles look old—it goes with their physiognomy—but this one looked even older, an almost prehistoric figure, with a face both wise and wizened and eyes that sidled to and fro under their horny lids. His shell was stubbled with barnacles and scored from the attacks of shark and sea scorpion; the tip of his tail had been bitten off. His broad flippers moved slowly as though inhibited by age or arthritis. But as he drew level with the mermaids' hiding place he halted, sculling backward, though no sound or movement had betrayed them.

"Denaero!" he called, as if to the sea at large. "I seek a mermaid named Denaero!"

There was a tiny pause—a pause for hesitation, speculation, doubt.

Then Denaero's voice issued from beneath the rock. "Who's asking?"

"I come from the albatross, Ezroc son of Tilarc. I have an urgent message for Denaero, Rhadamu's daughter."

"I am she." Denaero slid from the shadows alone, her hair clouding about her head. In one hand she carried a small dagger obtained from somewhere; the blade was shaped like an elongated leaf and glinted as if chipped from crystal. Carrying the weapon transformed her: suddenly she was no longer the half child, half woman Nathan had known but a deadly, alien creature.

He thought: *That's what fear does to people. That's what war does.*

"There are many mermaids in the sea," said the turtle. "You fit the description, but so might a dozen others. How do I know you speak truth, and I can trust you?"

"How do I know *I* can trust *you?*" Denaero countered. "I am wanted by the High King my father, or I would be if he knew I was still alive. There should be a reward for my capture. It's just an oversight that there isn't. You might be setting a trap for me."

"You are Denaero," the turtle said. "Ezroc told me you were spirited and contrary. You are indeed Denaero. Greeting, merwoman. I have a message—"

"Greeting," Denaero said perfunctorily. "What message? You said it was urgent."

"Ezroc said to tell you the northfolk are coming. They do not wait on Rhadamu's pleasure. The Spotted One leads an army south—I have seen them myself. There are perhaps three thousand selkies, with as many other creatures following. Seabirds fly above them in such numbers they are like a stormcloud riding down the sky. The selkies bear arms, though they rarely do so—arms they have stored a long time in secret places on the Great Ice. They have longswords of silverflint and pikes of hammerhorn, and arrows tipped with stingray barbs that will travel fast and far through the water. They may be unaccustomed to such weaponry but they have kept in practice, and they know they must fight for their lives. Carrionfish follow them; icthauryon and hydrosaurs are in their train. They smell bloodshed to come."

"I do not . . . want . . . bloodshed," Denaero said. "I must get word to my father, but . . . Tell Ezroc to meet me here. He must bring a selkie—not Nokosha, one more like Keerye—one who will help. We will need a lungbreather in case Nathan does not come."

I'll be there, Nathan vowed. *Somehow.*

"We have to try the plan . . ."

"What plan?" the turtle asked.

"Ezroc knows. Tell him—it's our only chance to stop the war. I'll see him here. Tell him . . ."

"I will," said the turtle. "But wars are easy to start, and very hard to stop. Once the killing begins . . ."

"It must *not*," said Denaero with all the determination of someone gambling on a forlorn hope. "Please go swiftly—as swiftly as you can."

"Don't worry," said the turtle. "I'm faster than you'd think, or the sharks would have had me years ago. May the tides of fortune go with you!"

He swam off at surprising speed, and Miyara emerged from the crevasse beside her sister.

"You can't stop it," she said. "What are we going to do?"

And, in mitigation: "At least Father will have to put off my wedding."

"You must find a way to warn him," Denaero said. "I can't: I'm dead. It's up to you."

"How? If I tell him I've seen you—"

"Say you got it from a smallfish, or a passing ray, or whatever. Use your imagination! Even if he doesn't believe you, he'll think about it—he'll check up—look into it. Go—go now!"

"What will *you* do?"

"Wait for the others," Denaero said. "We have a Plan." She gave it an audible capital letter.

"What plan?"

"Never mind. Just go!" Denaero prodded her impatiently out into the open water. When she was alone, she retreated close to the rocks, waiting with her hands pressed against her cheeks, staring out to sea as though willing Nathan or Ezroc to appear.

I'll be there, Nathan called, but he had no voice, no power, and the dark of the sea swallowed him, and he woke on other shores.

The
Horn of
Last Resort

Annie had had lunch with Pobjoy twice now, but because Nathan was working he hadn't realized, and she wasn't yet ready to mention it. He would ask questions to which she had no answers, and as it was, she wasn't sure there was anything to answer questions about. After all, it was only lunch . . . two lunches. Annie's knowledge of the etiquette of dating was very hazy. She had been with Daniel Ward from when she was eighteen until he died, and apart from her disastrous friendship with Michael Addison there had been no one since. Lunch, she decided, didn't rate very high on the dating scale. Lunch was a preliminary, a way of testing the water. A lunch invitation could be purely platonic in intent both from the viewpoint of the luncher and the lunchee. It wasn't like dinner, which happened in the evening, with the inevitable sexual undertones of any date that ends up in the dark. And Pobjoy hadn't attempted to hold her hand or take her arm, hadn't kissed her, not even on the cheek, although he had stared at her very hard a couple of times, a deep-in-the-eyes stare that might have meant something, or might just have been part of his standard interrogation technique. *He has no charm and no sense of humor,* she concluded partway through the second of the lunches. *He's determined to set limits on his imagination in case it takes him somewhere he's afraid to go.*

But he had *something*—a gravity, an intensity, a vulnerable streak hiding behind the grim armor of his outward persona. And by the end of that same lunch Annie had begun to wonder if the missing elements—charm, humor, imagination—were in there somewhere, left over from a more carefree past, creaking from lack of use.

"I come from an army family," Pobjoy told her. "Father, grandfather, and so on back into history. There was a Pobjoy with Gordon at Khartoum, another at Rourke's Drift. Wherever there was a last stand, we were there. I was meant to follow in the ancestral footsteps, but there wasn't enough money for Sandhurst and I decided to take a different route. Teenage rebellion. Didn't go down at all well with my relatives."

"Your act of teenage rebellion," Annie said, groping for clarification, "was joining the police force?"

"That's it."

"Most people," Annie pointed out, carefully, "play their music too loud, take drugs, drink too much, have sex with the wrong partners, run away to sea, whatever. Were you never tempted to do any of that?"

"I've been known to drink too much," he admitted. "I smoked for a bit. Tried a couple of spliffs."

"But you didn't inhale?"

"Yes I did. I—you're taking the piss."

"Just a little," Annie said.

He relaxed, laughed a bit—just a bit—asked her: "What about you? Did you do any of that stuff?"

"A few. I didn't run away to sea, though I thought about it. As a child, anyway. I wanted to be a pirate or a smuggler, but I was stuck in the wrong century, and besides, I wasn't sure I'd be brave enough. So I read books—lots and lots of books—where I could be a pirate, and a smuggler, and run away, and when I closed the book I was safe back home again."

"Is that why you sell books now?" Pobjoy asked.

"It isn't why I started. I trained in IT—that was the kind of work I was looking for when I first came to Eade. Bartlemy owns the shop: he said he wanted someone with computer skills to manage it. So I did, and . . . it suits me. I sell imagination, adventure, otherworlds. All the things you don't believe in."

"I'm a policeman," he said. "It's my job not to believe in things."

But he said it quite gently.

Later, back in front of her computer screen, Annie's mind wandered, though she wasn't sure where to. Around four she popped into the deli to arrange coffee with Lily Bagot. Lily had survived being married to Dave, who hit her, and going out with nice-but-dull Neil, acquired via an ad in the newspaper, and now she had Franco the toyboy and was happily scandalizing the village. If anyone knew about dating, it would be Lily.

I need advice, Annie decided. Bartlemy was her usual source when she wanted to discuss something, but she didn't think he'd be very expert on the twenty-first-century dating game, or its impact on teenage offspring.

The next morning, over coffee in the shop, she told Lily about Pobjoy.

"He's a cop," Lily said in a discouraging tone. "He wanted to arrest Hazel when that cup got stolen. And Nathan. How could you be going out with him?"

"I'm not going out with him," Annie said. "It was just lunch. Anyway, it was all a mistake, him wanting to arrest the kids. And he was right about the murders, wasn't he? And he was wonderful when Nathan was kidnapped by that boy from his school."

"All right," Lily conceded. "But you have to watch out for cops. My second cousin in London married one. He worked Vice. After fifteen years of marriage he left her for a hooker. It just goes to show."

"James isn't like that at all," Annie said, blushing faintly because she'd used his name. First-name terms may be the norm in contemporary society, but not for policemen.

"Have you told Nathan yet?"

"N-no. There isn't really anything to tell."

"Have you—you know?"

"No!"

"It's bloody difficult with kids around," Lily remarked sapiently. "I thought Hazel would get used to Franco, but she hasn't. You find yourself sneaking into the bedroom in the middle of the night trying not to be heard, like when *we* were the kids, dodging our parents. You'd have thought we'd have left all that behind by now. It's weird. Like—what's the word I'm looking for?"

"Irony?" Annie supplied.

"I expect so. It's all the wrong way 'round, isn't it? I wish Hazel had a steady; it would give her something else to think about. I love her so much, but she's always been a strange, secretive girl. I mean, at her age I'd been with Nick Cowley for nearly a year. You don't think she and Nathan—?"

"No," Annie said. "Not yet."

"Of course, *he* wouldn't go for *her.*" Lily sighed. "He's so good looking, so clever . . . Hazel's sort of—bright but not bright, if you see what I mean. Not good at the school stuff, but she's a smart girl."

"We think she's really special," Annie said, now completely sidetracked and uncomfortably aware she sounded like an American soap opera. That was the thing about children: they took over your life, they even took over conversations that were supposed to be about something else. "I know Nathan loves her a lot. I'm just not sure what *kind* of love it is. I don't think he's sure, either."

"It's their hormones," Lily said, as everyone does. "And ours. Life's a muddle, isn't it?"

Which, Annie thought later, really said it all.

"WHAT'S A Leviathan?" Nathan asked his mother over supper that evening.

"Sea monster," Annie said. "A very large one. I think it's meant to wake at the end of the world—or maybe that's the Kraken. I've a feeling it might be biblical, but I don't know the Bible as well as I should. Could be in Revelation. Are you planning to get up one morning covered in Leviathan-spit? Only I don't want the washing machine blocked up again."

"I'm not sure it can have spit if it's underwater," Nathan said. "D'you know what it looks like?"

"No, I don't. I've always thought of sea monsters as pretty standard—big marine dragons with lots of spiky fins, or finny spikes—but I imagine it could be a sort of giant squid. Or something with lots of heads, like the Lernean Hydra."

"What's that?"

"The one Heracles met: remember? Every time he cut one head off, it grew two more. Keep that in mind if you're thinking of confronting one. You don't want to start cutting off heads."

"Mm."

"How much danger are you in?" Annie asked, dropping the flippancy for a moment.

"Well," Nathan said candidly, "I'm in the middle of a war, but I think I *might* be able to stop it. I've got a plan—a diversion—but I have to get back there. It's been two nights now . . ."

"You will," Annie said, not certain whether she was glad or sorry, or just chronically terrified for him. "You always do. Am I allowed to ask what's going on? Where does the Leviathan come in?"

"Someone referred to it, and the priestesses were afraid. That means the Goddess is afraid. She's the Queen of the Sea—like Nenufar, only worse—so if there's a sea monster she's scared of, it might be a good thing. Or it might mean the Leviathan is so horrifying even the bad guys are afraid of it."

"Call Uncle Barty," Annie said. "Or Google."

After supper Nathan tried both. Googling elicited reams of information, including biblical sources—Job, not Revelation—several conflicting physical descriptions based largely on fiction, and random accounts of how the Leviathan would wake at the last trumpet and swallow whole continents, armies of seraphim and demons, and anyone else who got in the way.

Bartlemy was more specific. "We don't know what it looks like," he said, "but it's meant to be the largest monster in history or legend, even bigger than the Midgard Serpent, which is twined around the world with its tail in its mouth. God told Job, in one of those anything-you-can-do-I-can-do-better conversations between mortal and immortal, that he could catch Leviathan on a hook. There are scholars who take that to imply that this was a challenge even for a deity, and Leviathan must therefore be a creature big enough to devour the gods themselves. According to others, it has slept since the beginning of Time and will not wake till the end, when the forces of Good and Evil come face-to-face in the final great battle. Or not, as the case may be. The last-battle idea is a little out of fashion now. We favor a slow death for the universe, or possibly a reversal of the Big Bang. Whatever option you go for, hopefully it's a long way off. However, things will be different in otherworlds."

"There's a battle brewing," Nathan said, "but it isn't exactly Good versus Evil. Sort of a mix on both sides."

"It always is," Bartlemy said. "Were you planning to raise the Leviathan in order to put them off?"

"Something like that. But I've got other ideas as well—probably just as useless. D'you know what would happen if I did?"

"That's rather the problem," said Bartlemy. "You see, no one ever *has* raised the Leviathan, or at least not in this universe. Any description of what might follow falls into the realm of story or prophecy, and prophecy is a very uncertain guide to the future. Look at all those Greek kings who consulted the oracle at Delphi, adjusted their actions accordingly, and thus brought about the very fate they were trying to avoid. Besides, prophecy is often wrong. You just don't get to hear about the inaccurate ones. If I were you, I'd let sleeping monsters lie. For one thing, it would probably take a whole orchestra to wake a Leviathan. With nuclear weapons. The bigger they are, the deeper they sleep."

Nathan went to bed with that thought, hanging Hazel's vial around his neck, but he couldn't sleep and for the third night running he felt he was going nowhere. In spite of previous experience he was always worried he'd be unable to get back to his dreamworld adventure and finish what he'd started. He got up in the middle of the night and climbed up to the Den, out through the skylight onto the roof. The star was there—the Grandir's star—looking down at him, a fixed pinpoint of light. He found himself thinking of the shamans.

> *Mirror mirror of the night*
> *Who is evil in thy Sight?*

The verse had been in the language of the merfolk, but in his head it slipped easily into English, sounding like something from a children's fairy tale. He began making up his own verse:

> *Twinkle twinkle little star*
> *How I wonder what you are*
> *Up above the world so high*
> *Watching with your single Eye.*

This rhyming stuff is easy, he decided, huddling himself into his jacket against the chill of the winter night. *You, too, can be a priestess—or priest—of the dark; all it takes is a flair for poetry.* Not the Shakespearean kind, more the birthday-greeting-card variety.

And now he remembered that it wasn't just the countdown to war, it was the countdown to Christmas, and he hadn't done his Christmas shopping yet, and why was it girls were so difficult to buy presents for? He found himself thinking about another star—one that didn't belong in the sky—the star the three kings had followed, till it came to rest above a stable where a newborn baby lay in the straw. Was it blasphemy to wonder if that star, too, had come from another cosmos, and in a high tower beyond the Gate another Grandir had looked up at pictures on the ceiling—pictures of a sleeping infant who might be part of some ineffable plan to save a world? For no reason that he could explain the thought made Nathan's blood run cold. Supposing the whole of Christianity had mushroomed from that plan, just as the Grail legend had wrapped itself around the Cup of the Thorns and spread throughout the multiverse. Supposing Jesus himself had simply been a boy with a job to do, who had listened to a voice from an alternative universe and called it God. It was too terrifying to contemplate.

Nathan found he was trembling, though not from the cold. *I'm not the son of a god,* he told himself. *I'm not the savior of anything, I'm not special, I have no powers—all I can do is dream myself between worlds. I'm not going to die prematurely as a sort of sacrifice believing the sins of the world are on my shoulders.*

The thought steadied him. Of course, there were a lot of other ways he could die prematurely, particularly on Widewater, but there was no point in thinking about that. He scrambled down from the skylight and made himself a cup of hot chocolate to calm his nerves. Just for a minute, it was as if his whole view of things had flipped over into madness, and everything safe, everything normal, had been exposed as false and treacherous and insecure. He was walking on a thin skin of solid ground above quicksand, and for an instant his foot had gone through . . .

He pulled his imagination up short and told himself that any parallels between the story of Christ and his own were delusions of grandeur. Whether truth or legend, Jesus had been a good man who got hold of a good idea—Love thine enemy—and bequeathed it to the world in an attempt to make things better, and it was only human nature, not some diabolical scheme, if far too often it had made things worse. Bartlemy had always said that everything was part of a Great Pattern, and Destiny would give events a tweak, once in a while, to make them fall into place, but he, Nathan, was too small, too ordinary, to merit the attention of Destiny, and his part of the Pattern was surely only a careless squiggle out on the edge, nothing to do with the unknown mantra at its heart.

The chocolate soothed him, pumping serotonins into his brain, and he went back to thinking about Christmas presents, and once in bed he slept normally, without any dreams.

THE NEXT night Nathan was back on Widewater. There was a moment of the usual panic when he found himself solid, alone in the midst of the open sea, paddling to keep his head above water. Then Denaero was with him, and the panic subsided.

"Ezroc was meant to meet me here," she said. "I didn't know if you'd make it. I'm so glad you've come. The selkies haven't waited for our attack—they're attacking first—"

"A preemptive strike," Nathan said, and spluttered as a wavelet splashed into his face. "I . . . know."

"We *must* do something—try your plan—but the caverns are far below the reef, you won't be able to—"

"I've got a kind of charm here," Nathan said. "A magic potion. It might help. When we're ready, I'll try it. Can you—?"

Denaero was already supporting him, her webbed hands gripping him underarm.

"Is that it?" she asked, as he lifted the vial.

"Yes . . ."

"You must have powerful witches in your world."

"Not very," he said. "That's why I'm not sure if it'll work."

"Try it now!"

Ah well, he thought. *Here's to Hazel*. He pulled out the cork and drank it down in one go.

He expected it to taste awful, like medicine, since potions and medicines were vaguely connected in his mind, and all medicine was unpleasant. Instead it tasted mostly like water—water with an edge, the kind you get in advertisements, water that has trickled down from mountain springs and done various exciting things on its way to the bottle. It had a flavor of summer, and a flavor of shadows, and a tang of something familiar that Nathan couldn't quite place, something to do with childhood. He almost swallowed the pearl by accident. Then he recorked the vial and left it dangling against his chest.

He knew at once it had worked. He wasn't treading water anymore, merely floating, as much at ease as a jellyfish. He slipped from Denaero's grasp and turned to face her. "My God!"

"Which god?" Denaero asked with interest.

"Any old god! It *works*—it really works. Look!" He dived, somersaulted, came up for air that he didn't need. He couldn't decide if he was breathing underwater or if breathing was no longer a requirement. This was magic the way it ought to be, the storybook kind, the fairy tale—he was like Kay Harker in *The Midnight Folk*, who had flown with a bat, dived with an otter, swum with a mermaid. This was *enchantment*. He kicked and his body leapt from the water like a dolphin, crashing down in a cloud of spray. When he came up again, Denaero was seizing his arms, shaking him.

"What are you *doing*? D'you want every fish on the reef to come after us?"

"Sorry. Sorry . . ."

"I've been hiding here for a week—I've been so quiet, so careful—and now you come along and start splashing about like a baby whale—"

"Sorry."

"Stop saying sorry."

"Sorry." His chances of impressing Denaero, Nathan reflected, had always been practically nil. Evidently they still were.

"How long will the magic last?" she went on.

"Maybe twelve hours, maybe more. My friend—the witch—wasn't certain."

"She doesn't sound like much of a witch to me," Denaero said, flatly contradicting her earlier statement about the efficacy of his native witches.

They lapsed into a largely pointless quarrel that ended with Denaero apologizing for impugning Hazel's sorcerous skills and then glancing up, with one of her swift mood changes, her face lightening as Ezroc came winging down from the sky.

"I couldn't bring a selkie," he said. "There was no one I trusted, and Nokosha wouldn't listen. He's set on war. I'm glad Nathan's here, but—"

"He's taken a magic potion, which means he can swim like one of us," Denaero said. Having established his otherworldly credentials, Nathan realized there was little he could do that would surprise them. "We don't need anyone else."

"I've been wondering how we're going to move the boulder sealing the main entrance," Nathan said. "Considering it was put there by the Goddess—I mean, is it very big?"

"I've no idea," said Denaero. "This is your plan. You sort it out. First we have to get in through the secret door—that'll be difficult enough—then we'll deal with the rest, opening the caves and—"

"I thought you knew the way," Nathan interrupted.

"Yes, but I've never been inside. Only the High King and the shamans are allowed to do that, and they don't talk about it. It's forbidden to everyone else. There's a guardian on the door—"

"What kind of a guardian?" Nathan said with foreboding.

"I don't know exactly. Something nasty. I saw it once, but I was very young. I just remember lots of teeth."

"It wouldn't be—a dragon? I mean, this is the Dragon's Reef . . ." He had known all along there would be a dragon.

Unexpectedly, Denaero gave a peal of laughter. "We have dragons here," she said. "I'll show you one. They're very frightening . . . Ezroc, can you wait for us?" And, in words of familiar ill omen: "We may be some time."

"I'll wait, but not too long. Nokosha plans to attack with the dawn. I should be with him. The northfolk are my people—I have to stand by them. It's a question of loyalty—you understand?"

"Oh yes," said Denaero. "Men's stupid honor, and their stupid loyalties, and their stupid stupid wars. I understand."

"I'm not like that," Nathan said.

"You're from another world."

Nathan was silent, not certain his world was deserving of a separate category. The whole muddle of honor and loyalty and war and general stupidity was, he suspected, more or less commonplace throughout the multiverse.

Ezroc said: "It's not long till sunset. You shouldn't delay."

Nathan thought, too late, that they should have been better prepared—Denaero had her dagger but he needed a weapon of some kind, and explosives for moving the boulder, and all sorts of things he didn't have and couldn't get.

"Farewell," said the albatross. "May the winds of fate bring you long life and good fortune."

"The Force be with you," Nathan responded, unable, on the spur of the moment, to think of anything else.

"May the tides of destiny carry you to the pathways of the moon," Denaero intoned formally.

"Live long and prosper," Nathan quipped.

Finally, they dived.

And now this was magic indeed. The water no longer dragged or resisted him—instead it seemed to flow not just past him but through him, as if he were part of it, moving with its currents, rocked in its storms and its gentleness. He remembered how, at the end of Andersen's "Little Mermaid," the eponymous heroine had felt her breast melt into foam, and he began to comprehend what it meant to be merfolk, to be a creature not so much half fish as half sea, a spirit at one with its element. Little wonder they felt no pressure even at great depths, and their fealty to Nefanu was less worship than kinship—the same tides flowed in the veins of merfolk and Goddess alike. Humans, he had learned at school, are about 60 percent water, but he sensed the potion had somehow increased the percentage, melting his too solid flesh, transforming him into a being whose pulse beat was the waves and whose lifeblood was the surges of the deep.

And the water brought him messages—the rippled pattern of a nearby shoal of yellowstripe, flickering through the coral, the silent swoosh of a passing ray, the shifting coils of a moray eel stirring in its lair.

"Follow me," said Denaero. "I will show you the dragons of Dragon's Reef."

Now that he was so far down, he could see the form of the Western Reef more clearly: the ocean currents or some other phenomenon had eroded the rock in such a way that the upper section spread out like the cap of a giant mushroom while the supporting cliff had been eaten away. What remained was a species of thick trunk joining the reef to a broad plateau of rock below—rock in shelves and planes and strata— with here and there a chasm opening on blue darkness, so Nathan guessed the seabed must be much farther down. The reef was the highest point of a sprawling mountain ridge, a strange formation coral-grown and sun-touched, teeming with the life of the shallows, while far beneath was the eternal midnight of the ocean vales where creatures lived that never came up for light. Even under the overhang of the mushroom cap it was gloomy, though the potion seemed to have endowed Nathan with mervision, and he could distinguish rippling curtains of weed and the glimmer of tiny fish darting to and fro.

Denaero paused by one such curtain, parting the stems. "Look!" she said. A piece of the weed had broken free and hovered in the gap, a curling tendril like an S with too many bends, sporting leaves that fanned in the current and decorated with waving spines thin as gossamer. At one end was a minute encrustation like the head of a dragonet, with round sea-beryl eyes and tip-tilted snout. Denaero stroked beneath its chin with her fingertip, and suddenly Nathan saw it was real, though its camouflage was perfect, not a weed fragment but a miniature dragon as delicate as a butterfly, with leafy fins and sinuous body.

He had a feeling there were such creatures in our world—he must have seen them on television—but it was different, so different, when you saw them for real. The sea, he decided, with or without sorcery, was indeed a magical place.

"This is one of our dragons," Denaero said. "Isn't he beautiful? But I don't think he would be much good at guarding anything."

They swam on, descending farther, gliding above the lower stratum of rock. Overhead they saw the arch of the Dragon's Bridge, while below them the ridge was split by a long canyon with a path of sand visible between its walls. There the march of the lobsters had passed, but Denaero appeared untroubled by the recollection. Merfolk lived in the moment, Nathan thought; both her peril and her fear were forgotten, replaced by the anticipation of fears—and perils—to come.

Beyond the bridge, along the borders of the main reef, they plunged still deeper, past great bastions of stone, down into the dark. Denaero plucked a sea star from the rock and held it in front of her, a small nodule of light in the vast glooms of the sea.

The pressure here would be instant death to an unprotected diver, Nathan guessed, and for a second he worried that the spell might fail, but that was like worrying about an air crash when you were on a plane: there was nothing you could do, so why bother? He pushed the worry aside and went on.

"I didn't realize the reef was so big," he said to Denaero when they'd been swimming for some time.

"It's the greatest of the twelve," she said. "One reef for each tribe— one king for each kingdom—but ours is the largest. Even the Long Reef of Imarnu is shorter. That's why my father is High King."

After a while she continued: "The caverns are under the mountains. The main entrance was supposed to be somewhere along the top, but no one knows exactly where: the boulder would be overgrown with coral and weed now, indistinguishable from the surrounding rocks. It isn't a secret, you understand; it's just that nobody knows where it is."

"And the door that *is* meant to be secret?" Nathan said with emphasis.

"It's at the foot of the mountains. In the dark."

It would be, Nathan thought.

Now it was altogether black. The tiny glow of the sea star showed Denaero's hand, her arm, the swirl of her hair coiling in her wake. Every so often some small luminous creature would swim past, flourishing a glitter of antennae: ghost-shrimps, translucent worms, strange hairy fishy things whose filmy bodies appeared almost too insubstantial to exist. Their only substance was the light, the kernel of phosphorescence they carried within them like an internal lamp, gleaming in the ocean night. And once in a while Nathan had the impression of something far larger in their vicinity, as a long string of lights hove out of the blackness, like portholes on the side of a submarine. (He wasn't sure submarines *had* portholes, but even if they didn't, that was the image his brain supplied.)

He lost all sense of time. They seemed to have been swimming through the dark forever, in an unchanging midnight where the sun would never penetrate. In another state of being he had been afraid of the water—the blue rush of bubbles, the air expelled from his lungs—

now he was so much a part of it, he felt himself losing touch with the world above, as if the ocean deep was his long home and there was nowhere else he had ever been, nowhere else to be.

They had not spoken for what felt like hours. The vast silence of the undersea got inside them, making speech, like breathing, seem an alien thing, a function of other beings, in other worlds. Even Denaero appeared affected by it. As for Nathan, all the universes he had ever seen shrank to an atom of memory; he felt absorbed into the dark and the gigantic entity of the sea.

Denaero's voice came as a shock, intruding on the silence like the whisper of a bell.

"It's somewhere here," she said.

The light of the sea star showed the mountain roots sinking into sand, and details of the cliff rising like a wall above him. "I followed my father here once," Denaero volunteered. "With the shamans. I was very small, and I swam in their wave pattern. They never detected me."

She was always curious, Nathan thought. Going into forbidden places, making the wrong friends, doing the wrong things. Quibbling, quarreling, being difficult. And suddenly, in a distant sort of way, he was reminded of Hazel—Hazel who was farther away than the farthest sun, in another element, another universe—a speck of familiarity on the outer reaches of his thought. Hazel his companion, his ally and friend. And with the idea of Hazel came the awareness that the sea was not the only world, and somewhere every ocean came to shore, and the sands reached out beyond the waves toward daybreak and the realms of Land.

It was strange how, in every world, sooner or later there was some-one who reminded him of Hazel.

"Here!" Denaero said, on a note of triumph. "This is it."

There was a pointed arch cut into the rock, little more than a crude triangle tapering from a narrow base to the apex some seven feet up. By the faint purplish glow of the sea star Nathan saw that it framed a door—an ordinary door, apart from its shape, with a handle in the form of a whorled shell and hinges that seemed to be made of bone and fastened with leatherwrack, though in the dim light he couldn't be sure. Spongy growths padded the frame and in the center the carved head of a fish protruded, its mouth open in a threatening gape and set with a full complement of what looked like genuine teeth, long and curved and gleaming with a toothy gleam.

"It's a special door," Denaero explained, knowledgeably. "You turn *this* and pull, and it opens. I saw my father do it."

Nathan was about to say something mildly sarcastic when he realized that under the sea a door would generally be just a hole in the rock. "Clever," he commented blandly. "Where's the guardian?"

"I'm not sure. I think it might be—that." She indicated the fish head. "I was only a child when I saw it, and there's never much light. With all those pointy teeth, it *did* look scary."

"If there's no guardian," Nathan said, "what keeps people away?"

"They stay away because they're told to," Denaero said. "Anyhow, there's nothing to go inside for except air. The treasures belong to the Goddess: no one would touch them. And who wants to be in a cave full of *air*?"

"Well, we do," Nathan pointed out. "Is it locked? The door, I mean."

"What's . . . *locked*?"

"Never mind."

Denaero passed him the sea star and, taking the knob in both hands, twisted it and pulled. The door swung back sharply, throwing her against Nathan—she laughed her sudden laugh, making bubbles in the water. Nathan dropped the star, retrieved it before it could swim away, and they both peered inside. Beyond was a small stone chamber— perhaps three people might have stood there, huddled close together— and a second door, this time with no fish head.

"What do we do?" Denaero asked.

"I suppose we go in."

He stepped through the gap and tried the other door, but it wouldn't open. "What did your father do?"

"He went in," Denaero said, plainly struggling to recall things accurately, "he and two of the shamans. Then they closed the door. The other shamans waited for a while, then they followed him. I couldn't really see into the chamber—I was hiding behind those rocks over there—so . . ."

"Did you hear them chant a spell or anything?"

"I don't remember."

"All right," Nathan said. "Let's give it a go. In you come . . . then we shut the door." The sponges, he assumed, would make it watertight—or airtight. He glanced around and saw, set in a groove, a lever made of bone. The kind of lever that you pulled and something happened. He gave it a jerk—it was stiff from lack of use—and there was the whir of a pump jolting into action somewhere above, and a slot opened at the base of the door through which they had entered.

"What's going on?" Denaero demanded, clutching Nathan's T-shirt. He was getting used to being clutched in this way and managed not to focus on the closeness of her bare breasts.

"It's mechanical," he said, "though I suppose it could be operated by some kind of automatic spell. I don't know how else the pump would function. The water's being expelled from the chamber via the gap under the door; you can see the air coming in through that vent up there. When all the water's gone we'll be able to open the *other* door and get into the cave."

"How do you know?" Denaero sounded almost petulant. "You've never been here. You come from another world—a world of land. You can't possibly know how it works."

"It's logical," Nathan explained. "Anyway, in my world we use something similar to get people in and out of ships that can go under the sea."

"I've heard of ships," Denaero said. "But I thought they were meant to float."

Explanations only make things more complicated, Nathan decided. "You'd better *change*," he said. "You're going to need your legs for walking."

"But I can't walk!" Denaero protested. "How should I? *I'm* not a legwalker."

"You have the option of legs. You must use them sometimes."

"When? There's nothing to walk on."

"Why didn't you think of that before? You knew we were going into the caverns of air . . ."

"I just *didn't*. I was—I was thinking of other things . . ."

"You'll have to hang on to me then," Nathan said. "My turn to hold you up."

The water was draining fast. Denaero's tail seemed to dissolve, dividing into two, scales softening into the smoothness of skin. The forked tail fin shrank and paled into feet, placed unsteadily on the rock. As the level dropped Denaero's knees started to fold; she wound her arms tightly around Nathan's chest. "How can I balance?" she wailed. "My feet are too small. How can they support my whole body?"

"Mine do," Nathan said, half propping her up, half lifting her, trying not to focus on her nakedness. She was so slight, she weighed almost nothing. "Just keep holding on to me and try to walk on them, the way I do. Look, the slot's closing—the water's gone. We should be able to—"

But the second door opened by itself.

Nathan hobbled through, hampered by the mermaid, who was looking down at his feet to see how they worked. Exposed to air, the sea star no longer glowed, flapping helplessly on the rock where they had let it fall, but light came from somewhere, a pale light from a source a long way off, showing them that what they had entered was less a cave than an enormous void hollowed in the mountain. The roof was so far above them as to be almost irrelevant; great shadows dripped down the walls; here and there a clump of stalactites extruded from the darkness like a gigantic chandelier. The floor was split into huge shelves and steps, crunchy with the shards of splintered shells and the bones of sea creatures trapped there when the water was driven out. And it was dry. Dust-dry, bone-dry, dry as a tomb. Nothing lived there. A black frazzle of what had been weed sprawled close by, crumbling to powder at a touch. Nathan heard Denaero's breath wheezing in her throat.

"It's awful here," she whispered. It was the kind of place where you wanted to whisper, even though there was nobody around to overhear what you said.

"Will you be all right?" Nathan asked, wondering if he should send her back outside.

"Yes. It's only the walking—it's like knives cutting into my feet."

Nathan glanced down. "If you try treading on the bare rock instead of the shells," he said, "you'll be a lot more comfortable."

Together, they stumbled forward.

They began to see other things scattered among the debris on the ground—things Denaero stared at in fascination and bewilderment. Nathan, bemused by the potion, gazed at them with a disturbing sense of recognition, as if they were objects he remembered from long ago, whose use and style were now alien to him. They were made of wood and ceramic and metal, substances the mermaid had rarely seen—urns of chipped terra-cotta and tarnished bronze, goblets, caskets, candelabra, all gold and silver and studded with precious stones, swords, shields, helmets—sickles and chisels, forks and ladles, something that looked like a plowshare, something else that might have been a churn. Farther on there was part of a chariot with a single spiked wheel— "What's a wheel?" Denaero asked—and the hulks of broken ships, with curving ribs and fallen mast, one with a prow in the form of a swan; another, a dragon, the gold paint flaking from its scales; a third, a siren with flowing hair and outthrust bosom.

"Nefanu's treasures," Denaero said in an awed voice. "Aren't they amazing? I recognize the swords and stuff, but some of these things— what were they *for*?"

"They are terrible," Nathan said. He had seated the mermaid on a boulder to rest his arms and was studying something he thought was a barometer. These weren't the relics of a few island communities; this had been a whole civilization—a human civilization—with mines and palaces and agriculture, with art and technology, with ships and transport and armies, an entire kingdom above the sea. And all that remained were these dead things, preserved forever in a vast hidden crypt, to remind Nefanu of what she had done.

"The High King and the shamans have to come here every four seasons," Denaero said. "It's part of their duty to the Goddess. Do you think—do you think my father could walk, when he came in? I've never seen him walk."

"No," Nathan said. "I think he crawled. I think they all crawled. That's why Nefanu brought them here—so they could crawl to her on their useless legs, and bow down to her power."

There were other bones on the ground nearby, neither fish nor reptile. Nathan turned away, squatting down in front of Denaero.

"Put your arms 'round my neck. I'll carry you on my back; it's easier."

He picked her up and continued to make his way deeper into the cave, toward where he thought the light source must be. There was no sound but the padding of his bare feet and Denaero's breathing, close to his ear. She was accustomed to spending time above water, but the dry atmosphere clearly grated on her throat; he was impressed she didn't complain. The air felt heavy and still, the way air does when it has nowhere to circulate and has been shut up in a confined space for a long, long time. He thought he must have walked for more than a mile. Occasionally he glanced up, searching for where the principal entrance might have been, but the roof was coved, vaulted, shadowed, hung with curtains of frozen stone, too far above for him to make out any details. He speculated that they might be able to wedge the doors to the chamber where they had entered, letting the sea in that way, but he was afraid it would be impossible and his original plan already looked like a failure.

What had the Grandir said? Something about concentrating on his task, and not getting involved in local problems . . .

He must get the Crown. That, at least, would annoy Nefanu, even if he achieved nothing else.

"You must be getting tired," Denaero said.

"No," Nathan said stoically. Rugger and cricket had kept him fit, but after such a distance the weight of the mermaid was beginning to drag. And he had trouble picking his way among the items scattered across the cave floor: old cooking pots and broken utensils—a blackened chalice with red jewels peeping out of the grime—something with rusted spikes that might have been an instrument of torture or an agricultural implement. More remnants of a vanished world—a world within a world—which Nefanu had devoured in her insatiable hunger.

The bits she spat out.

By the time he saw the light source his arms were aching, but he was determined not to say so. The roof curved down to a point tipped with a crystalline formation that glowed bright as day, a mass of polygonal spines protruding in all directions like a giant cubist sea urchin. Below it on a smooth table of rock was something that didn't glow at all. A thorny, knotty, misshapen thing without luster or loveliness.

The Iron Crown.

Nathan set Denaero down on the edge of the rock and she twisted around, reaching out for it.

"Ouch! It makes my hand tingle—"

"You're werefolk; it's iron. Iron is inimical to you."

"What's inimical?"

"It—has a bad effect on you," Nathan explained. "You're a magical being, and magical beings don't like iron. The more magical you are, the worse the effect. Nefanu is a goddess: she couldn't even touch it."

"It's ugly," Denaero said. "It's ugly, and it gives me pins and needles. What's the point of it?"

"Power," said Nathan. "It's part of a Great Spell—something that could change whole worlds."

"Like mine?"

"Not this time." Nathan went to pick it up—and dropped it again with a yelp of pain. His hand felt as if it had been stabbed with a hundred pinpoints of fire. "I don't understand. *I'm* not magical—I'm just an ordinary human. I touch iron every day . . . well, I could. If I wanted. It shouldn't do this."

"Maybe . . . maybe it's the potion," Denaero suggested. "The potion made you magical for a little while—like me."

Nathan swore. "Nothing's working out," he said. "I can't figure out a way to let the sea into the caves, and now I can't even lift the Crown. What the hell are we going to do?"

The question was rhetorical, but Denaero answered it.

"What if you took off that bottle 'round your neck? It's part of the charm, isn't it? So if you remove it . . ."

"Once I'm back in the sea, I'm dead."

"Just take it off for a minute. Find out if you can touch the Crown, and then . . . and then . . . we can decide. Just a minute—what harm can that do?"

Nathan didn't know, and didn't want to know. He could be stuck here, unable to get out—he could die in the deeps of the sea—he could, if he was lucky, wake up, abandoning Denaero and the war he had started and still wanted to stop. *I can't always help you,* the Grandir had said. *If there's a risk, you have to take it,* he thought—he'd done it before, but that didn't make it any easier. Suppose his store of luck ran out at the crucial moment—it had been due to run out, he suspected, for some time. Hazel had discovered the potion, it had worked, Denaero had found the secret door, they'd managed to get into the caves—too much luck for one person. And now it was like that point in the pantomime when they ask the children to clap if they believe in fairies. *Do you believe in magic?* And he *didn't* believe in magic—he didn't believe in a spell that made him a merman for a day—he didn't believe in it, even though it had happened. He knew there would be a catch.

Nathan had read a lot of the right books—he'd read about spells that make heroes invincible and invulnerable—there was always a loophole somewhere. Samson's hair, Achilles' heel. The inevitable moment when you take off the Balaclava of Protection to kiss the princess and someone shoots you in the head. If he removed the talisman he knew, somehow, that all bets were off.

But he had come for the Crown. Without it, everything he had done was meaningless.

He took hold of the vial, hung around his neck on a piece of knotted thong. It felt suddenly heavy, dragging him down, as if there were a brick at his throat. With an effort, he lifted it up and pulled the thong over his head.

Nothing happened. There was no thunderclap, no lightning flash, no Nemesis emerging from the shadows. He set it down on the rock and picked up the Crown without adverse effect. He should have brought something to carry it in; then he wouldn't have to touch it anymore and perhaps he could replace the talisman. He looked around in the vague hope that Nefanu's collection might include a suitable receptacle.

Denaero, observing his actions with satisfaction, said: "Told you so."

Nearby there were other rock tables of varying sizes supporting items of obvious significance. A trident carved from what Nathan guessed to be whalebone—an enormous oyster holding a black pearl as big as a fist—a ring in the form of a crested serpent biting its own tail—a shell trumpet like the ones mermen blow in marble fountains, when a cascade of water comes out—a knife of bronze with a hilt in the shape of a skull.

"What are these?" Nathan asked.

Denaero wriggled off the rock and came toward him on hands and knees, like a child learning to crawl.

"Nepteron's trident!" she said. "It belonged to the God of the Sea, Nefanu's husband, only I think she killed him. And that's the Black Pearl—the largest and most perfect pearl ever found—there's never been another like it. There's a curse on it, though I can't remember why. I don't know about the ring—"

"It's gold," Nathan said. "That means it was made by humans."

He picked it up, trying it on his finger to see if it would make him invisible or something useful like that, but it didn't fit. It would only go on his little finger. Absentmindedly, he left it there.

"We have a few metal things," Denaero said. "We call them sea trove. They're very old. Uraki has a metal bit for Raagu. That knife . . . we used to sacrifice to the Goddess, when there were islands. My grandmother told me. There was a rock that stuck out of the sea, and the shamans used to sacrifice people there—not just humans, but merfolk, our own people. They used a special knife, a holy knife. Maybe that's it."

"I should take it," Nathan said reluctantly. "I could do with a weapon." But the knife looked ancient, evil, and rather blunt—and he was already burdened with the Crown. "What about the trumpet?"

"The triton? That must be the Horn of Doom."

"The Horn of Doom?"

"You know. The one you blow for the end of the world, or when things get so desperate the end of the world seems like a good idea. That used to belong to the High King, but the Goddess took it. She takes everything."

"Has anyone ever blown it?"

"I don't think so," Denaero said. "After all, the world's still here."

"Perhaps it would crack the cavern roof," Nathan said thoughtfully, "and bring the sea rushing in . . ."

"And then what would happen to us? I might make it, but you never would."

Nathan sat down on the rock beside the horn, turning the Crown in his hands. "I don't know how to do this," he said. "I suppose I thought, when we got here, there would be a switch to throw to unblock the entrance, or a spell engraved on the rock, or *something*. I thought inspiration would come, but it hasn't. We may have the Crown, but I can't carry it *and* wear the talisman . . ."

Denaero tried to curl up at his feet, forgetting that legs don't curl as easily as a tail. "I'll take that," she said, indicating the vial. "At least till we get to the exit. Maybe . . . maybe we'll find something, think of something . . ."

"Thanks," Nathan said. "But I'm afraid the only option is for me to wake up—in my own world. Otherwise I'm trapped here."

"You can't!" Denaero's voice shrilled into panic. "You can't leave me! I'd never get to the exit. I'm drying out already—my skin—look—"

"I'm sorry." Suddenly Nathan remembered Kwanji Ley, dying of the sundeath because he had left her in the desert. Would he never learn? "I'll carry you to the door, I promise. You take the vial—I'll take the Crown—just try not to brush against it . . ."

He jumped to his feet, hoping his strength would last. It occurred to him that he hadn't eaten for an awfully long time, and although he had felt no thirst while he was swimming, here in the cave he was beginning to dehydrate. When Denaero reached toward him he noticed there were blotches on her arms where her skin was growing red and flaky—her lips looked cracked—her hair dry and brittle, like shriveled weed. He had ceased to bother about her nakedness long before and felt only concern. He bent to lift her up—

That was when they heard the thunderclap. It echoed through the network of caves like a vast drumroll—the floor vibrated—dust rose— splinters of stone came pattering down from the roof. The light was extinguished, leaving them in utter darkness—then it blazed back in a dazzle of ultraviolet. He released Denaero, pivoting on his heel.

There was a figure standing there—a figure ten feet tall and spun from water vapor, translucent as a wraith, with night-dark eyes and hair that roiled like clouds in a hurricane. In the livid light its phantom form had the unnatural luminosity of chemical pollution. Power streamed off it like radioactive waves.

Nefanu.

Nathan groped for a course of action—the spark of an idea—but his mind blanked.

He knew in his gut he wasn't going to wake up. He feared he might never wake up at all.

IT WAS midnight, the witching hour, but Hazel didn't feel like much of a witch. She'd lit a couple of beeswax candles in front of her bedroom mirror—a fairly new mirror, the old one had been broken—and put on a CD of someone playing the electric cello, but it hadn't helped much. Beside her the piece of yellow paper remained obstinately blank, no matter what conjurations she used; even the title was beginning to fade. Something about the spell still niggled at her, and now that there was nothing to get in the way the niggle had grown to an itch, and she needed to scratch. She flipped through her great-grandmother's notebooks— pages and pages of how to cure headaches, or induce them, how to scry and spy, the odd love potion—*For love, read lust,* Hazel thought cynically—instructions for interpreting the Tarot, chatting with the spirits, sending curses, propitiating fate. *No wonder witches are going out of business,* she reflected. *Who needs magic when we have ibuprofen, electronic bugging, Viagra?* All of them, frankly, far more reliable than the dubious practices of witchcraft. As for fate, you make your own luck, Bartlemy had said, often and often. She had made her own luck once— out of pipe cleaners. Suddenly, she found herself looking for the Nenufar doll—recalling that because it had been soaked in river water it hadn't burned properly, just been a bit scorched. Perhaps she shouldn't have left it lying around. It should be here somewhere . . .

It wasn't.

One of the notebooks lay open at a page headed: A CHARM TO REVEAL THE TRUE NATURE OF THINGS. It sounded profound and philosophical, but when she glanced through it Hazel saw it was simply a way of learning if a gold coin was real or fake, that sort of thing. She thought for a minute, then fetched a basin from the kitchen, half filled it with water, added a few drops from a bottle, a sprinkling of powder from a jar. Then she said the words and slid the yellow paper into the liquid. *Probably only get soggy paper,* she told herself. But the paper shriveled away into floating stringy stuff, and when she picked it out of the basin she saw it was weed.

River weed . . .

Reed in the river pool
Weed in the stream . . .

She thought of the vial that Nathan was supposed to carry at all times, the gray pearl with its petroleum sheen.

Oh *shit*.

It was past one o'clock now, but she rang Nathan's cell phone. No answer. Then she tried the landline.

It rang a long time before Annie took the call.

"Sorry to wake you," Hazel said, "but I have to speak to Nathan. It's *urgent*."

Picking up on the undercurrents, Annie didn't protest. There was a pause while she left the phone to fetch him. Hazel waited, hanging on to her phone like the proverbial drowning man with the straw.

She mustn't think about drowning . . .

Annie came back.

"He's not there," she said.

HE WAS staring straight into her eyes—eyes ocean-deep, ocean-dark, like and unlike those of Nenufar. There was a purplish cast to their blackness like the aftermath of lightning in a midnight storm. And then the lightning came, leaping out of her eyes, crackling from floor to roof and back again. Nathan felt himself clutching the Crown and wondered fleetingly if that was wise.

"Let it go!" said the Goddess. "Or I'll fry you in the ashes of your own skin. It is not yours—let it go!"

Her voice, too, was Nenufar's, but harder, grainy with the breath of the wind and the surge of the sea. She had never needed to sweeten it for her worshippers, nor play the lorelei to bespell the unwary. She ruled; she did not have to seduce.

"Let it go!"

It's iron, Nathan assured himself. *She can't touch iron. Lightning is drawn to metal—but werespirits can't touch iron.*

"It's not yours," he said. "It was made by the ruler of another world—"

"It's in my world now. Everything in my world is mine!"

He was backing away from her, backing away sideways, trying to move clear of Denaero—so far, Nefanu seemed uninterested in her—and back-sidle to one of the rock tables with a weapon. The trident, the knife. He didn't know if it would do any good but he would feel much better with a weapon at hand . . .

"If it's yours"—he threw at her, recklessly—"then take it!"

Her form seemed to expand, growing another foot or so; more lightning forked from her eyes. He wondered how she got in—she was a goddess, presumably she could go anywhere, but she was a goddess of the sea, and this was a dry place, dust-dry and bone-dry and sealed tight against the incursion of a single drop of water. The rules of physics apply, even to the gods. She must have come through the stone chamber, as they had; there was no other way. Which meant her substance was finite—she couldn't draw on the sea to grow.

Her phantom figure looked awesome but transparent, as though stretched too thin. The lightning didn't touch him.

"You can't take it, can you?" he said. "You can't kill me. Your power here is limited—unless you call on the sea . . ."

Maybe he could provoke her into letting the water in.

She shrank again, growing denser. It wasn't reassuring.

"Very clever, little mortal," she said. "But I heard your plan—your futile little plan—your plan that *won't work*. I hear everything. The echoes tell me. Do you know what would happen, if these caverns filled? Do you know how vast they are, how deep they go, caves below caves, pits, chasms, an entire labyrinth burrowing down into the roots of the planet? If the sea came in, all the oceans of the world would fall. There would be land at the South Pole, continents to the north and west. The twelve reefs would emerge, driving the merpeople into the depths, only the depths would become shallows and the coral would die and bleach like bones in the sun, and a billion tiny creatures would lose their habitat, their home. There would be death, death everywhere, and what life would come to take its place? The humans are gone—the land creatures are gone. Even the weeds that grew there have vanished, leaving not a seed behind. Did your mermaid friend know that when she agreed to help you? Does she know the cataclysm that would follow, if the sea sank? You would make an eighth—a quarter—of my world into a desert, dry and lifeless forever."

"I didn't *think*," Nathan heard Denaero mumble. "I didn't . . ."

"There will be seeds," Nathan said, hoping he was right. "Seeds survive. There are still lungbreathers and legwalkers who will use the land. Others will come. Evolution—"

"Evolution takes a long time," said the Goddess. "I know: I've seen it. You want to slaughter my people—in the name of evolution?"

How the hell had he gotten into an argument about ethics?

"You slaughtered whole kingdoms! Look at all this stuff. There must have been a huge civilization—"

"You cannot bring it back. I am a goddess; I am supposed to kill.

Why would I have the power, if not to use it? I kill those who will not worship me, who follow my rivals. You are a mortal—your life is a little thing—you value little lives. Will you really wipe out half my world?"

Her math is going haywire, he thought, automatically—but this wasn't about math.

He said: "I want to—to restore the balance—"

"You want *revenge!*"

He knew she was right. He wanted revenge for the realms that had drowned, leaving their treasures here like bones in a charnel house. The realization horrified him. He faltered, finding no more answers, his arguments all run out.

But he would not give up the Crown.

"Leave it here," she said, and her voice changed, falling to a giant whisper, like the rasp of the wind in a canyon of ice. "I will let you go, back whence you came, such is the magnanimity of Nefanu. Return to your own gods—never come here again! The mermaid is mine—she must be punished. She will die here, slowly, withering, knowing, as the thirst devours her, what it means to be without the sea. One day I will bring her father here to see her skeleton. Such is the justice of Nefanu!"

"No . . ." He was backed against a rock—he felt the edge digging into his thigh. He reached out—his hand closed over the trident. The trident of Nepteron. He half lunged with it, half threw it. At that range, skill was unnecessary; he couldn't miss. It passed through her body with a crackle of sparks, clattered to the ground.

Nefanu laughed.

"Do you think such weapons can hurt me? I am the Sea—the Sea—"

Nathan wondered about hurling the Crown at her, but he knew it was his only protection—if he misjudged, or she was unharmed, she would kill him. He was fishing for inspiration when he felt the dream trembling around him. The portal was opening in his head, sucking him in. Words screamed across his brain—*Not now! Not now! I can't leave Denaero!*—and he struggled to resist, to focus, turning inward, *seeing* the portal, like a blur of interference on the blank screen of his mind, withdrawing from it, forcing all his thought, all his being, to pull back. Closing off his way of escape . . .

The effort left him reeling, faint, and sick. He had never managed it before—never wrested the dream into his control—but somehow he hung on to consciousness, to *thereness*, to the fabric of an unfamiliar world . . .

Denaero was peering around a rock, her breathing short and strained. The dehydration was aging her, pinching her cheek against the bone; her frightened eyes met his for a brief moment.

Nefanu had moved toward the rock where the Crown had lain. Seeing Nathan begin to fade—imagining she had driven him out—she let herself be distracted, staring at the vial he had discarded there. Picking it up—"What's *this*?"—uncorking it, letting the pearl roll into her palm . . .

"This came from beyond the Gate," she said. "Why? I have seen better pearls in an undersized mussel shell. There is power here, but . . ."

The rainbow sheen detached itself from the surface, swirling up into the air in a shimmer of dim colors. The pearl evaporated into a shadowy smoke that mingled with them, thickening, darkening. The shadow-shimmer became substance, a rippling, changing substance that shaped itself into a figure. Suddenly Nathan remembered why he didn't believe in magic. There were no shortcuts, no miracle solutions, no storybook spells. Only the small print you always forgot to read.

He said in English: "Oh bugger."

"What's happening?" Denaero asked.

"I know it sounds impossible," Nathan said, "but things just got worse."

"HE WANTED to be able to swim underwater," Hazel explained. "Like the merpeople. No need to breathe, no problems with pressure. He asked me—at least, he didn't exactly *ask* me, it was just a joke, but I thought . . . I found the spell on a piece of paper in one of Great-Grandma's books."

Bartlemy had driven over, and they were sitting in Annie's living room. Hazel was shaking.

"Effie Carlow would never have known a spell like that," Bartlemy said quietly. "Properly speaking, there *are* no spells of that kind. Such things are beyond ordinary magic. You must have realized that."

"I wanted to help," Hazel said, at her gruffest.

"You should have talked to me. If the potion works, it will be because Nenufar has put something of her self into it, her essence. When Nathan drinks, she will become a part of him. It's a form of possession."

Annie said in a voice that was almost inaudible: "No . . ."

"I doubt she intends anything permanent," Bartlemy said. "At a guess, she's using Nathan as a way into the otherworld—the world of sea. When the right moment comes—whenever that moment may be—she will leave him, and then—"

"What about the pearl?" Hazel said.

"The pearl is probably the nucleus. With it, she maintains her separateness while at the same time securing her bond with Nathan. If he loses it, or even puts the vial down for an instant, Nenufar will abandon him. The core of her self will be in the pearl: she could not risk being parted from it."

"I told him to hang on to it," Hazel gruffed.

"She might try to crack the vial," Bartlemy said. "If he's underwater at the time . . ."

"He's a good swimmer," Hazel said. "He was afraid of the water, after the accident, but he'll get over it. He's *Nathan*. He'll get over it."

Bartlemy forgot to offer comfort.

"Let's hope he has the chance."

THE TWO goddesses stood face-to-face, eye-to-eye. Nenufar Nefanu. They looked solid now, twin facsimiles of humanity. They were not exactly alike but in that confrontation their minor differences began to vanish, dissolving into similarities, as if they were trying to synchronize themselves, to achieve perfect duplication. Perhaps the process was involuntary, a kind of chemical reaction between near-identical opposites seeking an absolute equilibrium. Nenufar's hair curled into billows—Nefanu's smoothed into a waterfall of darkness—tiny variations in their features shifted and changed like worms wriggling beneath the skin. There was a brief, confused interlude when other shapes seemed to flow through them, peering out through face or breast or belly, becoming absorbed back into the core—shapes with tentacles and spines and scales, pincers, fins, fangs. Then gradually the two forms settled, until each was a mirror image of the other.

They said: "Nenufar. Nefanu," and name melded with name, voice with voice.

They reached out . . .

Their fingers entwined, entangled, melting into each other—the arms flowed together up to the shoulder. There was an instant when the two profiles were nose-to-nose, then they seemed to pour themselves into one, becoming a single body that, just for a few seconds, had two backs and no face—a blind thing horrible in its deformity that stood there, shuddering, as if wrestling with its own physical confusion. Nathan, still slightly faint from the effort of wrenching himself away from the portal, had dropped to the ground beside Denaero—he heard her sharp intake of breath at the sight.

"What's happening to them?" she demanded weakly.

"Not sure," Nathan said. "Maybe they'll implode . . ."

But they didn't. Once the entity had achieved what it felt to be its correct mass, its outward form appeared to melt—it became an amorphous column of not-quite-flesh, rippling and bulging with potential features like the water that was its main constituent, an elbow sticking out here, a knee joint there, a hand, a hip. Eyes swiveled around the head in separate orbits, finally coming to rest close by, more or less on a level. Then the whole column heaved—writhed—twisted itself into the shape it knew it ought to be, and the Goddess stood there again, the same but somehow *grown,* grown from within, two deities in a single being. Her strength, her aura, her very self was doubled—she was in truth Nenufar Nefanu, Goddess, demoness, witch . . .

She expanded upward into her own power, soaring toward the cavern roof, head thrown back in a terrible glee. The force that emanated from her was so potent the walls shook—the rock cracked as if in an earthquake.

"We are the Two in One!" she cried. "We are the Duality! We are the Sea—the Sea—"

Nathan recalled his words on the riverside and thought: *Dear heaven, this is my fault . . . all my fault . . .*

"What do we do now?" Denaero whispered.

"Die?" Nathan suggested. "She's out of control—the power's gone to her head. If the walls crack any farther the water really will come in . . . Save yourself: you must. Warn the others—the selkies, your own people . . ."

"Is this the hour of Doom?" Denaero evidently wanted to check.

"It looks like it."

"Then blow the horn!"

Nathan lurched to his feet, grabbed the shell trumpet. The ground vibrated; standing was difficult even for someone who was used to it. The Goddess's words boomed around the cavern like the thunder of great waves—"I will kill them all—the lungbreathers, the humans, the creatures that walk and crawl—I will drown the cities, sink the ships—the ocean will reclaim the earth—" She obviously no longer knew who she was or what world she was in. Nathan found the hole to blow through—it was in the side of the shell, not at the very top—and set it to his lips. His mind—as the human mind can—thought a dozen thoughts in a fraction of a second. What was he really doing?—blowing for the end of the world? Didn't the Archangel Gabriel have a bugle to blow for the last trumpet—or was it Heimdall on Bifröst Bridge, announcing Ragnarök? And there was Queen Susan's horn in the Chronicles of Narnia, that would summon help if you were in danger—the horn of another Susan, in Alan Garner's books, the horn you blew when all else was lost. The horn of last resort. Which horn was this? No more time to speculate. Just blow it and see . . .

The mouthpiece tasted stale and unpleasant, with a far-off tang of seafood several years past its sell-by date. He thought: *If I get through this, I'll probably die of botulism.*

He blew.

Nathan had never blown a horn in his life. There was a noise like air whistling in a tube, barely audible against the reverberation of Nefanu's curses.

"Blow!" Denaero urged.

He tried again, putting all his strength into it—the shell emitted a sort of squeak, but that was all.

"Give it to me! I've done it before—hunting with barracuda—but not—not in air—"

He saw there was blood on her lip where it had desiccated and split—her face was drawn—her hands unsteady. He knew she was an amphibean, but she had been too long out of water; she would never find breath enough for the horn.

"You can't—"

But she squirmed and crawled toward him, bruising her legs on the rock floor, snatching the shell trumpet from his grasp. She put it to her bleeding mouth, closed her eyes.

Nefanu looked down.

"Nooooo—"

The horn call wasn't loud, but somehow it overpowered all other sound, a low soft note that swelled and swelled until the air, the walls, the ground beneath them all thrummed with it. It was like the sea surge against the Rock of Ages, like the wind blowing down the long, long tunnel to eternity. Like the song of the whales echoing through the endless halls of the deep. Long after Denaero had run out of breath and dropped the horn the note went on, carrying into the caves beneath and the seas above, till that whole world throbbed. It was the sound not of endings but beginnings, a bugle call to wake the dead and summon souls from hell . . . Nefanu covered her ears; her lips gaped in a scream that no one heard. And then, when the horn music finally died away, there was another sound.

Water.

It came through the widening cracks, a drip, a seep, a trickle, a gurgle. It spread across the cave floor in wavelets, shallow but very swift, covering the ground faster than a rising tide. Denaero dipped her hands

in it—her face—rolled in it, trying to moisten every inch of her. The
Goddess, grown as high as the roof, cursed in every language of the
sea, pressing her palms against the cracks, seeking to close them with
power or brute force, but nature was stronger than magic, and the
water streamed in. Trickles became cascades, cascades became torrents.

Nathan thought, *Now would be the moment to wake up*—but he knew
he couldn't, the moment had gone for good, and somehow, in taking
control of his thought, he had severed his link with the Grandir. This
time, there was nobody to help him but himself . . .

The water was already three feet deep and Denaero had *changed*,
flexing her tail with relief. Her skin was starting to plump out again,
though the blotches would remain for some while.

She said: "Can you go home?"

"No—"

"Hang on to the Crown—I'll hold you—I won't let go, whatever
happens. If the water doesn't come in too fast we might make it to the
surface . . ."

"Leave me. You can save yourself—" He'd always thought it idiotic when people said things like that in films. It sounded idiotic now.

Denaero ignored the objection, unlashing the leatherwrack strap
that supported her knife. "Here—this'll help." The water was rising
faster—faster—in a minute Nathan would be out of his depth. Denaero
looped the weed under his arms, around his torso, through the Crown,
binding them together—he felt her breasts squeezed against his back.

He told himself he wasn't noticing, and then it occurred to him that
he was probably going to die, so he might as well notice and enjoy it.

But there was no time now—he was swept off his feet in the growing surge, carried across the cave, buffeted this way and that. Even Denaero could do little except try to steady them and lift Nathan's head
above water whenever possible. *Don't panic,* he thought. *Panic kills.
Breathe when you can* . . . He was weakened by the long swim—the trek
across the cavern—lack of food—lack of drink. They were getting
nearer and nearer to the roof, most of which was still holding. The
cracks were all at the western end where the walls must be thinnest;

Nathan, who had a good sense of direction, was almost sure it was the west. Nefanu, speaking now in the tongue of magic, sealed one rent, only for another to open wider.

"We must go—that way!" Denaero gasped, pushing against the current. "We need—out—"

The new rent yawned farther, farther—there was the head-splitting, mind-crunching noise of great rocks shifting and grinding, as if some ancient door in the fabric of the planet itself was slowly opening. The sea should have come through in a boiling tumult that would sweep them all to destruction—but there was something else in the gap, blocking it out, restricting the flow to a mere gush. Nathan and the mermaid were lifted up on the crest of the wash, plunged down again into a sudden valley of water. Briefly, they glimpsed a darkness filling the gap—a darkness solid as a wall, blacker than the blackest deeps of the sea. And in the darkness, eyes—not in pairs but singly, hundreds, maybe thousands, all different. Werefolk eyes, reptile eyes, *human* eyes . . .

My God, thought Nathan. *What did we summon?*

There was a smell—a stench—as if all the fish in the sea had been piled on a beach to rot. Nathan gagged, filling his mouth with water.

He heard Denaero say something that might have been *Leviathan*, but the sea swallowed her cry.

They never saw it clearly. That one glimpse—Nefanu's scream, searing air and water alike—a gulping, squelching, gurgling noise as if a giant quicksand had reared up, consumed a city, and was now smacking its muddy lips. Even as the thing retreated the backwash bore them toward it—Denaero, threshing her tail like a fury, propelled them into its wake like a flier heading for the epicenter of a hurricane. Nathan took his last breath even as they dived and the ocean poured over them . . .

A LIFETIME later, they broke the surface. Nathan coughed and retched a little and, against all the odds, found he was still alive. They had emerged from so near the cavern roof, he realized, they must have been above the levels of killing pressure. He had a dim recollection of the sea swirl rushing past, and the opening looming up in the cavern wall, and torn rock on either side, and the black solid mass beyond. He couldn't tell if it had scales or skin, only that it seemed somehow *rubbery*—he had a horror of rubberiness ever after—and the smell of it, the rotting fishy stink, tainting the water. It was too vast to see any shape. There had been an eye, flat and round like the eye of a haddock, but lidded . . . An eye so near he could have touched it. And then only the sea.

Denaero said: "Has it gone? I think it's gone . . . I knew it would shield us, when the sea came in. It was so big . . . I knew, if we could get close enough . . ."

Nathan couldn't talk.

"It was the Leviathan, wasn't it? It ate *her* . . . It *ate* her."

Something zoomed past underwater, grazing Nathan's calf. He managed a grunt of pain.

"What's that?" Denaero said.

Deflected by Nathan's leg, the javelin came to the surface some way off.

They were in the middle of a war.

Above the sea, nothing looked different. Nathan's first thought was that his plan had failed: in spite of Nefanu's death and the leakage into the caverns, it would take too long for them to fill and the level of the ocean to fall. After all, it covered the whole planet, so a huge volume of water would have to move before it sank even a foot. From what the Goddess had said, the final drop would be considerable, but Nathan remembered learning in a geology lesson that when the Mediterranean was sealed off and dried out it took a year to refill, and he could imagine the labyrinth of caves might take at least that long. *I should have thought of that,* he berated himself. *I've changed their world for nothing. They're still killing each other . . .*

Most of the battle was clearly happening underwater, but the surface of the sea churned from the tumult below—the waves still heaved from the backwash of the Leviathan's rising—bodies floated here and there, both selkie and merman. The shadow of the birds stretched across the reef from sky to sky, blotting out the sun. They screamed and swooped and dived, mobbing any merfolk who emerged above water—the noise of them was like the screech of a hundred saws sawing at a hundred metal bars. If Nathan and Denaero had been any closer, it would have been unbearable. Nathan realized how conspicuous they were with their heads bobbing about like marker buoys. "Undo the strap!" he said to Denaero, but she was already working on it. Even as he spoke, a group of gannets detached themselves from the flock and began streaking toward them.

"Ezroc!" he cried, hoping the albatross was within earshot. *"Ezroc!"*

And then he was there, plunging down from some hover point far above, fending off the assault with a squawk of warning. "Leave them! Leave them to me!" Denaero had unfastened the leatherwrack that bound them together, and as Ezroc settled on the water Nathan hung on to his neck.

"We have to stop this," he gasped. "Nefanu's dead—"

"What?"

"Didn't you hear the horn?" said Denaero.

"We heard *something*—there was this enormous surge, like the beginning of a tidal wave—the armies got mixed up—then it subsided and the fighting started again . . ."

"We raised the Leviathan," Denaero said, not without pride. "It *ate* the Goddess. It just swallowed her up—"

"The *Leviathan?*" The bird's head swiveled, trying to look in every direction at once. "Where? Where?"

"It's gone," Denaero assured him. "It ate *her* and vanished."

"What did it look like?"

"I don't know. It was too big to see . . ."

"Get on my back," Ezroc said to Nathan, pulling himself together. "We'll find Nokosha." And to Denaero: "You get hold of your father. I saw him over *that* way . . ."

"He thinks I'm dead!"

"Give him a nice surprise!"

Nathan climbed onto the albatross, the Crown once more looped around his arm, feeling weak from long effort, clumsy with exhaustion. He needed an adrenaline rush, but so far his body hadn't responded to the order. Denaero, revived by extended immersion, had evidently recovered her strength: she shouted something and dived.

Ezroc took off, calling to the birds in their own languages—in

Gannet, and Skua, and Common Gull. Gradually, the flock ceased their attack and rose into the air, spreading out in a giant V-formation behind him, a cloud of wings that swept across the ocean like a great wind, whipping the waves to spume. They no longer screamed but cried the death of Nefanu in all the tongues of the sea. For Nathan, the adrenaline kicked in at last—he forgot he was tired, he forgot he was thirsty—now he was king of the sky, riding at the head of his own storm.

"Nokosha!" Ezroc shrieked. *"No-ko-sha!"*

The spotted selkie emerged from the water, gazing upward with eyes glinting like the Great Ice. There was a long cut on his cheekbone; blood curled around him. A body heaved to the surface close by.

"I'm busy."

"Nefanu's dead!" Ezroc cried. "The Queen of the Sea is gone! There's no more need to fight—"

"Tell that to the merfolk!" Nokosha snarled. "When they stop trying to kill me, I'll stop killing them."

He disappeared, and the albatross wheeled low over the water, calling and calling in vain. For the first time Nathan could see something of the battle below—a phalanx of sharkriders with a leader who might have been Uraki on the great white, and around them selkies darting and diving, zooming in, falling back, more agile but less well armed, less strong than their mounted opponents. Manta rays surged up from the deep; walruses charged to cut them off—battle cruisers blocking submarine planes. Thin lines of javelins streaked the blue; blades gleamed in a searching sunray. Around the edge of the conflict, a scouting icthauryon snapped its jaws on a corpse, snatching an easy meal. Nathan saw Nokosha, spots visible even underwater, rallying a band of selkies to ambush the sharkriders, and suddenly the future was very clear. He and Uraki would fight—would fight and kill each other—out of some warped mutual respect—when they might have been allies, they might have been friends . . .

"We must stop them," Nathan reiterated, but there was nothing he could do.

They were too human to turn aside from war . . .

It was a moment before he noticed that the cry of the birds had changed. He looked around, uncomprehending, and thought for an instant the Leviathan had returned, because the approaching shapes were so big—as big as the biggest ships in our world. Blue-black bodies rising and falling in an inexorable advance, shattering the waves into foam clouds; vast tails lifting and thumping down on the water; blowholes spurting geysers of spray. There were twenty—fifty—a hundred of them, not a pod but a fleet, shouldering aside the scavenging icthauryon as if they were minnows. The horn had called them with their own music, and their song rolled beneath the sea like the boom of giant tubas and bassoons, and the battle parted before them, and warriors released their weapons to cover their ears from the din of it.

Nathan took up the birds' cry, calling till his voice was hoarse: "The whales are coming! The whales are coming!" and there were tears in his eyes though he couldn't spare the moisture, because he knew now they could stop the war after all . . .

THERE IS a sort of tradition that it always rains after battles, as if the heavens themselves are weeping for the dead. In a world of sea this has very little effect on anyone, since its inhabitants neither drink nor cry, but Nathan stretched out his hands to the squall and sucked the fresh water thirstily from fingers and palm. They were talking above water, a concession on the part of the merfolk—and an acknowledgment that their world was changing. The Dragon's Reef had always been near the surface, but now Nathan could stand on the rock with his head and shoulders exposed.

"*These* were the islands," he explained to Ezroc. "The islands you and Keerye searched for."

"The coral will die," Denaero said, remembering Nefanu's words in the cave.

"Yes, but more will grow as the lower rock stratum is brought nearer the sun. I think your father's halls should still be deep enough to remain covered. And the level will change gradually, over several seasons. The smallfish and other reef dwellers will have plenty of time to move. It won't be easy but when it's over there will be land again. You can learn to walk."

"Merfolk were not *meant* to walk," Rhadamu said. The shock of finding his daughter alive, while clearly pleasant, had shaken his regal authority; he was making an effort to reassert himself.

"Then why do you change?"

"For mating."

"Well," Nathan said, "the islands here will be yours. It would be a waste not to make use of them. But it's up to you. You've worshipped a psychotic goddess for centuries. Now that she's gone, you can make up your own minds."

"We will have no more war," Rhadamu declared heavily. "If the king of the selkies agrees—"

"I am not the king," Nokosha interrupted. "We don't have kings. I became the leader when my people needed one, but now . . ."

"Folk still need a spokesman," Burgoss grunted, wallowing in the water nearby. Like many of the northerners, he was uncomfortably warm. "Easy to lead us into a fight, harder to lead us out of it."

"We will make a treaty," Rhadamu ordained, seizing the initiative. "You will stay in your seas, we in ours. We will call it the Dragon's Accord."

"Perhaps we could fight sometimes without killing," Uraki suggested, plainly missing his aborted combat with Nokosha. "For practice."

He was sitting on Raagu, who regularly lashed from side to side, clashing his jaws on the rusted metal bit. It was not conducive to a climate of negotiation.

"In my world," Nathan said, "we call that *sport*. We have these games we play, one country against another, like soccer and cricket."

Nokosha sneered: "Games!"

"There's a lot of skill involved," Nathan said. "Of course, if you feel it's beyond you . . ."

"Don't try to manipulate me!"

"Describe this *sport*," said Uraki.

Nathan did his best to explain the principles of soccer—cricket, he felt, would be too complicated—and indeed, a few seasons later, a game of waterball developed in that world that became so popular, it was almost responsible for starting another war instead of becoming a substitute for one.

Meanwhile . . .

"What will happen to the shamans?" Denaero asked.

"Without the Goddess," Rhadamu said, "they have no voice, no basis for their authority. We will dispense with their services. Where they go, and what they do, is a matter for them."

"Won't they be punished?" Denaero said wistfully.

"For what?" her father said. "They served Nefanu, as did we all. Anyhow, there has been enough punishment. I do not punish you for surviving, nor will I punish them for losing the whole reason for their existence. Let them be. You have life; they, a living death. It will suffice."

Somewhat reluctantly, Denaero allowed herself to be persuaded.

"How will we cement this accord of yours?" Nokosha asked the king.

"We will engrave it on the first rock to emerge from the sea," Rhadamu decided. "We will cut the letters deep with ancient tools, and we will see to it that no weather erodes them, nor any weed grows over them, so they will last for a thousand years."

"We do not have this skill," said Nokosha, evidently intrigued. "What will you engrave?"

"A merman and a selkie, hands linked in a gesture of peace. Furthermore . . . among my people it is customary to seal an alliance or détente with a marriage. Of course, between hotbloods and coldkin this is not possible—a selkie and a mermaid could not breed—but it might be desirable for them to bond. Some kind of official arrangement. I have many daughters. I would be prepared to offer you one, in token of our trust."

"Th-thank you," said Nokosha, for once at a loss.

"Miyara might perhaps be suitable. She was promised to a fellow king, but that allegiance is no longer necessary. She is considered the loveliest of her sisters."

Somewhere below the water there was a screech of vexation and fury.

"We don't do things that way in the north," Nokosha said, recovering himself. "However, were I interested in such a connection, I would not aspire to too much beauty. I am hardly a pearl among my kind. I would prefer the boldest of your children, rather than the fairest. Your daughter Denaero—"

"*What?*" It was Denaero's turn to shriek. "Marry *you*? I couldn't—I wouldn't—"

"You will do as you are told," snapped Rhadamu.

"In my world," Nathan said—words the others were already beginning to consider ominous—"we treat women as equals. We don't tell them who to marry, or what to do."

"I *like* your world"—from Denaero.

"You cannot do such a thing," Uraki said, appalled. "The female of the species is always weaker. It is the part of the strong male to protect and guide her."

"We think intelligence is more important than brute strength," Nathan said.

He drew back, leaving them to their arguing; there's nothing like a peace treaty for causing a really good argument. Now, he knew, it was time to go home—if he could find the way. It wasn't going to happen anymore by some magical stroke of good—or bad—timing; he had taken control, and that meant he had to open the portal himself. At Bartlemy's suggestion he had always kept the mark of Agares, the Rune of Finding, written on his arm in indelible ink. It might help a little. He wanted to say proper goodbyes, especially to Denaero: they had been through so much together. But she was taking the first steps—or swimming the first strokes—toward sexual equality, and he thought it was best to let her get on with it. He found the albatross beside him, and

although the bird had no obvious expression he knew Ezroc understood.

"I have to go," Nathan said. "If I can. I've been here too long . . ."

"You won't be coming back?"

"I don't think so."

He had shared Ezroc's mind: it was a bond like no other.

"Get on," the albatross said.

And then they were flying, circling the group in the water. Denaero
looked up and waved, sudden comprehension in her face. Nokosha
made a gesture of acknowledgment; Burgoss raised a flipper; Uraki and
Rhadamu offered a brief salute.

He heard Denaero call what she believed to be the traditional farewell of his people.

"Live long—and prosper!"

He thought: *Maybe, from now on, they'll always say that . . .*
There are worse ways to say goodbye.

They rode the air, ascending in giant spirals toward the clouds.
Below, the water was shadow blue, still unbroken by a single rock, but
soon the islands would be there, the islands Keerye had dreamed of, the
Jeweled Archipelago, the Giant's Knucklebones, the islands of story
and legend that he and Ezroc had sought for long ago. The subterranean
caverns were filling and would never again be emptied. Whether the
deed was good or bad Nathan didn't know, but it was done, and he
couldn't change it now. Far off he saw the sun's rays parting the clouds,
streaming down toward the sea. And in the other direction the rainbow
appeared, arching across the horizon—he fancied they could fly through
it to all the worlds that ever were, and beyond, to a better place, a world
without war or hatred, Avalon, Nirvana, the kingdom of Faerie. He
closed his eyes, and for a moment, though he remained solid, he was
the bird, and the bird was him, at one in the magic of the flight and the
hope that somewhere there was a place where they would see Keerye
again, and tell him all their tale—somewhere there was a place where it
all came right . . .

And then Nathan found the portal in his mind, and it opened, not onto sleep but a spinning, reeling, dazzling rush through the borders of the cosmos, hurling him back into his own bed with a jolt that left him dizzy and star-blind.

He tried to sit up but sank back until the vertigo subsided. The Crown was in his hands. He was soaking wet.

Bartlemy was there—his mother—Hazel—all staring at him. For some reason, Annie seemed to be crying . . .

"It's all right," he said. "I'm back."

IT WAS Christmas. Annie and Nathan were having dinner at Thornyhill, joined this year by Hazel, who, having spent the day dutifully with her mother and an assortment of aunts, uncles, and cousins, had now left Lily tête-à-tête with Franco and come to dine off Bartlemy's cooking.

"I didn't eat *anything* at lunch," she revealed. "They all said I had anorexia—it's idiotic, I'm not even *thin*—but Mum said I was eating here, and Uncle Len said at my age, he'd have grabbed the chance to have *two* Christmas dinners, which is probably why he's as fat as a hog, and Aunty Christine looked all offended, so I took a mince pie and pretended. It was disgusting—Aunty Christine's the world's worst cook—I gave it to the cat, and she spat it out. It's awful when you have Christmas with bad cooking. I mean, the whole point of Christmas is the food."

"It's supposed to be the season of peace and goodwill," Annie murmured with the hint of a smile.

"Not in my family," Hazel said. "It's better since Dad left, but Uncle Kevin always gets drunk and starts to squabble with Aunt Lizzy, and Aunty Christine disapproves of Mum and Franco—"

"So do you," Nathan pointed out.

"That's different. She's *my* mum. It's nobody else's business."

"You'll get a good dinner here," Annie promised. "And no squabbling, especially between you and Nathan."

They had a wonderful dinner—roast goose with gooseberry sauce, potatoes done in the fat, sprouts and chestnuts, cabbage with leeks and bacon, then Christmas pudding with cream or ice cream, and Stilton if anybody had any room. Afterward, there was port, and presents. They had opened most of their presents earlier, before Hazel arrived, but they still had to exchange gifts with her, and Annie always made special crackers with gold paper and silver lace containing little extras for everybody. Even Hoover had a cracker, a very large one with a bone inside.

Hazel, to Nathan's surprise and satisfaction, was rendered nearly speechless by his present.

"I'm afraid I sort of stole it," he admitted. "Only it was probably stolen originally from somebody who died long before. I put it on in the cave and didn't take it off. It's way too small for me but it should fit you."

Hazel put the serpent ring on her third finger and said in her lowest mumble: " 'S beautiful."

She thought: *I have a ring from another world.*

It seemed to her that in putting it on her whole personality changed, becoming glamorous and mysterious.

Nathan added: "I'm pretty sure it's gold."

Hazel smiled. "I know how to check."

The snake's eyes were made of tiny jewels whose color altered when she put the ring on, turning from green to fire red.

"May I see it?" said Bartlemy. "Rings picked up in caves can lead to trouble—there are precedents, as we all know. There's something written on the inside . . . maybe Nathan can read it."

"I spoke the common language of Widewater," Nathan said, "but I never had occasion to read anything. Besides, this must have belonged to the human civilization there, and they could have had a language of their own. I'm sorry, Hazel: I don't suppose we'll ever know what it says."

"Doesn't matter," Hazel said. "I'm going to wear it all the time." And, to Bartlemy: "It isn't evil, or magical—is it?"

"After the dinner you've just eaten," Bartlemy said, "your chances of turning into a wraith are very slight."

Later, Nathan told Hazel about his scholarship ending—Annie had broken the news to him the previous week—and they discussed what he would do for the sixth form.

"Uncle Barty says he'll pay for me to stay on at Ffylde," Nathan said. "But I'm not sure I should. I mean, I love it there—I've got loads of friends—but maybe this is, like, a sign. Maybe I should have a change. Crowford College is really good—and I'd be with you and George."

"I'll never get into Crowford College," Hazel said. "They only take people with good GCSEs. You've got to be all academic and *motivated*."

"Uncle Barty says you can do it if you try," Nathan retorted. "It would be fun, the three of us together again. There's motivation for you."

"I always mess up," Hazel said somberly. "Look at my spell to help you on Widewater. All I did was saddle you with Nenufar. It could have been fatal. I'm bound to mess up my exams. It isn't *worth* trying— when I try, everything goes wrong."

"Your spell worked out for me, in the end," Nathan pointed out. "I couldn't have gotten into the cavern without it. And now the Crown's here, with the other things . . . and you've got a ring from another world. You can do *anything*."

For no particular reason, the snake's eyes turned from red to citrine yellow.

"It's like a mood ring," Hazel said. "I've seen those."

And: "I'll think about it."

THAT NIGHT—the night after Christmas—Nathan dreamed of Eos. He knew when he was on Eos, even if his surroundings were unfamiliar; by now, he had acquired a certain *feel* for that universe, a kind of instinct that told him when he was there. And he knew, too, that *he* was in control—or at least, that this visitation had nothing to do with the Grandir. He was in a room with dim mauve hangings and dim gray light and general dimness. There was a bed in a curtained alcove with the curtains drawn back. People came and went softly, the way they do when someone is very ill. Nathan thought that if it was him who was ill it might possibly annoy him—the tiptoeing and the carefulness and the library hush. He was insubstantial, observing, but for the first time he felt that if he wished to materialize he could: it would only take a moment of concentration.

In the bed was a man with long silver hair and an amazing beard, a beard that might, if he had been standing, have reached his knees. It was the beard of a wizard in a story, or an aged king from the days of legend, forked and plaited and white as snow. It was a beard that spoke of wisdom, and extreme old age, and possibly a permanent disinclination to shave. Even on Eos, Nathan was sure, there was only one beard like that. Osskva Rodolfin Petanax, first level practor and father of Kwanji Ley. Above the beard his face was unmasked and very thin, concave cheeks falling away from jutting bones, his eyes sunken deep in their sockets under tufted Gandalfian brows. They were closed, but as Nathan drew near they opened, and saw.

"Ah," he said, in a voice as dim and shadowy as the room. "It's you."

"You can see me?" Nathan knew he wasn't visible.

"The Gate is very near for me now. Already, it stands half open. I can see things that other men cannot."

"I didn't think people *allowed* themselves to die here," Nathan said. "I thought the magic kept you going . . . sort of indefinitely."

"We have outlasted the lesser races of this world," Osskva said. "The Contamination took them long before. But even we cannot live forever. I have seen seven thousand years come and go. It is enough. My daughter, whom I loved beyond all else, is dead. I am content to follow her."

"How old was she?" Nathan asked. "She must have been much younger—but the magic makes you sterile after the first fifty years or so, doesn't it?"

"It does indeed. I stored my seed, preserving it with certain spells for the right moment, the right partner. It is a method that senior practors use, though it is beyond the range of those with lesser power. Thus the great families conserve their talent and pass it on. But my Kwanjira was no spellmaster; she was proud, and difficult, and a rebel. Every family throws them up from time to time. Still, she was more to me than all the stars that ever shone . . ."

"Did you . . . have other children?" Nathan inquired diffidently.

"No. The magic does not work that way. You must save all your seed, all your fertility—that is the price. My first wife . . . did not forgive. But I waited for one of purer genetic makeup—I waited six thousand years for Zarabinda Ley. Her genes were perhaps not perfect, but she was as beautiful as the dawn. And so Kwanjira was born into a world without children, a world already on the edge of death. I thought . . . she would survive. I would have given everything I had, for her to live on. But she was rash, and angry—the fire of youth in a universe grown old. I think—I always knew she had no chance . . ."

"She was very brave," Nathan said uncomfortably, remembering how she had died, beside him in the cave. And there had been people waiting for her, he was sure of it—well, not exactly people but presences—friendly—kindly—only he didn't know quite how to explain that.

Perhaps he didn't need to. Not *now*. Perhaps Osskva already knew.

"Our Grandir," the old man went on, "I often wondered . . . He and Halmé . . . there were no children. I think . . . I understand now. His seed was required for another purpose. The Gate will open soon, very soon. Not into death but life—salvation. Salvation for all who remain."

"Are you the only people in this world?" Nathan said, remembering the term *lesser races*, wondering why he had not thought about it before.

"We are now. Once there were many, many peoples—too many to list them all. But we were the strongest, the cleverest, the ones with a natural affinity for magic. We came from Alquàrin, from Gond, from Rheegor—I forget. It was so long ago even the historians have ceased to speak of it. We ruled for a million years. The others blended their blood, their genes, mingled and degenerated, but not us. We remained pure. Somewhere, we will rule again."

Nathan considered debating the whole purity issue, but Osskva was dying, and he left him to his illusions. The purple eyes had closed

again; Nathan drew back. He found himself thinking of Eric, who had
never talked of *lesser races,* who had adapted to an alien world and its
backward inhabitants apparently without a qualm. But Eric wasn't a
first-level practor, just a onetime fisherman centuries out of a job . . .

A tall, dark figure interposed itself between Nathan and the bed. A
familiar figure, even from the back. Always familiar.

Nathan thought: *He doesn't know I'm here.*

"How long?" the newcomer asked someone else. One of those who
tiptoed, and whispered, and was careful in the imminence of death. As
if it was Death, not Osskva, who must be treated with respect.

Someone else said: "Not long."

Presently, the person added: "He talks to himself."

No, he doesn't, Nathan thought. *He talks to me.*

The Grandir said: "You may go."

It was an order.

Alone—more or less—he waited. He took off his mask, but Nathan
stayed behind him, unable to see his face. He felt less solid than a ghost,
but he knew the Grandir would be sensitive to his presence, and for no
reason that he could explain he did not wish to be seen there.

Eventually, the old man opened his eyes again.

"You have come," he said. "I thought you might."

"You had a daughter," the Grandir said. "One of the terrorists. She
was in Deep Confinement, but she escaped—somehow. None ever escape from the Pits, but she . . . I learned her identity too late to do anything for her."

"It doesn't matter," Osskva said. "Our children are our future,
even here. I knew, from the hour of her birth, that she would throw
mine away. She was willful—playful—reckless beyond reason. I will
pass the Gate before you, and my path will be other than yours. But
you—you have a future still. The future of our people. I have seen it."

"What have you seen?" the Grandir demanded.

"I have seen the child—the child of another world. He grows
taller—almost a man—he grows like the Destroyer in the forbidden
tales, who came to manhood in a year and a day to avenge the death of
a god. The youth is still on him, like dew on a flower . . ."

"The flowers have all gone," said the Grandir. "Only the desert endures. When did you see this child?"

"He comes and goes," Osskva said. "Twice—three times. The Gate is behind you—it stands ajar—ajar! He is beside it, holding the door. He shines like the dew in the morning—youth the Destroyer—youth that lasts an instant, an hour, and is blown out like a candle in the wind of Time. We have no youth anymore but he is there, holding the Gate, youth our savior, last of our children . . ."

He's rambling, Nathan realized. *The Grandir knows it. He will not turn—he will not look for me—*

"He is there!" Osskva cried, his voice growing stronger, trying to sit up. "*There!* Youth—the angel youth—"

The Grandir turned—

Nathan wrenched himself away, out of that world, into the dark.

He dreamed of a gate, an ordinary gate under a low stone arch. It was made of wood, bleached of all color by the sun, or the moon, or the light of forgotten stars. Flowers grew around it, tiny white flowers like jasmine, smelling of Forever. A lizard with scales like beads of glitter scurried across the boards . . .

He thought Osskva was beyond that Gate now, and Kwanji Ley—Romandos and Imagen—Keerye—his own father, Daniel Ward . . . So many, so many. There was no crack or chink between the boards but suddenly the Gate opened, less than an inch, and a light streamed through—a light he had seen once before, between worlds—a light that did not dazzle his eyes—a light that found its way inside him and touched his soul . . .

He woke up.

THAT NIGHT—the night after Christmas—Bartlemy sat in his living room, listening to the year tick away. Once this was Yule, the pith of the winter, the dark of the year—and people had always celebrated, because now the season was turning, the days lengthening, and they could look forward to spring. That was typical of the human race, Bartlemy thought with sudden warmth, to celebrate when things are darkest—to celebrate Hope, and Faith, and the belief that, with a little luck, the sun would rise in the morning, and for all the mornings to come. If there was a God Who cared—if there were Ultimate Powers watching over the worlds—he trusted they could see what they had made, the courage of these fragile, short-lived creatures, who shaped their world, for good or evil, and sang their songs, and feasted and fêted, because the hope of their hearts was stronger than the dark.

And the Christians had taken Yule, and given it to be the birthday of a man who had never seen snow on the pines or eaten plum pudding, who lived and died in the warm southern climes where winter never came.

So Bartlemy sat, sipping the dark red liquor he reserved for these occasions, pondering the nature of things, coming to no conclusions, for such ponders never do, but appreciating the conclusions he didn't come to. At his feet Hoover flopped his ears over his eyes and snored a doggy snore.

Presently, Bartlemy said: "Come in."

"Greeting," said the dwarf, stepping through from the kitchen, a bundle of dubious odors, rags of leather and hessian, clumps of hair. Knobbly fingers already held the wing of the goose, which vanished into his beard even as he seated himself crook-legged on the hearth rug. " 'Tis a black night," he remarked after a minute, around the goose, "and the fire looks muckle welcoming."

"The night is often black," Bartlemy commented. "Especially when it's cloudy. It's the nature of nighttime."

"Aye," said the dwarf pensively, as if this were a profound subject. "I'm thinking it mun be Yule, what the new religion calls Christmas. Nae doot that's why ye be roasting the goosey, and living off the fat o' the land."

"Nae doot," said Bartlemy. "But this is the twenty-first century, unless I've lost count, and in the New Year people will look at their waistlines and live off the lean. That's how they do things nowadays."

"The ways o' menfolk be strange to me," Login said. "But this New Year, the way I hear it, there may be neither fat nor lean. Let them feast now, while they can. There are dark times coming. Too dark for me. I'm hearing, ye ha' the cursèd Crown here, wi' the cursèd Cup, and the cursèd Sword. That bodes nae guid to man or dwarf. I told ye, the magister was mad—the hour he spoke of is a-drawing nigh, and I ha' no wish to wait here for the gate o' hell to open."

"You're moving on?" Bartlemy said.

"There's kin o' mine in the auld mines to the north, so I hear," Login explained. "Those places the humans abandoned make a home for dwarfs. And maybe I'll find my way to the Mines o' Gol, where my folk ha' dwelt ten thousand years—if the stories ha' no forgotten them. We can wait out the bad times—we ha' done it afore. But ye gave me a welcome, and cooked me fatworms—I wouldna gang without bidding ye farewell."

"And to you," said Bartlemy. "Farewell indeed."

"Tell the lad to be watching oot," Nambrok went on. "*They* may be gone, but there's too many eyes a-spying on him, too many ears a-listening. And the maidy—she's a bold one. Nae rose, just the thorns. She's a rare one, she is. I wish them luck, the both of them. I'm thinking they'll be wanting it."

"I'll tell them," Bartlemy promised.

A second helping of goose and half a plum pudding later, the dwarf was gone. Bartlemy closed the back door, though he didn't lock it—he never locked it—and went thoughtfully to bed.

ON NEW Year's Eve, he had another visitor.

Nathan and Hazel had gone to a party with the teenagers of the village where Hazel danced with Damian Wicks and Nathan ate marijuana fudge and bored Liberty Rayburn by talking about multiple universes. "He's one of those geeky scientific types," she told her brother Michael. "It's a waste: he's so *fit*. Of course, he's much too young for me." Annie went out to dinner with Pobjoy at the Happy Huntsman, the best restaurant in the county—though not on a par with Bartlemy's cuisine—but he was called away during dessert to attend a burglary at the house of a local bigwig. As she saw it, this was their first proper date—she still hadn't told Nathan—and she went home sober, long before midnight, deciding policemen made bad boyfriends.

Bartlemy's visitor came through Eade unnoticed by its inhabitants, his long coat flapping, the wolf-dog loping at his heels. The clocks were striking as he crossed the threshold of Thornyhill.

"A dark stranger," he said. "I may bring you good fortune. If there is any available."

"Ragginbone," said Bartlemy. "And Lougarry. A happy New Year to you both."

"I think not," said the tramp. "There is a darkness over the future that augurs ill for us all."

"Then let us drink to the present," Bartlemy said.

He opened a bottle of wine with the name of a rare French vineyard, a wine as golden as a June day, which tasted of sunshine, and laughter, and summers long gone by.

"I have seen too many summers," Ragginbone said. "There is always winter, waiting in the wings."

"And spring again after," Bartlemy rejoined. "Longevity has made you a pessimist."

"And you an optimist. Thus the capricious teachings of Time."

"Ah well," said Bartlemy. "I have lived longer than you, and seen too many sorrows. Only the hopeful heart survives."

And so they reran familiar discussions, familiar disputes, comfortable with their divergent views, at ease in each other's company as only people who have known each other for several centuries can be. Eventually Bartlemy began to talk of Nathan's adventures on Widewater, and the finding of the Iron Crown.

"Nathan," said Ragginbone. "Yes. That's why I came to see you. I heard a story about another Nathan—I would not have thought it significant, were it not for the name. There are few coincidences in the world of magic."

"If this is the tale of the Eastern witch and her son, who came here more than a millennium ago, I have heard it already."

"It concerns a witch," Ragginbone said, "but not from the East.

She came from the same land as this wine, a mere four hundred years past. However, if you are not interested . . ."

"Go on," Bartlemy said.

"I heard the tale from a kobold who resided in her house. Her friends thought he was a freak, a stunted human, but she was Gifted: she knew him for what he was, and enspelled him to be her slave. She was an aristocrat, or so she claimed, thrice widowed, a friend of de Montespan and Catherine La Voisin. La Voisin was one of those more cunning than clever, who deemed her power to be greater than it was— I met her once, before the end. She thought the spirits would save her from the fire. She had a pact with the Oldest, the one we do not name, but he abandoned her. However, this other woman, it appears, was a sorceress of a different caliber."

"She didn't get caught," Bartlemy deduced.

"Precisely. The *affaire des poisons* was exposed, and scandalized the French court—without La Voisin's charms, de Montespan could no longer hold the king's attention—but our heroine kept a low profile and passed unremarked through the debacle. She was a *marquise* from some Provençale backwater; her husbands had died far from Paris. The Parisians thought they had a monopoly on glamorous crime. Nobody could be mysteriously poisoned out in the sticks: they simply died. The widow had acquired the title from one, money from another, and came to the court to make an impression. She called herself something fancy, the way women did in those days—Margolaine or Mégaire—though she had been christened Marguerite. She had a son whom no one ever saw, save the kobold. He was assumed to be sickly, or insane, or living in the country. His name was Nathaniel." Ragginbone paused. "It was not a common name among the French aristocracy."

"What came to him?" Bartlemy asked, his wine glass untouched since the recital began.

"After La Voisin's demise Marguerite traveled to England. She claimed to have a cousin here, though there was no sign of one. She procured a house in London, admirers, friends. Nathaniel was kept locked in a suite of rooms on the top floor, away from all the servants but the kobold. They would hear him bellowing at night in rage or pain, and then they would run and hide, calling on God to protect them, for he bellowed in *two* voices—his own and that of his demon, or so they believed. They were uneducated and superstitious. According to the kobold, the boy had two heads. Siamese twins, I assume, with only a single body between them. But his mother appeared devoted to him, spending time with him every day, ordering the servants to scour the market for his favorite foods. She might have murdered three husbands, but her son was precious to her, for all his deformity." He paused again before offering his own comment. "One wonders why."

Bartlemy said nothing, stroking Hoover's neck, almost as though seeking reassurance himself—he who was always the one to reassure.

"She was not, I think, a woman much given to natural affections. You know how it is with the Gifted. The power warps us, corrupting mind and heart, until our generosity of spirit, our capacity for love, is all consumed in the desire for dominion. We become as the werekind with whom we consort, ruthless and cold. I was saved only by the loss of my Gift—you have made a choice, employing yours sparingly, seeking to do good in small things rather than great, and so you have remained human. Few among Prospero's Children have ever shown such restraint."

"Yet restraint is possible," Bartlemy said, thinking perhaps of Hazel and her reluctance to resemble her great-grandmother. "If mind and heart are strong . . . if the Gift is limited . . . if love already has a place there . . ."

"Be that as it may," said Ragginbone, the pessimist, "I do not think our Marguerite was restrained."

"What happened to her?" Bartlemy pursued.

"To her—nothing, or nothing unusual. But something happened to Nathaniel."

"What?"

"One day he disappeared. They went into the country in a closed carriage, leaving the kobold behind. Marguerite was tense, aflame with anticipation. She took with her a chest containing certain magical items and a sacrificial knife. The date was just short of Halloween. She returned without the knife, without the flame, without her son. His name was never mentioned again. When the kobold ventured to ask what had come to the boy, he was banished from her household. He remained in London, living with the werecreatures who infest cellar and sewer. I learned what Marguerite did from other sources, but it does not seem particularly relevant. She returned to France and went thence to Italy, marrying again, widowing again, involving herself with artists and writers. But they did not paint her or write about her. One of her husbands bequeathed her a disease that destroyed her beauty as Time could not, and she became a recluse, back on her estates in Provence. For all I know she may be there still. Stranger things have happened."

"Did she say where in the country they were going, when the son vanished?"

"She told one of the servants she was going to Scarborough—the kobold overheard her—but that seems unlikely. She set off south . . ."

"I daresay," Bartlemy said, "the kobold misheard." There was a chill inside him that he couldn't explain, the glimpse of a pattern he did not want to see. The Great Pattern had a purpose, a purpose he had always hoped and believed was good, but there were other patterns, shadowy designs hiding within and behind it, with a darker meaning, a meaning as yet obscure and unknown.

> *Are you going to Scarbarrow Fayr?*
> *Parsley, sage, rosemary, and thyme.*
> *Remember me to one who died there . . .*

"I thought the story might be . . . important," Ragginbone said. "That's why I came out of my way to see you. Tomorrow I must be moving on. Or rather, later today. Whatever the New Year brings, I hope you survive it."

"I hope we all do," Bartlemy responded.

After all, this was the season of hope. But he feared his supply was running low.

· · ·

IN THE small hours of New Year's Day, Nathan and Hazel had a fight in which the questionable charms of Damian Wicks became inextricably entangled with the older-woman allure of Liberty Rayburn, alcohol and fudge were mixed in with the brew, and the result was confusion, hostility, and mutual hurt. They parted company on not-speaking terms, and Hazel went home to find Lily in a clinch with Franco on the sofa, while Nathan discovered Annie in the living room watching TV, in a mood he didn't recognize.

"How was your party?" she asked him.

"All right, I suppose. How was yours?"

"It wasn't a party," she said. "I—gave you the wrong impression. It was dinner."

"Why—" Nathan stopped as realization kicked in. "Who with?"

"James . . ."

"Who's James? James who?"

Annie sighed. "James Pobjoy. The police inspector. He—he asked me, so I went. I had nothing else to do." *Coward,* she told herself. *Making excuses. You went because you wanted to.* "I shouldn't worry about it. He left before pudding."

"He took you out to dinner," Nathan was baffled, "and *left* halfway through?" Men had been challenged to duels for less, he thought, in the days when duels were in vogue.

"He couldn't help it. It was his job. There was a break-in during a party at some manor or other—I expect, with all the noise, they didn't hear the burglars. He had to go."

Nathan sat down abruptly. "Do you—do you *like* him?" he demanded.

"Yes," Annie admitted, limply. "I suppose I must."

"But . . . he's a policeman," Nathan said. "How can you like a *policeman?*"

"Don't be so prejudiced. He believes in justice—he wants to protect the innocent. Cynicism gets in the way sometimes, but he's a good man at heart, I know he is."

"He doesn't believe anything we tell him!"

"Well, you can't blame him for that. We've told him some pretty extraordinary things."

"Yes, but—"

"Bartlemy likes him," Annie said, by way of a clincher.

"Does he?"

"Yes, he does." She went on: "Anyway, you don't have to panic just yet. I may never see him again. This was our first date, and it wasn't exactly a big success."

But Nathan felt a weight of gloom on his heart that her uncertain assurance could not lift. He went to bed and slept badly, but without dreams.

In the morning he called Hazel, one problem displacing another.

"We aren't talking," Hazel said, when she finally answered her cell.

"We have to," Nathan said. "Something's happened."

They met at the Bagots', in the privacy of Hazel's lair. "I'm going to clear it up," she announced. "New Year's resolution. There could be some important stuff under all this—stuff. Have you come to apologize?"

"No. Yes. Whatever. That doesn't matter now. My mum went on a date last night—"

"Oh . . ."

"—with Inspector Pobjoy."

"*What?*"

"You heard."

When they had run through the subject several times without arriving at any helpful conclusions, Hazel said: "Now you know how I feel."

"This is different. Franco's a toyboy. Toyboys don't last. The inspector must be forty at least—she might *marry* him."

"It's only one date," Hazel said. "Your mum's always been sensible. She wouldn't do that."

"That's just it," Nathan said. "She's been sensible for too long. That's when people crack. Besides, women aren't sensible when it comes to relationships. Everyone knows that."

That might have restarted the previous night's argument, but Hazel, with rare tolerance, let the remark pass.

"We'll find a way to show him up in front of her," she said. "He thinks we're all barmy, so it shouldn't be too difficult."

"I hope not."

"There's no point in worrying now," Hazel went on, opting for a change of subject. "You've got more important things to think about. You've got a Great Spell to activate—or whatever it is one does with a Great Spell. You've found the Cup, the Sword, and the Crown. D'you have to dream them to Eos or what?"

"I don't know," Nathan said. "I've never been given a list of instructions. I just have to make it up as I go along."

"I wish we knew more about the Grandir," Hazel brooded. "I still think he's a power-crazed supervillain. Bartlemy told me, the Gift in humans comes from something called the Lodestone, which was in Atlantis thousands of years ago. He has this theory that it came from another world, a world with a high level of magic—that it was, like, a whole galaxy compressed very small, the way our universe was before the Big Bang. It gave off this force that changed everyone around it . . . Barty said, maybe the Grandir did that, to prepare us, to protect *you*. All that power—Atlantis overthrown—a whole new strand of human history—just for you . . . That's so scary it makes my head spin. Only a total megalomaniac would do that."

"Perhaps . . . he just sees things differently," Nathan said. "A different perspective. He's used to ruling an entire cosmos. Tinkering with the fate of one planet is no big deal for him." He didn't like the idea, mostly because it made too much of his own role. He didn't want to believe that Destiny had put the finger on him.

"If it's true," Hazel said, "he has so much power . . . No one should have that much power. *No one*. It's like God . . ."

"Do you believe in God?" Nathan asked carelessly.

"I'm not sure. If He exists, why does He let people make such a mess of things?"

"Free will," Nathan said. He had studied philosophy—from close up. "Gods shouldn't rule. They should simply . . . advise."

"The Grandir rules," Hazel said. "He acts like he's God. We're less to him than fleas."

"Fleas bite." Nathan's mind was elsewhere.

"How do you bite someone like that?" She lapsed into speculation. "I suppose . . . In magic, one of the ways you can break the hold of a master wizard is by using his spell-name. The Grandir keeps his name very secret, doesn't he? Everybody calls him by his title, even what's-her-face—the sister. You ought to try and find out his name—his true name. Names obviously have a *lot* of power in that world. Otherwise he wouldn't be so careful about it."

Nathan returned slowly from thoughts of his mother and Pobjoy. "How could I find out?" he said. "Anyhow, that wasn't what I came to discuss. About Mum . . ."

"I was just trying to change the subject," Hazel said. "Before you get really boring about it."

"You should talk."

The conversation ended, predictably, in a quarrel.

"Nathan needs to know the truth," Bartlemy said. "The Three are recovered, currently hidden at Thornyhill, but no doubt soon he will have to return them to the place from which they came. And then—well, we'll see. His task may be over—or it may not. However, he must know everything that has a bearing on his position. Without that knowledge, he is defenseless."

"I was going to tell him on his birthday," Annie said. "He'll be sixteen. It seemed—sort of appropriate."

"Ah yes," said Bartlemy. "In legends and folktales, it is at sixteen, not eighteen, that you become an adult. It is at sixteen that you prick your finger on a spindle, or slay your first dragon, or go out into the world to seek your fortune. But we live in a different age, an age where, in many respects, our children must grow up fast. Even in fiction, no one waits for sixteen anymore. It is as children that they go through the wardrobe, or seek the Philosopher's Stone. And Nathan has been killing dragons, metaphorically speaking, for some time now. He needs this knowledge. He is involved in a Great Spell, and what part he may have left to play I do not know—no one in our world knows anything about Great Spells—but there is a time of uncertainty approaching, perhaps of danger, and Nathan must have *all* the information we can give him, to know enemy from friend. Tell him tonight, before he goes back to school."

"I'll try," Annie said.

"No," said Bartlemy, with unusual firmness. "In this instance, trying is not enough. You *must* do this. For his sake."

The previous night, she and Pobjoy had managed an entire date, an uninterrupted evening of movies and pub, when he had laughed at two of her jokes and agreed to read a book of her choice— *"The Wind in the Willows,"* she said. "We'll start small"—and had kissed her goodbye, a kiss that had taken quite awhile.

"Remember," she had told him, "you're not to hold it against Mr. Toad that he's a criminal on the run. Go into the story with an open mind."

"I'll try," he had said.

Trying isn't enough, Annie thought unhappily after she left Bartlemy. *He's right. Sometimes trying just means I'll make an effort to show I'm willing, but it doesn't matter if I fail. I've put this off too long . . .*

At home, Nathan was finishing an essay with one eye, so to speak, and watching television with the other.

"We have to talk," his mother said.

Ominous words at any age. Nathan assumed the expression of someone who was bracing himself for bad news.

"You mean, about—about James," he said. "Are you going to marry him?"

"Good God, no! I haven't even . . ."

"Only I saw you kissing last night, and—"

"Nowadays," Annie said, "people do quite a bit of kissing without getting married. Society has gone downhill since the Victorians. If I saw you kissing a girl, I wouldn't expect immediate news of your engagement. I know you don't like James, but—if you just look at him as a temporary fixture, couldn't you give him a chance?"

"I'll try," Nathan said.

Those words again.

"Oh bugger," Annie said—she hardly ever used strong language.

"Funny how we always say that when we mean we won't really try at all."

"I *will* try, honestly, but—"

"Not you. Me. There's something I suppose I should have done a long, long time ago, but I kept putting it off, saying to myself: *Not yet, not yet.* And earlier today I told Barty *I'll try,* but I don't know that I meant it. And James said it last night, about Mr. Toad, but I'm not sure he meant it, either."

"Mum," Nathan said, "you're rambling."

"No, I'm not. It just sounds like it." She stood up. "I have to get something. I won't be a sec."

When she came back, he was making tea.

"I thought we needed it," he said, "if we've got heavy stuff to discuss."

"Yes," Annie said. "It's heavy."

She sat down again, waiting for the tea. When it came she said: "Have you ever . . . felt the need . . . for a father?"

Nathan looked startled. Whatever he had expected, it wasn't this. A lecture on drugs, contraception, safe sex, the meaning of life—but not this.

Were they heading back to Pobjoy again?

"Not really," he said. "Even though Dad's dead, I've always felt I had someone. You talk about him sometimes, and you loved him so much. And I have Uncle Barty." He added with a glint of humor: "I'm not short of male role models."

"This isn't about role models," Annie said with a sigh. "Daniel was kind, and good, and I loved him, yes, so very much. I told you we weren't married—we just didn't get around to it. My parents were old-fashioned: they disapproved—but they kind of tolerated the situation. And then he died, and you came, and they weren't so tolerant after all."

"That was because he was Asian, right?" Nathan said. "They didn't like you having a mixed-race child. You didn't exactly say so, but—I always thought that was why we didn't have anything to do with them."

"It's more complicated than that," Annie said. "I suppose I should contact them at some point—they're getting older now. I call my cousin every year, just to check they're all right, but being out of touch gets to be a habit, one it's hard to break. And going back would be . . . difficult. Painful. They never understood." She paused. "But then, I didn't understand, either."

"Understand . . . what?"

"About you. Daniel was in the car crash—the police said he fell asleep at the wheel, but I didn't believe it. He was always so *careful*. He wouldn't have driven if he was that tired . . . Anyway, they took him to the hospital, and I sat by his bed, watching him die."

"Mum . . ."

"No. Don't interrupt—please. I have to tell you. I have to tell you *now*." Her eyes were like dots in her face—gray dots in the blankness of her pallor—staring and staring into the past. "When he died, I *knew*. I felt him go. I went after him—through the Gate—I didn't know about such things in those days, but I do now. I loved him so, the Gate opened for me, and I followed him . . . I went *through*, between the worlds . . . and when I came back, I was pregnant."

"Are you . . . sure?" Nathan asked tentatively. "I mean, you could have been pregnant before . . ."

"Oh yes," she said. "I'm sure. I was so glad when I realized—so glad. And when you were born, even though I knew at once things weren't right, it was the happiest day of my life."

"What wasn't right?" It was his turn to stare, baffled by her tone. She talked as if he were a mutant, someone with six fingers on one hand, or thirteen toes, but he was normal—as normal as anything.

Except for the dreams . . .

"Here," she said, passing him the item she had fetched from her room. A photograph. A photograph he had never seen before. "That's Daniel."

"He looks . . . nice." An inadequate word. It was a gentle face but not weak, as honest and true as Annie's own. But . . .

"He's white."

"Yes," Annie said. "That was the problem."

"He's white . . ."

"When they saw you, my parents thought I'd been with someone else. But I hadn't. There was only that moment when Daniel died . . . My mind shut it off, sort of sealed it up, for years and years. And after the birth I started to see *Them*—the gnomons—I thought I was going mad. So we went away, and somehow we came here—it was an accident, or so I thought at the time—and Bartlemy took us in, and . . . you know the rest."

"He's not my father." Nathan was still gazing at the photograph. "Daniel Ward isn't my father . . ."

"When you were older," Annie said, "I tried to remember what had happened when the Gate opened. Love is so strong, stronger than death"—*oh Daniel, Daniel*—"I reached out for him, and Someone was there, waiting for me, in another place, another time. You were conceived—between worlds. Your father . . ."

"My father comes from another universe," Nathan said. "That's why I dream."

There was a silence that seemed to go on a long time. Nathan had left the television on mute and Annie watched the actors going to and fro, their faces moving in shock, horror, drama—all silent. And in this little room there was Nathan's face. No shock, no horror, no drama. Only the silence.

"Why didn't you tell me before?" The inevitable question. "Why did you—*lie?*"

Annie never lied. She saw herself in his eyes, diminished, degraded, touched with cowardice and deceit. It hurt her more than anything she had ever known.

"I wanted you to be normal." She was almost pleading. Pleading for him to understand. "I wanted you to have a normal life. Not to be saddled with all this doom-and-destiny stuff . . ."

"It's all right." His voice was curiously empty. "I can deal with it."

At least, she thought, snatching at crumbs, he's only seeing this from *his* angle. Not mine. He sees what was done to him—not what was done to me. And she was grateful—so grateful—for the blind self-absorption of youth.

He said: "It's the Grandir. It must be. *He's my father . . .*"

He wasn't looking at her, or he would have recognized the expression on her face. That look of *Nevermore*.

"I don't know," she said. "It's possible." She didn't tell him about the witch from the East who had sacrificed her own child. Right now, Annie felt as if *she* were standing there with the knife in her hand . . .

"I need to go and think," he said.

It wasn't late, but it had been dark for hours. She knew where he would go. Up on the roof, to look at the star.

"You can miss school tomorrow," she said. "We can talk about things . . ."

"No," he responded. "Normal boys go to school. You wanted me to be normal, remember?"

He said it without malice, but it stabbed.

He climbed up to the skylight, and Annie sat in the chair, waiting for him to come down, until at last she fell asleep.

UP ON the roof, straddling the skylight, Nathan didn't think. He just sat, his mind as blank as if it had been wiped. The sky was overcast, furred with gloom from horizon to horizon. All other stars were obscured, but *his* star was still visible, below the cloud, a fixed, unwinking light. The casual observer might have assumed it was shining through a gap, or, more accurately, might have labeled it a UFO, but Nathan surmised it was simply lower down. A spy-globe from another universe, watching him like a solitary eye. His father's eye. . . .

Images came and went in the emptiness of his head. The first time he had seen the Grandir, in his semicircular office—his face, unmasked, touched with concern—the feel of his hand, skin on skin—a bottle of cloudy liquid, glittering with leftover magic—Osskva's words as he lay dying: *You must save all your seed . . .*

And Osskva's words at the end, the very end: *We have no youth anymore but he is there . . . youth our savior, last of our children . . .*

I've always known, Nathan told himself, dully. It was part of the pattern, something so big and obvious he hadn't been able to see it—he had been too busy *looking* to actually see. Too busy jumping from world to world, caught up in action and danger, in questions and plans. If he had only stopped for long enough he would have seen, he would have known . . .

If Annie had spoken sooner . . .

But he didn't blame her. He couldn't feel, or wonder, or allocate blame. His mind—his whole being—was filled up with the hugeness of the truth, squeezing out all other functions. He just sat there, trying to absorb it, gazing numbly into the dark. The murmur of evening traffic on the Crowford road gradually died away. He was so still, a barn owl passed close by without a sideways glance, on its way to hunt in the river meadows.

The night went on forever.

When his brain woke up enough to nudge him toward bed he realized the window frame was cutting into his thigh and his leg had gone to sleep. He had to massage the feeling back before he could climb down and go to his room. He never thought to check on Annie, still curled up in the armchair downstairs. He never thought about her at all.

In bed, he groped for the portal—he could touch it now, he could manage the transition, he was in control. But when he arrived on Eos he found himself roaming the corridors of some vast empty building, peering into rooms and around corners, searching and searching, on a fruitless quest for someone who wasn't there. Around half-drawn screens he saw the cityscape of Arkatron, the curving walls like cliffs a thousand feet high, the poisonous sunlight reflected in the dazzle of a million windows. The occasional skimmer or winged xaurian soared the canyons in between. Inside, it was warm and soft underfoot, with soft lighting coming from no particular source and soft noises as automatic doors opened and closed for him. It was like a dream, he thought, only this dream was real. This was Arkatron, capital of Ind, the last city on the last planet in a world that was almost gone. There were few people left now. Only the empty corridors, the softness of the endless rooms. He walked and walked but there was nobody, nobody in the whole

312 · Amanda Hemingway

building. Beyond the windows the skimmers and xaurians were few,
and too far away to be clearly seen.

He thought, *I ought to go home,* but he had to find the way, and he
was so very tired, and the final effort drained him of all consciousness,
leaving him, at last, in the blackness of welcome oblivion.

AT HOME and at school, normal service was resumed. Nathan attended
lessons, played rugger, held conversations with his classmates; on week-
ends he did his homework, watched television, functioned. But his
friends thought him indefinably aloof, his teachers felt he was learning
on autopilot, and Annie noticed he spoke only when spoken to, as if,
somewhere inside, he had switched himself to another channel, or gone
into isolation, and the main part of him was no longer there. She talked
to Bartlemy, who said, "Give him time," and guessed Nathan talked to
Hazel, though what was said or how he said it, she didn't know. It was
as if he had pulled down a blind between him and his mother, and she
could find no way through, and the burden of her guilt seemed to grow
heavier every day. Guilt because she had left it too late to tell him, because she had been selfish, wanting to preserve his ignorance and affec-
tion intact, wanting to keep him innocent, in a world where no one can
afford innocence anymore—and guilt because she had allowed it to happen in the first place, the rapine and betrayal, she had opened the Gate
and let in the stranger and made Nathan what he was. All rape victims
feel guilt, she knew that; her emotions were commonplace. But it didn't
occur to anyone, even Bartlemy, that she would react that way; he was
caught up with otherworldly visions, with the Big Picture of fate and fa-
tality. *I see only the small picture,* Annie thought. *My picture.* She had
tried to follow Daniel, reaching out beyond life, beyond death—and her
body, her very womb had been invaded and abused. She had been happy
in the child who had come to fill her emptiness, spending long years on
the borders of denial, seeking to keep that happiness inviolate—and
now Nathan was in danger, weighted down with responsibility and
doom, and it was her fault. All her fault. How could she ask him to understand when all she herself understood was her own culpability?

To make it worse, it was January. The days were gray and short, the nights dark and long. February followed, as a matter of routine, and the world grew if anything colder, and it snowed even in the south of England, not just a light dusting on the hilltops but a real whiteout, and the electricity went off, and they huddled around the fire by candlelight, toasting bread over the flames. It might have been fun, an adventure of the small-scale, manageable kind, but Nathan declined the toast and went to bed wearing two sweaters and burying himself under extra blankets, searching for his father through a dozen different worlds. He was desperate to see him, talk to him, but the summons did not come, and when he was on Eos the buildings were always empty and the people distant, so he could not get close enough to question them, and he roamed other universes though he knew there was little point, not knowing where he was going or why, trapped on a mission to nowhere. Once, he was in the Eosian desert, under Astrond, the Red Moon of Madness, looking at the skeleton of a wild xaurian. Somehow he knew it had once been white. Another time he was in the Deepwoods of Wilderslee—he hoped to see Woody the woodwose, his childhood friend and playmate, but what creatures were there hid from him, and the slopes grew steep and the trees wild, and by a twilit pool among moss-grown rocks he saw a waterfay, watching him slyly from beneath her shadowy hair. And there were other worlds, worlds he had only glimpsed through the spy-crystals in the Grandir's tower, landscapes of ice and stone and sand, towering temples, jungles that sweated and steamed. There was a forest of giant purple mushrooms, and a house with a roof that curled up at the corners, and a lake of green water with a man sitting beside it who looked as if he had sat there for a hundred years. "What is this place?" Nathan asked, but not a muscle moved in the man's face, and his stillness and silence were as impenetrable as a wall. In all the worlds—in all the dreams—if there were people they were far away, or did not speak, though he knew he was visible, until he almost thought he was dreaming indeed, a recurring nightmare of an endless search for something that could not be found.

"Maybe the Grandir's doing it deliberately," Hazel said. "Building up the suspense—manipulating you."

He had confided in her because he required a confidante, but he barely listened to what she said.

"He wouldn't be so petty," Nathan replied.

When she heard the truth Hazel had been shocked but not, somehow, very surprised. It explained so many things that had needed explaining: Nathan's differentness, his specialness, his ability to cross the barrier between worlds—the Grandir's obsession with him. It was plain he had been conceived to fulfill a specific destiny—like the royal family, Hazel thought, whose role in life was mapped out long before any of them popped into existence. Sometimes, when Nathan talked about Nell or Denaero, she had experienced a sneaking envy of those born to princessdom, with kingly fathers and adoring subjects and a life that, whatever their tribulations, earmarked them as heroines from scratch. Hazel had an absentee father who had hit her mother when he was drunk, a little talent for witchcraft and none for anything else, and she knew she would never be a heroine—but she resented her own envy, and pushed it away, telling herself princesses were stuck with a life of duties and restrictions, and anyway she was a republican, and the French Revolution had been a good thing. However, Nathan wasn't a prince—she didn't know what the Grandir's son would be—and he seemed to have the duties and the dangers without the perks. In the past, though he had appeared increasingly mesmerized by the Grandir, it was the job at hand that had dominated his thoughts. Now Hazel feared he, too, was becoming obsessed—knowing the truth, it engrossed him to the exclusion of all else.

"Mum should have told me sooner," Nathan said broodingly more than once.

"Maybe *he* should have told you," Hazel suggested, but she made no impression.

"I suppose I'll have to stop thinking of him as a power-crazed supervillain," she remarked later. "Although supervillains *do* have sons who turn out to be good guys. Think of Darth Vader."

"Stop talking like Eric," Nathan said, taking her too seriously. "All that Good-'n'-Evil, turn-to-the-dark-side stuff—life isn't like that. Most people come in between. The Grandir may be a supreme ruler, but he's not a saint, he's not a monster, he's not a god. He's—he's *human*. Human writ large, but human. He cares about me, I know he does. I've seen it in his face."

"He uses you," Hazel said. "You were born for him to use."

"Yes. But he's got a universe to save. And he's also tried to protect me. We disagreed—he told me not to get involved when I was in otherworlds—he didn't want me running into danger. Just like a real father . . . Only I *did* get involved—I broke the—the *link* between our minds—I sort of took control of the portal—and now I can't find him. He must be waiting for me, trying to contact me . . . There are so many things I want to ask him."

"He'll be in touch," Hazel said in a strangely flat voice.

She was sure of it.

ANNIE AND Pobjoy continued to date, but infrequently. He was sent away to Lancashire over a case of people-smuggling that had ramifications in both areas, and when they *did* meet he found her preoccupied and unwilling to discuss her troubles. How could she tell him what she had told Nathan, when he was still so reluctant to believe in magic, and otherworlds, and their possible incursion on everyday existence? They kissed, and in kissing the barriers almost came down, and their doubts and differences started to melt away—but Annie always drew back, thinking of Nathan, though he was not thinking of her, feeling that now was not the time to risk widening the gulf between mother and son. And in consequence Pobjoy began to wonder if she truly liked him, and whether it was worth persisting, and—as usual—what was *really* going on in Eade. He read *The Wind in the Willows*, which he found unexpectedly gripping, though he was torn between his approval of Badger as a character and his disapproval of vigilante action by civilians, as advocated in the retaking of Toad Hall. Annie then gave him John Masefield's *The Midnight Folk*, because it had highwaymen and stolen treasure and many other ingredients guaranteed to appeal to the small boy in every grown man, and *Guards! Guards!*, because it was about policemen.

Pobjoy found himself thinking that surely dating never used to require quite so much intellectual effort. When he was in his teens and twenties, preparation had generally consisted of brushing his teeth, changing his shirt, and checking he'd remembered to pack the condoms. Reading hadn't gotten a look-in. But then his marriage had been short-lived, and he realized, looking back, that he didn't actually know if his wife liked to read, since he had never found the time to ask. Maybe, in the New Age, with its New Men, and its New Women—an age when you filled out a form on the Internet to assess compatibility, and chatting up a colleague could land you with a lawsuit for harassment—maybe this was how things were done.

He consulted the inspector with whom he was liaising in Lancashire, a man some fifteen years his senior.

"I dunno, lad," the man said. "Been married nearly thirty years. Easiest way. I'd be lost if I had to start again. My daughter's got a boyfriend in Tibet whom she met online—they've never seen each other but she says they bond spiritually. My son has a girlfriend with pink hair who's studying psychology and claims he's an interesting case. In my day a couple of pints and a grope in the cinema always did the trick. But you know what the French say: Ortra temps, ortra mouse. They do it with computers nowadays."

Which didn't help much.

Meanwhile, his sense of humor, carefully cultivated, grew like a bulb that thrives in the dark, ready to reach out into the daylight at some future stage.

MARCH ARRIVED, and the winter still hung on, like an unwanted guest who stays and stays, ignoring all hints that it's time to depart. It dug itself in with icy claws, turning the ground to permafrost, splitting the pipes, sharpening the wind till it seemed to cut to the bone. Puddles cracked underfoot, noses reddened, lips chapped, everyone got colds. Hazel decided she was warmer at Thornyhill, with Bartlemy's broth inside her and Hoover snuggled against her leg and a fire burning merrily on the hearth. Redoing her schoolwork was a small price to pay, and it meant she could talk to Bartlemy about her worries over Nathan, though careful not to cross the line into generation disloyalty. But Bartlemy had been around so long he didn't belong to *any* generation, so perhaps he didn't count.

"It's time to try and help," Bartlemy said, "though there's little we can do. Other universes are outside the province of regular magic. Still, we can ask a few questions and see if the answers have changed. You never know what we may learn."

"Do we light the spellfire?" Hazel said, happily abandoning her math.

"Not tonight. It is customary to burn fire crystals when you draw the circle, but in this weather I think warmth wins over atmosphere." He closed the curtains, rolled back the rug. Hazel, obedient to instructions, drizzled spellpowder around the perimeter, where the blackened scar of other circles showed clearly on the bare floorboards.

"Have you done this before?" Bartlemy said, with an absentmindedness unusual for him.

"N-no, but—"

"Very well. Just do as I say. I will initiate the magic, but you may summon the spirits and question them, as and when I tell you. However, this is a hazardous proceeding, so don't deviate from my orders, no matter what may occur. This is not the time for getting—as they say nowadays—creative. Do you understand?"

Hazel nodded and sat down again, no longer slouching in comfort but straight-backed and wary. Hoover came to attention, cocking an ear and opening both eyes. Bartlemy switched off the electric lights and the fire glow pooled in the center of the room, chasing the shadows into the corners. When the powder sputtered into a ring of flame Hazel had the impression the walls retreated, and the darkness drew in, and there was nothing beyond the firelight at all. Only the three of them existed in a dimension of their own, huddled around the perimeter of the spell.

"Call Eriost," Bartlemy said, meaning the Child.

Hazel spoke the words of summoning—words he had taught her

some time ago—but even before she had finished he was there. He—or she—or it. The choirboy face, the pale gold curls, the eyes as old as sin.

"Whence the haste?" Bartlemy asked, forgetting he had agreed that Hazel would be the Questioner.

The spirit did not seem to hear him.

"Well, well," it said, peering out of the circle as if trying to see through a thick mist, "a new friend—a hagling—young, so young. We will be playmates. I will dance with you on the sands of eternity until the tide comes in. Do you dance? Do you sing?"

"I dance a little," Hazel said, diverted, "but I don't sing, unless I want to scare people."

The Child laughed its silvery laugh. "I like that. We will have *fun* together. We will walk along the sands gathering seashells, and mermaid's finger bones, and drowned men's eyes. They turn into pearls, if you keep them long enough—did you know that? The poets say so. *Those are pearls that were his eyes* . . . But you must find the eyes first, and pluck them while they're fresh, or the spell won't work. Come with me—come away with me—"

"Ask questions, don't answer them," Bartlemy murmured. "Or it will spout nonsense all night."

"Who is there?" the Child demanded in an altered voice. "Is there a big fat wizard lurking in the shadows, whispering in your ear? Whisper whisper whisper—spin the coin, roll the dice—fiddlefeet and twiddlestrings . . ."

"Ask him how he responded so quickly," Bartlemy said. "It may not be important, but I think we should know."

"What does he say, the fat old wizard? Is he angry with me? Does he curse and spit?"

"No, he—how did you get here so fast?" Hazel asked. "I hadn't even finished the summons."

"I felt your call," the Child answered with rare coherence. "The wall between the mortal world and the place of the spirits grows thin. Soon it will fail, and then the circle will not bind me, and there will be no more questioning. Beware the Ides of March!"

"When is that?" Hazel said.

"The fifteenth," said Bartlemy. "Ask him—"

"Who knows?" the spirit mocked. "Who cares? The hour draws near at last, an hour long foretold.

Hickory dickory dock
It's time to break the clock
But heed the warning in the rhyme—
Breaking the clock won't stop the Time.

A night of magic approaches when all doors will open, even the Last Door that never opens for us at all . . ."

"Which night?" Hazel said, needing no prompt to hazard the question.

"*The* night," said the Child. "Is he still there, the Whisperer? Tell him we will come for him, him and all witchkind—we will make him dance with us until he grows thin, dance until his feet wear out—dance and dance—over the hills and far away . . . The fairies are coming back, out of the old stories, carrying their little green candles, lighting the way to Scarbarrow Fayr . . . Will you come with us, hagling? Will you take my hand and dance down the road to Faerie?"

"Dismiss him," Bartlemy said, evidently averse to even the wisp of a threat. "We have heard enough."

Hazel obeyed, a little grudgingly, and the Child faded in his usual haphazard fashion, leaving his eyes behind. Hazel got rid of them with a final Command and realized she felt trembly from tension, though nothing very frightening had occurred.

"Were there really fairies once?" she inquired skeptically. "With wings and sparkly hair?"

"Oh yes," Bartlemy said. "But you must remember, werefolk take many forms—often the forms we give them. They borrow our imagination, having little of their own. But what they borrow is not always what we wish to lend. There are goblins, piskeys, imps, gremlins, grinnocks, pugwidgies . . . I have seen some with wings, though they probably pulled them off a bird first. They might even sparkle—all that sparkles is not diamond, after all. But few would look good on the top of a Christmas tree."

"Who do we summon next?"

"No more spirits," Bartlemy decided. "I do not like that part about walls thinning. The old safeguards are slipping away . . ."

"But," Hazel said, frowning, "the spirits live in our world, don't they? They can't pass the Gate."

"Our world has many dimensions," Bartlemy said. "Some are more real than others. There are realms of folklore and superstition, which may linger on long after the original stories are forgotten. It is best to avoid such places. They hold many dangers for mortals, even the Gifted—especially the Gifted—but normally they are not easy to enter and are hidden from us by the very magics that made them. Few have ever trod the dark path to Tartarus or sailed to Tir na nog; the guardians may be sleeping, but the invisible doors are shut, and only a handful remain who could open them. However, the Spring Solstice is always perilous, and I fear—"

"The Solstice?"

"I suspect that's the night the Child was referring to. March twenty-first. It's not far off."

"But it's still winter!" Hazel objected.

"Spring is coming," Bartlemy said. "And maybe other things are coming as well . . ."

There was silence. Hazel wanted to try another summons, but she sensed a deeper unease in Bartlemy than the doubts he had expressed, and it disturbed her. Bartlemy was never uneasy.

The circle made a faint hissing noise, like the breath of a sleeping dragon. A log shifted in the fire with a swish of cinders. There was no sound from the night outside, no traffic murmur from distant roads. The rest of the world might have moved on, leaving them trapped in a single grain of being. The three of them around the circle, and the sinking fire, and the shadows creeping inward.

"We'll try one more thing," Bartlemy said. "But it may not work."

"Which spirit—"

"No spirit. This is a woman, or it was once. She may be dead. She may be incapable of responding. We will see."

"What's her name?"

Bartlemy told her.

Hazel recited the summons, but the circle remained empty. The fire was definitely dying; soon the only light to endure would be from the perimeter, a thin line of glimmer that barely kept back the dark. Within the spellring, there was a suggestion of . . . shapes, phantom forms too dim to be clearly seen, which might yet begin to solidify if the space stayed unoccupied for too long, or the shadows from which they came encroached farther, or Hazel spoke a wrong word, lost concentration, lost control.

She said: "There's something . . . trying to get through."

"This is magic," Bartlemy responded, unperturbed. "There's always something trying to get through. Perhaps . . . the name I gave you is too widely used. There could be a million of them. We will essay another."

"How many names does this woman have?"

"She may have several. What matters, for the Gifted, is the one she uses for spellcasting, for the self she wants to be. As I said, this is magic."

Hazel reran the incantation, this time with another name. In the circle, the phantoms faded. There was a long, dark moment when nothing was happening but she sensed the imminence of something, a prickle in the air, a teetering on the edge of things. Shadows gathered at the hub— grew denser—thickened into substance. And then there was someone there. At least Hazel assumed it was someone, since she had called a person by name, but it was so small—smaller than the Child—so hunched and twisted and shrunken, so bundled in dark shapeless clothing that for a minute she wasn't sure.

She said to Bartlemy, in a sort of stage whisper: "Is that *her*?"

"She is old," the wizard said. "Old beyond her Gift. It is not well to outlive your time."

If her face had been disfigured once, it no longer showed. It was brown and spotted and shriveled, like an ancient tea bag, jaws clamped grimly under knobbled cheekbones, huge yellow eyes, webbed with veins, peering from beneath papery lids. She was sitting in what appeared to be a wheelchair, not an efficient piece of modern machinery but something carved crudely from wood that, when she tried to turn it, emitted a creak like a scream of pain. Her hands were warped out of all recognizable handness, but they clutched the wheels of the chair like talons, as if, somewhere in the tiny mummified body, there was still an unnatural strength, a hungry, desperate spirit, a will to live out of all proportion to life. Her voice, when it emerged, was thin and hoarse, hissing through her toothless jaws like the wind through a keyhole.

"Connard! Connard de merde! Qu'est-ce qui se passe? Hein? Hein? Qui se passe?"

"Doesn't she speak English?" Hazel said, panicking.

"She should. She lived here once."

"Maybe you should talk to her—"

"Go ahead."

Hazel did her best to pull herself together. "Margolaine!"

"Qui est là? Qui parle? Putain—putain de merde!"

"Can you speak English?" Hazel asked doubtfully.

"Whore!" said the old woman, answering the question. "Whore and child of a whore! I speak English, Italian, Arabic . . . Who are you, to play zese games wiz me? Who are you?"

"No names," Bartlemy said.

"I am a witch," Hazel said. "I have—I have the power to call you. That's all you need to know."

"No manners," croaked Margolaine. "Ze witch should introduce herself. Zere is no *politesse* anymore."

"She's clever," Bartlemy said judiciously. "Be careful. She will trap you if she can. Your identity would not help her much, but it's safest to remain anonymous."

"My name isn't important," Hazel declared. "Answer my questions, and I will release you."

"Putain! I will not be questioned by you!"

"Then we'll stay here all night," Hazel said, glancing at Bartlemy for confirmation. He smiled. *"And* the next day."

"I piss on your circle!"

"Be my guest," Hazel said, almost beginning to enjoy herself. "You'll be the one with soggy knickers."

Bartlemy raised an eyebrow, but Margolaine appeared temporarily stymied.

"What are zese questions you wish to ask me?" she demanded. "I make no promise to answer, but—"

"We want to know about your son," Hazel said, echoing Bartlemy. "Your son—Nathaniel?"

"Nevaire!" cried Margolaine. "I nevaire speak of him—*compris?* It is *interdit*! *Espèce de merde*—" She shuddered with a spasm of what might have been rage, spitting more curses. Froth gathered at the corners of her mouth.

"You tell us about your son," Hazel said, "or we stay here all night. You know how it goes."

"*Putain!* Whore! You give me a name, or I call you a whore *all night*. You want that?"

"I don't care," Hazel said.

"You have no *honte*—no shame!"

Hazel rather liked the idea of being shameless, but a nudge from Bartlemy reminded her to stick to the point.

"Your son," she said. "Who was his father?"

The old woman champed her jaws—her eyes glared with a malevolence far beyond the strength of her meager body. *"Eh bien,"* she said, "we will speak of zese things, but only one time, and nevaire again. *D'accord?*" Hazel nodded. "Ze father was a magus, an emperor—more zan an emperor—ze ruler of anozzer world. He was a god among his people. His voice came to me through my spells, intruding on ze magic, saying he had chosen me—me alone, in all zer worlds—to be his bride, ze mozzer of his child. A special child, a child who would open ze Gate, at ze hour appointed, and unite me wiz my husband for all time. He teach me to make a great magic—we open ze Gate for a moment of time, *un moment éternel*—I am in his arms, in his love—his seed is in my body . . . Do you understand? *Peux-tu imaginer?* I was as ze *Sainte-Marie*, ze *Sainte-Vièrge*, but ze stupid priests, zey do not know what zey say. She was not *vièrge* after: how could she be? Ze love of a god, it is beyond such *conneries*—it fill you *à jamais*. I burned like ze stars—I shone like ze sun—you, who are little witch, wiz little spells, little dreams, you cannot know. To be loved by a god—no ozzer women in all time have zat, only me and zer *Sainte-Marie*."

Hazel listened dumbly. Bartlemy had told her nothing of Margolaine's history, but the picture was becoming all too clear.

She thought: *Annie . . . was it like that for Annie? Was that why there were no other men for so long?*

But now Annie was dating a police inspector, an unlikely successor in the celestial shoes—or bedsocks. And Annie had no Gift, no delusions of sainthood. Somehow she didn't think Annie would have seen it in quite the same way . . .

Margolaine's eyes were glazed, rapt with memory. Bartlemy touched Hazel's arm, murmured the question for her to repeat.

"And your son? What happened when he was born?"

Margolaine's old face scrunched into a terrible bitterness. "Ze magic was too strong. He was—*un monstre*. He had two heads—his own and his demon, ze evil spirit and ze good in a single *être*. But I love him—he is child of ze god—I love him though I know he is doomed."

"You had other husbands?" Hazel said.

"Zey were nozzing—little men, greedy, *lâches*—I took what zey could give me and watched zem die. I had been zer bride of ze god—wealth and position were my right. *D'ailleurs*. I had to look after Nathaniel."

"Why that name?"

"I do not know. It was ze name I had *au coeur,* when he was born. Maybe his father choose . . . He speak to me through ze smoke, in ze heartbeat of a spell. I come to England as he tell me, I find ze place—ze time comes, ze time of sacrifice . . ."

"The Spring Solstice?"

"It was spring, yes . . . In ze pagan days, zey make ze sacrifice, so ze corn grow tall. For us, it almost *Pâcques*—Easter—when *Sainte-Marie* must see her son die. Always, zere must be blood . . . I find ze place, ze hill zey call Scarbarrow, and I kill my son—my beloved Nathaniel. I

cut his throat, but ze ozzer head—ze demon head—still speak, still cry
to me—so I kill him, too, I kill him twice, and his blood run over me,
ze blood to open ze Gate, and bring me to my lover again . . ." Only
now did she start to tremble, her small body shaking like a leaf in a gale.
Hazel, cold with the horror of it, thought she could hear bones rattling
together under the skin. "But ze Gate is shut—it is shut! He does not
answer me—he does not come! I kill my son—*his* son—and he does
not come to me! I nevaire hear his voice again . . . I call to him, and call
to him, but he is gone . . . *Sacré Dieu de merde,* he is gone . . ."

Hazel found she, too, was shaking, though not in sympathy.
Bartlemy took her hand.

"Ask her," he said, "if she was *told* to kill the boy."

"I do not need to be told. I *knew.* It is ze ritual, as old as Time. In a
great cause, zere must be ze great sacrifice. Zere must be ze sacrifice of
love. For ze strongest magic, zere must be blood . . . to open ze Gate,
zere must be blood . . ."

"Where was the Scarbarrow?" Hazel said.

"South. Zere were woods . . . I have no map, I follow ze heart. Always, I follow ze heart. And now I have nothing—nothing. Nothing
for all time. My power is all worn out . . . I live on and on . . . wiz
nozzing. *Rien de rien de rien . . .*"

"Why don't you let go?" Hazel said, slightly startled by Bartlemy's
final question. "In death, the Gate would open for you, if not to the god
you once sought . . ."

Another spasm gripped Margolaine; sputum dripped from her
mouth. "I kill my son," she said, "for nothing. I think now it is not ze
god who wait for me beyond ze Gate. Maybe it is ze Devil . . . I feel
him zere, sometime, waiting for me—waiting . . . I will not go to him,
not while I can hold on to life. Inside zis body I am still strong, stronger
zan Death. I will nevaire let go . . ."

Hazel released her without thanks, with no courtesy farewell. She
wanted to find words of pity, but she felt none. Only disgust, and the
bigness of her fear, hanging over her like a cloud.

"Some people make their own hell," Bartlemy said. "There is nothing you can do for them."

"Nathan," Hazel whispered. "He wouldn't . . . Annie wouldn't . . ."

"No indeed." The circle was extinguished, the electric lights turned on. The room was a room again, not an isolated cell floating in the dark. Bartlemy bent to put another log on the fire. "Annie is hardly a mad sorceress seeking power beyond the world. I think the pattern became deformed, in Margolaine's mind, just as her child was deformed. And I fear she was not the only one. But Annie opened the Gate through love, with no thought of self, and so Nathan was born whole, and the pattern is clear—though we cannot yet see where it leads."

"Is it true—about the sacrifice?" Hazel said, her hands writhing in Hoover's shaggy fur. She felt it was true.

"Yes. But in the old days it was the king who died, not the prince. That was what kingship was all about."

"It's different now," Hazel said shakily, "isn't it? We don't sacrifice our royals. Well, not much . . ." She tried to laugh.

Bartlemy poured her a drink—the dark red drink he brewed himself, sweet and spicy, warming her with its own heat.

"You did well," he said. "And we may have learned something useful. That is worth a few horrors. Still, I had hoped to discover where the Scarbarrow lies . . ."

"Do I tell Nathan?" Hazel asked.

"It's up to you."

But she didn't think she could.

THE SNOW thawed, refroze, thawed again. The temperature inched up a degree or two. The spring flowers kept their heads down, staying in the comparative warmth of the earth. Nathan got a cold that went on his chest, and Annie decided to keep him home for a week or so, feeding him one of Bartlemy's tonics and lots of good food. Sometimes she could almost fool herself that their relationship was back to normal, unless she steered the conversation too close to the wrong subjects, when he would instantly withdraw from her behind a barrier of stillness and minimal communication. Hazel came to see him, and George, who caught his cold, and Michael and Liberty Rayburn, bringing a carrot cake from their mother and a couple of CDs they had downloaded specially. By the Sunday, Nathan announced he was well again and ready to go back to school.

"Keep him home a few more days," Bartlemy said for Annie's private ear. "Tuesday is the twenty-first. This may be the night we've been waiting for. Whatever he has to do, it's better he should do it from here."

"I'm not staying indoors," Nathan objected when Annie told him he wasn't going back to Ffylde just yet.

On Monday he wrote a history essay and went for a walk with Hazel.

"It's the Solstice tomorrow," she said. "Supposing . . . something happens?"

"Nothing ever happens," Nathan said. "Nothing's happened for ages. I look for the Grandir nearly every night, but I can't find him. I don't think I'll ever see him again."

Hazel thought: *Should I tell him—about Margolaine, and the boy with two heads?* But she couldn't summon up the courage.

They walked through the woods on that cold gray day, talking little. Afterward, Hazel would always remember that walk, and the things she had not said. The countryside was blanched by the long winter into every shade of pale: the grass was barely green anymore, the earth barely brown, the tree trunks colorless in the drab daylight. The whole world looked like an invalid who has stayed in bed too long, growing weaker and sicklier, hoping in vain that one day someone will throw open the curtains and let in the sun.

"Anyway," Hazel said, out of the blue, "it will be spring soon. That's what the Solstice is *really* about."

"How do you know?" said Nathan. "Just because it was spring last year, and the year before, doesn't mean it will come again. Some people think we're heading for another ice age. We've done so much damage to our environment. It's like the Contamination on Eos. We're only small-scale yet—just one planet—we may be extinct before we can take it further—but damage is what humans do. They could have taught us something, the Grandir's people. We might have learned from their mistakes."

Hazel shivered, though there was little wind.

"It *will* be spring," she insisted doggedly. "The day after tomorrow, it will be spring."

THAT NIGHT, something happened.

Nathan opened the portal more out of habit than hope—if *opened* was the right word. He would find the weak spot in his mind and pour himself through it, into another world—but although he now felt he could control the transition, he never knew which world he would be in, or where he was going when he got there. When his dreams had arrived at random they had seemed to have a goal, he had felt he was progressing, following some sort of plan, even if it wasn't his, but since he could dream to order the journeys felt purposeless, a vain ramble through a multiverse that meant nothing to him. The desperate search for his father had become the wanderings of a lost vagabond in the space–time continuum on a quest that would never be fulfilled.

He was not quite sixteen; his patience was limited and his attention span short. Nearly three months of nocturnal meanderings seemed almost interminable.

That night he was back on Eos. More twisty corridors, strange cellular rooms fitting together like bubbles in a lava lamp, a winding stair, not a spiral but a snake, uncoiling itself down a wide shaft studded with windows with the usual view of sheer buildings and intersecting sky, though there was no air traffic anymore. At the bottom a long passage like a tunnel burrowed straight through the heart of the complex— whatever complex he was in—with an archway at the far end filled with light and color. He was reminded of *Alice's Adventures in Wonderland* and the little door into the garden. But there were no gardens on Eos. He began to walk down the tunnel toward it, but it was a long way, and he broke into a run, and as he drew nearer he saw it *was* a garden, or a visual trick—there were green leaves, and flowers, and a light like the sun before it was poisoned—before it wiped out all the leaves and flowers for good. When he reached the arch there was a door of glass or crystal; he pushed it open and stepped through—and he was in the garden, it was real, it was alive, though the flowers were like none he had ever seen. Daffodil-trumpets a foot long, blossom-tassels in cream and gold, puffballs of milky petals emitting wafts of pale pink pollen . . . Somewhere above there was a domed roof that filtered the sun or gave off some light of its own, the light of spring in worlds where the seasons still turned, and spring always came around again.

The garden was circular. Paved pathways converged on a central point, where there was an arrangement of fountains with slender spools of water crisscrossing in an elaborate interplay. And there was the Grandir, sitting beside the fountains. Waiting for him.

He wore no mask or hood, and his customary black clothing had been changed for white. White jacket, white leggings, white boots. He seemed to glitter faintly in the spring light.

"You're my father," Nathan said.

The Grandir didn't hug him or even take his hand. On Eos, people very rarely touched.

"I would have told you," he said, "if she had not. It was time for you to know. Sit down."

Nathan sat.

The Grandir said: "Have you any questions?"

Of course he had questions—so many questions they were filling his mind and crowding one another out, and somehow he couldn't get a grip on any of them.

"Forgive me," the Grandir went on. "I have never done this before. I have lived almost fifty thousand years in earth time, ruled worlds beyond count, journeyed my own universe at thoughtspeed, done things no other man could do—but not this. This one thing. I have never talked to my son. It is difficult for me, too."

"We've talked before," Nathan said. "Twice."

"We had no time then," the Grandir said, "and you didn't know the truth. Now we have time, as I promised you. Not much, but a little. Time to talk, here at the end of the world. Father and son."

Do you love me? Nathan wanted to ask. *Are you proud of me? Am I the son you hoped for?*

Do you love me?

"I've got the Crown," he said.

"I know."

"Should I bring it here? With the Cup and the Sword?"

"No. The rest of your task is both simpler, and harder. We will come to that shortly. You have done well—beyond my expectation. I could have wished you had resisted the urge to interfere in the worlds where you found yourself, but you have the instincts of a ruler—the desire for justice, order, peace—and you have always showed both courage and resource. You imperiled yourself, and your task, but I helped where I could, and you survived in the end. You are my son indeed—the son I have not deserved. I betrayed Halmé that you might be born. She knows the truth now, and she will forgive me, but her heart burns. She is the most beautiful and beloved of all women; it is hard for her to come to terms with such a treachery, no matter how desperate the need."

Nathan stammered: "Why—why did you—how did you—"

"I needed a son who could open the portal—a son born of two worlds. I chose your world, your planet, when it was in its infancy; it resembles Alquàrin in the early days, the place from which my people came. But earthfolk had no natural magic, so I gave them a Gift—I performed a Great Spell when I was very young. You cannot imagine the power—almost, it destroyed me. An entire galaxy from my universe, crushed—imploded—into a fist of stone, cast into your world to change it forever."

"The Lodestone," Nathan said. "Atlantis . . ."

"Yes, I believe there was a place called Atlantis. But that was not the point. I wanted to engender your birth—to ensure protection for you, whenever you came—to prepare your planet for its destiny. Unfortunately, earthfolk appear to be unsuited to such power, incapable of handling it rationally. They are, perhaps, still too primitive; your civilization, after all, has barely tottered into the nuclear age, which for us is so far in the past we no longer think it worthy of recollection. If you had seen my cosmos in its heyday!—but the way we lived would have been beyond your understanding. To travel the galaxies at thought-speed, to communicate mind-to-mind, to select and control every aspect of your existence . . . But the Contamination destroyed it, in less than a millennium, and now there is little left. A few fragments of thaumotechnology, the dregs of a vaster world. This is the last garden that will ever be. There were stories once of a Paradise at the beginning of Time. This is Paradise at the end."

Nathan said: "It's beautiful," because it was expected of him. And it *was* beautiful, it was the most beautiful garden he had ever seen, but . . .

"The Gift," he pursued. "You were telling me . . . about the Gift?"

"Indeed. It was not a success. Initially I looked among the Gifted for your mother—twice, I tried with sorceresses of your people, powerful for their kind, but the passage between worlds was too traumatic. The children were born deformed, and in the end the women went mad; there was nothing I could do for them. Then the spells showed me another, with no Gift, but with the power of her own heart—a love strong enough to open the Gate for the instant that was all I needed. It seemed extraordinary to me that in a race so backward, so savage, so sickly and short-lived, there might be such love. It was desperate indeed to hazard so much on a creature of such frailty. But I had waited long—longer than you can imagine—and my world was already starting to die. Although my seed was potent, there was only sufficient left for one final attempt. I had sent the Ozmosees to your world; I used them to engineer an opportunity. The moment came, and I took it, and when you were born I knew I had not gambled in vain. I had selected the wizard Bartoliman already; he has the Gift but has used it in moderation and has retained power over his own self, if at the cost of his power over others. I sent you and your mother to him so he might be your guardian in my stead, gathering you all in the vicinity of the Grail. And I watched over you as you grew up, though you did not know it. I saw the shape of your mind, the temper of your spirit."

There was a silence—an eerie silence for a garden, a silence without the hum of bees or the chatter of birds. For this was a garden that grew by magic when all other growth had ceased, an Eden at the world's end—the memory of spring, not spring itself.

"I did not expect to love you," the Grandir said.

It was what Nathan had been wanting to hear, what he had searched for through all his dreams. For a second his happiness was so intense, it felt like a spear inside him, twisting in his heart. He could not speak.

"I planned so carefully," the Grandir said, "and for so many ages. But love creeps in through the chinks between plans, taking you by surprise. No ruler, no matter how powerful, can plan for everything. This has been a gift to me, and a burden, though it will cost me dear. As I sit here, in this garden, talking to my son—I would not be without it."

Nathan tried to meet his eyes, but he could not. He thought: *In our world, we don't say such things—embarrassment or inhibition gets in the way.*

Which world do I belong to?

The Grandir said gently: "You have asked me very little. Have you no other questions?"

"You've already answered the only one that mattered," Nathan said.

And then, out of nowhere, a question he had forgotten, or never thought to ask—Hazel's question. Always Hazel, intruding on his thoughts like a goblin, mischievous, malignant—a goblin popping up in this Eden where the spring made no sound.

"What's your name?"

Nathan thought for a minute the Grandir might be offended, but he only laughed. Nathan could not recall seeing him laugh before, yet it seemed he could laugh like lesser men. "My name! Ah, you would not understand. In your world, names are important—a little. I wanted you called Naithan because of its meaning, in many tongues—the gift, the God-given. It is the name that has been written into the spell since Romandos's day. But in my world, the name of a Grandir—his true name, his birth name—can be a weapon against him. It can even be used to counteract his spells or touch his thought. Among my predecessors, many have been careless or generous with their names, but I could not afford to take that risk. Even Halmé does not know it. Only my mother, who gave it to me when I first entered the world, and she carried it unspoken to her grave. It is a name of great import in any universe, but none other has ever used it, nor ever will." He paused. Smiled.

"You may call me Father. That, too, is a name none other has ever used . . . nor ever will."

"Father," Nathan said, trying it out.

In our world, he thought, *we say Dad, Daddy, Pop, Papa,* but such diminutives would not do for so solemn a moment, for a Grandir, for the ruler of a cosmos.

Father . . .

"It will serve," said the Grandir, "for what time we have left. I am proud to hear it on your lips."

What time we . . . Was he going to lose what he had found—so soon, so soon?

"Father—"

But the Grandir had gotten to his feet. "Halmé is coming. She helped you once, thinking I would not know it—she, who has no secrets from me! It was but a part of the pattern . . . Still, this is hard for her. She is the heart of my world, yet her own heart has been bruised, if not broken . . ."

She came toward them down one of the pathways, moving like a poem, her perfect head poised on her perfect neck. For a long while the subtle differences of proportion between earthfolk and Eosians had ceased to trouble Nathan; now it was his own people—the people he had grown up with—who looked wrong to him. Like the Grandir, Halmé wore white, a long flowing tunic over long flowing trousers. Her hair was piled up behind her head in a mass of knots and coils, bound with a strip of cloth with trailing ends that rippled as she walked. Everything about her rippled and flowed, but her face was still, frozen in hesitation—in doubt. When she saw Nathan, a light came into her eyes, though whether happy or sad he could not tell, and there was a tear on her cheek, a single tear bright as a droplet of diamond.

"I knew," she said, placing her hands on his shoulders. He was tall, but she was taller, well over six feet in earth measurements. "When first I saw you, I knew you for his son. My soul knew, though my mind did not. His child—by another . . . Yet I loved you from that moment. Isn't that strange? Almost as if . . . you were the son I should have had . . ."

"It is well," the Grandir said. Nathan noticed it was his gesture, rather than his touch, that lifted the hands from his shoulders, breaking the contact. "And now, the time has come. The time we have waited for. The Contamination has killed all life in my universe, save here. Even as we speak, it is closing on Ind, the last continent on the last planet . . . The night sky darkens; whole constellations have been snuffed out. By day the sun that once warmed us scorches like fire. Arkatron, city of forty million people, now has less than two hundred thousand, the last remnants of the greatest race who ever lived. If they are to be saved, we must act. Nathan . . ."

"Yes?"

"Take us to your world."

NATHAN STARED at him. In all his half-formed imaginings, there had never been a moment like this. He was still struggling to take in everything the Grandir had told him—still reeling from the implications—still flattened from the emotional steamroller that had thundered over his spirit. And now, at the climax of his short life, he was being asked to do the impossible. He could not disappoint his father now, but . . .

"I *can't* . . . I don't know how to—how to do that. I'm not a wizard, just . . ."

"Just my son." The Grandir's voice was as gentle and inexorable as the sea—and Nathan had seen what the sea could do when it made up its mind. "You've done it before. You saved a man who was drowning, when we closed off Maali. It was not what I needed from you, but it taught me you have the power and the will to use it. You transported the unfortunate Kwanjira Ley from the Pits—you took a princess for a walk in the woods, hardly an essential part of your task. You used the portal, even when you stayed in the same universe, switching yourself from A to B through a point *outside* being—and you were able to carry someone with you. You didn't know what you were doing, but you did it. Necessity was the driving force. And there is necessity here. The Great Spell must be performed in *your* world: the Three are there, the Cup, the Sword, the Crown—and the place was chosen long ago, marked with the impress of doom. Halmé and I must be there. Set aside your doubts. I have not failed you in the past; I know you will not fail me."

I wish I knew it, Nathan thought. The doubts were mobbing him, storming into his head—but he couldn't deal with them now. No time.

The Grandir said: "Link hands."

They stood in a circle; the Grandir took his right hand, Halmé his left. Being rare, the touch felt special—skin on skin—almost a meeting of souls. Nathan looked into Halmé's face and saw there the shadow of Imagen—Imagen in love, passionate and alive—stilled forever in those immortal features, time-frozen, fixed in a passionless perfection. Only when she looked at Nathan did a glimmer of that vitality return to her.

He remembered Lugair—the alien strain in their heredity. He must tell the Grandir . . .

"It makes no difference," the Grandir said, answering his thought. "Lugair, too, was part of the spell . . ."

And then Nathan looked into his father's eyes, and saw nothing else.

Emotion poured into him like a black tide—an urgency on the edge of despair. In his mind he glimpsed the lifeless wastes of the Contamination—empty lands, brown and sterile—gray deserts—great trees crumbling away, their dust blown on the wind until both wind and dust were gone—the red glare of dying suns—planets gripped in a starless cold, their orbits decaying around the heart of the universe—a heart that beat slower, slower, till it subsided into the stasis of the utter End . . . The visions opened his thought, unfolding it into the thought of someone who has lived almost fifty millennia, who has seen everything and done everything, and knows that everything is yet to see and do . . . Fear touched him, the penumbra of an endless night—the hope of a dawn beyond—and love, great love—for Halmé, the most beautiful woman in all the worlds—and for his son, valiant beyond the measure of his kind, who could not fail him now . . .

The world became a spinning dark, a tunnel that swallowed them at lightspeed—shrank—and vanished—

Nathan thought he passed out.

Scarbarrow Fayr

Annie knew, the second she woke up, that there was something wrong. It was a cold pale gray morning like many of the mornings that had preceded it, a winter sort of morning even though it was the first day of spring—winter seemed to be going on more or less forever that year—but her sense of wrongness was only heightened by the fact that nothing was obviously different, nothing out of place. Something must have happened, she thought, while she still slept, something she had been aware of on a subconscious level—a scream, a snarl, a minor earth tremor. A change in the tempo of the house. She could not see it but she *felt* it, her intuition sharpened by more than a decade of contact with the shady side of existence. She got out of bed, remembered that it was Tuesday. The twenty-first. And then she knew.

She ran to Nathan's room, entered without a knock. He was gone. She stood there, stupid with the onset of fear, trying not to lose her head. It had happened before, he had a tendency to go missing, in one world or another, but he had always turned up in the end. Only somehow this didn't look like *missing,* it looked like departure. The duvet was indented, as if he had been lying on top of it, like someone snatching a nap in a house not his own. The clothes he had worn the previous day were gone, including his sneakers—he must have slept in them. And the room was *tidy*, books stacked, oddments tucked in cupboard and drawer, unthinkable for a teenager. Unless they were going away. That was when you tidied up, wasn't it? *When you were leaving* . . . Nathan had been absent, inside his head, ever since she told him the truth. Now he was gone indeed, and she was filled with the terrible cold certainty that he was never coming back.

She rang Bartlemy, stuttering in her distress, fighting to stay calm. "It's the S-Solstice. You said—this was the day. I should've watched him—I didn't think, I expected it to be t-tonight—"

"You can't watch a fifteen-year-old boy all the time, you would drive him insane," Bartlemy said with quiet common sense. "Don't panic: we've been through this before. He'll be back. I, too, thought it would be tonight . . . Are you sure he hasn't gone for an early-morning walk?"

"No—yes. Of course I'm sure. He—"

"How can you be so positive?"

"The impression in the duvet. He never got up."

"All right. I'll come over as soon as I can. I have to check a few things first. Hang in there."

"Hanging," Annie said.

When he arrived, he found her in tears. For all her gentleness, he had rarely seen her cry, except over a sad film, or a novel, or a piece of music. She glanced up at him as he came in, pink-nosed and puffy-eyed, sniffling into toilet paper since Nathan had used up all the tissues the previous week.

"I've been thinking," she said. "I've only ever had him on loan, haven't I? His father always intended to take him back, when the moment came. Did he imagine I was going to—to sacrifice him or something, like that madwoman Kal spoke of? Does he think I'm some crazed medieval witch, trying to open the Gate of Death with my son's blood? He may not know me at all, but—but he should still know me better than that."

"Nathan's father must know something of you," Bartlemy said. "He knows you were able to open the Gate out of love, not as part of his spell."

"Love . . ." Annie's tears ceased; the back of her hand went to her mouth.

She bit it.

She thought: *I've hated him for so long. Supposing this is my punishment—to lose Nathan to him? And how can I harm him—should I ever get the chance—if Nathan loves him and wants to be with him?*

"Annie . . . ?" Bartlemy's voice interrupted the turmoil of her mind.

"These last few months," she said, "it's been as if—as if Nathan's almost forgotten me. He'll answer me when I speak to him—he's always polite—but he looks at me like I'm a ghost—like I'm transparent—not really there. As though he's looking at *me,* but seeing someone else . . ."

"He's had a lot to deal with," Bartlemy said. "He'll never desert you. You've been a wonderful mother under circumstances that haven't been easy—the best mother in the world."

"He used to say that," Annie said, catching her breath on renewed sobs. "But I lied to him—I *lied* . . ."

"You did what seemed right at the time."

"No—I was selfish—selfish and cowardly—you told me so, and it's true. And now he's gone for good . . ."

"Right," said Bartlemy with a brisk change of tone, becoming very down-to-earth. "One, I never told you anything of the kind. I simply recommended you find the right moment to talk to him, and eventually you did. Two, he hasn't gone for good, not if the Grandir wants to finish the Great Spell. The Grail relics are still in their hiding place—I had a look before I came over—and the magic can't be done without them. We're assuming the Grandir is Nathan's father, which seems to be the logical conclusion to draw. Anyway, having gone to some lengths to acquire them I'm quite sure Nathan will return for the relics, sooner or later. Meanwhile, how about some breakfast? I'll cook while you have a wash."

Annie blew her nose, rather more decisively than before. "Sorry," she said. "I'm being an awful fool. I hadn't considered . . . about the

Grail stuff. You're right: you must be. Only I'm afraid I'm not very hungry just yet . . ."

"Try," Bartlemy said. "The brain requires food as well as the body. And I think we will need to be very intelligent before this day is over."

NATHAN KNEW he wasn't asleep, but he didn't think he was properly awake, either. It was dark, a slightly paler shade of darkness than the dark between worlds, and there was a curious smell, a stuffy, damp, vegetal odor like the inside of a compost heap. He couldn't think what universe he was in, if any. And then he realized he could feel the Grandir's hand enfolding his—the clasp of Halmé's slender fingers— and he knew he must be *somewhere*, because during transition the senses didn't function normally, and although the handlink was there the feel of it had been lost.

He said: "Father, I'm not quite sure . . . where we are."

The Grandir released his hand—perhaps there was a gesture, unseen in the gloom. A ball of werelight appeared, hovering just above them, emanating a faint greenish glow that did its best to illuminate their surroundings. A rectangular chamber, not very large, with glimpses of stonework behind a gnarly matting of what appeared to be roots or stems. Crumbly pillars . . . a face, peering suddenly from the apex of an arch, with stumpy horns and wicked eyes above bunched cheeks— but it was only a carving . . . an alcove, where something might have stood, or was intended to stand, but it wasn't there anymore. The chapel of Josevius Grimthorn, built to house the Grail, buried for a millennium beneath the choking roots and briars of the Darkwood. Above, Nathan could make out the hole where, three years before, he had fallen through, though it seemed to be partly overgrown again and only a gray dimness leaked in from the daylight lurking somewhere up there.

The Grandir said: "This place belonged, I believe, to the man I originally entrusted with custody of the Cup. A small-time wizard, greedy and unscrupulous, but he did his job, though his descendants were less reliable. The Sword was well looked after in Wilderslee, even

340 · Amanda Hemingway

if the kings there could never leave it alone, and the spirit Nefanu proved an efficient defender of the Crown despite being relatively insane, but earthfolk, as always, seem to be—wayward. I understand the Cup was actually *sold* at one point. For *money*."

"People like money," Nathan said. "They don't have much magic here. They use money instead."

"We dispensed with it long ago," the Grandir said. "But these are trivial matters. The main thing is, we have arrived. Well done, my son. I knew you had the strength, and the will to use it. Halmé?"

"I'm all right . . . I think," she said, looking around her. "This . . . is our new world?"

"No," said the Grandir. "Just the loophole through which we entered. There is a portal here, not suitable for people as a rule, but it was used for the Cup. I imagine Naithan was able to force it wider . . ."

"I don't know what I did," Nathan said. He couldn't quite believe they were here—the Grandir, and Halmé. Even in the dark they seemed too large for this world, not just physically but in spirit. The Grandir's aura, the force of his personality, filled all the available space—it was like inviting a movie star into a bedsit. "Should we . . . get out of here?"

At a word from the Grandir the overhead roots drew back. Then they began to grow downward, knotting themselves into a ladder. The three of them climbed up. The wood above was deep in the leafmold of many autumns; snagging stems reached out to hook clothes, twig fingers poked down from the upper branches, catching at hair or, in extreme cases, trying to take out an eye. It was a dreary, untidy, unwelcoming sort of place.

Nathan had no idea what time it was, or even what day.

"What is this?" Halmé asked. "Is it a kind of garden?"

"It's a wood," Nathan said.

"I remember woods. There were flowers—some of them flew around, with petals for wings—and the leaves were green, and the trees were tall as towers . . ."

"It's winter," Nathan offered in mitigation.

"I think . . . I would like to go home," Halmé murmured.

"This *is* home," said the Grandir.

And then: "Come. We have things to do before nightfall." A snap of his fingers extinguished the werelight, which had followed them up from below. He turned to Nathan. "The place designated for the spell is not far from this spot. It was once called the *Scarbarrow*, in your tongue."

"Where?" Nathan said.

The Grandir told him.

"We will see you there after sunset. You must fetch the Three and bring them to me. Avoid any contact with your mother or the wizard you call uncle; I do not want you distracted. A Great Spell requires a level of concentration beyond your capacity to imagine, and this will be perhaps the greatest ever performed. Your part in it is small, but significant: I need you to be totally focused."

Even in Eosian, Nathan thought with a flicker of perfidious humor, the phrase sounded familiar. It was the kind of phrase teachers used at school when they wanted to press the right buttons—we want you *totally focused* on passing your exams, or winning this rugger match, or achieving certain academic standards. *Total focus here I come . . .*

But the Great Spell was too serious a matter for flippancy.

"My uncle has the Three," Nathan said. "I can't take them without asking him. Anyway, he's always home."

"He will be out," the Grandir said, with the certainty of one who *knew*. "You need have no qualms of conscience. He was only a caretaker. The Three are mine, or have you forgotten? Romandos made them, my ancestor of long ago. Bring them to me."

"I'll try." What had his mother said about those words?

But when he was with the Grandir, Annie and Uncle Barty seemed small and far away, people encountered in another life, another time. Which of course they were . . .

"We will meet at nightfall," the Grandir said. "I have faith in you, Naithan. Your task is almost over."

He strode off through the Darkwood with Halmé, and the trees parted to let him pass, and the briars wriggled out of his path like snakes.

Nathan started in the other direction toward Thornyhill Manor. Even though he was in his own world, somehow it didn't feel like it. He seemed curiously disassociated from his surroundings, as if he were in an alien universe in one of his dreams, the dreams he'd had recently of aimless wandering, searching, going nowhere. He knew what he was doing and where he had to go, but his actions felt almost robotic, as if the Nathan who was carrying out the Grandir's orders was divorced from the Nathan inside, a Nathan who watched from a distance, uninvolved, his brain in suspension.

He was following a plan laid down by one of his remoter ancestors in another cosmos perhaps a billennium ago, though time no longer had any real meaning for him. A lot of things no longer had any real meaning, when the man he had recently discovered to be his father—a supreme ruler on a scale unimaginable in our universe—told him he was nearly fifty thousand years old, and they jumped from world to world as casually as a subatomic particle in theoretical physics, and universes were two a penny and Doom was on the daily menu. It occurred to him he might be in shock and that was why he felt so strange—he'd felt that way ever since Annie told him the truth. People in shock, so he had heard, often went into a condition of mental and physical shutdown, to give their mind and body time to adjust to whatever had shocked them in the first place. Somewhere, he was adjusting, absorbing everything that had happened, everything that was happening. He wouldn't try to think about it yet. He would just get on with the job.

At Thornyhill he went in through the kitchen door. Hoover was there to greet him, tail wagging, but there was no sign of Bartlemy. The Grandir had been right, but then he always was. He had the Sight, or some high-tech, high-magic equivalent: he could see across the worlds, through windows in space and time. He had read his son's thoughts, admitted Nathan into his own. It had been the ultimate intimacy, an act of total self-revelation—but with a mind like the Grandir's there must still have been depths unplumbed, thoughts unexplored, veils past which he could not see. All he had been permitted, Nathan guessed, was a brief glimpse just beneath the surface.

He had started thinking again, even though his brain wasn't ready for it—thinking his mother must be worried, he should call her, leave a message, write a note. The drawing room clock said it was nearly five. Maybe Bartlemy was with her now. He felt as if he had been gone a century but worked out, with an effort, it was just a night and a day. No contact, the Grandir had said. Bartlemy would look after Annie. He could explain . . . afterward. When it was all over. The Great Spell— the end of a world—whatever *it* was . . .

He opened the secret compartment in the chimney and took out the three objects hidden there, wrapped in brown paper and bits of old sheet. There was a sports bag tucked in the cupboard under the stairs, one of his—he must have left it behind awhile ago—and he put the things inside. A section of the Sword protruded, but it was encased in its sheath and bundled in torn linen, so he didn't think it mattered. No one would be able to tell what it was.

Hoover watched him, head on one side, tail no longer wagging. He looked disconcertingly intelligent.

"It's all right," Nathan said. "I have to take these things—for the Great Spell. Uncle Barty knows . . . Anyway, I'll tell him later."

When the hour has struck, when the world has halted, when the knell of Doom is all tolled out . . .

Hoover clearly wanted to come with him, trotting after him out of the door, but Nathan said *"No"* in his sternest voice, tinged with a quaver of anxiety, and the dog, rather reluctantly, did not attempt to follow farther. At the idea of how the Grandir might react if he arrived at the location for the spell with his uncle's shaggy mongrel in tow, all the thoughts in Nathan's head began to tumble over, like a row of dominoes when someone flicks the one at the end. But he couldn't go there, not now, and his mind closed down again, and he was back in robot mode, walking through the woods with the bag over his shoulder, on his way to Scarbarrow Fayr.

Dark crept through the trees behind him, and as he reached the road there was a whistling call, somewhere nearby, a sort of eldritch piping, but he assumed it was only a bird.

POBJOY ARRIVED to see Annie about half an hour after Bartlemy had left. They didn't have a date, but he was back from Lancashire for a week and felt a sudden, overpowering need to talk to her—the sort of need that wouldn't waste time with preliminary phone calls but drove him straight to Eade, parked the car for him, and propelled him into the bookshop before he had had time to find an adequate excuse for the impromptu intrusion. On a subliminal level, he was thinking that Nathan would be at school and they could have some quality time together, discuss whatever it was needed discussing, maybe repeat their last kiss . . .

But one look at Annie's face changed all that. A pale winter face—wintry with the frozen top layer of her thoughts, with the deeps of inner chill.

She said: "I'm sorry, I can't . . . I can't see you right now. Sorry . . ."

"What's happened?" In Eade—quiet, sleepy little Eade—something bizarre was always happening. Robbery, kidnapping, murder. And certain individuals were invariably mixed up in it . . . "What's happened to Nathan?"

"He's gone," Annie said.

Pobjoy became a policeman—if he had ever stopped being one. His interrogation technique clicked in automatically. "How long? Have you reported it? Why wasn't he at school?"

Annie answered the questions, indicating her recognition of the auto-policeman phenomenon with a shadowy smile. "I don't want it reported," she said. "There's no point."

"He's only been missing a little while," Pobjoy said, hearing the standard reassurances coming out of his mouth and despising himself for them, knowing—*knowing*—that this time they didn't apply. "He's fifteen—almost an adult—and tall and strong for his age. I'm sure he'll be all right."

He was pathetic. There was a *crime* going on in Eade—a crime so large he couldn't see it, only the bits that stuck out around the edge—and the boy was involved somehow, up to his neck, perpetrator or victim. If he was missing, it was because he was in trouble, real trouble, and all he, Pobjoy, could do about it was bleat clichés to his mother like a bloody policeman's manual . . .

"We'll find him," he said, meaning it, and was shocked when Annie laughed.

The kind of laugh that cracks into a sob, only this one didn't.

"I don't think so," she said. "Not where he's gone."

"Annie—"

The shop door clanged. Hazel walked straight through into the house, barely acknowledging Pobjoy.

"Nathan isn't answering his cell phone," she said. "And it's the Solstice. And—" She took in Annie's expression. "—he's gone, hasn't he? *He's gone.*"

"Yes."

What does the Solstice have to do with it? Pobjoy wondered. But he didn't manage to ask the question.

The phone rang. In that taut atmosphere it sounded dramatic, portentous, the way only a phone ring crashing into a sudden silence can.

Annie picked up the handset, said *yes* a couple of times, and *I'm coming.* Put it down.

"I'm going to Thornyhill," she said, speaking to Hazel. Only to Hazel, Pobjoy noted. As if he didn't matter anymore. "The relics have disappeared—Nathan's taken them."

And to Pobjoy, as an afterthought: "Sorry . . ."

He followed the two of them outside to where the yellow Beetle was parked at the curb—Eade was the sort of place where you could still park in front of your own house without getting a ticket. Annie slid into the driver's seat; Hazel went to the passenger door.

Pobjoy said brusquely: "I'm coming with you."

"We don't need a policeman," Hazel said. "Especially not one who doesn't believe in the evidence."

She got in, slammed the door in his face. Annie had already switched on the ignition.

Thirty seconds later he went after them in his own car. Not because he was a policeman, not this time. This time, it was because of Annie—and because he wanted to know the answers, whatever the questions were—no matter how improbable those answers might be . . .

IT WAS dark when Nathan reached the hill, and he was having trouble seeing where he was going. There was a church at the bottom tucked into a fold in the hillside, a very old church, long neglected and un-used—local historians claimed the original building was Saxon, and various conservation groups were interested in it, but none of them had any money. In the dim light it appeared to be hunkered down against the cold, its stubby tower barely protruding above the pitch of the roof, darkness gathering behind the glassless windows. The churchyard beyond the low wall was overgrown—when spring finally arrived, it would be deep in wildflowers—and the gravestones leaned this way and that, as if their owners had dislodged them while tossing and turning in their eternal slumber. A cypress tree grew there, unclipped for a decade, stretching over the sleepers like a huge clot of shadow. On a summer's day it was a peaceful place where bumblebees and brown meadow butterflies came to browse, but that evening it looked different—*Creepy,* Nathan said to himself—with a thin mist oozing out of the ground and drifting among the tombstones. He almost thought he saw a light there, a tiny green flicker, but when he looked again it was gone. He hurried past and up the track to the hilltop.

There was a cluster of trees just off the summit, and the Grandir and Halmé were waiting there, shining faintly in their white clothing like tall ghosts. The Grandir took the bag from Nathan, unfolded the wrappings to check the contents. He did not conjure another werelight; evidently he could see clearly even in the gloom.

"It is well," he said. "Everything is ready. We have no need to mark the circle: it is already there."

The chalk lines showed pale against the turf, an arc bisected by a straight line, set within a circle. *Scarbarrow,* Nathan thought: *that must be an old name.* Perhaps there was a barrow once, before time and weathering had eroded the soil and it had sunken into the hilltop. He had always called it the Chizzledown, above the village of the same name. He remembered Eric telling him once that the chalk outline was a symbol of great power in his world, but he had paid little attention, since Eric didn't know what it meant, and anything could be a symbol if you stared at it long enough. Now he understood.

"The circle is the Crown," the Grandir explained. "The arc is the Cup, and the line the Sword. There should be a cross to represent the hilt, but it seems to have worn away. I had Grimthorn put the mark on the hill, more than fourteen hundred years ago in earth time. There is a weakness here in the fabric of the world—not an actual portal, such things are very rare, but the *possibility* of one. What we would call a magnopoint. It attracts magical energy . . . Are you cold?"

The previous night Nathan had gone to bed in a sweater but not a jacket, and he'd had no chance to pick up any more clothes. Now that he was standing still he had started to shiver.

"Take my hand," said his father.

Warmth flowed from his grasp, pouring through Nathan's body at pulse-speed.

"We have awhile to wait," the Grandir said. "I will say when it is time to begin. Meanwhile, let us sit."

They sat on the ground, cross-legged, in a triangle facing inward. With that unnatural heat in his blood, Nathan found himself impervious to the damp grass and the growing chill.

Presently, he asked: "Will the Great Spell . . . open a portal here?"

Against his will, he was picturing two hundred thousand Eosians arriving in the south of England, exiles who could never be sent home, asylum seekers as Eric had been, all needing to be housed and fed—proud people, intelligent and civilized far beyond the range of their hosts, some with what could be seen as superpowers . . . It was a picture that hadn't occurred to him before, and the sudden rush of panic galvanized his brain into action, unraveling scenarios in his head. The government in crisis—demonstrations by far-right groups—media coverage—the Grandir on TV . . .

It couldn't happen. He knew it couldn't. The Grandir, of all people, would plan ahead. He would never think short-term . . .

"No," the Grandir said. "That would hardly fulfill our needs. We would be mere refugees in your world, doubtless unwelcome as refugees always are, trapped in a primitive society, trammeled by the limitations of our environment. We would age as your people do, dying out in less than a century—freaks who might intrigue and even dominate for a few years but who would then be forgotten, swallowed up in the petty histories of your age, all our knowledge and potential gone to waste.

No—a portal, for us, would only be a shortcut to death. We need a universe with the magical levels of our own, and time—time to reestablish ourselves, time to start living forever. There is only one way forward— we must bring our own world with us."

Nathan's first flash of guilty relief faded. Human eyes didn't glow in the dark, but the Grandir's eyes shone in the deepening night as if lit from within.

"How?" Nathan said.

"The Great Spell." His father's voice was quiet with a sort of huge quietness, like the hush of a vast forest or the star murmur of an endless sky. "It is not for trivial things like opening doors. It can destroy a galaxy—or a cosmos—and it can regenerate, re-create, unite. I have read your memory: you saw what happened when the ancient goddess from your world met Nefanu on Widewater. The two beings fused, becoming a single entity. Given their parallel natures, it was an inevitable reaction. Your universe is, in all fundamentals, parallel to mine—save for the level of natural magic, which is far lower here, as I have explained. Your cosmos is expanding, ours is shrinking. Tonight, there will be an instant of perfect balance. The Great Spell will cause the two worlds to fuse, flowing into each other, melding into one universe that will incorporate the principal elements of both. My world will become yours, yours mine—and all that we have achieved will not be lost."

There was a pause that must have continued for a long time. Nathan struggled to think coherently, realizing too late that he was out of practice with both thinking and coherence.

You believed you were in shock? mocked an imp of thought at the back of his mind. *Try* this *for shock . . .*

"Will there," he managed, "will there . . . be any . . . *damage?*"

Stupid question.

The Grandir smiled. Nathan couldn't see his face anymore, except for the eyes, but he *felt* the smile, like a change in the texture of the dark. "Of course. I would expect about fifty percent destruction in both worlds. In mine that will make no difference, since it is barren from the Contamination, but here countless planets and civilizations will vanish—it is unavoidable. However, that need not concern you. Earth will be at the epicenter, the eye of the spell: it will remain untouched. Those who die will be billions of light-years away, what your people call, I believe, *little green men*. I will feel their death, as I feel the death of all things, but for earthfolk it will be but the repositioning of a few stars. You need not worry about it. Such troubles are on my shoulders, as they have always been."

Little green men . . . Nathan tried to imagine it—the annihilation of billions of worlds, of lives beyond count, peoples he had never known, would never know. But it was too big to take in, too big to think about. He was only an ordinary mortal, despite his paternity. He was earthfolk—when had he started saying that?—he could only think small thoughts.

Thoughts of Hazel . . . his mother . . . his little life in the village, with school, and friends, and an ordinary future lying ahead of him. Such a happy life, in all its comfortable smallness . . .

"What will happen," he said, "to the people here . . . on earth?"

"Your people, too, will become mine. I will care for them. I may even be able to teach a select few how to use their Gift without psychological harm. But they need guidance—their technology is crude but dangerous, they are prone to futile wars, and the planetary environment is already so badly affected it will take centuries to repair. However, these are small matters." *I like small*, Nathan thought. "Your cosmos is young, still growing. Once the union is complete it will continue to grow, and my power will grow with it, reaching out across the stars. I will have the space and time to achieve *anything*—ultimate order, a universal pattern not spun at random by a careless fate but developed from one Design, one Thought, one Man. In my world this was impossible—I was burdened by the errors of my predecessors, born too late into a cosmos already drawing to its end. But here . . ."

"What about the Contamination?" Nathan said. "Won't *that* be part of your new universe? Won't it take hold—here?"

"The impact of the Great Spell should eliminate it," the Grandir said; but Nathan noted the use of the subjunctive. "I have spent a thousand years on the calculations. The force generated by cosmic fusion should be enough—more than enough—to wipe it out. It was, after all, the affliction of an older world, battening onto a Time that was already running down. Just as a normal human is subject to the diseases of age, so it is with a universe. But your world is still young—*young* . . ."

And Nathan recognized the light of his eyes for what it was. Not aspiration, passion, vision—

Greed.

This is my father, he thought.

This is my father.

THIS IS MY FATHER . . .

What had Hazel called him? A power-crazed supervillain . . .

There is nothing like a cliché for getting it right.

Halmé had not spoken in a long, long while. Nathan wondered what she was thinking, if anything. She was the Most Beautiful Woman in All the Worlds . . . but that was it. It wasn't much to show for nearly fifty millennia. To move like a poem, and carry your perfect head like a queen—to be exquisite beyond all other exquisiteness—to exceed the standards of the past and set the standard for all women yet to come. And to be dead at heart, frozen in the shell of your beauty forever and ever . . .

Together, they would make a Brave New World. The three of them.

O brave new world that has such people in it . . .

Nathan struggled to his feet. "I can't—"

"Yes," said the Grandir, standing up in a single, flowing movement, so swift his body blurred. "It is time."

AT THORNYHILL, Bartlemy was trying to calm everyone down. It wasn't working.

"I can't think if you keep yelling at each other," he said, rather more sharply than was his wont. "Hazel, do you want to help Nathan or don't you? Because screaming about police harassment isn't getting us anywhere. James, I know you think we are all suffering from some sort of collective delusion, but if you want to stay and be useful, don't say so. Shut your mouth and open your mind. Annie—no, don't cry. Don't cry . . ."

"I'm not crying," she said. "It's just—I feel so *ineffectual*, hanging about like this, not knowing what to do . . ."

Pobjoy put a cautious arm around her, but she brushed it off, wiping her tears with her fingers, like a child.

Hazel said: "Nathan's got the Grail relics. He'll go back to Eos. There isn't anything we *can* do, is there?"

"We can *think*," Bartlemy said. "Quietly."

"What's the point of—"

"*Quietly.*" Hazel subsided. "We know Nathan took the relics, borrowing a bag from the stair cupboard, presumably to carry them in. That suggests he was taking them some distance—"

"Another universe?" Hazel said pointedly.

"Not necessarily. To get to Eos, all he has to do is lie down and close his eyes. He could have done that here, or at home. No real need for the bag. And Hoover . . . informs me that when he left he was heading *away* from Eade. He wouldn't curl up and sleep in the woods, certainly not at this time of year. Wherever he was going, it's in *this* world."

"Glad to hear it," Pobjoy muttered.

"He's talking in mutter," Hazel said. "He shouldn't be here. He's getting in the way."

"Never mind that," Annie said. "Nathan—oh God . . . Barty, you don't think he's going to the Scarbarrow? Kal said it was near here."

"He doesn't know about it," Hazel said. "I never told him. How do you—"

"How do *you* know about it?" Annie interjected.

"The Scarbarrow is . . . likely," Bartlemy said, leaving explanations for later. "I only wish we knew where it was. There are no barrows 'round here."

"Scarbarrow." Pobjoy latched on to the problem as something comprehensible, something he could analyze like a policeman. "I've never heard of it. That would be a barrow—with a scar? What exactly does that mean?"

"Some sort of mark, I imagine," Bartlemy said. "Cut into the ground, perhaps."

"Like the Long Man at Wilmington or the device on Chizzledown?"

"Could be. Yes, it could be. Chizzledown is near enough. No barrow that I know of, but—"

"Those Wicca nutters use it sometimes," Pobjoy said. "We've had complaints. Dancing 'round the hilltop in the nude and so on. They usually prefer midsummer—bit chilly in March. We rounded up a group of them last year, out of their tiny skulls on homegrown dope. They said the place exudes 'strong magical vibrations.' I'm not surprised, after what they'd taken."

"It *could* be Chizzledown," Hazel said, temporarily suspending hostility. "But Nathan wouldn't do any of that Wicca rubbish. Come on—let's go—"

"What about the Grandir?" Annie said. "Where's he in all this? *He's* the one who has to do the Great Spell—isn't he?—and he's on Eos. I'm not running off anywhere unless—until I'm sure. A scar could mean all sorts of things." She was talking with the wobbly determination of someone hanging on to her self-control by a single weak thread, fighting to stay rational in the face of a rising tide of insanity.

Bartlemy said: "It would be folly to chase after shadows. We need definite information."

"But if Nathan's in danger—!" Hazel protested.

"We don't know that for certain. The Grandir has always protected him."

"After what Margolaine told us—"

"Who's Margolaine?" Annie demanded.

"What makes you think Nathan is in *danger*?" Pobjoy interrupted, at his most inspectorial.

"Why—"

"How—"

"Who—"

"*Shut up.*" Bartlemy raised his voice, an event so rare the others fell silent out of sheer astonishment. "Now, let's sort out what we know.

Tonight is the Solstice—a suitable night for high magic. The Scarbar-row is the obvious location for the portal in this world. Nathan has set off on foot, with the Three, possibly toward Chizzledown—that's worth noting—which may be the modern name for it. The two names are clearly very similar. But the Grandir—the spellcaster—is on Eos, and Nathan doesn't have the skill or the power to attempt any magic by himself. However, what he *can* do—in extremis—is bring someone here with him. He did it with Eric, to save him from drowning. It occurs to me he might—*might*—have brought the Grandir to *this* world, so he can complete the Great Spell here. That would explain why Nathan was walking, not sleeping, when he left the house."

"The Grandir . . ." Annie's words came slowly. "In . . . *this* . . . world . . ."

"It's possible," Bartlemy averred.

"Then we must go *now,*" Hazel said. "We'll try Chizzledown first, then—then anywhere else that's likely . . ."

"There's another way," Bartlemy said. "Try to think like a witch for a change, instead of a frightened girl. We don't need to go looking for Nathan; we can bring him to us."

Annie said: "I don't understand."

"We draw the circle," Bartlemy explained, "and we summon him."

"But . . . he's a *person,*" Hazel said. "Can we do that with a person?"

"Of course we can, provided the magic is strong enough. He would normally return to wherever he's called *from* when the summons is over, but it is possible to draw him out of the circle and hold him here. It can be a traumatic process, but Nathan is well accustomed to—er—unnatural transportation: it shouldn't affect him."

He was rolling back the carpet as he spoke, unhurried but brisk.

Hazel said: "Shall I do it?"

"Not this time."

Shortly after, Pobjoy said to Annie, sotto voce: "Is this some sort of séance?"

"Not exactly."

The lights were out. The circle glimmered in the dark of the room. There was a fire smoldering in the background, but external sounds and distractions faded away. Bartlemy's voice reciting the incantation was both mesmeric and strangely soothing; Pobjoy found himself wondering if this was some form of hypnosis. In his teens and early twenties, he had been a heavy smoker and had once tried a hypnotist as a means of giving it up, but he had been told he was a poor subject, one of those people on whom hypnotism does not work, and he'd had to fall back on willpower. He waited with a sort of brittle detachment, speculating about what he had gotten himself into, what kind of grotesque con game Bartlemy was running. He hadn't seemed the type at all, but that was the thing about the best con men: not seeming the type was part of their stock-in-trade.

Then he saw there was someone in the circle.

The figure had come from nowhere, he was sure of it. A phantom figure that seemed to be made from smoke, its lineaments melting and changing against the suggestion of a skull. It wore a red veil, which it had pulled back to show the face; there was no other color about it at all.

He heard Hazel's hissing whisper: "What are you *doing*?"

"If Nathan and the Grandir are in *this* world," Bartlemy said, "the spells can see them. Greeting, Ragnlech."

"This is the hour of Doom," said the seeress, and something about her voice—the blended voices of the sisterhood—caught Pobjoy off guard, pressing long-forgotten buttons in his nervous system. He had been telling himself it must be a hologram, though he had noticed no sophisticated equipment anywhere in the house, but the voice was shockingly real. It seemed to come from the floor, or the walls, or the air itself.

A clever recording of some kind . . . ?

"I have no leisure for conversation with mortals. Release me!"

"Use the Eye," Bartlemy said.

"Time is running out. We are watching. That is our allotted task. We are watching for the end of the world."

"When will that be?"

"About midnight," said the seeress.

Hazel said "Fuck!" and then apologized hastily.

"What about Nathan?" Annie cut in. "Can you see my son?"

"I can only answer the Questioner," the seeress responded, and Pobjoy knew it couldn't be a recording; Annie's interruption was outside the script.

"Use the Eye," Bartlemy said. "I need your Sight."

Pobjoy saw the figure lift a small spherical object, like a marble, and place it in one empty eye socket. Unlike the rest of her, it looked solid, a milky globe with fine veining and the circles of iris and pupil marked on the side. Once fixed, it began to glow with an unhealthy radiance.

Pobjoy thought: *This is real. They can do special effects on film, but not in your living room. Not like this.*

This is happening . . .

Bartlemy said: "Can you see the boy Nathan?"

"There are barriers . . . One is there who will not be watched. The circle was drawn long ago . . . soon, it will burn. The spells are brewing . . . a Great Spell to shatter the worlds . . . This is the night of Doom."

"We knew that," said Bartlemy.

"Is it Chizzledown?" Hazel demanded. "Uncle Barty, ask her—"

"Tell me where this will take place," Bartlemy said.

"The Scarbarrow . . . Once, it was the door to Faerie, but now . . . He will not be watched! He has power—such power—power beyond measure, beyond any spirit in this world—" The Eye began to throb, expanding and shrinking to the rhythm of a heartbeat. The veins spread like cracks in the marble. "It is too much—too much power! Sisters, hold to me! We must—hold—No! *No!*"

Something like a lightning flash stabbed the core of the circle—the seeress screamed with a dozen voices—

Then there was nothing. The circle was empty. A wisp of smoke— ordinary smoke, without form or substance—drifted upward. There was a smell of scorching.

"What the hell—"

"What happened?"

"What—"

Bartlemy said slowly: "That was *not* on the agenda. I fear—"

"Is she dead?" Pobjoy asked, conscious the question sounded naïve.

"She is werefolk," Bartlemy said. "Strictly speaking, she was never alive. However—"

"Dead or alive, she's cooked," Hazel said brutally. "You said you would call Nathan."

"Annie?"

"Please . . ."

Bartlemy repeated the incantation. Pobjoy heard Nathan's name, among echoes of other, faintly familiar words, perhaps French or Spanish, a hint of Arabic, a rumor of Russian or Greek. England is a cosmopolitan country and he had heard many languages over the years, but never one quite like this—a language as lyrical as poetry, as sharp as a blade.

Again, Bartlemy called Nathan by name. But the circle was dark and empty.

"Why doesn't he come?" Hazel said. "He isn't—he isn't—"

"I don't know. If he lives—if he is in this world—he *must* answer." Pobjoy felt Annie's hand gripping his arm, her fingers pinching his flesh through shirt and sweater. "But the Grandir clearly has a Gift far exceeding mine. He may be blocking me in some way."

Pobjoy said: *"Who is the Grandir?"*

"A power-crazed supervillain"—from Hazel.

And Annie: "Nathan's father—"

His *father?* Pobjoy stared—glared—tried to understand.

"There's something else I can try," Bartlemy said, "though it may not work. I could summon the *place* . . . If it has a strong magical identity—what used to be called a genius loci—"

"How can you summon a place?" Hazel said. "That's impossible."

"Nothing is impossible. There would be a—connection, an instant when *there* and *here* overlap. We might be able to see—"

"Try," Annie said.

This time the summons was slightly different. Pobjoy heard both *Chizzledown* and *Scarbarrow* in the rhythm of the chant. For a couple of minutes there was no change. And then . . . the circle didn't actually expand, but suddenly there seemed to be a lot more space inside it—a breath of cold air off the open hillside—a piping call like the cry of a night bird. Chalk cuts showed faintly against a dimness of grass—an arc, bisected by a straight line . . . Within the circle, the hillside turned. Something was huddled on the ground—something they couldn't make out—and above it stood a man. They saw him for only an instant, but he was tall, taller than any ordinary human, dressed in white though his face was dark, and his eyes glowed, not like the eyes of a demon but like the eyes of an archangel . . . He saw the spellring, the Questioner, the watchers beyond . . . He made a tiny gesture, spoke a single word.

The circle exploded.

"I can't do it," Nathan said.

There was a silence on the hilltop, a night silence, breathless with the hush of the wind.

"You must," said the Grandir. "The choices have all been made."

"You chose," Nathan said. "Not me."

"With power comes responsibility. It is my fate to choose."

"You said . . . billions of people will die, whole civilizations—"

"You do not care about them," the Grandir said. "Your soul is not large enough. Earthfolk care only about those who are closest to them."

"Maybe that's true." Nathan wanted to express his doubts, to argue and out-argue—but no one could argue with the Grandir. It was like picking a quarrel with God. "Maybe I don't care. But I know it's wrong."

Almost, the Grandir sighed. "Your notions of right and wrong are so parochial. You must take a wider view. I will bring progress, harmony, order, not just to your planet but to the whole cosmos. And how can it be *right,* even by your standards, for my people to die? We have so much to give—so much wisdom, so much knowledge and skill."

"Who made the Contamination?"

The question hung in the air for a second like a raindrop suspended halfway to the ground.

"My father," the Grandir said at last. "There was a group of star systems who wished to secede from the Cosmic League—to destroy the unity my ancestors had built up over the ages. When their petition was refused, extremists among them resorted to violence. There were atrocities—innocent people were deliberately targeted—an entire planet was blown up. They used thaumotechnology, but my father came up with a way to distort the magical field around their power bases, so their spells would work against them. It was the fallout from this process that became the Contamination. At first he thought it could be contained within a single galaxy—the zone where the terrorists were operating. But we had learned to travel at thoughtspeed, which is far faster than light—a form of movement powered by magic—and so the Contamination was spread. My father tried to put a moratorium on such travel, except by the elite, but it proved impossible to enforce. When I succeeded him, I took sterner measures, and for several millennia the problem appeared to be under control, confined to a region we were able to keep in isolation. But it grew, advancing wherever magic was used, and in the last thousand years it has eaten up the universe."

"Your people destroyed their own world," Nathan said. "That doesn't—that shouldn't give them the right to take mine."

"*Your* people are destroying their own planet," the Grandir pointed out. "They know how to stop it, yet their elected rulers take no action. Destruction is the nature of humankind. We at least have learned from our mistakes. The lesson has been long and bitter; we would teach others to walk a different path. Don't you want that?"

"We have to—make our own mistakes." Nathan fumbled with ideas imperfectly thought out. "People have to—to work things out for themselves. Choose for themselves."

"Even if that means extinction?"

"Your people chose extinction," Nathan said. "Mine—might not."

"Argument is fruitless," the Grandir said. "You have your mother's genes—you were born in this world—in the end, your vision is too small to see as I do. You cling to your backward ethics like a child with a favorite toy. But it is time to be done with toys. You talk of choice, but your choices were made for you, eons before you were born. I am sorry—sorrier than I can say—that things between us must end in discord. I have planned for this moment so long, I and all my ancestors since Romandos's day. I did not know it would cost me so dear."

"Lugair killed Romandos," Nathan said, "because of Imagen. That wasn't part of the plan."

"Still you do not see. A Great Spell is like a story: it must grow over a long period of time, until all the different strands come together at the point of climax. Lugair's action was woven into the pattern. Romandos's blood began it, so his blood must end it. In a sense, what happens here tonight was dictated by Lugair. I did what I could, but the pattern cannot be changed."

He bowed his head; long black hair fell forward over his face.

Nathan thought: *We're father and son. Sons always argue with their fathers. Only it's usually about girlfriends, or schoolwork, or borrowing Dad's car. We're arguing over the future of a universe . . .*

Then the Grandir's words came home to him. He said: "Osskva told me—there was always a sacrifice. Must you—does it have to be you?"

"It should have been," his father said. "That's how the spell was shaped. I should have had a son with Halmé, a son whose genes were unadulterated, to carry on after me. I would have worn the Crown, died on the Sword, filled the Cup with my lifeblood. My son would have taken up my mantle, borne my burdens. But I am what earthfolk would call an avatar; without me, there is no future. I *am* the future. The spell could not be changed, but it could be twisted. I found a way, though it meant I would be the last of the true line. But I do not need an heir: I will live forever, or at least long enough."

"Aren't I—"

"You are my son, but not my heir. Instead of a true-born heir, I had a child of two worlds, who could travel the multiverse through the portal in his mind. You have no other power, but you have been using this ability since your infancy. I was able to conceal the Three in other worlds, but I could not pass the Gate; you went to retrieve them, and so you wove yourself into the pattern. But you were born to be more than a messenger. You have a nobler purpose . . ."

Suddenly the night was very still. The wind dropped; on the hill-top, it was almost completely dark. There was only the sheen of the Grandir's clothing and the pale form of Halmé a little way off, motion-less as a standing stone. Nathan thought the world stopped. The dark-ness crept inside him, filling his heart.

"Am I . . . the sacrifice?"

The Grandir's voice softened with the gentleness of sorrow. "I did not know I would come to love you," he repeated. "I did not know the price would be so high. Alas, gods have sacrificed their sons since time immemorial: it is the oldest legend in every world. I have condemned myself to an eternity of regret. But come: take my hand. We have these last moments to share. I would not waste them in pointless dispute."

Nathan felt the Grandir's handclasp, strong and sure. His father's handclasp. Warmth flowed into him, yet he was cold.

Cold as death.

"I don't . . . want to . . . share anything with you." It was a strug-gle to get the words out. "I am . . . my mother's son. Not yours. My *mother . . .*"

He couldn't pull his hand away.

"She served her purpose," the Grandir said. "As I told you, she had an extraordinary capacity for love, amazing in a creature of such frag-ile mortality."

Love . . . Annie's love for him—for Daniel . . . And he remem-bered the Grandir saying something about the Ozmosees—*I engi-neered an opportunity . . .*

"You killed Daniel," Nathan said.

"Of course. It was necessary. The spells indicated your mother would have the strength to open the Gate, but she needed motivation. Your race live so briefly and die so easily. Even you, my son, would barely have made it to a hundred. As it is, your life, though short, will be special—your legacy will change two worlds. What more could you wish for?"

Another seventy years?

"I don't want to die," Nathan said.

"I know," said the Grandir. "But this is the pattern Lugair made, when he slew Romandos with the Traitor's Sword. It can be modified but not changed—"

"*You* modified it," Nathan said. "You—fathered me, so I could die in your place. Like—*cannon fodder* . . ."

"I thought you understood." The Grandir's tone was tinged with disappointment. There was something in his manner Nathan recognized, a sort of lofty compassion. Like when he killed the gnomons . . .

What had Hazel said? *Compassion's cheap. It's what you do that counts.*

"This is painful for me," the Grandir said. "I had hoped you would not make it harder."

"Painful for you?" Nathan cried, and somehow he wrenched his hand free of his father's grasp. "*I'm* the one who's going to die! You're going to kill me—and it's *painful* for you? You say you care, but it's all just words. Caring doesn't mean anything unless it changes your actions. You use people—creatures—we're all creatures to you—you use them and kill them, and then say you're sorry, as if that makes it all right." The gnomons . . . the white xaurian . . . "You and Osskva talked about *lesser* races, but to you everyone's lesser. I don't believe you even care about your own people. They're just an excuse for you to take over my universe. You only care about yourself—yourself—yourself—"

"Enough," said the Grandir, raising his hand. Nathan's voice froze in his throat; his tongue felt like a lump of clay. "I don't need to listen to this. Your spirit is weak, your mind limited. Halmé and I have to prepare, to initiate the magics. It will be best if you sleep until the time comes . . ."

Sleep—dream . . . *dream* . . .

Nathan's thought flew. He had a millisecond in which to do something, come up with something, reach for the portal . . .

But he knew already where he wished to go.

"Sleep now," said the Grandir, and the darkness came, and Nathan felt himself pitching forward into oblivion.

POBJOY SAT up, slowly. The blast had flung him and Annie backward—he'd tried to shield her but there was no time—his head hurt where it had struck against the furniture. He touched his hair, gingerly, but couldn't feel any blood. It was pitch black—the explosion must have blown the fire out—but he could hear movement beside him, soft breathing, a murmur of discomfort.

He said: "Are you all right?"

"I think so."

She stood up, found her way to the light switch. The sudden brightness made him blink. Then he saw the wreck of the room, the toppled furniture and tumbled books, the charring of the floorboards, the burn marks radiating out from where the circle had been. The blast seemed to have been concentrated into a very small area; beyond it, there was more mess than damage. Bartlemy, nearest to the perimeter, lay still, his eyes closed. Hoover was licking his face. Beside him, Hazel staggered to her feet, blood trickling from a cut on her temple. She must have hit the corner of the table, Pobjoy guessed.

He bent over Bartlemy, feeling for a pulse in his neck.

Hazel said: "Is he alive?"

"Yeah." Bartlemy's clothes were singed, and there were what looked like second-degree burns on his hands, his chest, his face. They all had skin blotched gray with smoke stains.

"Can you call an ambulance?" Annie said. "I have to go. *Now.*"

"You can't—"

"Take care of him. Please. Hazel—"

"I'm coming."

"No—you should stay—"

"I'm coming."

Pobjoy got out his cell phone and called emergency services. He had seen the look on Annie's face. Even a policeman hesitates to get between that look and wherever it's pointing.

He said: "Give me a moment."

"Take care of him," Annie repeated. Then she was out the door. Hazel flung a quick glance at Bartlemy and ran after her.

In the Beetle they took off at speed. Annie had always been a sensible driver, conscientious and prudent, staying within the limits, but not that night. Trees lurched through the headlights as she swerved onto the road—her foot went down on the accelerator. Hazel fancied she heard tires—or brakes—or something—squeaking in protest on every bend. It wasn't a long drive, but the road was narrow and winding; once, they bumped onto the shoulder to avoid an oncoming car. Halfway along the Chizzledown lane the pavement ran out, and they were bouncing along a cart track toward the church. Annie pulled up, and they both tumbled out.

"We should've brought a flashlight," Hazel said.

"We just have to head uphill," Annie responded. "Uphill all the way."

There was a chalky path that showed up in the darkness, the same route Nathan had followed earlier that evening. They stumbled frequently on the uneven ground. Every so often they heard a whistling like a strange bird, sometimes to their left, sometimes the right. Hazel thought she distinguished the green glimmer of a glowworm, but there were no glowworms in March. When she glanced back, she saw a mist gathering behind them, crawling up the slope.

The fairies are coming . . .

She said: "There's too much magic in the night."

Annie said: "Good."

Hazel had a feeling if she had told her all hell was on the march, Annie would have said: *Good*.

Ahead, the hill crest was a dark curve against a sky dim with cloud. In a ragged gap a ragged moon gleamed briefly, a moon fraying at the edges as if torn in half. As they drew nearer, the rim of the chalk symbol came into view, glowing as though daubed with phosphorescent paint. Hazel thought: *The Grandir doesn't need to draw a circle. It's already there.* In the center, at the point where the sword line crossed the arc, stood the figure they had glimpsed at Thornyhill—a giant of a man even from a distance, all white save for the darkness of his hands and face. His arms were outstretched in the stance of a spellcaster; his black hair streamed in a sudden wind. The intrusion of Bartlemy's summons had been nothing more to him than a minor irritant, an insect buzz to be swatted with barely a thought. Close to his feet, the huddle on the ground obscured part of the sigil. And a little way behind him was a second figure, also in white. A woman. Halmé, Hazel deduced after a moment's reflection. Halmé the beautiful, queen of a whole world.

Strange how you could hate someone you'd never even met.

Hazel said: "What do we do now?"

But Annie had already started to run toward the circle . . .

NATHAN DREAMED. Across time and space, reaching back through the dark, into the light, before the stars began to die. The millennia spun past him like great Catherine wheels of time—hours, days, weeks whirled away into the spirals of history, lost in the flicker and dazzle of passing years, the contrail of flying centuries. He was aiming for one day, one hour—one moment among all the moments—narrowing his vision onto a pinpoint in eternity.

What he needed was to be *totally focused* . . .

The ages peeled away like onion skins, exposing the core. The beginning of it all. A child struggling into the world, daubed in blood and mucus, eyes squeezed shut, mouth open. He heard it cry—the first of all cries—saw tiny fists punching the air. He didn't think a newborn baby could make a fist, but this one did. Otherwise, it was a baby like any other, round golden arms, scrunched-up face, a tuft of hair, its only power in its lungs and its hold on a mother's heart. Hands placed the infant in her arms—he saw her profile as she gazed down at it, the faint, magical smile that curved her lips.

Very softly, she spoke its name.

So *that's* it . . .

He let go of the moment, and the dream receded, crowded out by the busyness of the past. The world was lost in a maze of other worlds—stars flared and died, galaxies imploded, nebulae did whatever it is nebulae do. And then everything was gone into the dark.

When Nathan woke, he was lying on an altar of stone, looking up into his father's face.

. . .

ANNIE NEVER made it past the rim. A ring of pale flame shot skyward with a noise like the hiss of white-hot snakes, enclosing the ritual in a cocoon of fire. For the second time that evening, she was hurled backward—the Grandir, screened by a force field of intensive magic, noticed her no more than a gnat. Hazel reached her as she picked herself up, beating at the barrier as at an invisible wall.

"I can't get through!" she screamed, the snake-hiss of the flames almost drowning out her voice.

"Look," Hazel said. "*Look* . . ."

She had seen it before, in the smoke-pictures, only this time it was far clearer. The Grandir moved his hand, and a hunk of rock shouldered its way out of the ground. It was roughly oval, flat and smooth on top, shaped in the remote past with primitive tools for a purpose long defunct. Another gesture and the huddle at the Grandir's feet floated upward, coming to rest on the flat of the stone, its limbs uncurling until it lay at full stretch. It was Nathan; she could see him plainly now in the glare of the magic. His eyes were closed but he appeared to be unhurt. The Grandir leaned over him, touching his face very gently, as if it was something fragile and precious. Then he straightened up and resumed the incantation.

They couldn't hear the words, but they didn't need to. Above them the clouds thickened, swirled into a bubbling brew like celestial porridge, spiraling inward toward a focal point directly overhead—a hole in the sky where the moon's husk drifted in a strange watery shimmer. They saw liquid moonlight fall to earth as tears—or maybe it was rain, a few thin shafts, glitter-bright, streaming down from the witch's brew of cloud. And all around the hill the mist was rising, fraying into wisps that danced away on their own. Shapes formed or half formed, diffusing into other shapes before you could be sure of them—filmy wings and pointy faces, bodies insect-thin, fingers long as claws. And here and there were gyrating fragments of skeletons, spun from air and vapor, things with cloven hooves and goaty horns, goblin feet and gargoyle masks. Spectral lights gleamed and vanished, held in unseen hands. Hazel peered behind her from time to time but never saw anything clearly; Annie seemed oblivious to everything outside the circle.

The phantom horde wound its way around the hilltop, and the not-quite-birdcalls became the skirl of distant pipes, and there was a soft drumming like raindrops or dancing feet.

The incantation grew stronger. Now they could hear the Grandir's voice, a deeper note behind the weremurmur and the silver hiss of the flame. Beside him, Halmé held the Sword, not by the hilt but with her hand around the sheath; in her other hand she carried the Cup. The Crown rested on the slab next to Nathan. The cloud-porridge churned faster; violet lightning stabbed from sky to earth. Hazel, glancing at Annie, thought she was almost unrecognizable, her face transformed by some huge emotion—fury, frustration, fear . . .

She said to herself: *We're going to watch Nathan die—and we can't do a thing.* Her own fury was a black gall rising inside her, a bile in her gut. Her clumsy witchcraft was no use against the Grandir's power; her rage was no use. The spell rolled on. The night had turned to nightmare around them, shadow beings from the other side of darkness thronging the hillside, capering, twirling—a carnival of specters. Somewhere, Hazel heard the voice of the Child, remote but very clear:

> *"Here comes a spindle to spin out your doom*
> *Here comes a candle to light up your tomb*
> *Here comes an angel to put you to bed*
> *Here comes a sword blade to cut off your head!"*

But she paid little attention anymore.

The spell rolled on, unstoppable as a tidal wave, mounting to a crescendo. The hole in the sky opened onto other stars, and a different moon sailed in the gap, a Red Moon of Madness. The Grandir bent over Nathan, opening his eyes with a word. A beckoning motion lifted his head; the Crown was placed on his brow. The spikes seemed to puncture his skin so the blood ran down his face. Halmé moved forward: the Grandir drew the Sword from its sheath—the Traitor's Sword, with a deadly spirit imprisoned in its blade, the Sword only his kindred might touch. Halmé laid down the sheath and stood there holding the Grail, bathed in the radiance of the spellfire—lovelier than

Blanchefleur, the cup bearer of legend, fairer than Helen who was the downfall of Troy. She did not look at Nathan, the son she might have born; only at the Grandir.

He pressed the Sword to his lips, kissed the cold metal. Then he raised it for the death blow.

Hazel screamed, or Annie screamed: neither knew which.

"Nooooo—"

No one heard.

Nathan's tongue was weighted; his body could move only at his father's Command. But he spoke the name in his mind, and his voice creaked into action—spoke it aloud, the name of names, the secret of secrets. And for an eyeblink, a heartbeat, the spell broke. The Sword flew from his father's grip and stuck quivering in the turf. The summit was plunged into night. Above, the cloud-brew boiled over, streaming in every direction at once—the Red Moon was blotted out. Nathan rolled off the slab and tried to get up, his muscles stiff from prolonged stasis, the Crown fallen from his head. The Grandir reached out with hands hooked into claws, grappling the magic back together, crying out new words of power, harsh with urgency, edged with fear. The circle blazed up again—

But the intruders had already crossed the barrier.

Hazel threw herself at Halmé, knocking the Cup from her hands, punching and scratching. The woman was far taller than her, far stronger, but in all her endless years of life nobody had ever raised a hand against her—she had been cherished, coddled, isolated, adored—and she reeled backward, unable to defend herself, paralyzed with shock. In her terror, she saw her attacker not as human but some evil goblin-creature who had leapt through the crack in the spell to seize on her. Hazel's nails raked Halmé's throat, tore the binding from her hair. She screamed for her brother—

The Grandir did not answer. Too late, he recognized the woman in front of him—the lesser mortal with her incredible capacity for love. The woman he had singled out, honored with his brief attention, used, all but forgotten. To him, the expression on her face was in an unknown language. He could have stopped her with a word, the twitch of a finger—but he needed all his words, all his grip, to hold the spell together. She reached for the Sword.

"No!" Nathan croaked. "Mum—you can't—"

But her blood was his blood, her touch was his touch, and the spirit in the blade felt her, knew her, sprang to meet the rage of her heart. Rage at the being who had used her without a thought—who would have slain the son he had given her. The Sword leapt in her grasp, knowing where it had to go. The blade sheered through flesh and bone, through sinew and spirit. The Grandir stared down at it, blank with amazement—he had lived so long, he had forgotten he could die like other men. He opened his mouth for the Command that would heal him, but the blood bubbled out, choking his words, and he fell back onto the grass. Even before he hit the ground, he was dead.

The spellfire went out in a howl of wind. Darkness poured over the hilltop—a darkness rustling with wings, pattering with flying feet. Faint lights bobbed and danced; faint images imprinted themselves on sight and mind, fading too slowly for comfort. There was the creeling of phantom pipes, the whistling that was not a bird. A pure choirboy voice was chanting snatches of song.

> *"Are you going to Scarbarrow Fayr?*
> *Hemlock, hemp, tormentil, and rue . . .*
> *Remember me to one who died there—*
> *Tell my love this grave is for you . . ."*

"The Crown!" Nathan cried. "Mum—Hazel—hold on to the Crown! It's *iron* . . ."

Somehow they found each other in the whirling dark—clung together, clutching the circlet of thorns. Halmé was shrieking in her own tongue "Help me! Help—" but shadowy hands plucked her, spinning her this way and that—Nathan glimpsed her loosened hair blowing in elflocks over the wild terror of her face. *She is beautiful—beautiful— her flashing eyes! her floating hair!—We will dance with her till the end of time* . . . For an instant sheet lightning blinked over the world—the shadows turned white, and they *saw—*

Then the night returned, and thunder rolled, and the piled-up clouds dissolved into a solid curtain of water, pounding the grass to mud.

It always rains at the end of the world. After battle, apocalypse, debacle, and death, the heavens weep for the folly of it all . . .

The three of them sat in the mud, wet and cold beyond bearing, empty at last of all horrors, holding hands against the dark.

Epilogue: Spring

The following morning Annie, Nathan, and Hazel went to see Bartlemy in the hospital, but he had gone. "He should never have discharged himself," the senior nurse complained. "He was severely injured. We couldn't stop him . . ."

They drove to Thornyhill, but there was nobody there. The stockpot that had been simmering on the stove since the night Annie first arrived had vanished; many of the rarer herbs, the bottles and jars of mysterious spices, the handwritten cookbooks sallow with age—all had been removed. There was no sign of Hoover.

Pobjoy said he would make inquiries, but his time was fully taken up with the discovery of a corpse on the top of Chizzledown, a John Doe with no papers or ID, stabbed through the heart apparently with a sword. The body was over seven feet tall, of unspecified racial origin, estimated to be in his forties or fifties though in superb physical condition. Pobjoy told the assistant chief constable, in confidence, that he had information from an illicit source that the man had been a people trafficker, operating mainly abroad, killed here because it was neutral territory, probably by Oriental gangsters—hence the sword—who had already left the country. In short, the investigation was going to go nowhere and wouldn't merit the expenditure of time and manpower.

"The path lab says the sword could be a samurai weapon," the ACC said knowledgeably. "Might have been one of those ritual killings. He looked a pretty distinctive character. Someone's bound to identify him soon."

"I don't think so," Pobjoy said.

A few days later Annie received a communication from a firm of lawyers in London, telling her Bartlemy had deeded Thornyhill to her, and enclosing a letter from him, and an accompanying parcel. He wrote:

> *I suggest you sell the house. I doubt if you would want to live in such an isolated location, but the proceeds from the sale will ensure you and Nathan financial security for some time to come. The bookshop with its adjoining property is already in your name, and I have arranged a fund that will continue to pay your salary for another two years. Without wishing to be premature, perhaps this may be considered a wedding present.*

"*Very* premature," Annie muttered.

> *I shall miss you very much. However, the death of the Grandir and the defeat of his plans*

How did he know about that? she wondered.

> *makes it clear you can look after yourselves far better than I ever could. You do not need me anymore, and I have injuries that require treatment—treatment I cannot obtain in Eade. It seems the right moment to move on. I would ask you to take the Grail, the Sword, and the Crown and bury them in the woods, well away from any paths. They have no purpose anymore but there may still be a vestige of power left in them, so dig deep, too deep for fox or badger to unearth them again.*

Tell Hazel I expect her to pass all her exams and have sent her
some books and other materials so she may continue her study of
magic, and learn, as I know she will, how not to use her Gift.

For Nathan and yourself, I include a few recipes; make use of
the spices and seasonings I left behind, and enjoy the wine. Think
of me whenever you bake a coffee cake or prepare a stew!

I will think of you always.

Meanwhile, let us say not adieu, but au revoir.

Barty

Annie cried a little when she finished the letter, though Pobjoy said, "I'm sure he'll be back," and Hazel suggested he might return looking completely different, like Dr. Who.

"I can't imagine Bartlemy looking like anyone but himself," Annie said.

They buried the relics the week after. It was an exhausting job, for the ground was hard, but Nathan and Pobjoy managed it between them. Hazel considered putting a spell of concealment on the place but decided it would only draw attention to it.

Afterward, Nathan told his mother: "If you *do* want to marry James, I suppose it's okay with me. Any father's better than the Grandir, after all."

"Premature," Annie reiterated.

The Grandir was eventually interred in the abandoned churchyard, after a special dispensation from the ecclesiastical authorities. It seemed appropriate. His murder was put in the cold-case file, where no one ever bothered to resurrect it. Nathan would visit the grave from time to time, more because he felt he should than because he wished to, and lay bunches of herbs on the ground: parsley, sage, rosemary, and thyme.

Nothing was ever heard of Halmé.

THE NIGHT before his sixteenth birthday, he climbed up to the roof to think things over. The star had vanished, and he knew in his heart that the world of Eos was ended—ended long ago—a dead universe suspended forever in a void of Time. Only Eric survived, growing slightly older, as people do, drinking lots of coffee, reading poetry, and still half believing every film he watched, especially those with the most dramatic special effects. Nathan searched for the portal in his mind, but it was no longer there—he had chosen his world, the world in which he would grow up, grow old, and although the multiverse was only a dream away, those dreams would not come again. Wilderslee and Widewater had disappeared into the cosmic labyrinth, never to return. Already they seemed dim and distant as the fantasies of childhood, visions that would remain with him as things more imagined than actually seen. The sun on the many-colored leaves in the Deepwoods, orange and gold and scarlet and pink—sharing wild strawberries with Nell beside the chatter of a stream—stroking the tiny dragonet under the Dragon's Reef—flying with Ezroc over the endless curve of the sea . . . the green of Denaero's eyes . . . the tangle of Nellwyn's hair . . . Hazel had taken to putting her hair up, though some of it still fell over her face. She was looking different now, more a woman than a child; it didn't occur to him that she had grown an inch or two. She even appeared quite pretty sometimes, which was worrying: it would attract all the wrong boys.

He was glad they would be together in the sixth form—he felt he owed it to Bartlemy, as well as Hazel, to make sure she got there. That way, he would be able to keep her clear of Damian Wicks and others like him.

He went to bed thinking not of the past but the future—an ordinary future, comfortable in its smallness . . .

On the evening of his birthday, they had a party at the Happy Huntsman. Everyone considered Annie was being very extravagant holding it there, but the only people who minded were those who weren't invited. Hazel came as a matter of course, and James, George Fawn, all the Rayburns, Ned Gable from Ffylde, Eric and Rowena Thorn, Lily and Franco, other teenagers from the village with dependent parents. They had champagne, and George was sick—it was practically a reflex with him—and Nathan and Hazel went out on the terrace together, shivering under the stars, for a moment of quality time on the way to adulthood.

"My star's gone," Nathan said, and: "Do you think anything magical will ever happen to us again?" He wasn't entirely sure he wanted it to, after the events on Chizzledown.

"Of course it will," Hazel replied, glancing at her ring. "Like Uncle Barty always said, we have infinity and eternity. That gives us space and time for *anything*."

"Anything?"

"Anything."

On an impulse, he kissed her. "That kind of anything?"

"That wasn't magical," Hazel said matter-of-factly. She wasn't going to tell him it *felt* magical, not for a long time yet. Maybe not for years and years . . .

The next day, against all the odds, it was spring.

About the Author

AMANDA HEMINGWAY has already lived through one lifetime—during which she traveled the world and supported herself through a variety of professions, including that of actress, barmaid, garage hand, laboratory assistant, journalist, and model. Her new life is devoted to her writing.